Discover the novel rea

'A poignant, engro
I can't stop think
mystery, but a
memory and family' Amy Tintera

'I will be thinking about [this book] for years . . . thoughtful, quirky, rich in character. A clever thriller told through the lens of memory' Gillian McAllister

'An elegant, twisting story of loss and longing, of the ache of the unknown and the drowning weight of past trauma' Chris Whitaker

'Cleverly crafted and deeply moving, this beautiful book is a genuine page-turner. It was original, it was gripping, it was shocking and I loved it' Alice Feeney

'A book that captivates heart and mind, it is powerful, thought-provoking, terrifying and exquisitely written. I loved every page' Hazel Prior

'The next must-read, must-recommend, must-discuss, must-reread novel. A miraculous literary thriller; shocking, daring, moving, haunting, infinitely rewarding' A. J. Finn

'Wonderful characters, an intriguing plot and beautiful writing' Emily Edwards

'A captivating, haunting and twisty story that explores the nature of loss and trauma, and the tricks that our memories play on us' Karin Slaughter

'A beautifully wrought story of shattered lives and the bond of true love that mends them' Veronica Henry

ABOUT THE AUTHOR

Sarah Easter Collins grew up in Kent and studied at Exeter University before moving to Botswana and later Thailand and Malawi. She now lives on Exmoor with her husband, son and two dogs. She is a graduate of the Curtis Brown Creative novel-writing course and holds a diploma in creative writing from Oxford University. When not writing, she works as an artist. *Things Don't Break on their Own* is her first novel.

THINGS DON'T BREAK ON THEIR OWN

SARAH EASTER COLLINS

PENGUIN BOOKS

PENGUIN BOOKS

UK | USA | Canada | Ireland | Australia
India | New Zealand | South Africa

Penguin Books is part of the Penguin Random House group of companies
whose addresses can be found at global.penguinrandomhouse.com

Penguin Random House UK,
One Embassy Gardens, 8 Viaduct Gardens, London SW11 7BW

penguin.co.uk

Penguin Random House UK

First published by Viking 2024
Published in Penguin Books 2025
001

Typeset by Jouve (UK), Milton Keynes
Printed and bound in Great Britain by Clays Ltd, Elcograf S.p.A.

The authorized representative in the EEA is Penguin Random House Ireland,
Morrison Chambers, 32 Nassau Street, Dublin D02 YH68

A CIP catalogue record for this book is available from the British Library

ISBN: 978-0-241-99931-8

Penguin Random House is committed to a sustainable future
for our business, our readers and our planet. This book is made from
Forest Stewardship Council® certified paper.

FSC www.fsc.org MIX Paper | Supporting responsible forestry FSC® C018179

For my beloved boy

1.
Supper with friends

Robyn

The match flares in the half-dark of our kitchen. As I lean towards the candles, light slips along the silver lines of the bowl that forms the centrepiece of the table. I stand back, making one final check of the linen, the glasses, the place settings, the eight mismatched chairs. Cat walks in.

'Okay,' she says, 'the twins are asleep. Sophie's in bed and reading. I've told her it's fine to come down so long as she takes herself back up. What's still to do?'

'We're pretty much there. Make yourself a drink.'

'I'm saving myself for when Jamie gets here.'

'Don't.'

'Last time he delivered us *forty-five minutes* on the engineering works between here and the coast. Remember? *Forty-five sodding minutes*. If he does that again, I'm feigning death.' My wife rummages in a drawer and pulls out a bottle opener. 'I honestly don't know what Willa sees in him.'

'He wants kids.'

'She's well aware there're other ways. Anyway, she's *got* to want more than that –'

'It's all she wants.'

'Basic compatibility for a start. I mean, why Jamie?'

'She's thirty-eight. You know it's a tricky subject.'

'Everything's tricky –'

'Cat –'

'This was meant to be a *family* get-together. *Sibs*. It's almost impossible to get Michael *and* Nate in London at the exact same time.'

'Willa's practically family.'

'Uh-huh.'

'She's been through so much.'

'Sure.' Cat gives me daggers, then just as quickly lets it go. 'I know.'

I look at the table, running a hand through my hair. 'D'you reckon everyone will get on?'

Cat pulls me to her. 'Course they will. It's nearly Christmas, plus we've been cooking *all* afternoon. They're duty-bound. By the way,' she says, turning me so my silver top glitters in the candlelight, 'you look truly lovely.'

'Thought I might dress up a little.'

'You always dress up for Willa,' she says, narrowing her eyes, 'your first love.'

'I should never have told you that.'

'Doorbell,' she says. 'I'll go.'

I hear voices in the hallway: Cat first, then Jamie's deep-toned reply. I lean against the table, face turned towards the kitchen door. And then there she is, Willa.

2.

The view from Tea Mountain

Robyn

There was a time in my life when everything seemed to be breaking.

This was the summer after I turned seventeen and I was home from school with Willa in tow. As soon as we arrived, the car broke down, which meant for the first three days we were completely marooned. 'So walk,' my mum said. 'It's only a couple of hours into town.'

Shortly after that Mum sat on her glasses and told everyone that she couldn't see a damned thing past the tape my dad had used to repair them. My mother compensated for her lack of sight by becoming even louder and more formidable. Willa jumped every time she opened her mouth, issuing orders and demands to whosoever was closest. To be fair, I'd done my best to prep Willa for meeting my family. *They're all completely barking*, I'd told her; *just be warned.*

Mum's favourite bowl broke too. It was the one that always sat in the middle of the kitchen table. Sometimes it had things left in it – keys, or fruit, or notes on scraps of paper – but mostly it didn't, because it was beautiful. It had a sandy-coloured rim, a central line of bright turquoise running through its middle and, at its base, a deep pool of cobalt glaze shot through with tiny green bubbles, like a blue hole in a sea. One day it was there. The next day, it wasn't. A different bowl had been put in its place, a bowl which, to the untrained eye, was *almost* the same, only the yellow glaze had a slightly greyer hue, the line of turquoise wasn't as clear, and the blue glaze had little flecks of burgundy in it. Still lovely, nobody was disagreeing with that, but definitely not the same bowl. Nobody owned up to that one. My dad shrugged, his expression hangdog. My brother shrugged.

'It wasn't me,' I said. I liked that bowl as much as anyone. Dad had made it, and, as I've said, it was beautiful. Anyway, it could have been anyone because we had a lot of visitors coming to the house around then, most of whom weren't even invited.

The plumbing broke and water flooded the kitchen. The stock fence broke and a whole bunch of sheep marched in off the moor, eating everything in sight. The gate to the chicken coop went as well.

Things were breaking. And the thing I broke was my arm.

I'd found a tin of moss-green paint at the back of my dad's workshop and had volunteered the two of us – Willa and me – to paint the kitchen cupboards. We put on old shirts and loud music. I'd picked out Madonna but Dad had insisted on Tina Turner, because, he said, there was no better music to paint to and, as it turned out, he was right.

I took charge of the high cupboards. I was stretched out at the top of a ladder with a loaded brush belting out 'What's Love Got to Do with It', one leg swung out behind partly for the counterbalance but mainly for the pose, when our dog Bach came wandering through. He was fifteen by then, with a completely white muzzle, arthritic legs, breath you could smell from ten paces and milky-blue eyes the vet said he couldn't do anything for. Yap, our other dog, a little Jack Russell cross, had taken to riding on his back like some sort of pilot. It didn't help

Bach to see any better but it definitely gave him a certain swagger, the air of a misspent youth in a circus. Well, anyway, Bach bashed into the bottom of the ladder and I was basically catapulted across the kitchen, landing with one arm twisted behind me and an excruciating pain shooting out from my shoulder.

It was the first and I think probably the only time in my life that I've ever been completely, totally winded. The air had been entirely knocked out of my lungs and I couldn't say a thing. There was noise, loud noise, but it wasn't coming from me. It was coming from Willa.

Everyone came running.

'Don't move her,' Mum said. 'She might have broken her neck.'

From my position on the floor, I now had an excellent view of the kitchen ceiling, which had acquired a splatter of bright green paint flicked across its entire length, like seaweed, even an entire kelp forest. Or a mystic dragon.

'Wow,' I said, 'that's amazing.'

'She's not making any sense,' Mum said. 'She's banged her head.'

'Perhaps you should call an ambulance, Nigel,' Dad said. My brother's name wasn't Nigel but I usually called him that on account of his general geekiness.

'I think it's a bit much,' my brother said, 'when your own father starts calling you Nigel.'

'It's a bit much,' I croaked, attempting the nerdy voice I used to imitate my brother.

'Just call an ambulance, Michael,' said Dad.

Mum dug around at the back of the kitchen pantry in order to find the first-aid kit.

'What's this?' she asked, emerging with a brown-paper bag she'd found hidden at the back. Inside the bag was her favourite bowl, in bits. She brought the pieces out one by one and placed them on the kitchen table, a look of astoundment on her face. 'I don't believe it,' she said. 'We'll talk about this later.' Shaking her head, she took a pair of kitchen scissors from the drawer next to the sink.

'That's it,' she said. She furrowed her brow, a vengeful look in her eyes.

'What are those for?' I said.

'We need to cut your shirt off,' Mum said. She snapped the scissors above my head.

'You definitely do not,' I said, trying to sit up.

Mum passed the scissors to Dad. My dad passed them back to my mother.

'Don't move,' she said. 'We need to see what's happened.' I thought it was pretty clear what had happened, given the angle of my arm. 'I can't believe you broke my favourite bowl,' she said, 'and didn't even say anything.' She started hacking up one side of the shirt while I tried to hold it down on the other.

'It wasn't me,' I said. 'I really like this shirt.'

'*This* shirt? This ancient thing of your dad's that you've requisitioned for painting?'

'Mum, *come on*. Plus, my bra's ancient. I *told* you I needed a new bra. It really wouldn't be too much to ask to have some nice bras. And I can go in the car. I'm okay. It just really hurts.'

'Cancel the ambulance,' Dad said. 'She can go in the car.' My brother returned to the kitchen and knelt by my side. Meanwhile my mother had cut away the last bit of my shirt. My entire family stared at my torso.

'What is *that*?' Mum said.

'Shit,' I said.

'Is that what I think it is?' She licked her finger and started rubbing at a little scroll of flowers and butterflies that spiralled up from my hip.

'Ow,' I said, 'arm.'

'Is that a tattoo? A real tattoo? I mean an *actual* tattoo?' The pitch of her voice was rising steadily. 'What on earth were you thinking? You actually got a tattoo? I don't believe it.' She looked directly at Willa. 'Did you know about this?'

Willa's eyes widened and she blinked rapidly.

'Okay,' Mum said, 'forget it, I'm not asking you.' She turned on my dad. 'You?' Dad instantly assumed the mild, doleful look he used when Mum was on the rampage. He shook his head. It was true, he hadn't known, although he had, in fact, signed the form giving parental permission. I'd told him it was something boring I needed for school. Picking my moment – his head under the bonnet, oil dripping everywhere, wrench in hand – I'd pointed out where he needed to sign, indicating the exact spot with my hand just so, coincidentally covering up the text.

'It *is* a bit of a surprise, Robyn,' said Dad.

'You do realize tattoos are permanent, don't you?' said Mum. 'You realize they're made with needles?' I attempted an expression that fell somewhere between *Gosh, needles, who knew?* and *Well, obviously that's not good*. 'Good grief. I can't believe it.'

'I quite like it,' Michael said. We all turned to look at him. He pointed at a small butterfly just below my ribs. 'That one there's a Marbled White – *Melanargia galathea*. Those chequerboard markings make it fairly unmistakable, though it's not always easy to tell the difference between the males and the females. The females have a slightly more yellowish hue. I suspect you've got a male there. They have false eyes on their underwings. They like grassland mostly, but recently I saw a female on some gorse, just yesterday, actually.'

At moments like that I loved my brother more than ever.

Days later, when a blanket of heat lay on the hill and it was too hot to breathe, too hot to sunbathe, too hot to think, Dad invited Willa and me into the pottery. Except for when he fired up the kiln, it was always cool in there. He needed our help, he said, with a small project. His studio was a few paces across the yard. It comprised an old stone building facing the moor with a long porch across the front and, its defining feature, the single word TEAS painted in metre-high letters on the roof. It was a word that could, on a clear day, be seen from a great distance. Tea Mountain, the locals called us. For them we were a useful landmark, but for tourists and walkers that word was a beacon, a shining invitation, beaming out at them across the hills. They weren't to know the old barn hadn't been used as a tea shop since Victorian times. Needless to say, we had a lot of random guests.

It was Willa's first time in the pottery, and while my dad showed her around I helped myself to some crank from the clay bins and attempted to model my family using my one remaining hand: my mother, short and round with thick glasses; my dad, tall and skinny and a little stooped, as if he were always just about to duck through a door; my brother with his wonky legs and lovable beaky face. I thought about making Willa too, but somehow clay wasn't the right material for her. She needed something more fragile, gossamer and glass. Something to capture all that flyaway hair and pale freckly skin. She was the most beautiful girl I knew.

Dad was showing Willa the rows of drying grey vessels, the warm brown ones already once-fired and the finished ones ready to sell. He opened jars of powdered glaze, showing Willa their dusty contents and explaining how the various combinations of manganese, bone ash and tin would magically transform in the heat of the kiln, how copper was green and cobalt was blue and antimony was yellow, and not to touch that last one because it was absolutely lethal.

My dad never hurried anything. Slowly the tour of the

pottery worked its way over to the bench where I was using a clay knife to get at the unremitting itch beneath my cast. He laid out the pieces of my mother's favourite bowl.

'So here's the thing,' he said. 'There's a Japanese process for mending pottery with tree sap which I've always wanted to try, where the cracks aren't hidden away, but made a thing of, made *deliberately* visible. What happens is you dust the lines of the repair with a powdered precious metal – gold, copper, whatever. The idea is that repairing something – something loved, something treasured – makes it even more beautiful. A nice idea, no? It's called *kintsugi*. What d'you think? Want to give it a go? I need you two to help hold the pieces in place.'

'Fine,' I said, deciding for both of us. It was too hot to do anything else. 'Let's do it.' I pushed one large shard towards another to see if they might fit. They did not.

'You ever worked with clay before, Willa?' Dad asked after a while. She shook her head. He glanced at her fingernails, bitten to the quick.

'You've got the right nails for it. I could teach you to throw, if you like. We could have you making a half-decent pot in a couple of days. Robyn here can do it in her sleep.'

I saw a momentary flash of delight fly across Willa's face, then it was gone. 'Are you sure?' she glanced from him to me. 'I'd hate to, you know, get in your way or something.'

'Nothing better than a willing student.' Dad was focused on a slab of pottery, drawing a careful line of glue along its edge. 'I'll bet you're used to a bit more action, generally, aren't you? I'll bet Robyn didn't tell you how cut off we are.'

'No, that's right, Dad, I *completely* got her here on false pretences,' I said. 'I told her we lived in a castle –'

'I'd hate to think of you getting bored here, stuck out in the sticks.'

'With servants. And a hot-air balloon.'

Willa opened her mouth to speak, then closed it again, her cheeks flushed. Her eyes met mine.

The bowl grew slowly, piece by piece. It turned out to be strangely satisfying, working out how each slab would fit with another, returning each bit to its rightful place. The time slipped by.

'I reckon this is how dreams work,' Dad said. 'Your mind picks up all the pieces of your day and puts them together to see how they fit. That's how dreams end up being so strange. It's when you put two bits together that don't belong.'

I caught Willa's eye and grinned at her. 'I do so love your ponderous little soul, Dad,' I said. 'You're a natural philosopher.'

By the end of the afternoon a quiet had fallen on all of us, something calming and meditative. Afternoon light sloped in through the window. Outside, swifts looped above bone-white grasses in air filled with the bright specks of insects. Bach nuzzled our feet. Yap curled up in a chair. Dad unrolled two little brown-paper twists and their contents flashed in the light. Inside was real powdered silver, real powdered gold. He offered Willa the choice. I would definitely have picked gold.

'Silver,' Willa said, straight off.

'Silver it is.'

And, finally, it was done. The bowl was transformed. Little silver-white lines wound around its surface, merging, dividing, and all of them reflecting the late-afternoon sun. Against the sandy rim they looked like the passage of water through a desert. Dad had been right. The bowl really was more beautiful than before.

'You can fix anything, given the right tools,' Dad said. His voice was gentle and he was looking directly at Willa. I widened my eyes and glared at him. Willa said nothing. She was still looking down at the bowl, her almost-red hair falling across her face. Perhaps she thought he was speaking to me. You never really could tell with Willa. She gave so little away.

'Tell me about your sister,' I said to her that night. We were lying in the grass with the dogs, bundled up in blankets, pillows under our heads, both of us looking up at the star-mottled underbelly of the sky. I'd known Willa almost a year by then, and never once asked her that question, not in the early days when she'd first pitched up at my boarding school, not since. We'd all worked out who she was. We'd seen the aerial shots of the house.

At first I didn't think she'd heard me. Or, worse, she'd heard me, but wasn't going to reply. I realized I was holding my breath. I was about to whisper *Sorry* when she cleared her throat and started to speak.

'Chatty, friendly. Kind. She had a really strong sense of right and wrong. And she loved animals. She would have loved these two.' Yap was nestled between the two of us, she stroked his ears, and he yawned in appreciation.

'And she was funny.' Her voice sounded raspy and thin. 'Witty, I mean. Quick-witted. Clever-funny. She was never at a loss for something to say, even when everyone else – *anyone* else – would have kept quiet. Not like me.' She turned her head to look at me. 'I always need to think things over first, you know? Like I'm always trying to work out if I'm wrong or if I'm going to offend someone, and by then the conversation's moved on. I've always been like that. Laika was the complete opposite. Whatever she was thinking, she just said, any old how. Dad always said she never stopped to think. But that wasn't it. She was thinking all the time. She was properly clever, I mean, not just bright but really, really bright. Gifted. That level of bright.'

'You're bright. You're the most academic girl in the school.'

Willa's hand went to a little silver chain around her neck. She felt around until her fingers found its tiny dolphin pendant. It caught the moon's light and glinted, like a torchlight in fog. 'Not like Laika. I do well because it genuinely matters to me. Lai never worked hard at anything; it all just came naturally to her. But she wasn't what you'd call academic, not in the traditional sense. It just didn't bother her all that much. She wasn't in the least motivated by the idea of coming first. If it didn't interest her, or if she didn't see the point, she just wouldn't do the work. Her school grades were pretty average – some of them were dire. Her teachers said she was the classic case of *could do better*. It used to drive Mum mad. She always says her biggest regret was leaving school without any qualifications. I think she . . . well.'

We lay in silence. I didn't want to risk looking at her in case she stopped talking. Instead I kept my eyes on the sky, where plum-dark clouds passed slowly under the stars like distant migrating whales and pipistrelles darted like tiny black fish.

'She was a fantastic mimic too. Honestly, she could pick up someone's accent and take them off within seconds. And she wasn't always kind with it either. She could be rude. And I do mean seriously, hideously, embarrassingly rude: confrontational. She never knew when to back down. She was fearless, completely fearless. She wasn't afraid of anything or anyone. She couldn't control it: when she got angry, she'd smash things.' I saw her shake her head slightly, then she lapsed back into a long silence. I wondered if she'd fallen asleep.

'I'm not meant to say things like that, am I?' she said. 'You know, that whole thing about not speaking ill of – well, you know. But anyway. That's who she was.'

I reached for her hand under the blankets and she shifted on to her side to face me. 'On the news they described her as a likeable and popular girl with masses of potential and lots of friends and a loving, stable family. I don't know, perhaps you saw. It's like reporters keep a list of stock phrases to describe teenagers. They're always *plucky*, or *brave*, or *tragic*. Even the photo they used didn't look a bit like her, not at the point she disappeared anyway. I wouldn't have recognized her from the TV, so how was anyone else meant to? She didn't even have any close friends. Laika could be a complete pain in the arse. Dad used to tell her she was pig-headed and bolshy. And she was too, at times. She was irritating and argumentative and difficult, but she was also wonderful and absolutely brilliant.'

'In other words, a real person.' I squeezed her hand.

'Yes. She was a real person.' Willa took a sudden deep breath. I heard a crack in her voice. 'And I really, *really* miss her.'

'Oh, God,' I whispered. 'I'm so sorry. I shouldn't have asked. I shouldn't have said anything.' I thought, perhaps, she was about to throw back her head and howl. But she breathed deeply again and held her breath several times, then exhaled slowly.

'It's not you,' she said, her voice small but controlled again in the dark of the night. 'I'm glad you asked, honestly. I mean that. I think about her all the time. All the time. I mean every hour, every minute, every second of the day. But nobody ever asks about her as a person. I know people don't know what to say, or they're afraid I'll get upset. I get that, really, I do. But it's not even been a full year –'

She turned on to her other side, away from me. I rolled on my side too. I put my arm around her waist and she found my fingers and held them. Moving slowly, I tucked my knees up behind hers and put my cheek against the back of her neck, my nose buried in her hair. The night rolled on. I think I slept. When I woke again it was still dark, but I somehow knew Willa wasn't sleeping. I held her tight.

'Did she look like you?'

'Not really. If anything, she looked more like Dad. Her hair was darker than mine. I look more like my mum.'

We were both awake for the dawn. In every direction, as far as the eye could see, the grass was covered with the silver-white webs of funnel spiders, each with its own central spiral tunnelling down into the grass. And every strand of every web was hung with tiny drops of dew, like tiny beads on tiny silver chains, and every web was connected to the next, to make one giant, floating, delicate carpet, and all of it was covered with countless tiny sparkling orbs, reflecting the world in miniature.

'They'll find her, Willa.'

'They won't.'

'You don't know.'

'I do know,' she said. 'I know.'

3.
Supper with friends

Robyn

Willa slips into the kitchen. She gives me a quick, uncertain smile, then glances once towards the sound of voices in the hallway: Jamie talking to Cat. I pull her into a hug. Her hair smells of rose and amber and something else, something summery, orange blossom perhaps, clementines.

'About this morning,' she says, her voice a low, urgent whisper, 'I –'

She breaks off as our five-year-old, Sophie, bowls into the room, throws her arms around my friend's waist and almost knocks her off her feet. It will have to wait.

'Let Willa get her coat off,' I say, smiling as Willa bends with the grace of a dancer to present Sophie with a book and a soft grey rabbit in a paisley waistcoat. I watch her pass a hand over our daughter's dark hair and stroke her cheek. Willa looks stunning, truly beautiful, in a deep forest-green wrap dress that contrasts wonderfully with the almost-red of her hair. Large diamonds sparkle in her earlobes. She is all cheekbones and hips and legs.

'Wow,' I say, 'you look *amazing.*'

'Check these out,' Cat says. She comes in from the hallway, clutching an enormous bouquet filled with white roses, peonies, thistles and sprigs of eucalyptus, followed by Jamie cradling two expensive-looking bottles of wine. He bends to kiss my cheek with a delicacy somewhat unexpected in such a large man, his breath hot on my cheek and holding within it the sweet-sour tang of an earlier drink.

'Robyn,' he says smoothly, in the low tones of a late-night radio host, 'it's always lovely to see you.'

Willa offers to take Sophie back up to bed, leaving us to entertain Jamie. He dwarfs my fine-boned wife. In the cluttered space of our Victorian kitchen he looks too large, too tall, like some luxury cruise liner jammed into a narrow Venetian canal, and I immediately find myself willing him to sit. I pull back a chair and flash a smile at Cat as he lowers himself into it. He crosses one leg over the other, ankle to knee, scoops up a handful of almonds from a bowl and ladles the entire lot into his mouth. I edge round the table to sit next to him while Cat arranges the flowers in a vase. He leans back and, in a languid gesture, drapes one arm heavily over the back of my chair. I lean forward, putting my elbows on the table.

'Why don't I take charge of the wine?' he says. 'Make myself useful.' He examines the label on one of the bottles. 'Pass me a corkscrew and I'll open this one, if you like.'

'We've got fizz too,' I say. 'Or perhaps you'd like an aperitif? Vodka? Gin? I make an amazing Martini.'

'You're okay,' he says, popping the cork and pouring himself a large glass of velvety wine. 'This will do.' For a crystallizing moment I can't think of a single thing to say to Jamie, a man I've known now for almost two years. I need Willa back, her grace and beauty and familiarity, to be our common ground. He takes a long drink of the wine, and I follow his eyes as they make a slow sweep of our kitchen and its detritus of family life – the drawings and photographs on the fridge, kindergarten notices, the pile of small shoes by the back door, a stray abandoned bear. I push a plate of canapés in his direction and he selects a small square of rye bread topped with cream cheese, red pepper and caviar. A fish egg glues itself to his lower lip and, when he next starts to speak, I can't stop looking at that little black speck.

'Interesting kind of fix,' he says, running a finger over the silver lines of our favourite bowl. He breaks into a grin. 'Couldn't afford a new one?'

I smile. 'Kintsugi, it's called. It's a technique that signifies healing and forgiving. Mending things with love. My mum and dad gave it to us when Cat and I got married.'

'Dear oh dear,' he says, sounding amused. 'They reckon you two argue, do they? Better watch your back, then, Robyn, Cat's probably fairly handy with a spear.'

My mouth drops open and Cat turns from the stove so fast that her elbow sweeps a side plate off the worktop. There's a loud crack as it hits the floor.

'I'm sorry,' she says, '*what*?'

'What did I miss?' Willa says, coming back in.

There's a beat. One of the many things I love about my wife is her grit. She speaks her mind, calls out bad behaviour, challenges people, stands up for what's right. I've never known her to let a racist comment go past unremarked, not ever, not once. But now she glances once at Willa and then, clear-eyed, at me. '*Nothing*', she says, a small but definite signal to let it go.

'You should kin-thing that,' Jamie says. Cat plucks up the broken pieces, raises the lid of the pedal bin and drops in the bits. You'd think she hadn't heard.

'Let me get you a drink,' I say to Willa. 'G and T?'

Jamie looks at the tray of canapés with wolfish eyes. 'She's not drinking,' he says. 'She'll have water.'

'I'll have one,' Cat says. 'Actually, why don't you make it a double?' She turns back to the hob and the kitchen fills with the warming scents of ginger and lime. I place a tall glass within her reach and, as I move close to nuzzle her cheek, she throws me a look and mutters, 'Jesus fucking Christ.'

I squeeze her arm and turn back to our guests. To Willa I say, 'I thought you might want to sit next to Michael tonight. He always asks how you are.'

'The egghead, hey? So you two are great pals, are you? Darling, you never told me that.' Jamie fills up his glass and, smiling broadly, growls, 'Should I be jealous?'

'Who's he bringing?' Willa says.

'Some girl called Liv. I don't know much about her. I get the impression she's a bit younger than us. He did say she reminds him a bit of you.'

'*Me?*' Willa's eyes widen. 'In what way?'

'Not a clue. His messages always read like flipping telegrams, like he's paying for every word.'

'Doorbell,' Cat says. 'I've got it.'

Flushed from the cold and ushering a slim woman ahead of him, my brother lumbers softly into the kitchen. 'Liv, meet my little sis,' he says, 'and this is the lovely Cat.' Michael embraces my wife with genuine warmth, kissing her on both cheeks, before enveloping me in a bear hug. I bury my head in his woolly brown jumper, wrap my arms around his back and inhale deeply. How does Michael always manage to smell of home? Heather and applewood; peat, grassland, wet dog. He embraces Willa too, landing an awkward kiss somewhere between her cheekbone and ear before quickly introducing her to Liv. Then he turns to Jamie.

'Jamie,' Michael says. 'Good to see you.'

'The man of the moment,' Jamie says, flashing Willa an amused look. He leans across the table to shake Michael's hand and then rises out of his chair to meet Liv, an affable smile on his broad, handsome face. He bends to kiss her cheek, offers to take her coat, admires the flowers she's brought and, still smiling, questions her about their journey into London. Liv replies affably, but I think she looks somewhat ambushed by all that attention: I see her glance at Michael, giving him a slightly quizzical smile. She's young, well, younger than me anyway – maybe in her early to mid thirties. And, yes, I can see what Michael meant when he said she reminded him of Willa. Liv's colouring is darker and she's not as tall, but she certainly has Willa's slender frame and fine hair. She has a similar sort of beauty, with full lips and an oval face with high cheekbones. Then I look over to where Willa is standing quietly off to one side, behind the main nub of the group, as still as a painting. She's also watching Liv, really watching her, in fact, her grey eyes taking her in.

And not just watching Liv, I think. Willa is examining her.

Willa is transfixed.

'Nate and Claudette are running late,' Cat says, looking up from her phone.

'Claudette?' Jamie says.

'French,' Cat says, 'doesn't speak a word of English.'

'*What?*' I say. 'You never told me that. You're kidding, right?'

'I'm not, seriously. Nate just sent me a text. How's your French?'

'Rusty. I've barely used it since school. You?'

'You *know* I did Spanish. Sounds like you're on your own there, then.'

'You're joking. *Bloody hell*, Cat.'

'Anyway, they're stuck in traffic,' Cat says. 'I'll stick the wontons on the table, just to stop everyone from starving.'

Jamie pulls out the chair opposite his own and, with a flourish, offers it to Liv. Slowly, she sits.

'So, Liv,' I say, 'how did you meet Michael?'

Liv tucks a stray lock of hair behind her ear. 'I'm at the university,' she says, 'writing up my doctoral thesis. Michael said you're at Bart's?'

'I'm a radiographer. I mainly work with cancer patients –'

'I'm an ambassador for Pearl River Wines,' Jamie says, refilling his glass. He waits for Liv to look at him again, then lowers his voice, smiling. 'But my genuine passion is for conservation.'

Liv hesitates. Then she says, 'Antiques?'

'Lions.'

'Interesting,' she says. She sounds polite.

'It is,' Jamie says. He leans across the table. 'I'd love to tell you more.'

I throw a look at Cat, but she's busy checking her phone. 'They're still about ten minutes away,' she says. 'Sorry, everyone. It's bloody typical of Nate to be late.'

I think Liv looks grateful for this quick change of subject. 'At least he let you know,' she says. 'Don't you hate it when people don't do that?' A dark expression moves across her face. 'You're waiting and waiting and then you end up worrying that something truly awful's happened –'

Hang on, I think, *where's she going with this?* 'Drink anyone?' I say. 'Liv?'

'– and you're never going to see them again.'

Too late. Willa stares at Liv. She makes a sound, a small, high *ha*, and the rest of us seem to take a collective intake of breath. Cat looks at me fast.

Jamie shifts in his seat. 'Willa,' he says, his voice low, and I've a feeling he would reach out and put a giant hand firmly on my friend's arm, were it not for the fact that I'm sitting between them.

Willa stares at Liv, hard-eyed and silent. She makes that sound again, the small *ha*, but lower now, softer; an expelled, held breath. Then, speaking slowly, her eyes still fixed on Liv, she says, 'My sister disappeared when she was thirteen.' With some force, she adds, 'I mean, she just *vanished*. We didn't have a *clue* –'

Cat makes a tiny movement. I catch her eye and she throws me a *Do something* look, a microscopic expression of alarm. I reach out and take Willa's pale hand in mine.

'Her birthday was a month ago, November the third.'

'That's always going to be a difficult date,' I say; 'anniversaries are hard.'

Willa stares at Liv. 'She was just a *child*. She'd be a grown woman now, thirty-six. She would have changed a lot, of course.' She gives a high, humourless laugh. 'The awful thing is, I could pass her on the street and not even *recognize* her. She could be *anyone*.' Her grey eyes dart around the group, then land again on Liv. 'I mean, she could be you.'

There is a moment of stunned, horrible silence.

A bell chimes from the hallway.

'They're here,' Cat says, rising rapidly from the table. 'Finally. Thank Christ for that.'

Nate, apologetic, loud, shaking off the cold night air like a cat, strides into the kitchen. He's tall, with closely cropped hair, dark freckled skin and a wide mouth that breaks easily, fluidly into smiles. He drops the hand of the woman he's with to hug first me and Cat, then Michael and Liv. Then he makes to move towards Jamie and Willa, but Cat touches his arm and shakes her head. Jamie is talking to Willa quietly by the back door, holding her close, and secretly I'm relieved to see him stepping up to comfort her. It's obviously what she needs. We give them some space.

'Et voilà,' Nate says, 'je vous présente ma magnifique Claudette, ma petite amie.' He introduces his girlfriend to Cat and translates his sister's warm welcome into French. Based on past experience, Claudette is not the woman I'd expected him to bring: most of Nate's previous girlfriends looked like models. Claudette isn't tall; rather, she's my height or shorter, with a lithe, impish body and cropped, boyish hair, a strong nose and a full mouth. Her clothes – black jeans, white blouse and a thin orange chiffon scarf draped loosely round her neck – are worn with the sort of easy chic that I've always envied in the French. Behind tortoiseshell-rimmed glasses, her eyes move evenly around the room, taking in my brother and Liv, me, then glancing at Jamie once, and then again, where he still stands at the back of the kitchen with his arms folded protectively around Willa.

'And, Robyn,' Nate says, turning to me, 'I'm right in thinking you speak some French, right?'

I nod with as much enthusiasm as I can muster. 'I can certainly give it a go,' I say, turning to Claudette and smiling; and then, with some hesitation, 'Bienvenue, Claudette, je suis ravie de te recontrer.'

'Moi de même,' she says, talking rapidly, gesturing with her hands. 'Je suis désolée d'arriver en retard. La circulation était chaotique, mais je pense que l'on a pris une mauvaise route.'

She's lost me completely. Something about poor circulation maybe? I think I heard the word 'circulation' in there somewhere. And possibly something about eating? And *mauvaise* – she's been sick perhaps? She had food poisoning?

'Oui,' I say, putting a hand to my lips, 'um –' I turn to Nate for help and realize that he is almost crying with silent laughter, as is Cat.

'Claudette speaks excellent English, Robs,' Nate says. 'She's practically fluent.'

I look at my wife, then back at Claudette, who shrugs and says in perfect, if softly accented English, 'Thanks for having us and I'm really sorry we're late. That honestly wasn't my idea.'

'You were in on this,' I say, turning to a grinning Cat. Nate's arm is slung around her shoulders, the siblings delighting in the thrill of their guile. 'I hate you all. Come and eat before I throw the lot of you out. And that,' I say to Cat, 'includes you.'

While everyone finds their seats, Cat and I load dishes on to the table – crab cakes and steamed red snapper with Thai basil and lime, bowls of pickled cucumber sprinkled with tiny red chillis, vegan curries of varying spiciness, vegetables tossed in coriander and soy, sticky rice and lots of bright, fragrant dips. We top up our guests' wine and water glasses and, to my relief, the room is filled with talk. No one is sitting where I'd planned.

Nate's positive energy is a joy. He talks about their life in Paris, his work teaching music, his band, their gigs, the project that has brought him to London. He describes how Claudette was teaching his yoga class, the months it took him to persuade her to go on a date. Claudette raises her eyebrows, cocks her head on one side and looks more amused than flattered. Cat and I exchange a look. This is a first: to our knowledge, Nate never chases anyone. It fits that she's a yoga teacher, I think: she's completely self-possessed, the picture of studied serenity. I can totally imagine her in the lotus position, eyes shut, meditating. I steal glances at her and I realize she's doing the same – I see her looking carefully at Cat, at me, at Liv, angling her head down the table to where Willa sits at the other end. Her focus is fascinating. When she talks, and when she listens, she gives each person her full, undivided attention, as if they're the only person in the room. I watch her take small portions of the various curries. She doesn't touch the wine.

'What's your thesis about, Liv?' Cat says, as later we clear the table of the main course and bring out a long wooden platter filled with slices of mango, strawberries and watermelon scattered with mint.

'I've been looking into the corruption of memory,' Liv says, 'by which I mean how memory can be changed, altered with time. I'm a psychologist.'

'Oh,' I say, genuinely surprised. I had somehow just assumed that Liv worked in the Zoology Department with Michael.

Michael looks at me and smiles. 'Go on,' he says, 'say it. You thought she'd be studying the sex lives of limpets.' I laugh. He knows me *far* too well.

'Interesting stuff,' says Claudette, turning dark, tranquil eyes towards Liv.

'It is,' Liv says. 'It really is. I've been looking into false memories. It's truly extraordinary how easily the human brain can be tricked into believing it remembers something that didn't happen. You'd be amazed.'

She has our attention now. We all sit up a little.

'Even on a simple level, we can have wildly differing memories of a single event, where you'd be right in thinking that everyone experienced the exact same thing. Take this supper party, for instance. If in six months' time, I asked you individually to recall tonight in as much detail as possible, it's more than likely that you'd each give me a slightly, perhaps even a *wildly* different account – with variations in everything from what everyone was wearing and the order in which people arrived, to what we ate, what we discussed and who said what.'

'I don't really see how that would work,' Jamie says; 'we're literally sitting around the same table.'

'You'd be surprised,' Liv says.

'Do it, then,' Jamie says, 'six months from today. Count us in.'

'But if we knew we were going to be asked to recall everything, wouldn't that fact alone alter the way we processed tonight's events? People would be actively trying to remember everything as it happened,' Nate says.

'Definitely,' Liv says.

'More than that,' Cat says, 'wouldn't it even alter the way we *acted* tonight? Right down to what we said? We'd all become hyper self-aware. Nobody would want other people remembering that they were the one who'd come out with something stupid. We'd all be trying to outdo each other with our fierce wit and intelligence.'

'Totally,' Liv says, 'no doubt about it.'

Now Willa joins in. 'So what factors influence how we actually remember events?'

'Good question.'

'Drugs, alcohol,' Jamie says.

'Sure,' Liv says, 'they're a given.'

'Dementia, ageing,' says Claudette.

'Yes. And there's some fascinating research being done in that area. But now we're really crossing into neurology, because we're talking about irreversible changes to the brain's structure. Similarly with brain injury. Also, there's your general health and we know the quality of your sleep affects memory too, not to mention other environmental factors such as distractions – physical, mental, what's going on around us. Also, prior events, whether they've been consciously noted or not.'

The yellow light from the candles plays on our faces and I find myself taking a mental snapshot of the scene, each of us trapped like insects in amber, leaning into the centre of the table, absorbed in the discussion and in each other. Michael looking at me. Cat and Jamie looking at Liv. Willa looking at Claudette.

'Then we get on to other factors: state of mind, wish fulfilment, stress. Embarrassment. Humiliation. Guilt.'

'You mean reworking events to fit our own narrative,' says Cat.

'Exactly. And now it gets really interesting: transference of memory, by which I mean absorbing other people's memories, taking possession of them, as if they belonged to you. And, as it happens, this is my area of research. We all do this, to some extent. For instance, we all have that one story that gets slightly embellished in the retelling and, over time, the exaggerated story becomes the version we actually believe, indistinguishable from the original in our own minds. And here's another example, and you don't have to answer this out loud, but did you ever date someone who, when you look back, you think of as highly irritating?' There's an awkward laugh, and a pause in which no one meets anyone else's eye. 'Well, it's a bit like that,' she says. 'You've shifted your perception of them. Your memory is colluding with your subliminal desire to put that person firmly outside your emotional reach. And this shift in thinking happens on a cultural level too – take Princess Diana, for example – she was treated like a saint when she died, whereas now she's very often described as if she were slightly unhinged. How did that shift in thinking happen on a national – even a global – scale?'

'We've been collectively manipulated,' Cat says, 'to remember things differently.'

'Precisely,' Liv says.

'It's important research,' Michael says, 'given we're constantly bombarded with information, much of which comes with a certain agenda attached. We need to know the extent to which our memories are reliable, and, equally, the extent to which memory itself can be deliberately constructed.'

I look at my beautiful, brilliant brother and smile. He sounds so flipping earnest and I love him for that. He's always been that way, Michael. Even as a kid he was that person, a small, ardent professor of life, even then, when we were both so utterly unfettered by life's responsibilities, entirely free to do whatever we liked. How green I must have been, somehow imagining my summers would always be like that: just an endless stream of warm, carefree days that seemed to stretch on forever. Then Willa came to stay and everything changed after that. Michael was there too, that summer, and I wonder now just how much he still remembers of that time: how much he saw in the first place, how much he missed.

Me? I remember it all.

4.

Summer break

Robyn

When Dad taught Willa how to throw a bowl, even Michael came to watch, which just goes to show that we were all a little in love with my friend. Mum said she had *very nice manners*, which meant she called her Mrs Bee. She called my dad Chris. I watched my brother's eyes following her around the house. I'd never seen my brother pay attention to *anyone* before, let alone one of my friends. After all, he was nearly four years older than me. He used to call me *Kid*.

'Don't they have girls at Oxford?' I asked him when Willa was in the shower. 'What makes you think she'd be interested in *you*?' In my head those words had sounded playful and fun, but that's not the way they came out. I grinned. I poked him in the ribs. 'Just joking,' I said.

Michael even invited Willa into his bedroom to look at his rock collection, a grey cardboard box filled with a variety of specimens, some from the moor but others from far more exotic locations. Each one was nestled in a tiny bed of cotton wool: malachite, azurite, obsidian, rock rose, and Brian, a yellow pebble I'd found in the river and gifted to my brother, writing his name on a tiny paper slip in the same miniature handwriting that Michael used to label everything else. Willa trailed slow fingers over the fossils on his windowsill.

'Do you ever collect birds' eggs?' she said. She would honestly ask the oddest questions at times.

'You mean from nests?'

She nodded.

'Well, no,' my brother said. 'First off, that's illegal. But, more than that, it would be wrong.'

Willa nodded again and moved on around his room. For the longest time she stared at a map of the oceans that Michael had pinned to the wall.

'Show me where there are blue holes.'

'Blue holes? Sure. The one everyone's seen pictures of is here' – Michael pointed towards Belize – 'but there are others too, less well known, not as big or impressive. There's one off the coast of South Africa. One here, near Egypt. The Caribbean. There're lots of them, actually, even inland ones. Here – Oman. They're all just sinkholes, but aerial photos make them look really impressive – like you're looking into an abyss.'

Willa seemed to sigh and for a beat we all stood in silence. Then I showed her the line my brother had drawn on the boards of his floor, marking the point I wasn't allowed to cross until I was almost thirteen.

'She was a contamination hazard,' Michael said. 'She contained glitter.'

Later, finding a quiet moment alone, she asked me about Michael's limp.

'He was born like that,' I told her. 'He had a bad case of talipes equinovarus – you know, club feet? Plus, some other stuff going on with his hips. He had a whole bunch of operations when he was a kid and not all of them went well, so both his legs were in plaster for ages, years, in fact. I walked before he did.'

'That's awful.'

'Don't,' I told her. 'It's not a big thing. Okay, so he was never going to play rugby or run marathons or whatever, but that's it. It's literally never stopped him doing anything. And get this – I was *so* jealous of him. Dad used to walk around with him balanced on his feet, to build up his muscle strength. And believe me, Willa, I've never been allowed to forget that I had a massive tantrum about that one time, shouting and screaming, hurling myself on the floor, banging my little fists, the works. Turns out *I* wanted club feet too, so *I* could be walked around on Dad's feet. Then, of course, he grew up to be a complete genius. Left me standing. No wonder I got into sport. It's the only thing I've ever been able to beat him at hands down. So. There you have it. I was a brat,' I said, grinning at her, 'which, of course, happens to be the natural role of little sisters.' Willa gave me a small smile.

'I suspect it is,' she said.

In the pottery Dad slammed the clay on to the wheel and showed Willa how to get it going.

'I can't do it,' she said, as her bird-like hands were dragged wildly around. 'I'm not strong enough.'

'You can,' Dad said. 'You're stronger than you think.'

He showed her how to focus on her core and work from there, to still her mind and body, then to power her thumbs down into the very middle of the clay, opening it from mouse-hole to foxhole, then widening into whirlpool, vortex, and eventually, fantastically, to a black hole with all the rings of Saturn spinning up its sides. Then the entire thing collapsed and hefted itself off to one side of the wheel like a midnight drunk.

'Sorry,' she said.

'There's no need for *sorry*,' Dad said; 'you're learning. Have another go.' He scooped up the folds of wet clay and threw them into the recycling bin. Then he slammed another slab hard into the centre of the wheel and off she went again, and again. I knew her back and arms would be aching like hell, but she wouldn't give up. She made pots with strange lumps and heavy rims and thick bottoms, and Dad sliced each of them off and dumped them into the bin like wet rags.

And then it happened.

'Stop right there,' Dad said, slowing the wheel to a crawl. 'That's it. That's the keeper. That's the one.' In its centre was a perfect pot, with thin, grey, even walls and a lovely open shape.

'That,' my dad said, 'is a thing of beauty.' Willa grinned. It had taken her three hours. I'd known she was going to be good.

'Okay,' Dad said, 'get out of here. Take a break.'

The pot had to dry out and be biscuit fired, which meant that it wasn't until the last night of her stay that we could finally glaze the thing. The day had been too hot to do it, the air as languid and still as a sleeping lizard, so we waited until after supper.

The raku kiln lived on bricks in the yard and looked a bit like an old metal dustbin, which it was. Fired up, it radiated a fierce heat. Willa's pot sat inside its glowing chamber, and Dad, usually so calm, fussed around the outside like a jackdaw, constantly checking the temperature and the seals.

'Okay,' he said, 'we're on.'

He kitted out Willa in a long leather apron, some goggles and a pair of thick gauntlets that almost covered her entire arms. Using metal tongs, he took the lid off the top of the kiln and lifted out her pot, now glowing orange-white with heat. 'Open that one,' he said, pointing to another smaller dustbin; 'that's the reduction chamber.'

'Reduction of what?' Willa asked.

'Oxygen. Watch.'

It was full of woodchips. Dad positioned the glowing pot

inside. Sparks and flames instantly burst out in every direction, hissing and sputtering. We all leapt back. Little spits of fire flew across my dad's forehead and small puffs of smoke popped around his head. He clamped down the lid over the pot and stood back, a wild grin on his face.

'Give it a few minutes,' he said. A small part of his hair had withered into wiry crisps and one of his eyebrows was smoking. There was a long black smudge across his brow where he'd wiped his glove across his face.

'Kiln Face,' I said.

Dad stood with his hands on his hips. He couldn't stop smiling. After a while, he gave the metal tongs to Willa so she could pick out her pot. It was still glowing a bit, smoky dark with wood ash and with a few curls of burning wood clinging to the surface. But we could already glimpse the glaze, iridescent and glittering beneath the blackened areas of ash, the colours of a bluebottle. Dad told her to plunge it into a bucket. The water hissed and spat. When he picked it back out, wild crackles had shot across its surface, thin and wiry in some places, dark and deep in others. The base of the pot was a deep copper umber and its rim a bright cobalt blue. It was absolutely lovely.

'Wow,' Willa said, her voice thrilled, 'thank you.'

'You did it,' Dad said. 'It's your hard work. Take it home. Give it to your mum.'

And that was it. It was just a normal summer. We hadn't done very much. We'd sunbathed in the garden and watched buzzards make lazy turns of the thermals above; read novels, painted our nails, listened to music and swum in the river. We'd walked the dogs to see wild ponies and had distant sightings of skittish deer. At night we'd sat in deckchairs with my parents and brother and looked at the stars. The weeks had just floated away.

Everyone offered to take Willa to the station on her last morning, so in the end we all went, even Michael, despite the fact it was practically two hours each way, so all three of us rammed into the back of the Landy. My brother sat jammed behind my mum, wearing a newly ironed shirt with long sleeves and a button-down collar, the burnished mahogany of his hair gleaming in the sun. *He's brushed it*, I thought. *Oh, Michael.* He smelt of fresh linen and something else too, something nice. I sniffed in his direction. *Aftershave.*

On the station platform, I hugged Willa and she hugged Michael, even though his arms stayed clamped fast to his sides. Dad patted her shoulder and Mum held her tight for a moment and then got a little weepy and that set me off too. She'd stayed with us for a month after all, and that made her family as far as my lot were concerned. Dad had given her a pitcher from his pottery as a leaving gift, a tall, rounded vessel in a deep sea-green with an elegant curving handle, which he'd wrapped up together with her pot. He checked the package was safely wedged on the baggage shelf, then we all waved until the train rolled out of sight. And then she was gone.

Back in the car, Mum sat with her hands on the steering wheel, staring ahead. 'Lovely girl,' she said finally. She turned in her seat so that she could look at the rest of us. 'Is it not at all odd that –' She stopped. She looked at us. She took a breath. 'If it was me,' she said, 'if I was her mum, I know it's far, but if it was me, I can't help thinking I would have come to pick her up. I just don't think I would have made her get the train.' She stopped. Then she said, 'After all that has happened to that family.'

'She's seventeen, Mum,' I said. 'She's not a baby.' Don't ask me why I felt a sudden need to defend her parents – I'd never even met them.

'Perhaps,' my dad said, rearranging the crux of my thoughts into more diplomatic form, 'they don't want her to be afraid about going anywhere on her own.'

'I mean, she's got to get across London on the Underground,' Mum said, 'with all that baggage.'

There was a silence.

'I'm just saying,' Mum said, 'all I am saying is, if that was my daughter, if Willa was my daughter, I wouldn't want her doing that. I just wouldn't.'

And there was no arguing with that.

5.
Supper with friends

Robyn

A sound like a small bell pulls me back into the room: a fingernail tapping on glass. Jamie catches my eye and smiles, then nods at his empty glass. I pour him another glass of red.

'Now think about your *earliest* memory,' Liv says. 'Okay, done that?' She looks around the table. 'What is it?'

Jamie leans back, placing both hands flat on the table. 'Easy,' he says, 'sitting on my dad's knee, drinking beer from his pint. I can even remember what I was wearing – stripy top, blue shorts.'

'How old would you have been?'

'Two, two and a half max.'

'Michael?'

'I remember Robyn being born. I would have been three years, eight months and, let me think, fifteen days old. Mum had her at home. Apparently Mum hadn't realized how far along she was and suddenly it was all happening. Dad had to deliver her with one ear clamped to the telephone, following instructions from a midwife. I remember seeing her head coming out, then her body. They let me cut the cord.'

'Oh my God,' Willa says.

'That's not the worst of it,' I tell her, laughing. 'I was *enormous*. Almost nine pounds.'

'What about you, Robyn?'

'Me?' I say. 'I don't know, it's all pretty vague. There're a few things, I suppose – laughing so hard I got the hiccups. Trailing Michael around.'

'True,' Michael says, 'she was like an imprinted duckling. She wouldn't leave me alone.'

'Willa?' We turn to where Willa is sitting at the end of the table. She shifts a little in her seat.

'I remember my dad tickling me. Bit embarrassing – I wet myself –' Her story is interrupted by Claudette having a fit of coughing and Nate jumps up to pour his girlfriend a glass of water.

'I'm so sorry,' Claudette says, 'Willa, to interrupt your story. I had a little something in my throat.' She pronounces Willa's name *Weela*. She taps her chest, just below her clavicle. 'I do apologize. Do go on.'

'Yes, do,' Liv says, looking at Willa intently, 'go on.'

Willa blushes deeply. 'That's it, really,' she says.

Liv holds Willa's eyes for a moment, gives her a small half-smile, and then moves on. 'What about you, Claudette?'

'I remember breaking my arm. And also eating cake.'

'Cake?' Jamie asks, smiling broadly. 'Was it a special cake?'

'Yes,' she says, 'a birthday cake, and it was covered in thousands of tiny sugar flowers. And I was putting each tiny flower on the tip of my tongue – just like so – and I remember *oh*, the taste was magical, so sweet. Outside, it was very hot, but I was inside, somewhere dark and cool, a small room, with long shelves full of food –'

'A pantry?' Cat says. 'Or you can say *larder*.'

'Yes, *thank you*. I was inside a pantry. And the big cake was on a cool marble shelf, and I was sitting *under* that shelf. And I remember looking up and seeing the slab of marble had blue lines running through it, like those little veins you see here –'

'*Wrist*,' Nate says.

'Yes, under the skin of your *wrist*. And I had a little handful of tiny sugar flowers, and I was eating them, on the cold pantry floor, underneath that shelf.'

There's a pause, all of us momentarily held inside the tale by the lilt of Claudette's accent and the softness of her voice, her dream-like storytelling. Cat rests her chin on her palm, watching. Jamie shifts in his seat. I think I am holding my breath.

'Was it your own birthday cake?' Willa asks.

'Non,' Claudette says, breaking the spell, 'it wasn't mine. For me, I have a winter birthday, in March.'

'And about how old were you?' Liv asks.

'I was six.'

'Six,' Liv says. 'Well, that would work as an explicit memory. We can divide early memories into two types: explicit and implicit. An explicit memory is one that involves recall of specific times, places, events. Yours too, Michael. The details are very defined and, to be fair, what you've described is the sort of major, one-off event that would stay in a child's mind. Robyn, Jamie, Willa, you're describing *implicit* memories: unconscious, emotional recollections. These are more like an amalgamation of your total early childhood sensations than memories of specific events –'

'Not a chance,' Jamie says. 'The memory I described had *exactly* the sort of specific details you've just mentioned – right down to the colour of my shorts.'

'Sure,' Liv says, 'but you also said you were two. If that's correct, it's far more likely to be an implicit memory or, even more likely, not a memory at all but a description of something you've been told about, or a photograph you've seen. There are exceptions, of course, but, generally speaking, explicit memories start later.'

'I remember it exactly,' Jamie says. 'It's an *explicit* memory.'

Liv says, 'It's possible. But, to be honest, it sounds far more like a generalized, happy childhood sensation.'

'Explicit,' he says. 'The entire thing is guesswork anyway. Supposition and conjecture.' He throws back the last of the red, then crosses his arms, the picture of a sulky adolescent, spots of high colour on his cheeks.

'Coffee, anyone?' Cat says, meeting my eye and widening hers. '*Jamie?*' It's abundantly clear to the entire party that he's as pissed as a fart. He's been through both the bottles they arrived with, and then some. Nate and Michael exchange a look: tolerant but unimpressed. Liv looks concerned, Claudette a little repulsed. 'Weela,' she says, moving her eyes away from Jamie, 'how do you two know Robyn and Cat?' Her voice is lemony-sour.

'I met Robyn at boarding school,' Willa says quietly. 'They gave me to her to look after.'

I grab the chance to lighten the mood. 'You make it sound like you were some sort of exotic pet,' I say, smiling. 'They used to assign everyone an official buddy when they first arrived. I was meant to show her around, get her used to the routines. But I've always maintained their real intention was for Willa to be a good influence on me.'

'And was she?' Cat says, throwing me the evils.

'God, no,' I say, grinning. 'She corrupted me completely.'

Jamie leans back in his chair and laughs so loudly at this we all look at him. *He hasn't got a clue*, I think. At least it's cheered him up. One good laugh and he's back in the room, starting a conversation about his and Willa's renovation project, and – God help us – his commute. Cat widens her eyes and mouths – *Kill me now* – and I almost start to laugh. I don't: a single glance at Willa stops me in my tracks. Her face has grown as grey as a February cloud.

The light from the candles flickers. I look round the table:

Jamie, boorish, holding court, his voice growing increasingly strident and loud. Our poor other guests have grown as quiet as the spectators in the background of an Old Master's painting: impartial witnesses, faces half hidden in the dark. Claudette frowns as she listens, leaning towards Jamie with a look of confusion, but Liv keeps her eyes on Willa, her expression, I suspect, almost purposefully blank. Willa herself is silent, pensive, lost in thought.

My beautiful, brave friend, I think, *how did you end up like this?*

6.
Small bones

Willa

What people don't always understand about the British press is this: they are vile. When Laika disappeared, it took only hours for them to locate our family home and less than twenty-four before the first of them turned up at my school. After that, everything changed. Rabid packs of them gathered by the school gates, shouting my name, shoving microphones and cameras into the faces of my teachers and friends. They wouldn't leave. By the time a few of them got inside, masquerading as cleaners, the school had had enough. It would, perhaps, be in my own best interests, the head told my parents, if I were to move.

I'd been at that school since I was seven, and I'd loved *everything* about it. The last thing I wanted was to go somewhere new. But there wasn't really a choice.

That's how I met Robyn.

She was waiting for me in the headmistress's office and my first thought was that she didn't look like a sixth former at all. I thought she looked about fourteen, at most. Then I realized that, at that moment, I probably didn't look any older myself, because at that school you had to wear a uniform all the way through, even in the sixth form. At my old school we were allowed to wear our own clothes in the sixth form, as a mark of our seniority. I'd worked for that privilege, *earned it*, with a full set of A grades at GCSE. Being forced back into uniform was the final indignity. I already felt hollowed out.

And here was Robyn, wearing a faded grey skirt that stopped somewhere mid thigh, far above the stated regulation length. Mine was on the knee.

Robyn was my assigned buddy. I hated the word instantly, sitcom slang, I thought, picturing American Girl Scouts marching cheerily off to camp, grown men slapping each other's backs, smiling dogs with wet, lolling tongues. Worse still, we were going to share a study-bedroom in the boarding house. Up to that moment, not one person had mentioned I'd be expected to share a room. It occurred to me that the showers were bound to be communal, all of us girls washing together in a steam-filled room like in some film from the seventies, horror-slash-porn. *Jesus*, I thought, *I will literally kill myself.*

I didn't need a buddy anyway. What I needed was a ghost-rider, someone to sit inside my brain and work my limbs, to answer questions when they were directed at me, to navigate my life. When people spoke to me, their voices were too quiet. I could see their lips moving, but their voices seemed to come from other rooms. Nothing made any sense.

Robyn had dark, shortish hair which she sometimes plaited into two stubby pigtails which stuck out from the back of her head at odd angles. She was shorter than me, with strong-looking limbs. On our first tour through the school she'd asked if I liked to play tennis. I said maybe, but that I wasn't very good. She asked me what sports I liked and I told her that I'd taken ballet as a child, then she grinned and spun round in a pirouette. 'Like this?' she said. She jumped into the air, kicking her legs into a split. 'Like this?' Then she told me she was the captain of the senior girls' hockey team.

Our tour ended in the boarding house. Robyn had one half of our study-bedroom, I had the other. The room was small, with clean, functional furniture. We each had a single bed, a cupboard with an integral chest of drawers, and a desk with a pinboard attached to the wall. Robyn's board was covered in stuff: photos of her parents and brother, a drawing she'd made of her dogs, a black-and-white postcard of Virginia Woolf, and an old ticket stub to some minor West Country music festival, where the headline act had been Joan Armatrading.

I didn't put anything on mine. There was no way I was going to put up pictures of Laika for the cleaners to gawp at or, worse, sell, and I didn't have any pets. I didn't want to put up pictures of my parents either, especially since they were still being featured on the news. No one at that school paid the slightest attention to the TV, but it was always on in the communal sitting room, as background noise. Groups of girls sat around on baggy sofas, laughing, eating toast smeared thick with Nutella, and there, two nights after I arrived, I saw my parents on the screen at a press conference, in front of a poster-sized image of my sister, a photograph that showed her with long dark hair and the serious eyes of a deep-water fish. My father had a thick arm angled round my mother's shoulders, and my mother herself sat stock-still, a grey cashmere wrap folded around her shoulders, staring ahead, in the manner of the sole survivor pulled from a wreck. An unseen voice asked if they had a message for their daughter, and my father, looking straight into camera, said, 'To whosoever has my child I say this: Bring. Her. Back.' A discharge of camera shutters, flashing bulbs. My mother's bloodless face.

Of course, that was while the press still thought the story had legs. In time there were no fresh developments to report, no new arrests, and after that I didn't see them any more.

I missed my old friends, their sophistication, the brightness, the cleverness of their talk. I missed our weekend trips into London, visits to shows and galleries and shops. The girls at my new school mainly came from rural backgrounds, and boarded only because their homes were too far away to travel in from every day. We had nothing in common. But I didn't need friends anyway. And I definitely didn't need rosy-cheeked Robyn, who, when she smiled, had actual dimples in her cheeks.

There was, of course, a point to my going all the way across the country, almost as far west as it was possible to go, to start again somewhere new. My parents had thought no one would recognize me.

But everyone knew who I was.

That was my fault. I drew attention to myself. I didn't mean to, but I kept thinking I'd seen her. She was *everywhere*. She'd be in a thick pack of younger girls ahead of me in a corridor or else running, a distant figure on the other side of the sports field, or that girl leaning out of a top-floor window, waving to a friend. Every dark-haired girl made me do a double-take. Once I ran after a girl and touched her on the arm, making her turn to look at me, startled at first, then perturbed. When I walked down the corridors, conversations stopped, and began again only after I'd passed. Eyes followed me. People whispered. I was given excessive praise in the boarding house for small tasks such as making my bed, keeping my shoes polished, tidying my locker, having neat hair. The teachers were overly kind. They spoke to me as if I were a little slow and marked my work a little generously.

That I didn't need. Fact: I didn't need anyone's help to know how to be the best in the class. Work was the one thing I could throw myself into. I was taking English, maths and history. Robyn, to my surprise, was taking four subjects: all the sciences and English too, just because, she said, she loved books.

Sometimes she was in the English class with me, but at other times she wasn't, because on her timetable it clashed with biology. Any classes she missed she made up in her own time. I'll admit I was a little envious about that. I asked if I could start another A Level too, French perhaps, but my housemistress said no, I had enough on my plate. The problem was that they didn't know me at that school. They had no idea what I could do.

In the evenings, Robyn would work silently at her desk, sucking on teaspoons of Marmite and, with my back to her, I would work at mine. On our first graded paper for English, 'Discuss the difference between appearance and reality in *King Lear*', I scored 81 per cent. Robyn scored 92.

'Can I see your essay?' I asked. I wanted to know where I'd lost marks.

'Sure,' she said. She showed it to me. She'd made some good points. *Really* good points. Okay, I thought. Fine. I need to do better.

In the mornings, Robyn often wasn't there when I woke up; she liked to go running before school. I would open my eyes and have the room to myself. That was the only time, ever, that I spent time on my own. I could look at the ceiling and think about Laika. Where was she? How was she? Doubt had been cast on the kidnap theory. Why kidnap a girl and then not demand money for her return? Every single TV report had mentioned Dad's haulage firm and the fact he owned a whole bunch of London lock-ups, plus the photos taken of our house from a helicopter clearly showed the pool, so my family was obviously wealthy. Some of the grubbier papers postulated that she had been trafficked. Horrifying thoughts filled my head. I imagined her chained by her wrist to a metal bedstead in some grungy bedsit, half covered by filthy sheets, men in a queue by the door. And once those thoughts had sidled into my head, I couldn't get rid of them. I would see her at the bottom of a lake, her dark eyes open to a distant wavering moon, pale limbs floating in the dark. Or else covered by leaves in a wood, beetles crawling through her skull. I imagined her swimming, strong limbs tearing through waves. I imagined her saying *Fuck you. Fuck you. Fuck the lot of you.*

For our second English essay, 'Discuss loyalty and disloyalty in *King Lear*', I scored 89 per cent. Robyn got 93. In our third assignment of the term, 'Lear's youngest daughter is admirable, but not entirely: discuss', I beat Robyn's 90 per cent by a clear five marks.

No one asked me a single thing about Laika, not once. I began to wonder if the entire school had been put under instruction not to mention her to me. Either that, or no one cared. But it was better than being at home. No journalists for a start, or baggy-eyed detectives endlessly repeating the same questions, going round in circles. My father had become increasingly infuriated by them: their lack of progress, the evident lack of a successful conclusion and their focus on *blatantly inconsequential details*, such as the long lock of Laika's dark hair they'd found behind the cistern in our bathroom.

She's been snatched off the street, my father said. *In what conceivable way is it relevant if there's a bit of hair in the house?* He told them they wouldn't survive in business: things didn't work like that when he was running the show. He didn't like the detectives as people either, the shabby way they dressed, the sloppy way they drank their tea, the tone of their voices, the vile, loaded, intrusive nature of their questions.

She's my daughter, for Christ's sake, of course she's not sexually active. She's thirteen.

Of course she wouldn't run away. Use your eyes.

You're the fucking detectives. Bring her back.

Would she have gone anywhere without telling them? *Never*, my father said, *she's a child, she did what she was told.* Did she have a boyfriend? *Absolutely not*, my mother said, *she hadn't even started her periods*.

They interviewed me as well, always with my parents there for support, one on either side. *Tell us about the morning she disappeared*. I looked at my father.

'Just tell them, Willa, exactly what happened the morning she disappeared,' he said.

So I did. I told them exactly what happened the morning she disappeared. I told them how it had been the very first day of the new school year, how Laika had been late getting up, how I didn't like to be late, not ever. Especially not on the first day of the new school year, and also because I was starting my A Levels and I was looking forward to seeing my friends, so I hadn't waited for her. How I'd walked to school on my own.

'I know this is hard,' the policewoman said; 'nobody blames you.'

That's what my parents said too, even when the detectives found Laika's bloody handprint on the underside of my bedroom door-handle, and I had to explain how it got there. I told the truth but don't know if they believed me, because after that crime-scene investigators went through the fabric of the entire house, fibre by fibre. They sat in my father's study, reading through his papers, going through his receipts. They took his computer away.

Then the police asked me to walk with them the way Laika and I usually walked to school. On my own, they said, just them and me. I really didn't want to go. I'd noticed the tricky way they spoke to my father, asking the same questions over and over from slightly different angles, like they were somehow trying to trip him up. And I get tongue-tied at the best of times.

'You're an intelligent girl,' my father said. 'You know how to handle a few direct questions. If you feel at all worried, just imagine I'm there, walking alongside. Be clear, be direct, be polite.'

He placed a large hand on my shoulder, softly reassuring. I looked him in the eyes.

'All right,' I said. 'Okay.'

I went. Two officers came to the house early the next morning and we set off at exactly the same time that Laika had left. Just go the way you'd normally go, they said, do what you'd normally do, don't change a thing. On the way they asked new questions. What was Laika like as a person? Down the road, up an unmade lane, over a stile. Would I say we were close? Through the woods that skirted the golf course, past the pond at Hole 9, through a field, up another lane, into the school. What was her relationship like with our parents? Did anything significant happen in the days leading up to her disappearance, anything out of the ordinary? Anything I could think of, no matter how small. Also, who cut our hair? Then they went back and, on their own this time, they searched with dogs in the woods, with divers in the pond. I saw it on the news.

I thought they might want to interview me again, but, as it turned out, that was it, my one chance to talk. They seemed more concerned with my father than either my mother or me.

My mother insisted the police interview the neighbours too, but all the houses had long driveways and were set far back in their own private grounds, so, with the exception of the one neighbour who'd spotted Laika talking to my parents' builder that morning, nobody had seen a thing.

My mother drove all the way down from East Sussex at half-term. As a nice surprise, she said, instead of driving all the way home and then back again in a week, we were going to be driving on to Cornwall to spend the week at a spa. My mother put on a bright expression, as if this were a real treat. I did the same for her. During our first few days we sat around in soft white robes picking at salads, watching strangers as they went from treatment to treatment, glowing. My mother asked me about school. I'm not sure she heard my replies. She threw back glasses of gin and went to bed early. I badly wanted to ask her things. I wanted to discuss all the things we'd been bombarded with, all the routes of enquiry followed by the police, even the terrifying, lunatic ideas dreamt up by the tabloids. More than anything, I wanted to know whether she shared my own secret fears, the ones I didn't even know how to voice. In the strange, clear light of the indoor pool, her face looked waxy and baffled. Unsaid words hung between us like steam.

Finally, my mother mentioned that my father was looking for a new builder, since the work on the conservatory had stopped.

'What, *now*?' I said. 'Who cares about a sodding sunroom?'

'He seems obsessed with the thing. Says he wants it done by Christmas.' My mother sighed, then said, 'I think it just gives him something else to think about. The investigation has really got under his skin. He hit the roof with the inspector last week and now they've impounded his vehicles.'

We were sitting on loungers at the time, by the side of the indoor pool. As for Ian Cox, she said, the builder who'd started the project, she wanted the police to interview him again, to put him under duress. He'd been forced to admit that he'd seen Laika that morning, and that he'd been speaking to her: a neighbour, Felicity Williams, had *witnessed* them together, *talking* at the end of our drive. That made him the *last* person to have seen her. Which was clearly significant. He *had* to know more. My mother kept her eyes on the water as she spoke, following the slow movement of its surface. She was angry. Angry at Cox. Even more angry at the detectives who'd interviewed him and then let him go. He knew *something*. They just had to get him to say so. Something was wrong about the man, and she'd known it straight off, even when she'd first met him: he was taciturn, uncommunicative. She hadn't liked the way he'd looked at any of us; he had sly, avaricious eyes. She should have trusted her instincts, insisted on hiring someone else, no matter the cost. Someone more honest. More trustworthy.

'Do you honestly think it was Cox?'

My mother gave me a look of pure astonishment. '*Of course* it was Cox. He followed her out of the house. He's *seen* talking to her, then, minutes later, he's captured on CCTV, driving out down the road. And no sign of Laika. Not a trace. Not on *that* camera, not on *any* camera. And apparently there's CCTV *everywhere*: at the golf club, at the train station, the bus station, on the high street, at the school, *every*where. The police say they're *impossible* to avoid. And she didn't appear in *any* of them. Not one. So *Cox* took her, of course he did. He bundled her into his van.'

'But the police said it couldn't have been. He has an alibi.'

'He's *lying*, Willa. Or someone is lying for him.'

'But there's no way she would have gone with him willingly. Laika wasn't a victim, she would have fought. And the police *told* us that. They said if she'd been in that van then they'd know.'

'Then they are *wrong*. No one can simply vanish, Willa. He would have had sheets of plastic in there or something. Knocked her out and rolled her up. It was *Cox*.'

On the Sunday night she drove me back to the school. For a while we sat looking at the boarding house, its façade shadowed a deep blue against a darkening sky. There were bright rectangles of orange light in the windows and, inside, cheerful girls who'd never had a bad thing happen to them in their entire lives. We both sat staring ahead. Laika had been missing for seven weeks and five days.

I said, 'She's not coming home, is she, Mum?'

My mother went very quiet. She turned her face to mine and the night's shadows filled her eye sockets, the bones of her cheeks. She'd lost so much weight it scared me. I reached for her hand.

'Do you want me to come home?' I said. 'I want to. I want to come home.'

'No,' she said, 'absolutely not. What I want is for you to get your exams. That's essential. And, also, I want you right here, where I know you're safe, away from' – her hand made a vague movement before coming to rest on her arm – 'all that.'

'But what about you, Mum? What about you?'

My mother seemed to gather herself. When she spoke again, her voice was firm.

'It's very important to stay positive, Willa. No one's given up. I certainly haven't and you mustn't either. The police promise me they are doing everything in their power. You have to believe she's coming home. She *is* coming home. And, when she does, I will be right there, waiting for her.'

I hugged her, then got out of the car, feeling lost, as miserable as I'd ever felt in my entire life. Still wearing her seatbelt, my mother leant forward and peered out through the open car door. She paused, looking at me, her eyes shifting between mine.

'You would tell me, Willa, if you knew anything.'

It wasn't a question.

'Mum –' I said. She waited. I looked up at the flinty sky, then back. 'Of course.' Exhaustion made my bones hurt. My head slumped.

'Darling girl,' she said, 'don't go back in like that. We will find her. Meanwhile, *chin up*.'

Short autumn days rolled rapidly towards winter. The clocks changed and the afternoons grew dark and wet, and cold.

Fierce winter storms came through. The windows shuddered in their frames.

Every morning I lay awake on my bed, looking at the ceiling, thinking about Laika. The summer felt like a lifetime ago, another planet, somebody else's life. I thought about how we used to muck around in the pool together, ducking each other under, counting to see who could hold their breath the longest. Laika was amazing at that. She truly loved swimming. She said she was going to be a free diver when she grew up, that she would dive the world's blue holes just by holding her breath. She practised by diving into our pool and holding on to the filter at the deep end, and then I would wait, counting aloud, slowly at first, then faster. One minute passed. Two. When I couldn't bear it a second longer I would swim down and forcibly drag her to the surface.

'What d'you do that for?' she'd say. 'I was fine.'

'You're an idiot,' I said. 'You'll get brain damage.'

I tried to keep her safe. I really did. I told her, keep your head down, don't bring unnecessary attention to yourself, just do what you're told, all the things that just came naturally to me. But I was so busy keeping her safe from herself that I forgot to warn her about the outside world. I should have told her that there were people out there, men, women even, who could harm her.

So much was my fault.

My parents were known for their extravagant parties, over which my father would preside like some munificent dictator, handing out compliments to the women and fine cigars to the men. None was more lavish than the one they held to celebrate my mother's thirtieth. It was a stinking-hot day in July. In the early morning a catering company arrived with truckloads of food that they carried into the house on huge oval platters – bright red lobsters, black-eyed prawns with hard pink tendrils and eggs clinging to their undersides, slippery blue-grey oysters in pearly shells, slices of red-centred beef, knuckles of pork, ham, then desserts to be kept in the cool for later – custards covered in raspberries, stiff white meringues, trifles, slices of chocolate ganache topped with specks of real gold, a cake. My mother sped around the house, issuing instructions to the hired help and inspecting everything, positioning each dish on starched white tablecloths, then repositioning them somewhere better. Bottles of Bollinger chilled in vast silver buckets that glittered with bright beads of condensation; crystal glasses stood arranged in perfect rows. A team of waitresses arrived in black dresses and lace-edged aprons, sommeliers to serve the wine, a musician with a harp. The house was filled with the powerful scent of roses, gladioli, Casablanca lilies. My sister and I were buttoned into matching smocked dresses that looked sweet on her and too young on me. We had our hair tied tightly into bows. We were not to touch *a thing*.

Shortly before midday my mother reappeared in an outfit my father had bought her especially for the occasion: a pure white dress with a plunging neckline and a wide belt at the waist, topped by a tiny bolero jacket with long sleeves to stop her from burning: *a little Joan Collins number*, according to my mother. The entire thing was covered in little sparkling crystals, and in her white stilettos she looked taller than ever. I thought she looked like a goddess. My mother was the most beautiful woman in the world, I'd always thought. We all thought that. My father called her his PP, his Prized Possession.

Soon the guests started to arrive, mostly men from my father's various clubs and their wives, also our neighbours, a couple of minor politicians, and an ageing actress who'd once had a bit-part in a Bond movie. My father's latest secretary arrived wearing a scarlet dress that was so short and so tight my mother had to tell us not to stare. Laika pronounced the word 'secretary' as *sexetary*, which made the guests laugh like mad, so she repeated it at the top of her voice until my mother asked her to stop.

Gifts wrapped in bright paper and tied with thick ribbon bows were piled on a table in the hall. Doughy Aunt Deedee, my father's sister, arrived with her stocky, thick-necked husband, their three boys and two mean-faced Dobermanns, which my aunt kept on leads. My cousins Max, Angus and Freddie, miniature versions of their father, stood in a group with their freckly arms thrust into trouser pockets. They were the only other children who'd been invited. I was nine, so they would have been in their teens.

The noise from the party grew ever louder as ever more people arrived. Laika and I trailed around the edge of the adults, hot, tired, listless, bored. The food, which had looked so beautiful on the platters, was strange and inedible. Laika whined that there was nothing on those vast tables she liked to eat. She wanted to throw a ball for my uncle's dogs, but each time she went close they showed their teeth and then Deedee would bark at Laika to leave them alone.

'They don't like six-year-old girls,' she said, and then, with a stage wink to the other adults, 'They find them highly irritating.'

Eventually she said to my mother, 'Do something about her, will you, Bianka?' and when my mother appeared not to hear, Deedee sent all five of us cousins off to entertain ourselves at the bottom of the garden.

I was glad to be away from the sun trap of the terrace. There were mature trees on the lower slopes of the lawn, beneath which there were always cool puddles of shade. Max, Angus and Freddie were evidently less thrilled to find themselves with two girls in tow. Max had a tennis ball which he was kicking about, slamming into trees, throwing over Laika's head to Angus and Freddie. They never let her catch it. Laika tugged at my arm. She wanted to go in. I wanted to go back too, but didn't dare until we were called. I held her hand in mine. I could hear the adults in the distance, talking in loud, ugly voices, laughing in great static bursts like machine-gun fire. I could see the dogs sleeping under the chairs.

The ball sailed over our heads, over and over. Then Freddie hurled it skywards and it landed in the upper branches of an old oak tree, and stayed there, high overhead.

We stared up at the tree, its high thick canopy of dark green leaves and rugged cankers and gnarled bark.

'You bloody idiot,' Max said, 'our one source of entertainment.'

'I'll get it,' Angus said; 'that tree's easy.'

'I don't think you should,' I said, but nobody was listening except Laika, who looked up at me, wide-eyed, then back at the towering tree, its huge trunk narrowing away into the distant sky. Angus already had his hands on its rough surface. He felt with his fingers for places he could grip, flattened his legs against the trunk, tested his weight on the trunk's jutting lumps and slowly edged his way up, eventually finding his way into its lower branches.

'It's easy from here,' he called down, 'loads to hang on to,' and we watched as he went higher and higher, hauling himself up on the tree's thick, crooked branches.

And then he was high, too high, impossibly high. He would break his neck if he fell. My heart scudded in my chest.

'Come down,' I shouted. 'You shouldn't be up there.'

'Found it,' he said. He turned around and waved the ball. 'The view's great,' he said. 'You should come up.'

'Come down,' Laika called. 'We'll get into trouble.'

My cousin lurched to the side of the branch and I gasped. Laika squealed.

'Ha, ha,' he said, 'got you.' His brothers laughed.

'Hey,' he shouted, 'there's a bird's nest up here. Eggs, baby birds too. They've got their mouths open really wide. They're all like, squawking. They sound exactly like Laika.'

'Come down,' my sister called again, her voice small and reedy with fear.

'All right,' he said, 'keep your knickers on.' His brothers laughed. The ball plummeted towards us and then bounced off the grass in a hard shock, flying back up to fall and bounce again. Max caught it on its third bounce and stuck it in his pocket. Then I watched in silent terror as Angus edged his way back down the tree. Eventually he made it to the lower branches, scrabbled his way down the last parts of the trunk and jumped to the ground.

'Welcome back,' Max said. 'How was your trip?'

'Fantastic,' Angus said. 'I got you a gift.' He reached into his shirt pocket and pulled something out. He opened his hand. Dwarfed inside his palm was a single, tiny, speckled egg, the brightest, palest blue I'd ever seen, the colour of an April-morning sky. Laika's small face became bright with wonder. The egg was so perfect. She held out her hand and Angus tipped it into her palm. She looked at me, her little mouth opening into an *o* of delight, then back at the egg.

'It's warm,' she said.

'That's because it's alive, stupid,' Freddie said. 'It's got a bird in it.'

'Who's got a penknife?' Max said. 'Give it here.' He plucked the egg back out of Laika's hand. 'Find something sharp.'

Freddie and Angus kicked around by the base of the tree,

picking up small sticks and discarding them. A small dread filled my stomach. I looked up at the house.

'Can I see the egg again?' Laika asked.

'You can see something better than that,' Max said. Angus had handed him a small, sharp-edged stone.

'Don't,' I said. 'You shouldn't do that. Put it back.'

'Do what?' Laika said.

Above Laika's head, Max began tapping.

'What are they doing?' Laika said to me. She looked up at the boys, wobbling on tiptoe as she tried to look at the special blue egg. 'Don't break it.'

'Don't,' I said. 'Stop it.'

'Don't be such a girl,' Freddie said; 'this is science.'

The tiny egg began to split. Max peeled away the shell, piece by broken piece. Inside was curled the tiniest thing – all red transparent skin and tufts of grey fluff. Between two thick fingers, Max picked up one pink leg and dangled the hatchling by its miniature claw.

'Stop it,' Laika said. 'Don't do that. You're hurting it.'

'It's really gross,' Freddie said. 'It looks like Frankenstein.' The baby bird's tiny monstrous head lolled on a neck too thin to support it. Its skull was almost entirely taken up by two dark, hazy discs under the skin where its eyes should be. Then it gave a shudder. It opened its tiny pale yellow beak and moments later its entire body seemed to pound as it started to breathe.

'Fantastic,' Angus said. 'It's properly alive.'

'You've got to put it back,' Laika said. 'It needs its mum. It's got to have food.'

'Here,' Angus said, 'hold out your hands.' He dropped the tiny creature into Laika's palm. 'Go on, then, if you care so much. You do it. You put it back.'

Laika looked at the boys, up at the tree, at me. Then she looked up at the house, and before I could stop her she bolted, her little legs flying across the lawn. '*Mum*,' I heard her shout. 'Mum!'

'Don't go up there,' I yelled. 'Laika, *come back*.'

But Laika was already halfway up the lawn.

'There goes space pup Laika,' Freddie said, 'off on a mission to Mars.'

'You shits,' I said. I turned and ran, the braying of their laughter following me up to the house.

By the time I got to the terrace, Laika was already weaving her way between the adults, her hands cupped carefully before her, in them the tiny baby bird. She found our mother talking to Aunt Deedee, both of them sunk into patio loungers softened by thick cushions, glasses in hand, their voices spirited and a little slurred. I hung back, afraid of my aunt's dogs, both of which had sat up on Laika's approach and were watching my sister, squinting at her through small, tight eyes, their triangular ears stiff and alert.

'Mum,' Laika said.

'Don't interrupt now, Laika,' my aunt said. 'Manners, please. Wait until you've been asked to speak.'

'It's an emergency.'

My mother turned to Laika, her features softened by sun and champagne. The bright sun made her grey eyes shine like mirrored glass, and there was a small smudge of red lipstick just above her upper lip. 'What is it, darling?' she said.

'Look,' Laika said. 'It needs help.'

My mother peered into my sister's hands, saw the tiny pulsating creature, its skinny hairless wings and strange, foetal head, and recoiled.

'Darling,' she said. 'You shouldn't pick up things like that. It could be sick. Put it back, please, wherever you found it.'

'But, Mum,' Laika said, her voice rising, panicky-scared, 'we can't. Its nest is all the way back up the tree.'

'Sometimes baby birds do fall out of their nests, sweetheart. And then the mummy birds pop along and collect them.'

'Don't indulge her with nonsense, Bianka,' my aunt said. 'It just encourages her. Tell her to go and wash her hands.'

Laika stood between them, her eyes filling with tears.

'But, Mum,' she said.

'For goodness' sake, Laika,' my aunt said, 'just put it down. You're spoiling your mother's party.'

My aunt reached into Laika's hands, plucked out the tiny bird and put it on the ground. Instantly both dogs raced forward and, in a single swift and bloody lunge, one of them snatched up the baby bird in its jaws. I thought I heard the sound of soft bones popping. The tiny bird was gone. There was a moment of silence before the terror and shock fully registered, then Laika threw back her head and howled. She kept her empty hands held in front of her as fat tears coursed down her face and rivulets of snot streamed from her nose, her chest heaving with the same giant shuddering breaths that had pounded the baby bird. She was loud, too loud. My parents' guests turned their heads towards the source of the noise.

'Oh dear,' one woman said, 'someone's a little overexcited.'

And now she had my father's attention.

Seeing him look towards the source of the commotion, my aunt waved a hand at my father and, in an exaggerated gesture, pointed at my sister, widening her eyes.

My father came towards us. I stood back.

'All right, foghorn,' he said, 'that's enough.' He smiled at their guests. 'Come on, let your mother enjoy her day.' He took my sister firmly by her upper arm and almost lifted her in the direction of the kitchen door. 'Go into the house.'

I went to follow.

'Just stay here,' he said, 'and let her calm down.'

And so I did. I stayed on the terrace, kicking my heels, by the edge of the adults.

I should have gone to her. *Of course* I should have gone to her.

I don't like to think about what happened after that.

7.
A doll in a music box

Willa

The days stepped relentlessly towards November the third. I couldn't stop them. I'm okay, I told myself. I'm okay.

But I was not.

Night after night I lay awake, staring at the ceiling while Robyn slept, her breath calm and steady in the night.

Dread flooded me. *I should have looked after her*, I thought. *Everything is my fault.*

My stomach flooded and pooled; I felt sick all the time and I couldn't eat. I couldn't slow things down. I could feel blood speeding too fast through my veins, thudding in my temples and scudding down into fingers and toes that seemed to pulse with every beat of my heart. Each morning I hauled myself out of bed, showered and dressed, and went through the day like an automaton. Lack of sleep left me fuzzy-brained and stupid. I couldn't concentrate in class, or on my homework, or on anything anyone said. My chest was too tight to breathe, as if bound by great bands of elastic.

I began counting seconds in my head, starting from one, then up, each number relentlessly following the next, thirty-one, thirty-two, thirty-three, and on and on, sixty-five, sixty-six, sixty-seven, counting the seconds that Laika ticked away from me, drifting, untethered. When I lost count, I started again from one. At night I felt as if I were sinking into the mattress, or else floating above it. Exhausted, my body snatched moments of sleep before my mind dragged me back into the harsh landscape of consciousness.

And then my mind hooked on to Laika's last birthday and stayed there. November the third. Her thirteenth birthday, that is. Not her last birthday.

It can't have been her last.

In the early morning I'd slipped along the landing to her room and climbed into her bed.

'Shove over,' I said.

It was still dark. Sleepily, she pulled the duvet around the both of us and I drew her into a hug.

'Happy birthday, sis.'

'Bleuh.'

'I got you something. Here.' She took the little box from my fingers and held it, her eyes fast shut.

'What is it?'

'Open it.'

'What, now?' she said. 'I'm asleep.' Her body was warm under the duvet.

'Open it.'

'God, Willa. This had better be good.' She sat up in bed, huffing, and turned on her bedside light to open the box. I'd given her a tiny silver dolphin pendant on a silver chain, its leaping body curled into a crescent moon.

'Hey,' she said. She turned the tiny dolphin in her hands, smiled at its smiling face. 'I love it.'

'To keep you going until you get to swim with real ones,' I told her. 'Remember that, when you're diving your first blue hole. Here, put it on.'

I fastened the clasp around her neck and we lay back down in the warm cocoon of her bed. She reached out and turned off the bedside light. I wrapped my arms around her back and tucked my knees up behind hers. Outside, I could hear rain drumming against the window, wind tearing through black trees.

'I'm never going to take it off,' she said, her voice sleepy and low, 'not now. Not ever.'

That year the third of November fell on a Sunday and so my parents held a birthday lunch for Laika. To our joint dismay, Aunt Deedee and her husband had also been invited. Even worse, Cousin Freddie was back from his uni for the weekend, so they brought him along too.

The party began in the lounge, where a huge fire roared in the grate and the Sunday papers were arranged in a neat pile on a low table. The adults sank deep into the sofas, gripping their pre-lunch drinks, Campari for Deedee, gin for my mother, single malt whisky for the men. Laika and I stood with our backs to the fire, warming our rear ends, beneath an oversized studio photograph of the four of us, in which my mother and I were smiling and my father and Laika were not. Freddie stood with us, his thick-lidded eyes fixed on the far wall, beer glass in hand. I knew the rules, so did Laika: one of us had to start a conversation. I made a sidelong glance at Lai. She made a face.

'Freddie,' I said, 'have you seen any good films lately?'

His eyes moved to mine. 'Last night I watched a documentary about wolves.'

'Really?' I said. 'Gosh, how very interesting. What did you learn?'

He turned his face back to the wall. 'Things I didn't know about wolves.'

We stood in silence. I glared at Laika. Her turn to have a go. He was only here because it was her flipping birthday.

'Freddie,' she said, 'what are you studying?'

'Consumer behaviour.'

'Consumer behaviour?' Laika paused. 'Are you *kidding* me? You mean *shopping*?' I threw her a look, and she returned to her talking-to-unwanted-guests voice, saccharine-sweet. 'So how's it going? Any good?'

'S'alright.'

Silence again. *Jesus*, I thought, *this is hard.*

'I see you're in the papers again, Laika,' Freddie said, 'space dog.'

'That's not funny,' Laika said.

'Not everyone gets named after a dog.'

'Too much gas and air for you, Bianka,' Deedee said, joining in from the sofa, 'that was the problem. Naming a child after a dog. Honestly.'

'I think it's a very pretty name,' my mother said, her voice bright, 'and, as you all know, November the third happens to be the very day the dear little thing shot up into space, on her very first mission.'

'And her last,' Laika said.

'I thought we were calling you Leica,' my father said, 'as in a very nice camera.' The adults indulged him with a short peal of laughter. It was a well-practised line; one they'd all heard before.

'Laika was a real little hero,' my mother said, 'an absolute trailblazer.'

I could feel my sister stiffening beside me. I sent her a look. *Don't*, I thought, *just don't. Let it go.*

'She wasn't a hero,' Laika said. 'She was sent on a suicide mission. She was never coming back.'

'Now then, darling,' my mother said, 'that's not really the part of the story you should be thinking about.'

'That is the story,' Laika said. 'The entire story. The only story. No, wait, actually, you *are* right, there *is* more.'

I screwed my fingernails into the flesh of my palms.

'First, they went out to look for a little stray dog, and they caught a really sweet one. It turned out Laika *loved* people. She'd do anything, *anything* for them. All she wanted were little scraps of love and kindness. And is that what she got? *No.* What they did to her was *obscene*. They shoved her into tinier and tinier capsules for weeks on end. She couldn't stand up. She couldn't even turn around. She must have hurt so much, trapped like that, unable to move, but even *then* she came out with her tail wagging. And then they shaved her, opened her up and shoved a whole bunch of electrodes into her heart.'

'We all like dogs,' Aunt Deedee said.

'Yeah, right,' Laika said. 'I remember. Some people like them more than kids.'

'Don't be rude,' my father said. His voice carried a warning we both understood.

Laika took a step forward. I stayed where I was. 'And then they fixed her inside some tinny rocket and wired her up and shot her into space and you know what? She was *terrified*. Her heartbeat *rocketed*. And you know *why*? Because it was like a *furnace* inside that rocket. *Laika was literally being boiled to death.*'

'That's enough,' my father said.

Laika, stop, I thought. I threw her a look she ignored. 'And you call that a hero? A hero makes an active choice. A person *chooses* to be heroic. And they can *choose* not to. Laika didn't have a choice. She didn't have a choice about anything.' Laika's voice buckled, tears fell from her eyes. 'She was just a little dog. She trusted people. And they fucking killed her.'

'Go to your room,' my father said. 'I will not have that language in my house.'

'For a fucking science experiment.'

My father jumped to his feet, instantly followed by my mother. She snatched his sleeve.

'Bryce,' she said, *'it's her birthday.'*

My father looked at my mother's hand, then into her eyes. They held each other's gaze. His eyes travelled momentarily towards Deedee, then moved back to my mother. He tugged his jacket out of her grip. He looked again at my sister.

'I said go to your room.'

I stood still, my heart yammering, while Laika walked straight across the room towards the door, her chin held up and directly ahead.

'And stay there,' he said. 'Don't think we want you at the table. And *you,'* he said, jabbing a finger in my direction, 'you stay here.'

My mother met my eyes for a moment. Then my father took her by the upper arm so gently it barely looked like he was touching her at all, and slowly, slowly, turned her away.

'Bianka,' he said, his voice soft and low. 'How's that lunch doing?'

My mother touched her arm. She dropped her eyes to the floor. 'I'll just check,' she said. She walked towards the kitchen door. 'It should be ready in a mo.'

Silence filled the room.

Freddie said, 'Laika's always entertaining, right?'

My mother and I ate the lunch in silence. It was my father's favourite, roast lamb.

That's the truth. At Laika's last birthday meal, she wasn't even there.

There is no such thing as midnight, not really. In the hazy loam of the night, I kept my eyes on the glowing second hand of my watch. It was one second to midnight, then, instantly, one second past. And then it was the third of November and somewhere, somewhere far away, I didn't know where, Laika was turning fourteen. I groaned and put my arm across my eyes.

'Willa?' A soft voice, Robyn, in her pyjamas, bending over me in the dark. 'Are you okay?'

'I'm fine.'

'You're not, though,' she said. 'I can see that.' I felt her sit down, half perching herself on the edge of the bed. I took a deep breath, then removed my arm. Her face was fuzzy in the dark, her expression concerned.

'Talk to me,' she said.

I turned my head so it was facing the wall. I closed my eyes.

'I'm okay,' I said.

She reached out a hand and lightly stroked my hair. My skin prickled under her touch. I kept my eyes shut. Her fingers were slow, light, hesitant, soothing. Eventually she said, 'Okay, if you need anything, or if you want to talk, I'm right here, okay? I'm just across the room.'

She made to move. I said, 'Don't go.'

She stopped, half standing. She sat back down.

I said, 'Will you – I mean, could you, would you – stay here, with me, just for tonight? Please?'

I lifted the covers a little. Robyn hesitated a moment, then slipped in. Slowly, she put her head on the pillow next to mine. The bed was small. I turned on my side so I had my back to her and she curled her legs up into mine. Then she put her hand around my waist. Under the covers her fingers found mine.

'You're okay,' she said. 'You're okay.'

I could feel her warm breath on the back of my neck slowing as she drifted back off to sleep.

And I slept too.

It just became something we did. It wasn't complicated. It wasn't even a thing we discussed. For the rest of that term, at night, I slipped into her bed or she into mine. I hadn't realized how much I'd been longing for physical touch. With Robyn next to me, I could finally sleep.

The days got easier too. Sometimes I would spot Robyn in a crowd of other girls, or we'd pass each other in the corridor and she'd catch my eye and smile. Her presence somehow made me feel better, safer, more myself. I needed the uncomplicated steadiness of her. Laika was there too, always, always at the back of my mind, but I could think again, I could concentrate. I was okay.

When I went home for the Christmas holiday, I missed Robyn with a force that took me by surprise. I missed the nights with our arms around each other, waking up with her in the grey early dawn.

And being home was strange. Without Laika there, everything felt different. And it actually *was* different. The extension my parents had started in the summer had been completed. The last I'd seen, it had just been foundations. Now it was a vast, elegant structure with large-paned windows, a tall lantern roof and three sets of double doors that led on to the terrace. The whole thing had been my father's idea, and, like all his projects, designed on a grand scale. If ever my mother, sister or I had referred to it as a sunroom, he had corrected us. It was, he said, a conservatory. And now, to my utter astonishment, it wasn't just finished but *decorated* too, with a vast gold Christmas tree at one end. I couldn't believe it. We had a *Christmas tree*. With Laika *missing*. I looked at my mother, mouth open in surprise.

'Deedee,' she said.

Throughout that entire holiday my mother, father and I crept around each other like solitary foxes, each of us holed up in our own defined territory. My father, always a shadowy figure in our lives, kept to his study; my mother to the den, curled up on the sofa watching *The X-Files* with a gin. And, as for me, I mostly stayed in my room. I didn't even really want to see my old friends.

'*Go*,' my mother said, when for the umpteenth time they invited me out. 'It will be good for you.' I did it for her in the end.

We met in a café in town. Sixth form life clearly suited them. They looked older, more stylish, sophisticated. They cooed over me like a bird with a broken wing, asking me softly about my new school, were there any nice shops within reach and did everyone talk like farmers? After a while one of them mentioned the hordes of reporters that had plagued their school gates. Then they all joined in. They asked me about things they'd heard on TV and wanted to know if I had any inside information. How had Ian Cox got away with it? The man was clearly as guilty as hell. You could tell that just by looking at his photos, a definite pervert: he had an evil face. Plus, when the police had searched his home, they'd found a whole bunch of depraved stuff: porn, horror films, drugs, women's jewellery, even a hunting knife. Did I know that? The whole thing was on the news. He kept a hammer in his bedside drawer. They leant forward, tipping their heads in a way that made their hair fall in glassy waterfalls. So sorry, they whispered, so awful, just tragic. And in our town too. That's what no one could really believe – it was such a *nice* place. Turns out nowhere was safe. It had definitely made people think twice; everyone was a little more wary. In fact, the whole thing had been hard on everyone. Their parents had collectively developed a deeply irritating need to know where they were *all of the time*, and it was unbelievably tedious. Then they spoke about the shows they'd seen, the school cabaret, the sixth form ball, the lights on Oxford Street and what they were getting for Christmas.

⋆

Christmas Day itself we spent at the house of Aunt Deedee and my cousins, where the atmosphere was as brittle and fake as the fine glass ornaments. There wasn't a place for Laika laid at the table. No one had bought a gift for her either. Not even me.

I saw in the New Year on my own. My mother stood on the threshold of the house, hesitating, with my father already halfway down the stone steps.

'Are you sure you'll be all right?' she asked. 'We don't have to go. Just say if you'd rather I didn't leave you. I could quite happily not go.'

'Be honest,' my father said. 'We can stay if you want.'

'Go,' I told them. 'You'll just be down the road. I'll be fine.' I smiled at my mother. 'Don't worry, Mum,' I said. 'I'll keep all the doors locked, promise.'

At nine o'clock I stood in the shadow of an unlit window as they arranged themselves in my father's Mercedes to drive the quarter-mile to the Williamses' house.

Then I went into Laika's room.

I turned on the light and stood in the doorway. It was exactly as she had left it, her clothes still draped on her chair, the covers still on the bed. I pulled up the duvet and looked underneath. I lay down and buried my head in her pillow and tried to pick up her scent. Then I turned over and looked at the ceiling. After a while I pushed my fingers down between the mattress and the bed frame and felt all the way along. Nothing. I stood and lifted the mattress. Nothing. Way too obvious.

I looked round the room. I felt under her clothes in each of her drawers. I checked the pockets of her jeans. I looked at her desk, my eyes drifting over pens, pencils, tubes of paint, a notebook full of drawings, a dictionary, a copy of *Jonathan Livingston Seagull* left upside down on its spine. I had no idea what I was looking for. Still I went on. I picked up her desk chair and lifted it inside her wardrobe. Then I stood on it and, on tiptoe, felt along the top of the inside frame where there was a tiny gap between the wood and the plaster of the wall, the space she used to stash the notes she lifted from my father's wallet, rolled up into tight little tubes. Nothing.

I went back to her desk and looked through the jumble of things she'd left on the top of her chest of drawers – the hair ties and clips meant to tame her unruly hair, beads, a peacock feather. A china cat. A felt mouse. She was so *messy*. There wasn't an order to any of it. I opened her pink jewellery box, a relic from childhood, and jumped as a small pink plastic ballet dancer sprang up and shuddered into life, turning on its stand to tinny music. Amazing the thing still works, I thought. I listened to the tune, feeling rushed backwards through time as an image filled my mind: my mother one day pretending to be that doll, turning jerkily on the spot with a strange, fixed smile on her face, while Laika and I danced around her, giggling like mad. It was funny, because, as children, we honestly believed our mother was the clumsiest person on earth. She always told us she couldn't walk through a doorway without accidentally banging into it. Bruises bloomed like flowers on her arms. *Silly me*, she'd say, when we pulled up the long sleeves she always wore, when we traced their outlines with small fingertips, when we tried to kiss them better.

I snapped the lid shut.

Almost immediately I opened it again. There was something bright in there, something I'd not noticed before: a discarded thing in a child's jewellery box, just one trinket among many others, easily overlooked.

With slow fingers I lifted out the object and held it up: a tiny silver dolphin, curled into a dive, shaped like a crescent moon. I stretched out the little silver chain. It was broken. The ballerina kept turning.

I love it.

I'm never going to take it off.

Something like static seemed to hiss and spit inside my brain, scattering my thoughts.

I folded my hand around the dolphin and squeezed my eyes shut. There was too much noise, so much noise. I slammed the lid of the box. The music stopped but the buzzing inside my head carried on. Blood was rushing in my ears. I felt impossibly hot, like I was burning with fever. I went and stood by the window. I put my head to the cool glass, then the flats of my palms. Then I stood there, thinking, overthinking, not thinking at all.

The minutes clicked past midnight. Distant fireworks lit up the sky, momentarily illuminating the outline of the stone steps and the dark garden, the black water of the swimming pool, the dark shadow of the pool house, the long sloping lawns and the flowerless winter beds, the leafless webs of oak and laburnum, and, all around the perimeter, the towering wall of rhododendrons.

I stood there for a long time. The last fireworks faded into the night. I left Laika's room, snapped off the light and quietly shut the door behind me. I hid the dolphin and its broken chain deep within my school bag. Then I sat on the stairs, waiting for my parents to come home.

The morning I was due to return to school I was packed up and ready to go straight after breakfast. I found my mother sitting in the kitchen. I sat next to her. I placed the tiny leaping dolphin on the table between us.

My mother's hand flew to her mouth. 'Where did you find it?' Her voice was breathy and came out in a rush.

'In her bedroom.' I pushed the chain around so she could see the break. My voice was low, urgent. 'Tell me about that morning, Mum. What happened after I went to school?'

She glanced once in the direction of my father's study, then back at me.

'You left. I nipped next door to give our new neighbours some flowers. I was only quick. I wanted to give her a lift to school so she wouldn't be late. When I came back, she was gone. Your father told me she'd left for school.'

'You left them on their own?'

'*No*, the builders were here, pouring the concrete floor.'

I felt a prickling heat rising fast up my neck. I looked towards the conservatory. I said, 'Oh my God.'

Something was building in my chest – something that would burst out of me, urgent, savage, uncontrolled. I opened my mouth. '*Mum* –' I stopped. From the hallway we heard my father's study door opening, his footsteps in the hall; both of us glanced towards the kitchen door. As my mother's hands reached for mine the edges of her silk blouse pulled back, exposing the white skin of her wrists. Automatically I checked them for marks. Then I gave her fingers a quick squeeze and before my father arrived in the kitchen I swept the silver dolphin off the table and folded it into my palm.

8.
The Fermi Paradox

Willa

The January term started with a blizzard. The school cranked up its ancient heating system and the radiators threw off so much heat you could almost see it blistering the air. One minute we were frozen, the next we were dripping with sweat.

At night our room was so stuffy we could barely breathe. We threw off the duvets first, then our pyjamas. In the middle of the night I watched Robyn as she stood naked, tugging at the metal hooks of the ancient sash window. She rammed it up a few inches and a cool river of chilled air flooded in, fresh and bright and clean.

'Better?' she asked, looking round. I nodded. 'I'll leave the curtains open.' The moon touched her hips, her small breasts, the dark tuft between her legs.

'You're so beautiful,' I said. The words were out of my mouth before I realized I'd said them aloud.

'I'm not.'

'You are,' I said.

'I have a runner's body. I could do with a few more curves.'

'Wish I had a runner's body.'

She climbed back into bed, and I shifted over to make space.

'Thank you,' I said.

'For what?' She turned on her side to face me. I leant on my elbow and moved a lock of hair from where it fell across her eyes.

'For everything,' I said. 'For being you.'

Her eyes moved between mine, her face an open question. The cool air pooled between us and my skin brightened, prickling into goosebumps. Her eyes were clear and dark in the silver-grey light.

With a finger I drew a line down her breastbone and across the small curve of her belly. I watched her little nipples harden. I put my head next to hers on the pillow, my hand on her hip. The air was full of unanswered questions.

'And now it's cold,' I said.

'Come here.' She put a hand on my neck and her fingers found their way to the dent at the base of my skull. A slight pressure in the weight of her hand, an invitation or not. My choice. I moved my hips towards hers. Our eyes held, our faces almost touching.

It was me who closed the space, me who put my lips on hers, and her lips that softened, then opened, the tip of her tongue finding mine. All of me shuddered.

'You okay?' she asked.

'Yes.'

Words whispered in the dark. I put my hand to her breast, felt the perfect shape of it, so light and warm and round. Beneath my palm I could feel the nub of her nipple, a little nipple, so much smaller than mine, something amazing.

She moved her hand on to the small of my back, her hand warm, stroking, her fingers making light circles on my skin. For ages she drew circles on my skin, I on hers. Then it was me who rolled on to my back, my legs that opened, and her fingers that moved downward, opening me, exploring.

Words breathed rather than spoken, like cirrus clouds, tiny puffs of air.

There

Don't stop

You

Then an opening of warm, infinite spaces inside me. Soft-edged shapes that bloomed in my mind like giant peonies, undulating, moving, each one blossoming from the centre of the one that came before, on and on, then everything opening, rising, filling, emptying, and flooding, until I arched my back and gripped her wrist *Stop*.

My breath, holding, then releasing, then holding.

My eyes shut.

And then opening again, and there was Robyn, still there, still real, still looking at me with such tenderness and wonder that I wanted to cry. My beautiful friend Robyn. My good friend Robyn.

Robyn, who could make everything okay.

I think, perhaps, I slept more deeply than I ever had before that night, my arms around her, my head buried in her neck. Robyn must have too, because with a jolt I realized I could hear the morning wake-up call. That meant our housemistress, Mrs Turner, was at that very moment walking along the corridor, knocking briefly on doors before swiftly opening them, delivering a cheery greeting into each of the rooms, *Good morning, good morning*. We were naked. We were both in the same bed and we'd both overslept.

Robyn heard it too. She hesitated for one brief second before leaping out of the covers. She threw a duvet over me while scrambling for her abandoned pyjamas. Moments later our door opened.

'Morning, girls. How was your night?'

'Great, thanks, yep, really good, actually.'

'But it's so chilly in here.' Mrs Turner looked down at me where I lay with the duvet pulled up to my chin. 'Poor Willa's frozen.' She moved across the room to try to shove the window shut. Robyn stood in the middle of the room, dragging her fingers through dishevelled hair. *Fingers that smelt of me*, I thought. *In Robyn's hair*.

'No run this morning, Robyn? It's not like you to still be in bed at this hour.'

'Too icy, miss.' Robyn widened her eyes and grinned at me behind Mrs Turner's back. 'It's more inviting inside.'

Mrs Turner gave up on the window. She looked at me and smiled, tipping her head on one side, and, softening her voice, said, 'And how are you, sweetheart?'

'I'm all good, thanks.' I smiled. Mrs Turner smiled. She moved to the door. Then she stopped. She turned round. She looked from me to Robyn and back again, a puzzle in her eyes.

'Have you two swapped beds?'

Laika was missing. Laika was missing and I missed her with a raw, incomprehensible grief that sat inside my every cell. And yet the truth is, I would count the next eighteen months as some of the happiest of my entire life.

It was a world that existed entirely inside that room, and if I could go back and relive every single moment of it again, I would. I still do. But now I only ever remember it in snapshots.

Once, laughing. The sound burst from me one morning and was so strange and unexpected I immediately clapped a hand over my mouth. I hadn't known that I could ever laugh like that again. But there it was.

And music. Singing, dancing to Robyn's ridiculously retro tastes, 'You're Simply the Best', 'Always on My Mind', 'Don't You Want Me, Baby?'

Celebrating our birthdays within a month of each other, both of us turning seventeen.

Robyn's tender kisses. The curve of her clavicles. The nubs of her spine. The small of her back. The stretch of skin over her hips. The tip of her tongue. How much I wanted her. The way she made me come.

She must have guessed things, I suppose, but she never let on. I think she was too good, too kind ever to ask. Or perhaps she was scared of making things worse. But she must have guessed *something*. I know she must have, because she was always there for me, holding me, talking to me, when I woke from dreams in which I was pushing through rivers of thickening concrete, forever trying to reach a half-submerged shape. Never getting there, crying out. Night after night after night.

And, once, this: Robyn talking about something, lying on her side, facing me, her voice rippling with laughter, teasing, her fingers dancing over my skin, her hand playful, then her tickling fingers jabbing into the skin of my ribs and my instant *No*. The command flew from me fast and hard and unbidden; my voice loud, edged with panic. Just as fast I grabbed her wrist with my hand. We froze like that, me holding Robyn's hand in the air, my eyes fixed on hers. I wasn't smiling.

Robyn looked at me, her smile fading. I opened my hand and let go of her wrist. Slowly Robyn put down her hand, keeping her eyes on mine.

'Whoa,' she said. 'Sorry.'

I started to speak. 'Sorry –' I stopped. 'Don't tickle me. Anything, just – not that.'

'Okay,' she said.

She lay back down. I put my head next to hers on the pillow. Her face was as gentle as ever. My eyes moved over hers. I felt I had to say something, to explain.

'I –' I stopped again. She put a gentle hand on my arm.

'It's okay,' she said, 'really. It doesn't matter. You don't have to say anything.' She let a long moment lap between us. 'But you could tell me anything, you know. Anything. I swear I'd never tell a soul.'

'Go on, then.' Sitting up, I slipped the chain off my neck and placed it in the palm of her hand, folding her fingers over its tiny dolphin. 'Swear.'

She grinned. 'Fine. I, Robyn Bee, do hereby swear –'

'Solemnly swear –'

'Do hereby *solemnly* swear that *you*, Willa Martenwood, could tell me *anything* –'

'Anything?'

'Anything, and I would never tell another soul.'

'Thank you,' I said, smiling. She dropped my necklace back into my hand. I put it back on and lay down again, two heads on one pillow. 'That means a lot.'

I could have told her anything.

I could have told her *everything*.

I just never did.

The day school finished for the summer, Robyn's mother picked us up in a battered blue Defender, and in the two hours it took to drive to their home I honestly don't think she drew breath. Sometimes she talked to us, sometimes to passing sheep and the flocks of pheasants that periodically flooded the road; at other times to the Land Rover itself, Bertie.

I'd never ridden in a Defender before. The three of us sat rammed together on a bench seat in the front, and there were bits of moss growing on the inside of the windows and holes in the floor where you could literally see straight through to the road. The thing lurched wildly as it went round corners, and we went with it. I clung on to Robyn until she pointed out a handle on the dash she called the *Oh shit* bar, then I clung on to that.

Before long we were off the main roads and on to single-track lanes. We crossed river after river, sometimes on ancient stone bridges, and sometimes actually plunging through the water, Bertie reeling like a drunk over the riverbed's rocks. We wound our way through valleys so thick with trees the landscape looked almost Jurassic; everywhere was hung with vines and drifts of lichen, and the forest floor was thick with ferns.

Then Mrs Bee was saying, 'Come on, Bertie, you bastard,' and, as the oaks gave way to open moorland, we began the final ascent to the house, up the steepest hill imaginable, on a stony unmade track.

And then there were dogs barking and running alongside, and we drew up outside a lone stone cottage with a slate roof. Straight off two men appeared from the house. The tall thin one with curly greying hair, a big nose and wide grin I guessed must be Robyn's father, and the other her brother, a young man with a shy smile and a limp. All of them were talking and hugging, and the two dogs were jumping at Robyn and practically howling with joy when she bent down to kiss the top of their heads. Then her dad and brother were hauling our bags into the house and we followed, scattering cats, ducks and a goat in our wake.

I swear to God we must have gone back in time. The house was somehow alive, as if the actual physical building was living and breathing. Chickens and dogs marched through the kitchen, and there were hundreds of bats in the attic that streamed out from under the eaves at dusk. It wasn't a big place, and everything seemed to spill from the inside to the out: there were pots of geraniums and herbs by the back door, boots and dog beds, even the scent of the kitchen escaped into the garden – the smell of yeast and coffee and cinnamon and apples. Upstairs, the bedsheets smelt of marzipan, the towels of cucumber. And not only did they not lock up at night, they didn't even *shut* the front door. Outside, there were long views in every direction.

Everything was old, in fact the bathtub was seriously ancient.

The loo flushed with a chain, and the plumbing was treated like some sort of prehistoric creature in need of special care, a job which Robyn's dad, Chris, performed regularly with a wrench and a bucket, coaxing the pipes to splutter and gurgle their way back to life. Nothing was wasted in that household. Scraps went to the animals or the compost, and everything else was repurposed as seed trays or flower vases or saved for later, just in case. Everything had some sort of value, it seemed. Even the smallest thing mattered.

Meals appeared at a kitchen table that was hewn from a long plank of pale oak with an undulating surface, like a sea on a calm afternoon. Robyn's dad had made it. In fact, it turned out he'd made pretty much everything in that house and nothing was what you'd call perfect, no surface was flat. All the wood was full of dips and knots and bumps. Not one of the legs was square.

'You shouldn't overwork wood,' he told me, spotting me running my hands over the kitchen worktops one morning. 'It takes away its soul.'

For a house in the middle of nowhere, it wasn't a quiet place at all. It was full of noise and had a regular stream of visitors too, some of whom had made the climb because they'd spotted the word TEAS faraway on the roof of the pottery and others who arrived simply by word of mouth. Whoever they were, Robyn's mum, Caro, coaxed stories out of them. We met a group of dinner ladies from Truro, an archaeologist from Hexham, a professor of physics from Kansas, a stripper from Southend. Caro was fascinated by everyone. If they liked dogs, they were welcome.

Every once in a while someone would arrive who didn't speak English, and those were always the visitors that Robyn and I enjoyed the best. Not only did their appearance entail Caro's performing a series of increasingly complicated mimes, but when they came to pay they'd be completely bemused by her absolute refusal to accept even a single penny for the tea and cake. Then, after that, it just got worse. Before they were allowed to leave, Caro would produce a tatty old exercise book for them to write in. On the first page she'd written PLEASE ASSIST FUTURE VISITORS BY WRITING THIS IS NOT A TEA SHOP IN YOUR OWN LANGUAGE BELOW –

'Mum,' Robyn said one night as she flicked through its pages, 'you *do* realize you only ever give this book to people who don't actually have a clue what they're being asked to do, right? Look at this entry, somebody's just written *Bizarre*.'

The next month just went. I barely had time to think about home. We were somehow always busy. It was only at the end of my second week that I realized they didn't actually have a TV – *Absolutely no point*, Robyn said, *there's no reception*.

In the evenings, after supper, the whole family just sat around the kitchen table and talked, or sometimes played cards for buttons and coins. Big debates happened there too, discussions on art, politics, music, current affairs, anything really. Other things too, specific things, some of which I'd never even heard of before: Maslow's Hierarchy of Needs, the Bechdel Test, Hooper's Law, Schrödinger's Cat, Dunbar's Number, the Barnum Effect; and, once, argued passionately by Chris and with more examples than you'd think strictly necessary, Frank Zappa's musical genius. Mostly these discussions were started by Caro in a passing comment delivered casually, a small thing thrown into a ring. But just as quickly each idea got picked up and passed around. Every point was acknowledged, then instantly challenged. I soon realized you had to think fast and back up your arguments with good evidence, or else Robyn's brother, Michael, would pick them to bits with a precision that was needle-sharp. Robyn's dad, I thought, listening intently with his head cocked on one side, looked a bit like a raven, but he spoke like a priest, adding his own thoughts to ours in a voice that was measured and soft. Nobody ever lost their temper. Nobody shouted. Nobody stormed out. It took me a while to understand no one ever got angry about anything. If I'd have figured them out sooner, I would have owned up to accidentally breaking a bowl. I should have said something straight off, of course, but Laika and I knew better than to own up to *anything*. Nonetheless, I felt a deep shame for letting the moment pass. They were so generous about it. They must have known it was me.

That family. Caro, who always claimed to be exasperated by the ramblers that appeared at the door, but who then insisted they stop for tea and who had, in fact, already baked something, in anticipation of their arrival. Chris, who lived in plaid shirts with worn collars, and who seemed genuinely interested in everything we had to say. Beautiful, hesitant Michael, who, for someone so unbelievably clever, was the only person in the house who didn't seem to have clocked that Robyn and I were sleeping together. Robyn's parents never said anything, but I just knew they knew. It was nice, not having to explain, to just feel accepted. There wasn't a chance I'd be telling my own mum and dad.

They were both so kind. Not only had Chris spent an entire afternoon teaching me how to throw a pot, and later how to glaze and fire it raku-style, but the night before I left he gave me a gift from his pottery too. It was a tall, round pitcher with an elegant curving handle and a deep green glaze, the colour of the Atlantic, he said. It was by far the most beautiful thing I'd ever been given in my entire life.

'Make sure you use it,' Chris said to me. 'Put flowers in it or water for the table, anything, I don't mind. Just promise me you'll actually use it. Art's meant to have a *purpose*.'

'He's a potter,' Caro said; 'he makes functional objects. He would say that.'

The sky on my last night with the Bee family was dark and clear, so after the firing we just sat outside in deckchairs. I'd never seen such amazing stars in my entire life.

'No light pollution here,' Caro said, as Michael pointed out the three stars of the Summer Triangle, Deneb, Vega and Altair. Later, we just sat in silence and watched the slow turning of the sky. Yap, their tiny terrier, was curled into a soft comma in the middle of my lap. I buried my hands under his warm little body.

'But where is everybody?' Chris said, in a strangely emphatic voice, widening his eyes.

Michael laughed, then looked at my blank face. 'He's quoting the origin of the Fermi Paradox.'

'The what?'

'The Fermi Paradox, after Enrico Fermi. That's what he said about the problem with aliens, allegedly.'

'Sorry – aliens?'

'Okay, so the theory goes, given we know the universe is infinite, then that means there's an infinite number of possibilities for the existence of extra-terrestrial civilizations, so, logically, a bunch of them must be way older and more advanced than ours, right? Right. So the question is, why haven't any of them made contact? You'd think at least a few of them would have shown up by now. That's the crux of it. In a nutshell, the Fermi Paradox basically states that there's a contradiction there somewhere. The question is, where the hell are all the buggers?'

We lapsed back into silence. I looked up into the luminous sky and its infinite spaces, its infinite possibilities, its infinite hiding places.

Laika, I thought, *where are you?*

9.

Lamb

Willa

My mother had said she would drive down to collect me, but I told her I'd be okay on the train. The truth is, I wanted some time to myself, to process things. To think. By the time I arrived home, something in my life felt changed. The taxi slowed to a crawl as we went up the gravel drive and came to a stop halfway round the grass circle. I paid, tipping the driver as generously as my funds would allow, and he hefted each of my bags up the curved flight of stone steps, placing them just outside the solid oak doors. I let myself in. Then I stood just inside the front door. I don't think I'd ever really thought about the cavernous spaces of my parents' home before. The hallway alone was vast, a home to my father's collection of antique Chinese artefacts. Midway down, placed in the exact centre of a dark mahogany table – where no visitor could miss it – was the jewel of his collection: a huge mirrored black urn from the Qing Dynasty. A gold dragon with furious eyes snaked over its surface, a snarl on its strange, almost-human face. My mother once told me in a quiet aside that she thought the piece was grotesque, but my father cherished the thing. He'd been given it by his golf club as a show of appreciation, after he'd helped to fund their new club house. On either side of the hall, smaller, decorated porcelain vases and elaborate carved jade sculptures were arranged on polished half-moon tables between parallel sets of double doors, all of which opened on to other big rooms. A wide, carpeted staircase led to the upstairs.

I took off my shoes, dumped my bags and took out the raku pot from its layers of wrapping. Holding it in both hands, I walked barefoot through the empty hall, cool Carrara marble under my hot feet, my damp toes making prints on the tiles that just as quickly evaporated, fading into nothing. Well, that's what you'd think, but actually they don't. It turns out a partial print can be found months, even years later, if it's on the right surface. Each naked footstep says *I was here*. Nothing ever totally disappears. There will always be a trace.

The house felt strangely silent after the constant ruckus of Robyn's home, where there was always music playing, dogs barking, Mrs Bee talking, chickens fussing, visitors scraping chairs on the flagstone floor. I went through the house, looking for someone, anyone. Everywhere smelt of furniture polish and air freshener. The lounge was empty. There was no one in the study. I went into the kitchen, then stopped. My father was standing with his back to me, oblivious to my presence, and for a moment I looked at him the same way I'd looked at strangers through the window of a train. I saw him open the freezer and tip a couple of ice cubes into a cut-glass tumbler already half filled with a honey-coloured liqueur. Then he turned, raising the glass to his mouth and stopped when his eyes met mine.

'I didn't know you were back.'

'I've only just arrived.' I stood for a beat. The pot felt heavy in my hands. 'I've got something for you. For you and Mum.' I smiled and walked forward, holding the pot towards him. After a moment he put his glass on the kitchen island and took it from my hands into his.

'What is it?'

'It's a pot,' I said. 'It's raku. You can put it in the middle of the table.'

My father glanced momentarily at the glass kitchen table, where peach-coloured silk flowers and imitation sticks of hazel spilt out of a tall vase, then back at me.

'Your mother usually deals with that sort of thing.'

'I made it,' I said. 'Robyn's dad taught me. He's a potter.'

'Christ, how do they afford the fees?'

'Robyn's on a full scholarship.'

My father examined the pot, flipping it upside down to look at the underside. 'That's the intended look, is it? Rough.' He put it on the table. 'Very good, Willa. Your mother's digging or something, somewhere down the garden.'

I walked on to the terrace and hollered *Hello* and a voice shouted back *I'm here*. And then my mother was running towards me, opening her arms. I stepped into them and she held me for a long moment, her hands thick with peaty soil.

'I was in the greenhouse,' she said. 'I didn't hear the car.' When she drew back there were tears in her eyes. 'Wonderful thing,' she said, 'sweet, sweet girl. Come and tell me all about it.' Then she kissed my hair and together we walked back inside the house. I gave her the pot and, tears coming again to her eyes, she said it was the most beautiful thing she'd seen in her entire life.

We ate that evening around the long cherrywood table in the dining room. My parents sat together on one side, I sat opposite my father on the other. Unbalanced by our odd number, Laika's absence felt like an invisible presence. My mother sat stiff and upright in her chair. Between the three of us sat a dish of the palest veal, served in a milky cream sauce.

Watching my father carefully, I said, 'I can't eat that.'

His face went very still. He picked his napkin out of his lap and, with a look of total absorption, folded it in half, then half again, until it made a neat, exact oblong. He placed it next to his plate. He met my eyes.

'I'm veggie now. I should have said.'

'When did this come about?'

'A while back.' *Seconds ago.*

'Is this some fancy idea you've picked up at the pottery?'

'No.'

My father tapped the napkin with his fingertips.

'And what, exactly,' he said, 'are you trying to achieve?' I kept my eyes on his. A long moment seemed to pass. Eventually my father gave me a chilly smile. 'Well, then,' he said, 'you'd better make the most of the vegetables.'

My father dictated the meals we ate. He took charge of the grocery order himself, which he had delivered straight to the house. We had foie gras, oysters, lobster, suckling pig, fillet steak. My mother never knew what was coming; she just made meals out of whatever arrived. My father also took care of all the household bills. For anything else we needed, he gave her cash. My mother didn't even have a bank account.

Laika couldn't bear the idea of eating anything with a face. The truth is, she'd been stashing meat in a bag in her pocket for years, then taking it down the garden to give to the foxes. I knew it. My mother knew it. My father did not.

At least, he didn't until the day he did, on a hot Sunday the previous June. My father was carving at the head of the table, putting strips of limp meat on our plates. Each wet slice oozed pink transparent juice. He liked his meat barely cooked, so we all had it rare. Mealtimes were often taken in silence: my father always said if ever he felt a sudden need to listen to women yakking, he would happily visit the typing pool at work. But he made the odd exception.

I saw Laika looking at her glistening plate with disgust. She was trying to place her veg on the very edge, away from the fatty meat. My father watched her too, a slow look of comprehension dawning over his face.

'Nice little spring lamb this one, right, Laika? Fresh as a daisy. Only yesterday, there she was, jumping around with all the other nice little lambs, when some ugly sod whips her off to a slaughterhouse and mashes up her brain with a bolt. And here she is on our plates.'

Laika didn't look at him. She pushed up some peas with her fork. It was almost impossible to keep them from slipping back into the blood.

My father's tone changed. 'What in God's name, Laika? You're not a child.'

Laika's eyes narrowed. She looked at her plate.

'Show some appreciation. There are children out there who'd kill for a decent meal.'

Laika looked up. I thought, please don't say *Send it to them*.

'I understand that,' Laika said. 'I know.'

'Right, then. Don't play with your food.' My father stuck a fork into some meat and raised it to his lips. He chewed, not taking his eyes off Laika. 'Go on. I'm watching.'

Laika speared some carrots and ate them.

'That's it,' my father said. 'Meat next.'

'You don't have to watch me.'

'You're acting like a baby, so I'm treating you like a baby.'

Laika put down her fork. 'I'm not a baby.'

'Do you need me to feed you?'

'No.'

'Right, then.'

My mother said, 'It is possible she's not terribly hungry, Bryce. She had a very big breakfast.'

My father slammed the top of the table and my mother and I both jumped. 'How many times, Bianka? I will not be told *how* and *when* to discipline my child.'

My mother dropped her eyes to her plate. Laika ate some peas.

'Eat some meat.'

Laika placed her knife and fork together. She looked up. She said, 'I'm not hungry.'

My father slowed his voice. 'You'll eat what's on your plate. And you will clear it.'

'I'm a vegetarian.'

'You're a child. You don't get to decide what you eat.'

She held his gaze. 'I'm not eating meat.'

My father put down his knife and fork. 'While you're living in my house, Laika, under my roof, you'll eat whatever you're given.'

'No, I won't. Not any more.'

'That's what *you* think.'

'That's what I *want*.'

'What you *want* doesn't come into it.'

My father stood up. He walked around the table and stood behind my sister. She sat upright, looking dead ahead.

'Eat,' he said. He held a piece of lamb to her closed lips. After a few seconds he took hold of Laika's hair and yanked it so hard her head snapped back. She opened her mouth in shock and my father shoved in the meat. She immediately spat it back out. It landed in a bloody lump on the white tablecloth. My father moved his jaw. Still holding her hair with one hand, he stabbed the same piece of meat back on to the fork and jabbed it again at her sealed lips. Shimmering lines of fat streaked down Laika's chin. She kept her eyes shut.

My mother said, 'Bryce, for God's sake, please.'

'One of us has to ram some manners into this child and it's becoming all too clear it's not going to be you.'

My father threw the fork back on to Laika's plate and it bounced off, clattering on to the floor. His eyes moved to me.

'Why aren't *you* eating now?' he said. '*Eat.*'

My own hunger had evaporated. I glanced at Laika, sitting with her eyes closed, then at my mother. She made a tiny movement with her head, a microscopic nod. Her hand shook slightly as she raised her own fork to her lips, as if demonstrating for me what to do. She took a small bite of the meat. Another tiny nod. I copied her example, forking up some meat and attempting to chew it enough to force it down my throat. After what felt like an age, I swallowed. My father said, 'Show me.' Feeling my cheeks colouring, I opened my mouth. 'Good,' he said. 'Thank God one member of this family does what she's told.'

Laika opened her eyes.

'As for you, Laika, you'll sit there until you've cleared your plate. Every bite.'

And Laika sat there. She was still there the next morning, in front of a plate of cold food swimming in congealed white fat. She was still sitting there on the Monday afternoon, her face grey with exhaustion. My father accompanied her to toilet breaks, and late in the evening she was sent to her room and told to stay there until the next day. When she came down for breakfast on the Tuesday, the plate was brought out again. She hadn't consumed a single thing in forty-eight hours.

My father stood over her, his arms crossed.

From my position halfway up the stairs, I saw my mother go into the lounge and remove my father's collection of whisky tumblers from the drinks cabinet. She picked one up and appeared to look closely at the cut of its heavy glass. Then she rolled back her arm like a county cricketer and took aim at the fireplace. The glass shattered on the marble surround. My mother paused. Then she selected a second glass and threw that one too. Then another.

It took six glasses before my father came to investigate.

'What's this,' he said, a quiet smile on his lips, 'some sort of protest?' I looked through the banisters, holding my breath. I'd never seen my mother act like this, not ever, not once. Her face was fixed into a strange expression: moonstruck, dazed. I had no idea what she would do next, what either of them would do. I folded my knees into my chest. I kept very still.

My mother didn't say anything. Like some sort of living mannequin, she moved jerkily past him into the hall. She paused by one of the half-moon tables, selected a jade figurine from a table and, after a moment, took aim and lobbed it at the opposite wall. With a loud crack, the green head separated from the body and ricocheted into a porcelain vase. Both items smashed on the marble floor, and the sound of the shattering pieces echoed around the hall.

His voice soft, my father said, 'There are all sorts of ways to pay for broken vases, my dear.'

My mother glanced at him. She picked up a jade elephant.

'Go on, then,' my father said, 'do your worst.'

My mother raised the elephant to her shoulder and took aim at the wall. Then she seemed to change her mind. Her eyes moved around the hall. She swivelled her feet until she was facing the black Qing urn.

'You had better deal with me first.' My father's voice had changed from amusement to quiet fury.

My mother looked at him, then back at the urn. She raised her arm.

'*Enough.*' My mother lowered her arm. 'Let her eat sodding vegetables for all I care. But that's it, Bianka. I won't be ordering her anything else.' He turned on his heel and stormed into his study, slamming the door behind him.

Laika had won.

I'd always been my father's *Golden Girl*. That's what he called me, as if, alongside my mother, I was not his flesh and blood but simply some sort of prized possession. It was nothing to do with the colour of my hair. I'd spent seventeen years doing exactly what I was told. He'd always told us that families were private spaces, that our home lives were never to be discussed with anyone else, full stop. It was, he said, his house, his family, we were his children and his rules applied. But at Robyn's house I'd seen how families were meant to function, and it wasn't like ours. Other families didn't operate like ours at all. Now I started testing him in small ways. Not eating meat was one. I said I'd lost receipts. I rearranged his books and CDs. I answered back. *What are you going to do about it*, I thought, *make me disappear?* But nothing worked. I just couldn't get him to react. Finally I played Frank Zappa in my bedroom at full blast until he stormed in and told me in no uncertain terms *to turn that shit off*.

A small but satisfying result.

The summer before she disappeared, my sister had spent the entire time bugging me to play chess. It was a pretty boring activity as far as I was concerned, because she could beat me hands down.

'Do we have to?' I said, when yet again I saw her setting up the board. 'I don't have the strategy.'

'You've got strategy in spades,' she said. 'Your problem is that you don't see the point.'

'What's the point?'

'Patricide,' she said. 'You have zero interest in killing your father.'

Work on the conservatory had begun that August. The builder in charge was a taciturn man with flaky red skin called Ian Cox, who, on his first visit to the house, had stood looking at the garden with stony eyes.

'Bloody hell,' he said, 'some money round here.'

'I don't know what I'm doing wrong,' my mother said to us as the work progressed. 'It's impossible to get a smile out of the man. Po-faced, that's what he is. He doesn't even look me in the eye. Perhaps he's one of those types that just doesn't like women.'

One afternoon Laika and I retreated halfway down the garden. It was hot and we lay in our bikinis in the shade of a laburnum tree with the chessboard between us. Up at the house a mechanical digger began scooping out bucketloads of soil.

I kept half an eye on the chessboard and the other half on our mother as she carried out a tray loaded with mugs and cake. She touched Cox lightly on the arm as she spoke to him, smiling beatifically, as if the builder were some dear old friend, and not just some bloke they'd employed to do a job.

Laika moved her queen. 'Do you remember when we were little and Mum made us walk around with books balanced on our heads?'

'It was meant to teach us deportment.'

'Whatever. If I have a daughter, I'm not ever making her do that. Books are for reading.'

A cloud passed under the sun and I sat up and pulled on a jumper.

'Don't look now,' Laika said as she took my knight. 'Deedee's arrived.'

We watched from a distance. Deedee stood on the terrace gesturing at my mother, the noise from the digger drowning out her words. Then my mother turned and waved at us with both arms, as if marshalling jets.

'Shit,' Laika said, 'is there any chance we didn't see that?'

'Nope.'

We took as long as we could to amble up to the house.

'Dear God,' my mother said. 'Laika, put on some clothes. You shouldn't be parading around like that. We've got workmen here.'

'You make it sound like builders are natural-born perverts,' Laika said.

'I'm just saying you're not children any more. Anyway, it's your lucky day. Aunt Deedee has very kindly brought you something.' I could see my mother trying not to smile.

'I've been having a bit of a clear-out,' Deedee said, 'and I've found some very nice bits and pieces from my younger days. Far too good for the charity shop.'

'That's very kind of you,' I said, leaning on Laika's foot.

'Gosh, how lovely,' Laika said, 'how exceptionally generous.'

Deedee looked pleased. 'I've left a bag in the hall. I'll let you girls go and have a rummage, shall I?'

'Thanks, Deedee,' I said. I grabbed Laika's hand and we turned and walked fast towards the house.

'Bagsy you get anything with sweat stains,' I said.

'First dibs on the giant knickers.'

We hefted the bag up the stairs and turned out its contents on my bed. I'd expected the worst, but I was wrong. It was a surprisingly good haul.

'Look at this beauty,' Laika said, holding up a blouse with bouffant sleeves and a high frilly collar in a faded tangerine.

'Put it on,' I said. 'No, wait – look at this jumper – can you believe that pattern? Put that on too. Here – try it with this nylon skirt. And those socks with the multicoloured sheep.'

'Now this is more like it,' Laika said, pulling out a pair of faded black jodhpurs. 'Hey, and look at the heels on those boots. Some of this stuff is seriously cool. Vintage. I'm going for the jodhpurs. And the frilly shirt.'

I pulled on a white, layered ankle-length sundress and used a wide belt to cinch it in at the waist.

'That actually doesn't look too bad,' Laika said, 'if you were thinking of auditioning for a part in a musical. Put that enormous hat with it. You look like a wedding cake.'

'We need make-up,' I said. On a roll now, we marched into my mother's bathroom and, giggling madly, helped each other load up our faces with foundation, then eyeliner, mascara, blusher, cherry-red lipstick.

'I look ridiculous,' Laika said, inspecting her face. 'I look like a clown.' She pulled a couple of poses. 'You look okay.'

'Come on,' I said, 'let's show Deedee.'

Laika looked at me and raised her eyebrows. 'Seriously?'

'Why not? Just keep a straight face, okay?'

We tottered downstairs. I had to hold up the tiers of lace fabric so I wouldn't trip and Laika could hardly walk in the high-heeled boots. I went first out on to the terrace, where my father, who was supervising the work, was standing with Ian Cox, both men with their arms crossed across their chests, businesslike. I gave a twirl.

'Very nice, Willa,' my father said, 'very *Stepford Wives*.'

'*Stepford Wives*,' I said. 'What's that?'

Following my lead, Laika made her entrance. She flung open her arms and wheeled around, staggering slightly in the high heels. She was giggling, enjoying herself. Standing in the middle of the terrace, she wiggled her hips and strutted like a catwalk model, striking different poses, her dark hair wild and tumbling about her head. The pale tangerine blouse billowed like a sail. I stood on the edge of the terrace, loving the show, the fun Laika was having. The two men watched.

'Good God,' Deedee said, appearing in the doorway. 'What's she up to now?'

'What's going on?' my mother said, following behind.

My father replied, keeping his eyes on my sister. 'Laika is flirting with me,' he said.

I watched Laika's face fall the moment the words were out of his mouth. Turning, she pushed past Deedee and my mother and stumbled into the house, wobbling unsteadily in the heels. I followed her. She pulled off the boots and threw them hard across the kitchen. One bounced off the utility-room door and she bolted upstairs.

'Oh, my girl,' my mother said.

'Stay here,' I said; 'I'll go.'

I raced up the stairs. Laika was in her room, tearing off the clothes and hurling them across the room, her cheeks burning with shame. I stood in the doorway, plucking at the fabric of the white dress.

'Don't say anything,' she said, 'don't even speak to me.'

She was down to her bra and knickers, the little dolphin necklace swinging wildly at her throat. She pushed past me and into the bathroom we shared. At the sink she scrubbed at her face with soap until her cheeks were blood red and raw. I put out a hand and touched her arm.

'Lai.' She turned her streaked face to me, her cheeks slick with rivers of black mascara.

'It's always me,' she said. 'Don't you get that? It's never, ever you, never the *Golden Girl*. Even when we're doing the exact same thing. It's always *me*.' She turned back and scrubbed again at her face. 'Like I would *flirt* with *my own father*? It's sick.'

'I don't think he meant it like that.' My words sounded weak, even to me, a lie.

She turned on me. 'Who the fuck are you now, his pet monkey?' She stood up and glared at me, her entire body tense with fury, her eyes red from the soap. 'I *hate* him.'

She pushed past me and stormed to her bedroom. Then she turned and stood in the doorway. Through gritted teeth she said, 'You're never going to understand. You do everything you're told. You never question anything. You're a puppet.

Somebody pulls a string and your arm jerks up. Someone opens your mouth and you spew whatever they want you to say. You never stand up for me. You never stand up for you. Nothing matters to you. You haven't got the guts to stand up for anything or anyone in your entire life, not ever. I hate the fucking lot of you.'

She slammed the door so hard it rattled in its frame. I stood by the door, frozen, holding my breath in case someone downstairs had heard.

Laika only came down the next day, silently materializing next to me by the kitchen sink in a T-shirt and shorts but otherwise looking like she'd just got out of bed, her hair still an unbrushed mess of wild dark curls. I put my arm around her shoulders and we stood in silence, gazing through the window. Some new neighbours, Graeme and Sheila Bowman, had come over to introduce themselves, and my parents were standing with them on the terrace, inspecting the pale yellow brick my father had chosen for the extension. Spotting the two of us through the kitchen window, my mother called us out to say hello.

'Jesus,' Laika said, 'do we have to?'

'Yeah, we do,' I said, 'for Mum.' I dragged her outside.

'These are my daughters,' my mother said. 'This one is Willa.'

'What a pretty name,' Sheila Bowman said. 'Very unusual.'

'She was meant to be a William,' my mother said. 'And this one needs a haircut.' My mother took hold of the long, tumbling cords of Laika's unbrushed hair and twisted them into a sort of high bun around her own fingers. Unable to move, Laika stood scowling, the milk-white skin of her neck exposed, as if waiting by a guillotine. Her fringe covered her eyes. 'I've been telling her for weeks, but she's not exactly cooperating.'

'My hair's fine,' Laika said. She sounded sulky. I glanced at my father. His eyes moved briefly between my mother and sister, his mouth set in a line.

'Well,' my mother said, 'you're definitely going to need one before you go back to school.'

'What a beautiful garden,' Sheila said, 'and a swimming pool too. You lucky things. We've only got a tennis court.'

'Count your blessings,' my mother said. 'A tennis court is *so* much easier to maintain. All that faffing around with test strips and the like – it's a total pain.'

'Really?' Shelia said. She sounded amazed. 'Don't you have a little man?'

'Oh, I don't have help.' My mother's eyes flashed fleetingly towards my father. She instantly gathered herself. 'What I meant was, we don't *need* help.' She smiled warmly at Sheila. 'But, believe me, those chemicals are *filthy*. One time I accidentally wiped my face after I'd been handling the chlorine and the pain was *excruciating*. I honestly thought I was going to lose an eye.' No one said anything, so my mother added, 'And the pool house is a bit of an eyesore as well.'

At the mention of the pool house, Laika looked at me and rolled her eyes. Whatever it was, a 'pool house' it was not. Rather, it was a squat, airless bunker used to store chemicals, with a roof so low you couldn't stand up inside. It didn't even have any windows.

My mother went on, 'We only really keep it for the girls.'

There was a moment of silence. Sheila Bowman gave my mother a mild smile.

My mother said, 'Have you moved from very far?'

'From Cambridge. It's been forced on us really, to put distance between us and Graeme's job. It's all very tiresome.' Sheila made a face at my mother.

'Oh?'

'Graeme's a director at Huntingdon Life Sciences.'

My mother looked blank.

My father said, 'Biomedical research.'

My mother said, 'Oh.'

Laika's eyes moved from my father to Graeme Bowman.

'It all became terribly uncomfortable,' the woman said. She widened her eyes at my mother, as if they shared a common understanding.

'Oh?'

'Bleeding-heart activists, that's the problem,' Graeme said. 'The animal-rights people. They're a complete bloody menace. Roadkill on our doorstep. Broken glass. Faeces through the letter-box. Couldn't get away from them. Obviously I'm telling you all this, but even here we'll keep a low profile. You wouldn't believe the tactics they use to find out where you live.'

'You'll be all right here,' my father said. 'That's the primary advantage of a gated community. Makes for a very safe neighbourhood.'

'What do you do?' Laika said to the man.

'Why don't you girls run inside?' my mother said.

Graeme Bowman looked at Laika. 'Various types of animal research: medical, pharmaceutical, cosmetic. Mainly we use rats, mice, rabbits, beagles of course, chimps, pigs. Cats. And don't believe that rubbish you hear about our sourcing them from shelters or stealing people's pets: that's a load of nonsense. We've a substantial on-site breeding facility: we produce our own guinea pigs, as many as we want. The fact is, it's important work, necessary, and, dare I say it, a number of the experiments are genuinely fascinating. But try telling the sodding campaigners that – excuse my French, ladies – they're completely obscene.'

Laika said, 'You experiment on animals. Isn't that obscene?'

A beat of silence, then, 'I apologize for my daughter,' my father said; 'she really can be exceptionally naive.'

*

Two days later the entire road knew exactly who the new neighbours were. Somebody had thrown a couple of bricks through their kitchen windows.

The news arrived with us at breakfast on the Saturday. Graeme Bowman came round, driving up to the house in a large black Lexus. He pulled two pale yellow bricks out of a bag and my mother quickly produced a kitchen towel for him to put them on, so they wouldn't scratch the glass table. He said he hoped my parents wouldn't mind the intrusion, but he'd remembered that our extension was being built from pale yellow brick. Would my parents mind if he checked to see if these bricks matched those? It was such an unusual colour. But of course not, my mother said, what a dreadful business it was, and how unfortunate to think how quickly those awful people must have located their home – and to think of the *lengths* they must have gone to, and how concerning it was to think they had perhaps even been on our property as well, stealing bricks.

My father collected a brick from the pallet. He placed it next to the others on the towel. It was a perfect match.

'Would you like a coffee?' my mother asked. Mr Bowman wouldn't – he had to get home. They had a glazier coming.

'But Sheila's feeling pretty low,' he added. 'No doubt she'd like a bit of company. Come back with me, have one there with her. I'd appreciate that. It would do her good.'

'Now?' my mother asked. She blinked rapidly.

'If you've got the time.'

My mother glanced at us, then at my father. 'I would, of course,' she said, her voice unnaturally slow. She paused, her eyes still blinking rapidly, then added in a rush, 'But I was just about to take the girls out.' When neither man replied, she added, 'To the hairdresser.'

'Go on, Bianka,' my father said, his voice indulgent and

warm. 'Of course she'd love to go for coffee, Graeme. Perhaps Willa would like to go too?'

'I've got stuff to do.'

Looking flustered, my mother gathered her things. She spoke, looking more at Laika than at me.

'I won't be long,' she said.

My father smiled. 'Take your time.'

Mr Bowman left the bricks where they were, on the kitchen table. My mother slid into the passenger seat of his car and Mr Bowman closed the door behind her with a soft thunk. Moments later the Lexus slid back down the drive, gravel crunching under its tyres.

Laika instantly made to leave the kitchen. My father caught her by the arm. 'What do you know about those bricks?'

Laika's mouth dropped open. 'Me?'

'Yes, you.'

'How should I know anything about that?'

'Don't answer back.'

'I thought you were asking me.'

'Don't take me for a fool, Laika.'

'You think it was me? That I broke their windows?' Her face was the picture of wide-eyed astonishment.

'That's exactly what I think. You've made your halfwit opinions perfectly clear.'

'Dad,' I said, 'that's not fair. Lai wouldn't do that.'

'Laika, look at me when I'm talking to you.'

Laika looked up. Her hair hung over her eyes. She said, 'It wasn't me.'

'I said *look at me*. Take that hair out of your eyes.' His voice became low, dangerous. 'And if your mother says you need a haircut, then you'll get a haircut.'

My father jerked my sister towards the knife rack. He grabbed the kitchen scissors, then dragged her over to the stairs. Twisting round, Laika started hitting him with her free arm, landing blows on his chest and legs. I heard her shout, '*Get off.*'

'Dad,' I said, breathing fast, '*stop*. Don't do that.'

Laika said, 'Help me.'

I did the only thing I could think of. In bare feet I ran to the front door, hurtled down the steps and took off down the long curve of the drive, stumbling as sharp pieces of tiny gravel jabbed into my feet. I turned on to the road. The black car was already out of sight. I stopped dead. By the time I caught up with my mother it would be too late. I had to go back. I turned, breathing hard. I had to save her myself.

I ran back to a house that was strangely quiet. I found them upstairs. Laika was sitting on the closed lid of the loo in our bathroom, and our father was cutting off her hair. Her fringe had already gone, cut high along her hairline, revealing giant brown eyes like those of a deer, and now he was beginning on the rest, shearing chunks of long hair off in great sheets, making a hard uneven line above the level of her jaw. Dark locks of hair fell about her, into her lap. On to the floor.

Without even looking at me, my father said, 'If you want a trim, Willa, then stay. If not, then I suggest you leave, right now.'

Laika was sitting quietly, her face empty of emotion. She wasn't fighting any more. Like an animal before slaughter, she closed her eyes. I could barely recognize her. And I don't just mean how different she looked without her hair. I mean it was as if some essential part of her – her spirit, her soul, that part of her that truly mattered – had simply *gone*.

I couldn't bear to see her like that. And, anyway, I could only make things worse. That's why I left, I told myself, why I obeyed his instruction to leave; why, yet again, I did what I was told. I went to my room and shut the door. A few minutes later I saw my father through the window, dragging Laika across the lawn towards the airless bunker we called the pool house. I stood at my window, my hands pushed flat against the glass, knowing I'd let both of them down: not just my sister but my mother too. I knew what her reaction would be. She'd throw herself at him. She'd cry, she'd plead. She'd beg. And none of it would change a thing; the outcome was always the same. He'd punish her too. And then she would hit the bottle.

My father shoved Laika inside the pool house and locked the door, pocketing the key. Only then my sister seemed to regain her fire. Even from all the way across the garden, even from inside the house, I could hear her slamming her entire body against the solid door, her distant voice bellowing *You fuck*.

That was the Saturday morning. On the Sunday morning, he let her back out. She was withdrawn and hardly speaking that day, but at some point in the grey early hours of that night she turned up in my room, shaking me awake from a deep sleep and shushing me urgently when I nearly cried out. It wasn't just that she was pale and bloody, it was that I hadn't instantly recognized her. That awful haircut my father had given her – best described as a severe bob – made her look like a stranger. She needed me that night. Then the next day she was gone, vanished on her way to school.

So I did see her again that weekend. But when I think about the last time I saw my sister, really saw her, I always think about the quiet emptiness of her being as she sat on the seat of the toilet, with her hair falling on to the floor. The moment she closed her eyes.

That's when she went. That's when she really disappeared.

10.

Driving lessons

Willa

A year to the day that Laika vanished, Robyn and I began our final year at school, putting in our university applications and cranking up the work to make sure that both of us would achieve our first choices. We'd aimed high: medicine at Imperial for Robyn and English at UCL for me. That way we'd both be studying in London: Robyn's idea.

I knew what Robyn felt. She was always watching me, then smiling, her lips curving upward. I knew from the way she touched me, the way we kissed.

I knew she loved me. She told me all the time.

It was me that started it. And me who sabotaged it, me who pretended I didn't know what I was doing. And I chose my moment too, just a couple of days after her eighteenth birthday. A couple of weeks before our final exams.

It was a spring morning. Back from a run, Robyn was getting dressed, miming to 'Tiny Dancer' in her knickers, arms above her head as she swayed in the blue light of early May, her unbrushed hair falling about her face, turning, smiling, turning, smiling. The window was open and a perfect day filled our room. There was birdsong outside. Robyn went to the window, leant on the sill and stuck her head out, taking big lungfuls of clean bright air.

'Listen,' she said, 'can you hear that one? That's a mistle thrush.'

'How d'you even know something like that?' I said. 'I wouldn't know a blackbird from a robin.'

'That's easy,' she said. 'Want to know the difference?' She turned round and coyly presented her breasts. 'Blackbirds don't have these.'

She turned back, laughing, gazing out of the window. I looked at her back, the nubs of her shoulder blades like little wings, her little boyish hips, the lace edge of her pants.

And, out of nowhere, a voice, mine, said: 'You know, this doesn't make us gay.'

She didn't turn. I thought, perhaps, she hadn't heard me. I said it again. I elaborated.

'I mean, this is great, but it's not real. Obviously I'm not an actual lesbian. It's really nice, though, as an experiment. But I wouldn't say I'm gay.'

Another beat. By the time she turned round, her hands were folded in a tight *x* over her breasts and her eyes were as bright as a morning sea.

'God, no,' she said, 'me neither.'

Sometimes I remember it like this:

Me: I don't think I'm actually gay.

Robyn [turning instantly, laughing]: Hell, no, me neither.

And other times, in the middle of long nights lying next to Jamie, after Robyn met Cat, after they moved in together, after they bought a house, after they had kids, this:

Me: I don't think I ever want this to end.

Robyn [turning, smiling]: Neither me.

She didn't argue or cry or try to make me change my mind. She was a bit quiet, perhaps, I thought. She didn't come to my bed again, but our final exams were coming up and it was ridiculously hot for May and she said she needed her sleep. And that was the sensible thing, I told myself. There was time to repair things. I could make it up.

The first of our final exams was the Shakespeare paper for English, so Robyn and I would be sitting it together. That morning both of us were on edge, a little excited, a little scared. I thought *So much rides on these next three hours.*

I sat at my desk doing some last-minute revision but I couldn't really concentrate. I kept looking at my watch. In thirty minutes we'd be going to the examination hall, twenty, fifteen, ten. I was so nervous I couldn't keep still.

With five minutes to go I leapt up. 'I really need the loo.'

Robyn laughed. 'Go on,' she said. 'I'll wait here. Be quick.'

Every bathroom on our corridor was occupied. Knowing the next closest one was on the ground floor, I dashed down the stairs, two steps at a time, and ran through the empty day room, glancing at the TV as I went past, which as ever was switched on, its volume turned right down. I stopped short. On the screen was a photograph of Laika. A breaking-news message on the news ticker ran continually across the top of the screen. I read: HUMAN REMAINS FO . . . Something pounded through my chest. The image changed to a lock-up. Police cars and an ambulance out the front, a tent. MARTENWOOD WARE . . . Grim-faced men in white boiler suits. Another vehicle, this one moving at speed past banks of reporters, flashing cameras pressed up against the windows of the car. My eyes went again to the moving message on the top of the screen. I read FATHER OF MISSING . . . then back to the image – fuzzy dots started blurring and colliding. I read ARREST.

I felt as if my heart had stopped. And Mum, I thought,

Mum – where's Mum? I scrambled for the volume, and accidentally hit the on/off button instead. The screen went blank.

A voice behind me said, 'Willa?' I spun round to see my housemistress smiling at me. 'Chop, chop,' she said, putting a hand on my shoulder. 'It's a bit late for nerves.' She almost pushed me into the pack of girls flooding along the corridor and into the exam hall. Stupid, dazed, barely thinking, I sat at my desk, head in my hands, my head full of noise. I didn't know what to do. I couldn't think at all. I turned in my seat, craning to see Robyn. I needed Robyn. Robyn, the only person in the world I could talk to, who could help. But she wasn't anywhere – her seat was empty. It was only as the exam was about to start that she flew into the back of the hall. She caught my eye, her face flushed red. Shaking her head, she mouthed, *Where were you?*

Moments later, the exam began. Mindlessly, unthinkingly, automatically, I opened my paper and read: *The death of Lear's youngest daughter is the shocking climax of cruelty in Shakespeare's exploration of evil. Discuss.*

I didn't write a thing.

'What happened?'

What happened? Laika is dead.

I opened my eyes. I was sitting on my bed with my shoulders and head against the wall, stupefied and numb. Robyn was standing in the doorway of our bedroom. She looked furious.

'*What?*'

'Where were you? We were going together. To the *exam*, remember? I *waited* for you. You said you were coming back.'

'Sorry. Robyn –'

'If I'd been another thirty seconds they wouldn't even have let me in. I could have failed the entire bloody exam because of you.'

'Robyn – I can't do this right now.'

'It's always about you, isn't it?'

'*What?*'

'I mean, we've been together for nearly eighteen months and then you just go and dump me like –'

'I didn't *dump* you.'

'You said this – us – wasn't even *real*. Everything I've done, everything I've felt – I mean *everything* – you called it an *experiment*.'

'My sister –'

'*Just for once* this isn't about your sister,' she said. 'It's about *us*.'

'Keep your voice down. People might hear.'

'People might hear *what*? That there's an *us*? So, what, it's fine for us to have sex so long as nobody knows?'

'That's not what I –'

'Let's find out, shall we?' She stuck her head out of the door and shouted, 'HEY, EVERYBODY! WILLA AND I HAVE SEX.'

Straight off a voice shouted back, 'WE KNOW,' followed by peals of laughter.

I jumped up and slammed our door. 'What the *fuck*.'

She glared at me, almost smiling, her face flushed with heat. Then a cloud passed over her eyes, a gradual understanding. Her mouth changed shape. She shook her head. Quietly she said, 'You're embarrassed, aren't you? I embarrass you. *This* embarrasses you.'

She gave me a chance to say something. Every chance. My mind just wouldn't operate. Couldn't. There was just too much going on in my brain. Too much chaos. Too much disaster. She waited as the silence swelled between us. And I just kept looking at her.

She walked to her desk and picked up a thick ring binder, the words HUMAN BIOLOGY surrounded by hearts drawn in fluorescent pink marker. She said, 'I'm going to revise in the library. Perhaps while I'm out you should ask to swap rooms.'

And then she left.

I pulled my purse out of my locker and picked up my school bag. Then I walked down the corridor, keeping my face fixed dead ahead so I didn't meet anyone's eye. I ran down the stairs and out into the midday sun. Then I walked, fast, but not so fast that I might attract attention, down the wide tarmac drive until I'd passed the school gates. I kept going until I found a phone box. Then I called a taxi and when it picked me up I asked the driver to take me to the station. From there I took a train to London, then the tube and then another train from Victoria. My mother met me at Lewes wearing dark glasses and a headscarf, plus a Burberry trench coat which, despite the warm evening, was buttoned up to the neck. I could stay one night, she said, and then she would drive me straight back to school. I said, 'Absolutely not.'

All we knew was this: the body was female, it had been found in a Martenwood warehouse and it had been there some time.

And this: my father was being interviewed by the police.

That night my mother holed herself up in the den with the curtains drawn tight. She was there when I went to bed, and still there early the next morning, slumped on the sofa like a discarded ragdoll, mouth open, hair dishevelled, mascara smeared beneath her eyes. Beside her, an empty gin bottle rolled on its side. I covered her with a blanket, switched off the TV and righted an old black-and-white snap in a frame. It had been taken by some paparazzi at a club in London, and had later appeared in the back pages of *Tatler*. In it, my mother, on her twentieth birthday and at the height of a brief modelling career, is dancing on a table, holding a cigarette in one hand and the neck of a bottle of champagne in the other. Wearing a miniskirt, long boots, a white vest top and several long chains of beads, and she'd been caught mid laugh with her eyes shut and mouth open, the beads and her long hair flying round her head like ribbons flung from a maypole. In it, she looks startlingly beautiful, young, wild and completely, deliriously happy. My father is in the photograph too, standing half shadowed in the background with his eyes fixed on my mother, grinning broadly and applauding, his expression somewhere between wonder and animal desire. According to the story, that's the night they first met, but things must have moved along fairly fast. My mother's modelling days came to an abrupt halt, and not even ten months later I came along. I held the picture up close so I could look at her face. Even from a black-and-white photograph you could tell she was plastered, and it occurred to me that there must have been a time when my mother was a happy drunk. I couldn't ever remember her being like that. Where other people would become truculent or loud when they'd been drinking, my mother would slip into a quiet despair. Booze made her cry.

I didn't know what to do with myself. I stood in the doorway of the conservatory, gazing at that expanse of white marble, that spotless white surface, the rigid, grey pool of cold concrete that lay underneath. I thought about that one, single chance I'd been given to talk to the police on my own, the morning we'd retraced her footsteps to school. What I could have, *should* have told them: what happened with the scissors that night, how culpable I was, what *I* had done. I should call them perhaps, ask for another chance to talk. But how could I start telling them things now that I hadn't mentioned before? I was scared. Things were already bad enough.

Finally I could hear my mother moving around, the TV switched on, then straightaway off. I went back with two mugs of tea.

'Mum,' I said, 'I want to ask you something. It's important.'

I gave her the tea. She placed it on the floor and crossed her arms.

'Yes,' she said, 'I am all ears.'

I realized I hadn't planned how to phrase what I wanted to say. I paused, looking at her. After a moment, I said, 'D'you think –'

'Do I think he did it? Is that what you're asking? Do I think your father killed Laika? How could you ask such a thing, Willa? How could you even *think* such a thing? Of course he didn't do it.'

I said, 'You don't think –'

'No,' she said, 'not for one second do I think.'

It was rare for my mother to ever sound cross. I said, 'I'm sorry – I don't . . .' My voice trailed off.

'Your father couldn't get away with murder, Willa. He doesn't have the wherewithal. He'd get caught and he knows it. He'd make all sorts of stupid mistakes.'

A thought fluttered through my mind too fast for me to net it. I blinked, trying to catch the sense of what she'd said.

'Take this away, will you? I'm not in the mood for tea.' I took the still hot mug from her outstretched hand. It was clear the conversation was over.

'Can I get you anything else?' I asked.

Without looking at me she said, 'I could murder a gin.'

A police liaison officer turned up at our house in the morning. They hadn't yet managed to identify the body, but they did know this: it wasn't my sister. The dental records had been conclusive. I clutched my mother, wiping away the tears streaming down my face.

My father was released. He arrived home grey and uncommunicative, then spent the following week holed up in his study with the door slammed shut. During those strange, strained days my mother hung by me like an orbiting moon. Something about her continual presence reminded me of being a child. Then one morning, after my father had appeared in the kitchen in pursuit of fresh coffee and my mother, wearing rubber gloves, had manifested from somewhere upstairs, I realized just what it was: it had been exactly like that when Laika and I were small. When my father was at home, my mother was always close by. If we weren't out, either at school or attending an endless stream of holiday clubs, she was by our side. She brushed our hair and read us books and sang to us while we took baths. She never, ever, let us be around him on our own.

But now he said he wanted a word, alone, with me. I followed him into his study, not looking back in case I met my mother's eyes. He shut the door. Then he sat back in his black leather chair and steepled his fingers. I stayed standing, pinned to the wall.

'I thought we should have a little chat,' he said in an equable tone; 'thought I'd better check in with my little *Golden Girl*, make sure you're doing okay. Can't be easy for you, what with that girl's body being found, all these rumours flying around, me being taken off by the police. God knows what's been going through your mind.' He leant back, one arm supporting the elbow of the other, his thumb resting on his jaw. 'You know what I've always appreciated about you, Willa? You always tell the truth. That's a good trait. A trait I appreciate. Makes you someone I can trust.' His voice soft, he added, 'You're a good girl, Willa.' I felt myself filling with a sort of violent headiness, like vertigo, or the plummeting sensation that comes before a faint.

'Tell me something,' he said, 'did you think that was Laika?'

'*What?*'

'You didn't somehow imagine that Daddy had chopped your

little sister into pieces and stashed her body inside one of my own warehouses?' His voice was mild, almost amused.

'Jesus, Dad, *no*. Of course not.'

'How about your mother?' He gave me a benign smile.

'She wouldn't ever' – *he doesn't have the wherewithal* – '*ever* think that.'

'You're sure?'

'One hundred per cent.'

My father pursed his lips. Then he nodded, a look of quiet satisfaction on his face. 'Okay,' he said, 'good to know.' I blinked. I felt as if thousands of spiders were crawling out of the back of my shirt. I forced myself to stand still. He crossed his arms, his eyes still holding mine. 'Your mother' – he paused, as if searching for the right words – ' has been known to entertain some pretty odd ideas at times. I would hate for you to be – *infected* by that sort of thinking. Anyway. We probably shouldn't bother her with this conversation, I think. Better we should keep it between ourselves, tell her we were chatting about school. We wouldn't want to worry her. You understand me, precious?' I nodded, standing very still. He looked at me for a long time. Finally he said, 'You will be all right, Willa.'

He looked down at his desk. I turned, reaching for the door-handle.

'And, just so we're clear,' he said, 'I did not.'

I stopped. I looked back, my breath caught in my throat. My father was leafing through some papers. He didn't look up. When he didn't say anything further, I turned again to go.

'You're a good one, Willa,' he said, almost half to himself. 'If all women were like you, my life would be a damn sight easier.'

A day later, the police liaison officer was back.

'Based on what we know so far, we suspect it's a migrant,'

he said. 'Some poor kid from the Philippines or Vietnam. Somehow ends up inside a long-term lock-up.'

'But how did she get there?' my mother said. 'That *poor* girl.'

'People smugglers, almost certainly. It's a growing business. Mr Martenwood, we're going to need to interview your drivers, in fact, your entire workforce. All of them.'

My father said, 'Jesus Christ, do you have *any idea* what that's going to do to my business? Some little whore steals a lift from me and I pay the price.'

Two days later, my father let my mother and me know that he intended to take a trip to South-East Asia. He planned to sell Martenwood Haulage and wanted to investigate possible business opportunities abroad. He couldn't say when he'd be back. The morning after, a driver came to take him to the airport. I stood on the stone steps beside my mother, her arm around my shoulders, my chest tight. I felt as if I'd been holding my breath for weeks.

The day was already warm, the sky a peacock blue. My mother watched the limousine as it disappeared down the drive, a rigid smile fading slowly from her face. She stood for a long time after the car finally disappeared from sight, a fingertip pressed tight against her lips. I thought she looked unspeakably sad. The metal gates they'd installed swung open, and then shut. My father was gone. My mother sighed, and the look of exhaustion seemed to slip off her like a cloak. She pulled herself upright. She put her arms around me and clasped her fingers tight together. She looked at my face. Her eyes roved over mine and I waited for her to say something momentous.

After a moment she said, 'Did you ever apply for that provisional licence? I really ought to teach you to drive.'

*

We practised every day. My mother put down the roof of her convertible and we went hiccupping up and down the gated road, first at a snail's pace, then gradually faster. My mother was a relaxed instructor. Wearing a spotted sundress, headscarf, dark glasses and red lipstick, she appeared completely oblivious to the bucking, jerking motion of the car and the fact that I didn't appear to be making any progress. Occasionally she'd shout *clutch* but mostly she kept up a stream of commentary about our neighbours, which she interspersed with lines from *Dynasty*, all of which were delivered in a slow American drawl. I'd say, 'I keep forgetting which one is the indicator and which one is the wipers,' to which she'd reply, 'Felicity Williams has most definitely had work done, *you overrated cowboy.*'

Later she based my lessons around trips out – to country houses, the coast or tea shops in little local towns. Despite my appalling skills behind the wheel, she always looked like she was enjoying herself. She smiled a lot that summer. She laughed. She sang along to her George Michael CDs. She wore short sleeves.

One warm afternoon we drove miles to see a crop circle that had appeared in a field. We stood looking at a vast yellow meadow beneath a sky filled with banks of lavender clouds. In front of us was a small section of flattened ground, but, from where we were standing, it mostly looked like a normal field of wheat.

'It's incredibly disappointing,' my mother said. 'I really wanted to see the whole thing. I suppose you'd only really be able to see the entire design from up there.' She pointed at the sky, then leant her elbow on the top of the fence rail and popped her chin in her hand. After a bit, she said, 'My entire life feels like that sometimes. Like I'm only ever seeing a tiny part, when what I really want is that bigger perspective.' She paused. 'Still, it's truly astonishing to think that aliens have landed right here, in this very spot.'

'Mum –'

'I'm joking, Willa.'

We stood in silence, both of us leaning on the wooden fence. After a while she said, 'I've been thinking about starting a business.'

'Really? Doing what?'

'That's where I get stuck. I have no idea. What could I actually do?'

'Something you know about. Something you enjoy.'

Her eyes drifted over the field. 'Maybe I could start my own gin company. Something super-special, aimed at the top end. Boutique, obviously, with a lovely label and a really upmarket bottle – heavy weight, you know the type I mean: the sort that could give someone a really good clonk.'

'You'd have to come up with a name.'

'Yes. Something upbeat and full of possibilities – Adventure Gin, or something.'

I said, 'Or Misadventure Gin.'

'Yes! *Misadventure* Gin. Wonderful, you clever thing. With the tag-line *Death by Misadventure*.' She let out a hoot of laughter.

'That makes it sound like you'd want your customers to drink themselves to death.'

'I was thinking more about the clonking-over-the-head bit.' She turned and gave me a buoyant smile. 'What?'

'I'm not sure gin is the best idea, Mum. You can't run a successful business if you drink all the stock.' My mother pursed her lips and looked away. 'Sorry,' I said, 'I probably shouldn't have said that. I didn't mean –'

'I know exactly what you meant, Willa. You think I'm a lush.'

I didn't know what to say, so I squeezed her arm by way of apology. 'Why d'you want to run a business?'

'So that, if it comes to it –' She stopped and the bright expression slipped off her face. After a long silence, she said, 'If your father wanted a divorce, we'd have to sell the house and then how would she ever find me? How would she know where I was?'

I put an arm around my mother's waist. 'I keep thinking I see her, Mum. I've lost track of the number of people I've run up to, shouting her name. It never is.'

My mother drew me into her. 'Oh, darling.'

A warm wind ran over the surface of the wheat, turning it into a golden sea.

I took a long time to find the right words. Eventually I said, 'The police thought that girl was Laika, didn't they? They thought Dad had killed Laika.'

'But he didn't, Willa. He *can't* have. It's just not possible. I was gone *minutes*. And, anyway, she *left the house*, Willa, we *know* that. Felicity Williams *saw* her talking to Cox.'

'But what if she went back?'

'Then something would have been out of place. But it wasn't: everything was exactly as it had been. Cox had gone, your father was in his study, and everything was quiet. If anything had happened, I'd have known. I would have noticed *something*. No. Whatever happened to Laika that morning, it didn't involve your dad.' My mother paused. Then she said, 'Sweet girl, do you honestly think I'd have stayed with your father if I'd thought he'd killed Laika? Or let him anywhere near you? Good grief, Willa, I would have been the first person to have told the police. Trust me, murder is not his modus operandi.' She gave a short, humourless laugh. 'Torture, maybe. Murder, no.'

I took a breath. I said, 'What about you, Mum? What about when Dad comes back? How will things be for you?'

My mother looked away and let a long moment pool between us. Keeping her eyes on the distant horizon, she said, 'He doesn't hit me any more.'

The world seemed to tilt a little on its axis. For the first time in my entire life, something unspoken had been spoken, a secret truth known by our family alone.

She turned to meet my eyes. 'It stopped after Laika disappeared. And I honestly don't think it will happen again, really, not ever. I think he feels under scrutiny, like everyone is watching him these days: our neighbours, the police, the press, the entire world. Even more so now.' We stood in silence, watching a group of crows passing between the field and the towering mountains of cloud. Then my mother said, 'I can't leave him, Willa. I couldn't when you were small – I was terrified that he would somehow get custody, that he'd somehow spirit the two of you away.' I saw her eyes fill with tears and she quickly brushed them away. 'Even if we'd been awarded joint custody, you two would have spent half your holidays with him, *on your own*, and every other weekend with him, *on your own*, and there was no way, *no way* . . .' Her voice cracked. She breathed deeply through her nose, pulling up her chin.

'Mum –'

'No, don't feel sorry for me. I'm not asking for that. Anyway, I had *you*, my beautiful, beautiful girls. I'd never, ever change that.' She shook her head. 'I know what they say about women like me: *Why don't they leave?* Ignorant pricks. *Of course* I couldn't leave. I had to protect the two of you. And now I *won't*. Do you understand that? I am *not* leaving her home, Willa, I am *not*. I just can't. It's where she knows, where she would come back to. And anyway, you don't need to worry about me any more. I'm safe. I've become untouchable.'

I put my arms around my mother's waist and she pulled me close. Then we turned and looked again at the hypnotic drifts of wheat, bending and lifting in waves like a living, breathing thing. A break appeared in the clouds and all at once the late-afternoon sun streamed through, drenching the world in brilliant light, turning the stalks of wheat into long, flaming tapers. In that moment everything looked beautiful. The entire landscape had changed.

On the way home a rabbit ran in front of the car and, in order to avoid it, I swerved and drove us into a ditch. My mother kept talking as the car slid sharply down the bank and came to an abrupt halt in a clump of hogweed.

'God,' I said, 'I didn't mean for that to happen. Sorry.'

My mother said, *'You know something, lady? You inspire revenge.'*

'Are you quoting *Dynasty*?'

'Every time you come into my life something terrible happens to me.'

'What are we going to do?'

My mother looked at me, her expression unperturbed. 'Did I tell you?' she said. 'Deedee really has got enormously fat.'

We left the car where it was and walked home along the lanes, and when we got in my mother called a recovery company and asked them to please go and drag it back out.

That summer, that is, the summer I left school, when my father first took off overseas, neither my mother nor I had any idea how long he'd be away, but, as it turned out, she and I had almost two entire months on our own. He finally returned at the end of August. I couldn't say what he'd been up to in that time. He never said.

The summer was at an end. Over the next few weeks the skies turned grey and autumn set in. A soundless atmosphere descended on the house, and I decided it was time to look for a job.

Throughout that summer, Robyn had called my parents' home repeatedly, leaving multiple messages on the answering machine. When I didn't call back, she wrote me long letters on lined yellow paper. She wrote again in September, before she went to uni. She'd missed out on her place to read medicine by two grades, she said, but she'd found a place to read radiography through clearing and so she'd be in London; perhaps we could meet up.

I often think about watching her walk out of our little study-bedroom that day, the back of her head, the way her two stubby little plaits stuck out at odd angles, the crooked line of her parting. The next time I saw her she didn't wear her hair like that any more. It was almost four years before I could face seeing her again, and by that time everything had changed.

11.

Supper with friends

Willa

Cat opens the door, the warmth of her smile instantly dispelling the wintry air of Forest Hill. She gives me a quick hug and her lips brush my cheek. 'Lovely to see you,' she says. Then she turns to Jamie. 'Hi,' she says, her voice falling through the keys of a minor scale, 'come on in.' Jamie and I step into the hallway and I hand over a large bunch of flowers.

I like Cat, of course I do. She's quick-witted, plain-speaking and terrifyingly smart, plus she exudes a sort of artless confidence that I'd love to have, the worldliness of the well travelled, I suspect. Cat's mother is Irish and her father is from Queens, New York, and she lived in both those places as a child. Her parents still live in the States. Her mother lectures in Urban Design at NYU and her father writes for the *New York Times*. Despite the physical distance, they're really close, and Cat and Robyn take the kids out to see them at least once a year. Cat herself is an architect. I've seen Cat discussing the future of sustainable housing and fire-safety measures and I've also seen her doing the Cha-Cha at house parties dressed in a gold jumpsuit. I can see why Robyn loves her, what the fascination is. And it's not like she and I don't get on. She's just . . . I don't know. She's very different from *me*.

'You look nice,' she says, giving a single glance to the green dress that has cost me almost a week's wages. Cat herself is wearing cropped velvet leggings.

I leave her with Jamie to sort out his coat while I whip on ahead to find Robyn. Before the others follow me in, I want to grab a quiet moment with her, without either Cat or Jamie around, just to tell her what I've been thinking since I saw her this morning. I don't get the chance. I've barely made it into the kitchen before Sophie, their eldest, hurtles in, throws her arms around my waist and snatches that time away. Much as I'd hoped for that small moment, I can't mind too much. I always love seeing Sophie. She's a true delight, and seems completely tickled by the little gifts I've brought her. She takes my hand and drags me straight back out of the kitchen and up the two flights of stairs to her little attic bedroom. Then she makes me lie with my head beside hers on her pillow and together we look at the glow stars that she tells me her uncle Michael has stuck on to her ceiling, a task, I note, he has completed not randomly but organized into proper constellations.

I turn my head and smile at my precious, brilliant goddaughter, a child still young enough to smell of talcum powder and soap.

'What?' she says.

'Nothing.'

I run a hand over her dark, curly hair and down across her cheek. She is the most wonderful child I know, beautiful in every way, as joyful and uncomplicated as Robyn herself. I shut my eyes. The pain is almost physical. There is nothing, *nothing* I long for more than this.

When Michael arrives, I watch the warmth of the sibling hug he shares with Robyn with no small pang. All that understanding, I think, all that shared history. All those strong, unspoken bonds. The tsunami of grief I once felt for Laika's absence is more like a quiet wave these days, something that resides deep inside me, lapping somewhere at the edges of my mind. It's been so long, but it's there. It's always, always there.

Michael hugs me too; I've known him for years. Then I turn to meet his girlfriend, Liv, biting my lip as some secret part of me steps forward. *Get a grip*, I tell myself, this is *Michael's girlfriend*. But the thing is, Liv is a very attractive woman. She barely needs the touch of eyeliner that outlines her eyes; she's just one of those women who is startlingly beautiful in a completely natural, unstudied way. She brushes a stray lock of hair away from her face and tips her head on one side, listening carefully to Michael as he speaks. According to Robyn, Michael said she reminds him of *me*. That's nice, I think, she's lovely. I'm flattered we've been compared.

I'm not the only one watching Liv. Robyn is too. In fact, with the exception of Cat, all of us are watching Liv, including, I note, my boyfriend. I watch Jamie rise from the table and pull himself up to his full height, then move towards her with the fixed gaze of a cat watching a bird. Greeting her, he liquifies into charm personified, his voice lowered to almost a purr, a slow smile edging across his face. He seats her opposite him, pours her a glass of wine and pulls her into conversation. I wait to feel the dark burr of jealousy but it doesn't come. I think, *You big tart*, but not with any particular rancour. I don't actually feel anything.

'Nate's running late,' Cat says. 'Sorry, everyone.'

'Oh, don't worry,' Liv says. 'It's not like he's vanished off the face of the earth.'

Everyone looks towards me. Individually, their movements are so small, so underplayed, that they could easily be missed. It's just that they do it en masse, and Liv looks around, aware, of *something*. Eyes move from her to me, and in that beat of silence I feel for her. I know what it's like, that feeling, to be the outsider, the one person left out.

'My little sister disappeared,' I tell her, 'twenty-two years ago. She was thirteen. Abducted, probably. Someone took her, we think.' My breath catches in my throat, and my words come out sounding strangely low and hoarse. 'They never found her body.'

Suddenly I feel as if I want to cry. It's hard, this story, even now, even after all these years, and I swallow as something awful moves through me, something deadly swimming up from the past. Because now I'm remembering the very last time I ever saw Laika, standing in front of me in the furred early hours with blood on her hands. That's what I always remember: her hands. I never remember her face. That's something nobody ever tells you, that the face of a person you once loved can fade like an unfixed photograph. The awful truth is this: I have no real idea what she'd look like now. When I try to imagine her as a grown woman, an adult in her mid thirties, I can't. The only mental images I have of Laika are as a blurry thirteen-year-old, fuzzy and featureless, as if even then she was already fading from my memory somehow, becoming unrecognizable, slipping away to the point where I could unknowingly walk past her any day of the week.

Jamie's finger drums the table.

'She could be anyone,' I say to Liv. 'She could be you.'

There is a moment of silence in which I think I could have explained myself better. After all, Laika could conceivably still be out there, somewhere, maybe, perhaps. I'd like to think she is. I should have told Liv that there was a time when I used to run up to people, total strangers, accosting anyone about the right age and height, girls with scruffy dark hair. *Tell her*, I think, and I'm about to elaborate when the doorbell chimes and Cat leaps to her feet. Nate and his girlfriend arrive in the kitchen, and then, as everyone leaps up to meet them, Jamie takes hold of my arm. 'Here,' he says, pulling me towards the back door, 'a word.'

He barricades me tightly into his arms and puts his mouth next to my ear. 'Willa, darling,' he says, 'are you completely off your fucking trolley? I mean, Christ almighty, what was *that*? You can't just walk up to random women and accuse them of being your *sister*. It makes you look like a lunatic.'

A lunatic? *Wow*.

'Screw you, Jamie,' I hiss. 'Don't even think about telling me how to behave.'

Jamie releases me from his grip and stalks back to the other end of the table, sits himself down and throws back a glass of red. I stay where I am, pretty much as far away from him as I can get. *A fucking lunatic?* I glance at Robyn. Then Liv. Then I shut my eyes, weighted by a certain truth, one I've spent the last few months ignoring: whatever I once felt about Jamie has gone. I don't want to be with him any more. In fact, perhaps I never really did. Perhaps Jamie never really wanted to be with me either. Perhaps the two of us just fell down some sort of rabbit hole together, both of us chasing a belated dream of having kids. And a child, a daughter, is something I have wanted so badly. Him too, I know that. He told me he wanted children just as soon as we met. If I'm honest, that was part of the appeal. *Was* the appeal. And we've tried. In fact, that description pretty much sums up the history of our entire sex life: we tried. We *tried* to connect somehow, through lukewarm touches, tense bodies and distant minds. We *tried* to conjure up desire. We *tried* for a baby. It's been the one thing that's kept us together, really, that trying. I probably should have ended things a while back, but the truth is time's not on my side. If I have to start all over again, trying to meet someone who wants kids as badly as me, then I won't have a child of my own, not ever. That would be the cost.

But that's not a good enough reason to stay with anyone, and definitely not Jamie. It wouldn't be fair on either of us. *Oh, God*, he and I need to talk. Not here, obviously, bang in the middle of a supper party, not tonight, but we do.

I am so far into the warren of my thoughts that I've barely followed the conversation going on at the table. I should be making more of an effort, I know. Everyone is tucking into the food. I'm seated opposite Cat's brother, Nate, a musician who's been busy entertaining the rest of the party with stories of his life in Paris. He's clearly besotted with his girlfriend, Claudette, his eyes dancing down the table to where she sits diagonally across from him at the other end, on the same side of the table as me. Cat said she didn't speak English, but clearly she does, and I catch an occasional oblique glimpse of her as she joins in with the conversation. Everything she says sounds wise and calm and softly spoken. That beautiful French accent.

Over desert, Liv tells us about her research into memory and now I really start to listen. We all do. It's riveting stuff – *everything* depends on it. To my amazement, she tells us how fallible our memories can be, how our minds rework things, how key things we remember from our childhoods may not even be true. Wow, I think, that's a strange thought. No, worse, it's a *horrifying* thought. I think back to all the things I remember happening as a child, things about which I've always felt so sure. Now I think, *But what if those memories are wrong?* What if there's another story, buried somehow, underneath the one I think I know?

Yet again I think back to that very last night: Laika, waking me in the middle of the night from deep sleep, bright lines of blood drawn along her palms. She thrusts a pair of scissors at me. *Do it*, she says, her thirteen-year-old face wavering like a mirage at sea.

But what if that's not *true*?

I have to break in. 'But how can we *know*?' I say. 'What factors are involved?'

'Good question,' Liv says, smiling at me.

I drag my chair to face down the table so that I can concentrate on her answer. Cat, Robyn and Nate lean in too, and Michael hangs on Liv's every word. Then Michael edges his chair back a little and finally – finally – I have a direct view of Claudette. She has cropped hair and glasses and, behind those, a face so familiar that the breath is knocked from my lungs.

My God, I think, *it's Laika*.

12.

London

Robyn

I first met Cat when I was twenty-two, and I was attracted to her straight off. The first time we talked, she told me she was gay. I instantly thought that was wonderful, her being so open about her sexuality. Plus, she was sexy, beautiful, with a long skinny body, little breasts and an amazing smile. I remember thinking how self-assured she appeared, how well she'd nailed that tricky veneer of outward confidence. Then, as I got to know her better, I realized it wasn't an act. Cat was, quite simply, comfortable in her own skin.

She was two years older than me, accomplished, hard-working and brilliant. I liked her fast intelligence and the way she spoke her mind. Also her voice, her accent, the elegant lines of her legs. She was straightforward and decent. She was also, as I gradually came to understand, incredibly perceptive. Cat saw everything.

At the time I was a few months into my first graduate job, working long hours and living in a shared house with friends I'd met at uni, whereas Cat rented a tiny flat, most of which was taken up by an enormous drawing table. Her place was barely big enough for one fully grown adult, let alone two, but it had a good feel: I liked the narrow stairs to the fourth floor, Cat's clean architectural drawings on the white-painted walls, her moss-green bedsheets, the faded colours of her vintage throw. Sure, the kitchen overlooked railway tracks and a dump, but it was still quite special compared with the shared house I was in: far less frantic and relatively quiet.

As the months passed I began spending more time there. Cat was easy company: talkative and astute, plus if I stayed over it meant we could make the most of our precious days off. If they fell on the same day, we'd get up early and head off to the gym or get out of the city altogether, but my shift work meant that didn't always work out. If my day off fell on a weekday, I'd go for a run after she left for work and then hang out at her flat for a bit before heading home. And, as much as I loved the buzz of the hospital and the constant horseplay of close friends at the house, I secretly enjoyed those occasional moments of borrowed solitude. They were a gift.

It was a Friday in April, and we'd woken up to a clear bright day. Cat was heading off for an early-morning meeting on site, and after a run of nights I had the day off. I was thinking I might even head back to bed for a bit, take a mug of tea with me, read a chapter of my book. I'm sure that's what I was thinking. Almost certain anyway. Meanwhile I hung by the bedroom door, watching Cat pull on her boots.

She looked up. 'What's with the goofy smile?'

'What goofy smile?'

'Whenever you're nervous, you kinda pull this really goofy expression.'

'Do I?' I made my best attempt at looking normal.

'So what are you up to today?' Cat bent over to check the contents of the messenger bag she used for work.

'Seeing an old friend. She's invited me out for coffee.'

'Who's that, then?'

'Just someone I used to know at school.'

'Does she have a name?'

'Willa.'

Cat straightened up. 'Is this the Willa whose sister went missing?'

'Uh-huh.'

'Who's basically responsible for your not getting into medical school.'

'Did I put it like that?'

'You've certainly told me about that giant pang you get whenever groups of medical students come through.'

'Do I?'

'There's that smile again.'

'Hell,' I said. 'Who'd want to be a doctor anyway? D'you have any idea what sort of hours they do?'

'I've lost count of the times you end up doing a double shift.'

'Only because of staff shortages. The timings can be tricky. I mean, I'm not going to abandon a patient mid treatment, am I? Anyway,' I say, grinning to lighten the mood, 'I've no idea what I'd do with a doctor's salary. All that dosh.'

'You could move out of that shared house for a start.'

'Whaddya mean? I *love* that house. The lingering smell of takeaways. All that decorative mould on the ceilings. Random strangers barging into my room late at night. People's pants on the stairs.'

'We could get a place *together*.'

Her words hung in the air for a moment. Sure, I loved Cat, but we'd never really spoken about the future. I don't know why. It was just the sort of conversation I'd been keen to avoid. Now I edged my way round the drawing table and put my arms round her neck.

'Should I be worried?'

'Cat,' I said, 'are you jealous?'

'*Hell*, yes. I didn't know you two still saw each other.'

'We don't. I haven't seen her since we split up. That was *four years ago*, Cat. And, honestly, we're only meeting for coffee.'

'So I'm going to work and you're meeting up with some woman who comprehensively stomped all over your heart.' She turned away. 'You might have told me.'

She was right. I should have told her.

'I should have told you.'

Cat tipped her chin back. 'Are you going to tell her about me?' In reply I pulled a goofy smile, and, when she continued to study me through narrowed eyes, I said, 'Of course.'

We had arranged to meet in a tiny café near Regent's Park. Willa's idea. I arrived first. I sat at a table and watched the window. People passed by on the street. Perhaps we wouldn't even recognize each other. The minutes ticked by. I checked my watch. She was late. Perhaps she's not coming, I thought, perhaps she's changed her mind. She'd done that before. And perhaps, I thought, meeting her at all was a really bad idea. Because no matter how much I'd downplayed it to Cat, the very idea of seeing Willa again made my entire body feel prickly and bright. I should just go.

But then she was there, standing in the doorway, smiling at a woman with a pushchair, four years older and at once both exactly the same and completely different. Her eyes moved over the other customers, and for a moment I felt invisible. Then she stopped, our eyes met, and I stood too fast, knocking my chair off balance. Grabbing it mid fall, I set it back up and stepped round the side of the scrubbed pine table. Willa came forward, holding out her arms. I kissed her cheek, she mine, and we hugged, first with the distance of years, then, after a beat, properly, with warmth and feeling. I could smell the familiar wild orange scent of her, the soft heat of her skin, and for a moment I was transported back to our tiny study-bedroom, back to a time of infinite possibilities. I didn't want to let her go. Finally we pulled away from each other and sat down. She took a sip of the coffee I'd bought her and said thank you, and how delicious it was. I knew it must already be cold. Everything about her was lovely.

There was a pause. I had no idea where we could even begin.

She smiled, looking at me with those dove-grey eyes. 'Where did you say you're living now?'

Cat's tiny Peckham flat jumped into my mind. *Obviously I'll tell her about Cat*, I thought. A little later. It was too early in the conversation for that.

'I'm still in a shared house with a bunch of other people I met at uni. Oh, and some rats. It's in Croydon. What about you?'

'With Mum. Dad too when he's at home. I'm trying to save, but, you know, impossible dreams and all that. How anybody ever manages to buy a place of their own beats me. Especially on what I'm earning.' She smiled broadly, her voice bright and nonchalant. 'Turns out GCSEs count for absolutely zip as far as getting a decent job is concerned.' Too bright, too unbothered. She was forgetting how well I knew her. 'I temp, mainly. Right now I'm working as an assistant to a retired opera singer. She's in her eighties and she's fabulous, a real diva. I organize her schedule and stuff.'

'That sounds fun.'

'It is really. I shouldn't complain. She's got a bunch of *terribly* theatrical friends. Honestly, you should see them gossiping about their heydays. They're all on the sherry by nine.'

Willa gathered her hair and pulled it over one shoulder. I caught a glimpse of the pale skin of her neck. Her clavicles.

'I'm sure you're perfect in that role. My mother describes you as *that lovely Willa*. She always said she'd never met *anyone* with better manners. *Such a lovely girl, so polite.*' I could hear myself gabbling. I stopped. My face felt fixed in an odd smile. I cleared my throat. 'They send their love by the way.'

'It was a special time.'

My breath seemed to catch in my throat – *hhh* – and I felt a sudden urge to tell her how I still kept that beautiful summer hidden inside me, a secret place I went to sometimes, full of sun-warmed memories that passed through my mind like low-flying swifts. A lifetime ago.

'How are you enjoying your job – it's radiotherapy, right?'

'It's good. Busy. Challenging at times. But rewarding, really rewarding.'

Willa's voice dropped. 'I feel absolutely responsible that you didn't make it into medical school.'

'God, Willa, don't be ridiculous. I just didn't get the grades.'

'That was my fault.'

'It absolutely was not. Honestly, I never even think about it. I love my job.'

She didn't take her eyes away from mine, and I realized that she had prepared a speech, something she needed to get off her chest. I let her speak.

'I shouldn't have run away like that. I should have told you what was going on. I'm honestly so sorry.'

I paused, feeling as if I were stepping around some hole half hidden in the ground. 'I felt truly terrible when I heard about your dad. It must have been an awful time for all of you. How are they doing?'

It took her a moment to answer.

'You never met my parents, did you?' Her eyes moved somewhere else, somewhere distant and pensive. She chewed a moment on her lip. 'Dad's away a lot now. He goes away for weeks, sometimes months at a time. We never know when he's going to reappear. Mum's –' She glanced at the other customers at tables dotted around the café. 'Can we get out of here?' She drained the last of the cold flat white. 'I could do with some fresh air. Let's walk.'

It was a late-spring day, almost summer, the lawns of the park a deep emerald green, the cobalt sky and cords of willows mirrored deep within the lake. We walked in the direction of the Japanese Garden, side by side, not touching.

I thought, *I'll tell her about Cat. In a bit.*

'You heard about Mum's restraining order, then?' she asked. I hadn't expected her to mention that. 'It's okay, Robyn. It was in the papers. There's nothing the tabloids like more than reporting the antics of some bat-shit crazy woman, and, believe me, that's something I'm qualified to know. She's not allowed to enter the street where Cox lives *at all*, nor any of the surrounding streets. Nor is she allowed within thirty metres of his van, or to call his home, that of any of his relatives, or go to the homes of anyone he does work for. Here, let's sit.'

We sat together on a bench overlooking a small wooden bridge hung with trails of lilac wisteria. Her hair moved lightly in the breeze. She was so beautiful, and so totally oblivious to the fact. The man on the bench opposite couldn't keep his eyes off her.

'Is it possible?'

'The police don't think so. They reckon it could have been a hit-and-run and the driver took the body as a cover-up. Either that or someone else took her. But as far as they're concerned it's not Cox. A whole bunch of people have sworn he was with them. The problem is, Mum just won't accept that. If she keeps on harassing him they could put her inside.'

'Your poor mum.'

'It's driven her mad. I don't mean mad, that's unfair. I mean she carries this quiet suffering with her all the time. She hides it, though.' Willa briefly chewed on her lip, staring vacantly, somewhere far off. Then, slowly, she added, 'She's always been good at hiding things, Mum.' She turned to look at me. 'I'd love for you to meet her. You'd like her, really, she's lovely. She's kind, thoughtful, decent. She's funny too, even now, after everything. She loves cooking and gardening and the *X-Files* and Jilly Cooper, and, okay, get this – she's a *massive* George Michael fan. What I mean is, she's *normal*. But after Laika went missing, the press made her look completely deranged. Which is hardly surprising, given the sorts of headlines the tabloids were printing: PSYCHIC SAYS JUNGLE-LOVING LAIKA KILLED BY JAGUAR IN PARAGUAY. Remember that one? It's *cruel*, that's what it is. They just made things up.'

'Your poor, poor mum.'

'Even now they do it, the tabloids, I mean. Laika was on the cover of the *Mail* last week. It's like a scab they keep picking, a useful fallback for a slow news day. And it's not like it's proper investigative journalism or they're doing anything that's actually going to find her; it's just repackaging her story again and again in different ways, feeding the public's appetite for sensation. None of it helps.'

I paused. 'And what about you? How are *you* doing?'

'Me?' She opened her mouth, then shut it again. I waited. Eventually, she dropped her voice. 'I still think I see her sometimes. I'm always doing double-takes, but it's never, ever her. And then I dream about her too – dreams where I see her and I *know* it's her but I never can get to her.' She shakes her head. 'And it's awful because it's like *I'm* the one who's the problem, not her, because *I'm* the one who can't move or speak.' She put a hand on my arm. 'But also that means she's *alive*, Rob, I *know* it. She's *somewhere*. It's just that I can't reach her.'

A group of pigeons were startled, and rose chaotically into the deep blue of the sky as the man sitting across from us approached our bench, his eyes still fixed on my friend. We both looked up, and Willa promptly set her own face into a friendly, expectant look. Looking directly at her, he said, 'Do you want to watch me wank off?'

'Thank you,' Willa said, 'but I honestly can't think of anything worse.'

'You okay?' I said as we walked towards the tube, so close our shoulders brushed.

'I'm fine,' Willa said. 'Poor man. He's obviously not well. You never know what's going on in another person's life, do you? We should probably tell someone, though. There's kids about, and anyway, he needs help.' We walked a few more paces. 'Though on the subject of odd sexual practices, I had a date last night with a dentist, Greg. He seemed nice enough and we'd been out a few times, so, long story short, I ended up going home with him. Well, everything was going okay, I thought, but then he burst into tears the moment he came. Wept for a good ten minutes. Completely inconsolable.' She stopped walking and turned to face me, her expression somewhere between baffled and amused. 'I mean, is that *normal*?'

I blinked. 'Wow,' I said, 'I honestly wouldn't know.' I grinned. 'Though you are *very* lovely. It was probably that.'

'Though, now I think about it, he also thought the Booker Prize was something to do with gambling. I don't think I'll be seeing him again.'

At the entrance to Great Portland Street tube, Willa hugged me close.

'I feel bad,' she said, 'like we've only spoken about me. Can we do this again? I really, *really* want to see more of you.'

'Me too,' I said.

'And will you do something for me?'

'Of course.'

'I want you to meet my mum. I want you to see what she's really like, that she's not the total fruitcake the media made out. *Promise me*, Rob. It would mean so much.'

'Sure –'

'Come and stay for the weekend, then. We'll make a date.'

She reached into her bag for her travel pass. She kissed me on the cheek and I felt my face pulling into a strange smile. Then she was gone, and I hadn't told her about Cat.

But she'd told me about Greg. As I walked away from the Underground, I folded my arms around my chest. Over my ribs. Above my battered, broken heart.

We next met in a bar near St Paul's. I came straight from work and was a bit late, aware the smell of the ward was probably still clinging to my skin. I spotted Willa at the bar, talking to a woman with long dark hair, and she looked so involved I almost didn't want to pull her away. I stood by the entrance, looking at them there. Then I reminded myself not to be stupid. Willa wasn't gay. She'd told me that herself. She didn't like girls. And I had news too, I knew that. A promise to keep: something I had to be honest about. Something she had to know.

'I've met someone,' I said, the moment we sat down, 'actually we're moving in together. We're going to see some possible flats this weekend.' I grinned wildly in her direction. Willa grinned back.

'That's wonderful,' she said. 'You look unbelievably happy. Your eyes –'

'She's lovely,' I said. 'I can't wait for you to meet her.'

'Oh,' she said.

'What?'

She paused. 'I hadn't realized you meant a girl.'

I laughed and pushed her arm. *Come on*. I mean, honestly. It was always going to be a girl. 'As soon as we've found a place, you'll have to come over.'

The flat we found was in a tower block near Lewisham: reasonable transport links into Central London, big enough for the two of us, cheap enough to allow us to save. I told my mother the area was *lively*. I told my father it was *liberal*. I told my brother it was good enough for the time being.

And I kept my word, inviting Willa to come and meet Cat almost just as soon as we'd moved in. The August air was still warm at seven, and we'd thrown open all our windows. Laughter, shouting and snatches of music freewheeled into the flat from the street below, together with the heady scent of street food, mixed in with bus fumes and weed. In our kitchen, an area of the living room partitioned off by a narrow worktop that doubled as our dining table, Cat was stirring a big pot of callaloo while I pretended to tidy the living space.

'Robyn?' Cat said, looking up. 'You've been plumping those bloody cushions for about five minutes. Are you –'

'Door,' I said, 'hang on.'

And then there was Willa, standing on our little welcome mat, holding a small plant in both hands and blinking rapidly.

'I'm here,' she said, her voice containing a small note of panic; then, in a whisper as the words *Just fuck off* bounced up the concrete stairwell from the floor below, she added, 'I don't think they mean *me*.'

I ushered her inside, and there was a moment when time seemed almost to stop. Cat walked forward. Here was Cat, this brilliant, amazing woman whom I loved, I really did. And here was Willa, whose presence filled me with such complicated feelings I didn't know how to turn them into words. And here they both were, in the same room, at the same time. As planned.

For some baffling reason I'd engineered this, and now it was happening.

'Willa,' I said, 'this is Cat. Cat is –' I stopped. They both looked at me. 'Making us her grandmother's totally amazing saltfish patties for supper. And, Cat, this is Willa, who –' I stopped again, thinking I should really have thought through the introductions prior to Willa's actually arriving at our place. Cat narrowed her eyes.

'Robyn, are you intentionally trying to make this as weird as possible?' To Willa she said, 'It's lovely to meet you.'

Willa laughed. She held the plant out to Cat.

'It's a succulent,' she said, 'apparently they're almost impossible to kill.'

We showed her around the flat, our bedroom, the little bathroom and the very small second bedroom which now housed Cat's drawing table, explaining how the lime-green and egg-yellow walls would be painted over just as soon as we found the time. Then we ate, and after, as the air finally began to cool, the three of us collapsed together on the brown corduroy sofa Cat and I had rescued from a skip.

I knew Cat felt odd about meeting Willa. She hadn't come straight out and said anything directly, but I knew. Nonetheless, she did *everything* to make her feel welcome, even getting her laptop to show Willa the plans she was drawing up for her very first commission.

'It's going to be the best toilet block ever,' I said.

'It is,' Cat said, grinning. 'It really is.'

'While you've got that open,' Willa said, 'would you mind if I showed Robyn my new website?'

'Sure,' Cat said, 'go ahead.'

Willa took the computer and balanced it half on her knees, and half on mine. Obviously she hadn't purposely meant to exclude Cat, but still, I could see how it might have looked like that. Cat glanced at me then, and after a moment she hauled herself up off the sofa and walked stiffly towards the kitchen. Meanwhile Willa had opened a site called findlaika.com.

'Oh, wow,' I said.

At the top of the first page there were two photographs. One was familiar to me: it was the one the press still used sometimes, showing a startled-looking teenage girl half hidden behind a thick fringe. The other was a slightly fuzzy image of two much younger girls, the taller of whom, smiling and dressed in a yellow frock with a Peter Pan collar, was instantly recognizable as Willa. She had her arm around the shoulders of a younger dark-haired girl who was squinting into the sun, one arm held across her forehead and half her face in shadow.

'It's a bit amateur, I know, but it's the best I could manage. It's for Laika more than anything. I just hope, you know, if she ever Googled her name . . . or somebody might recognize her – she could have amnesia, right? It's got a mailbox too, so people can contact me directly. Actually, could I make you an admin? That way we can talk about anything that comes in. And also look at this.'

She scrolled down until a further image filled the screen, an e-fit impression of a serious-looking young woman with large brown eyes and closely cropped hair.

'It's an age-progression image of what she might look like now, at twenty. What d'you think?'

'I thought she had long hair.'

I began reading the post below the e-fit. Dated just a few days before, it was addressed directly to Laika herself.

'My beloved Laika,' it read.

> Not a day goes by when I don't think of you. This week I came across a new word: syzygy. Even before I looked it up I knew it was going to mean something amazing: I mean, you can tell

that just by looking at the word. Syzygy. How fabulous is that? So you don't need to go to the trouble of finding a dictionary, I'll tell you right now what it means: it's an alignment of planets. And, ever since I read that, I keep thinking that someday the planets will align and you will appear. And then we'll spend our entire time laughing and talking and everything will be wonderful. What I really mean is, everything will be normal, and that's honestly all I want. For things to be normal. I know you are out there, somewhere. I hope you know how much I miss you and how much I wish you were here. And I hope that, wherever you are, you are surrounded by animals and the sound of the ocean.

My beloved sister, I miss you so much.

All my love,
Willa xxx

Willa looked at me with eyes full of such feeling that for a moment I felt speechless and lost. I took her hand and held it, touch closing the years between us. I was filled with an almost unbearable sadness for her. How hard it must be, I thought, to keep believing, with so very little to go on, when the whole world thinks she's dead. We sat like that for a while, both of us lost in thought, until I felt that strange sensation of being watched. When I looked up, Cat was staring at the two of us from across the room, her face unsmiling and tense. I gave Cat a brief awkward smile, then squeezed Willa's hand, patted it and let it go.

13.
Vapour trails

Robyn

That September, Cat and I each took a week's holiday so we could freshen up the flat. We started on the Friday night and were shoving the furniture about when somebody banged on our door. Cat opened it, and Willa was there, her face witchy-wild. She came straight over to me.

'I've got a hit on findlaika. Just now.'

I sat down beside her as she pulled a laptop out of her bag. The mailbox on her website was already open. I scanned the message quickly, and then again, more slowly.

'Shit.'

It read:

> Hello, my name's Katie Taylor and I'm writing about your sister. I'm in Thailand right now and I'm sure I've seen her. She's on Phuket, the island? I'm attaching a pic. Sorry it's not great but I was trying not to make it too obvious that I was taking it. She's with another girl on Patong beach, at the top end near the Sheraton? Only I think you'll have to act quick because the police here don't like stuff like that. What do you want me to do? Do you want me to say anything? Attaching my contact details. Message me back. Love and hugs, Katie xoxo

Below the message was a photo of two young women.

'How would she get to Thailand?' Cat said.

I realized my eyes were darting around the screen, trying to absorb all the information as fast as possible, and I forced myself to slow down and take a proper, considered look at the two girls in the image. It was night, and they were sitting on a neon-lit pavement, cross-legged on mats. Both were wearing thin, strappy dresses that hung loosely about them, revealing grungy-looking bra straps and thin limbs that were either tanned or dirty, or perhaps both. They wore leather sandals and each had multiple string bracelets tied around her wrist. On the left of the picture one girl, with bright chestnut hair and brown eyes, sat upright and stared directly at the camera, an eager, open look on her face. The other was looking slightly down and away, as if lost in thought, her face shadowed by the night and a mass of long, messy, dark hair. Between the two of them was a bowl and the edge of a ragged cardboard sign with the words: PLEASE HELP.

'She's *begging*,' Willa said. 'It's just awful.'

'Which one is Laika?' I said.

'How would she get to Thailand?' Cat asked again.

'This one.' Willa tapped her finger on the dark-haired girl and we both moved our heads closer to the screen.

'That's her?'

'It's definitely possible. Obviously she would have changed a lot. The angle's a bit –'

'She'd need a *passport* to get to Thailand,' Cat said, 'and a visa.'

'Are you sure?'

'I don't know.' Willa turned her eyes to me, her voice high and silvery. 'I don't know. I can't tell. But those could definitely be her cheekbones. And that could definitely be the line of her jaw. I really, honestly think it is. It is. It's *her*.'

'Tell the police,' Cat said, 'or call the British Embassy. They can contact the embassy in Bangkok.'

'I tried the embassy, but they told me they're short staffed. There's some giant festival going on or something, a holiday, I don't know. This is the first proper lead *ever.*'

'Willa,' Cat said, 'hang on, slow down a bit. You don't know for certain if that's her; it's not a clear photo. Why don't you ask this Katie person to send another picture? A close-up. What if she's wrong?'

'What d'you mean? There's an actual *photograph.*'

'A debatable –'

Willa turned to me. 'Tell me what *you* would do.'

'Well –'

'What would you do if Michael needed your help?'

'*Michael?* I'd help him, obviously.'

Willa held my eyes for a long moment. 'Yes, you would, wouldn't you?' She paused. Slowly, she said, 'You would. Right. Okay, then.' She stood up. 'So that's what I'll do. I'll fly to Phuket.'

'Willa,' Cat said, speaking slowly, 'wait. You're not really about to jump on a plane, are you?'

Willa looked her straight in the eyes. 'Why?' she asked. 'Wouldn't you?'

We all stood looking at each other for a beat.

'With your mum?' I said.

'No. I can't ask her. She –'

'You can't do this alone,' I said. 'I'll come with you.' Cat's eyes widened.

Willa looked once at Cat, then back at me. 'Can you leave tomorrow? Or Sunday? If there's an available flight.'

Thoughts flew round my head – tickets, visas, cash. Jabs? 'How long can you spare?'

I looked at Cat, then back at Willa.

'A week.'

Cat turned on me the moment she was gone.

'What the *hell* just happened?'

'I couldn't just let her fly to Thailand *on her own*.'

'I get *that*. And I also get that Willa *wants* that girl to be her sister. But it was impossible to tell *anything* from that photo. You're really going to fly halfway round the world on account of one inconclusive photo and the word of some girl you don't know from Adam? How does this *complete stranger* have *any idea* what Laika would look like now? What if it's a giant hoax? Also – think about this, Robyn – what if by some miracle it *is* her? How the hell does someone who's been *abducted* end up *begging* in Thailand? And, more importantly, why the hell would Willa even believe that? And if by some remote possibility that really is Laika, and she knows who she is, then you do get that she is *choosing* to be out there, right? She's *choosing* not to come home. And if that's the case, what's going to happen when you two turn up out of the blue? Have you thought about that? Like I said, the best way forward would be to call the police.'

'But Cat –'

I turned, running a hand through my hair, my loyalties torn between Willa and Cat. Willa was going. And I couldn't let her go on her own, there was just *no way*. Or could I? *Should* I? Everything Cat had said made good sense, and, hell, of course I knew there were a thousand reasons why Cat wouldn't want me to go. If I went, I would be letting Cat down, badly. But, if I didn't, if I changed my mind now, if I told Willa she was on her own, where would *that* leave things? I'd probably never see her again. How was I meant to choose? My eyes fell on the pile of painting equipment stacked neatly against the wall: our own week's plans flung out of orbit. At least we could leave the painting for another time.

'Can we –'

She cut me off. 'You're clearly going,' she snapped. 'We can talk about us when you get back.'

A week later I let myself back into a flat that smelt new and different, bright and alien with the sharp tang of fresh paint. I found Cat in the tiny spare bedroom, working at her drawing table.

'Hi.'

'Hi.' Cat looked up and held my eyes. I hung by the door, feeling grubby. Everything felt wrong. Eventually Cat said, 'So it wasn't her, then.'

'No. She did look like her, though.'

'How would you know?' Her voice was stony.

Jet lag fogged my brain. I grabbed for something, anything to say.

'And she wasn't really begging. Well, she was, but not because she was in any genuine need. They call them begpackers, apparently. They're just cheapskate tourists who want total strangers to fund their trips. Turned out the rest of that sign had a smiley face and MAKE OUR DREAMS COME TRUE.'

'Right.' An uncomfortable silence filled the small room. For a long time she looked at me. Finally Cat said, 'I've had a lot of time to think this week.'

'Don't say it.' My voice came out in a rush.

'Say *what*?'

I was going to lose her. 'Oh, Jesus, Cat, I'm so, so sorry.'

'Are you? Because I don't want to spend my life with someone who's completely wrapped up in somebody else.'

I felt like I was falling. 'Nothing happened.'

'*Pah*,' she said. 'That you feel the need even to mention that is pretty telling. Anyway, that's not the main point. If you're not fully present in this relationship, I need to know. Now.'

'I couldn't just let her go *on her own*.'

'I *get* who you are, Robyn. I know you'd drop everything to help out a stranger, let alone a close friend. But –' She paused. 'It's pretty obvious that Willa *is*, or has been, more to you than that. I need to know where I stand. And *you* need to decide who I am to you or that's it. I'm not playing second fiddle.'

Our two worlds hung, suspended like threads. I loved Cat, wholeheartedly, and, in that moment of nearly losing her, I knew it without a fragment of doubt. Cat, who worked hard and played hard and lived her entire life with honesty and conviction. Cat, who could always find the right words when it mattered, who could dance like a disco queen and laugh like a drain. Cat, who was candid and honest, and who desired me – desired *us* – in ways that were open and wholehearted and real. And I loved her, everything about her: everything she stood for, everything she was. She was the person I wanted to be with, and not just now. She was the person I wanted to be with for my whole entire life.

I never told Willa how close I'd come to losing Cat that time, but something changed in me after that. Some cardinal thing that had stayed with me for so long – stalked me, *haunted* me – quietly slipped away. I opened my hand, and let it go. From that point on, everything would be about Cat. So when Willa continued to invite me down to Sussex to stay, I told Cat I wouldn't go at all unless she came too. Admittedly, it took a bit of persuasion, but finally she agreed.

So we both went. Willa and Bianka, her mother, were waiting for us at the train station at Lewes, standing together by a silver convertible, both of them dressed in tank tops and shorts.

Her father was away again, somewhere or other, Willa had said, sounding offhand; it would just be us four.

The car roof was down, and on the way to the house I sat in the back with Cat, wearing mirrored shades and feeling for all the world like some kind of minor rock star as we whipped along the lanes, laughing like loons and all of us singing along to 'Freedom' as it blasted from the CD player.

'Mum's a George Michael super-fan,' Willa shouted above the music. 'When we were little she used to sing us Wham! songs in the bath, using the shower attachment as a microphone. She *literally* cried when they split up.' Bianka laughed. It was amazing. She looked *exactly* like Willa, just older: she had the same slender frame, the same smile, the same grey eyes and almost-red hair.

In time we turned into a private estate, waiting first for a metal barrier to rise and then driving slowly past huge houses, until eventually we pulled up at a pair of high metal gates. Bianka pressed a button on some gadget and they swung open. We'd arrived.

That house truly shouldn't have come as such a huge surprise. Like everyone, I'd seen news footage of the place, the shadow of a helicopter circling a large white mansion and garden, its flickering blades moving over a glistening sapphire pool. I'd *known* it was going to be big. But the inside was something else. We followed Bianka and Willa through a heavy set of dark oak doors, arriving in a huge entrance hall that felt more like a museum than a home, where beautiful things were arranged on polished tables in such perfect order that I half expected to see small cards giving the date and provenance of each object and little DON'T TOUCH signs beside each thing. The difference in temperature from the warm day outside was remarkable too. Inside it felt – *chilly.* And not just physically cold either. Glacial.

'Wow,' I said, my voice sounding too loud as it bounced off glass, porcelain and marble floor tiles. I lowered my voice. 'This is' – I cast about for a word – ' incredible.' Lowering my voice further, I said, *'Amazing.'* I rubbed my arm, aware that my skin was prickling into goosebumps.

'Come through to the garden,' Willa said, her voice as quiet as mine.

We followed Bianka and Willa through that hall in a strange sort of hush. Bringing up the rear, I hefted my bag further up my shoulder, for fear it might brush against some priceless heirloom. I had the strangest sensation of being watched, and, in some respects, we were. A quick glance towards the ceiling revealed the fixed gaze of security cameras in almost every corner, and on almost every surface there were framed photographs of the man I knew must be Willa's father, in which he was mainly posing with various well-known faces: politicians, actors, celebrity chefs. After Laika disappeared, I remember seeing Willa's dad on the TV during press briefings, looking awful, turbulent and grim. Now I could see what he must usually look like: a solid combination of conviviality and steel, something like a statesman, perhaps. Formal, certainly. They certainly had formal taste.

Through one doorway was a drawing room with a massive stone fireplace, above which a giant photograph showed Willa and Laika standing stiffly beside their parents, positions they'd clearly had to hold for some time: Laika and her dad weren't even smiling. Other walls were hung with florid oils of stags and pheasants, all bearing the wild-eyed expressions of creatures who just knew they were about to be shot. From the hall we went into a vast kitchen with carved Baroque-style cupboards and trippy marble work surfaces, and finally into a conservatory tall enough to house real palms. Cat turned to me and mouthed *Fuck*. The entire place looked as if it had come straight out of the pages of some glossy magazine.

Bianka unlocked a set of French doors and we stepped out on to a wide stone terrace, overlooking a huge garden which I guessed must end at the distant line of rhododendron bushes that grew as thick and tall as trees. It was only then that everyone started talking in normal voices again.

Once Cat and I had got over our astonishment, the four of us had a lovely afternoon. Bianka made us a salad, and, as we ate on the terrace, I began to realize she was exactly the person Willa had described: funny and generous and genuinely interested in the two of us. I liked her a lot. The time passed easily, so we must have already been there for a couple of hours when the gates to the road silently pivoted open and a large, black limousine started crawling up the curve of the drive.

Willa said, 'Oh,' and Bianka, without saying anything at all, jumped up and rushed into the house.

'Shit,' Willa said, 'this is what he does.'

'Who does what?' Cat said.

Willa, blinking rapidly, said, 'Dad. He never gives us any warning. We never know when he's coming home. Sorry. Can you –' She stopped. 'Look, stay here a minute, will you? I just need to help Mum a sec –' She grabbed our plates and dashed after her mother, leaving us alone on the terrace.

'That was odd,' Cat said.

I stood up and brushed myself down, waiting to say hello. I've *always* loved meeting people's parents, just as I've always loved for people to meet mine. Cat stood too, and we turned our heads towards the open doors of the conservatory. *Hang on, what?* I did a double-take, then glanced at Cat. Inside, Willa appeared to be splaying a group of magazines into a perfect half-moon. Cat threw me a questioning look. Was it some kind of joke? If *my* dad had just arrived home, I'd be running out to meet him. As for tidying up – *splaying magazines* – that would be the *last* thing on my mind. Why would she even *think* about that? It occurred to me then that I knew very little about Willa's father. She'd told me lots of things about her mother, and Laika, of course, but she'd hardly ever said a word about her dad. Something felt odd.

Even more bizarrely, when Bianka and Willa reappeared on the terrace just a few minutes later, accompanied now by a large man with a head of thick silvered hair, both had changed into floral tea dresses, long enough to cover their knees.

'I hear we have company.'

I held out my hand, grinning. 'I'm Robyn,' I said. 'This is Cat.'

'Bryce.' He smiled at us warmly, leaning forward to shake our hands. 'Great to have you with us,' he said. 'I do hope you'll be comfortable. You must let my wife and daughter know if there is anything you need. Anything at all.'

'Of course,' Bianka said. 'Now, then, girls, as I was saying, I'm afraid the old pool was drained years ago so we can't offer you a swim. But what we can do, is go for a walk.'

'That's right,' Willa said, looking at her dad. 'We absolutely promised we'd take them to see the white cliffs.'

They had?

'Look at that,' Bianka said, her voice as shiny as the delicate gold watch on her wrist. 'The time must have run away with us. We had better get going.'

Moments later we were back in the car and driving towards the coast. Willa and her mother sat glassy-eyed and silent in the front seats of the convertible. There was no music. I tried throwing out one conversational opener after another, but my words just got swept away by the wind. Eventually I gave up. Bianka parked the car and the four of us walked along the top of an airy cliff. The distant Channel of filmy sea rumbled and hissed hundreds of metres below us.

'Wow,' I said, 'look at the *views*.'

Bianka looked around and seemed slowly to come back into herself, as if she'd just wandered out of a wood. 'It's the highest chalk sea cliff in the UK,' she said. 'One hundred and sixty-two metres.'

'Lovely, isn't it?' Willa said. 'This is my go-to spot whenever I need to think.'

'I don't know,' Cat said. 'Personally I find it completely terrifying. Why aren't there any fences? Bloody hell – look at those idiots taking photos right next to the edge. One misstep and they'd be over.'

'How about I run and get us all some ice creams?' I said. We'd arrived at a bench. 'I spotted a van in the car park.'

'Let me get them,' Bianka said.

'No, no,' I said, 'our treat. This is on us.'

'Let me help,' Cat said quickly. 'You two stay here and enjoy the view.'

It was only when we were halfway across the grass that Cat, keeping her voice low and her head straight ahead, said, 'What's with the frocks?'

I pulled a *Don't know* expression, my mind scrabbling. There was something else different too, something I hadn't been able to put my finger on, and only now did it dawn on me exactly what it was.

'Willa's not wearing her dolphin,' I said. 'She *never* takes it off.'

Ten minutes later, making our way back with tall waffle cones stuffed with ice cream, we realized we could hear shouting, but it took us a long moment to connect the commotion to our friends.

Cat said, 'What the fuck?'

From halfway across a wide expanse of grass, Bianka – *Bianka* – appeared to be *kicking* a man with a dog, and it was *her* voice whipping towards us across the grass, *her* voice shouting *You fucking fucking bastard*.

We started running just as Bianka hit the man square in the face. He staggered backwards, then fell, hitting the ground with a thud. Instantly she straddled him, pinning him to the ground, all the time yelling *Let go of the fucking dog*, while Willa tugged at her shoulder, screaming at her mother to get off. Now Bianka had her hands tight round the man's neck, strangling him. As his face turned scarlet the man let go of the lead and, finding itself free, the little dog shot off across the grass. Willa shouted *Jesus, somebody get the dog*, then, at Bianka, *He's let go*, but Bianka didn't stop. It was almost like she *couldn't* stop. Cat and I threw the ice creams to the ground and the three of us physically had to pull her off. The man bolted, shouting *Crazy fucking bitch* as he went.

By now people were running towards us, but the man was already gone. It was all over.

Wild-eyed and panting, Bianka was looking about her, the silk tea dress ripped open across the front. 'The dog,' she said, breathing heavily. 'The dog.'

'What's going on?' some woman asked, and a man with an American accent said, 'I reckon that jerk was trying to steal her dog.'

'Should we call somebody?' the woman said. 'The police?'

Then somebody walked up and said, 'Here. I've got your pup. Lucky for you it didn't run towards the edge.'

Another woman put a comforting hand on Bianka's shoulder. 'I'm all right now,' she said. 'Thank you. I can take it from here.' Evidently, she wasn't on her own, and, as there really was nothing more for people to see, the people who had gathered round just faded away. Bianka sat down on the bench with the dog on her lap and loosened the string around its neck. It was a black, scruffy little thing and small too, just a puppy. Willa sat beside her. Cat and I stayed standing.

'What – *happened*?'

'That *bastard*,' Bianka said, 'was *kicking* his dog.' She closed her eyes and buried her head in the puppy's fur.

I leant down and touched its soft coat. 'Looks like you just acquired a pet,' I said.

'Oh, no,' Bianka said, tears welling in her eyes. 'I couldn't keep it.'

'Why not?' I said, instantly picturing their large, secure garden.

Bianka's head made a strange jerking movement. 'I just couldn't,' she said. She kissed his little head. 'Anyway, we should probably get him to a vet.'

At supper that night, which was served in a formal dining room, Bryce asked how our afternoon had gone. Good question, I thought, *get this*. I sat up and looked across to where Bianka sat in a fresh dress and immaculate make-up, fascinated to know how she might even begin.

'Very good, all things considered,' Bianka said. With a delicate motion, she dabbed at her lips with a napkin. 'The weather was perfect for an afternoon stroll.'

'We had ice creams,' Willa said.

I paused, my fork halfway to my mouth and glanced at Cat. Neither Willa nor her mother was making eye contact with either of us.

Bryce looked back at his plate, then glanced back up. 'How d'you get that scratch?'

Bianka touched her cheek with her index finger, running it

along the length of a thin red line. 'I had a little to-do with some brambles,' she said. 'I really must get them cut back.'

'Is it just me or did today get really, really weird?'

Cat and I were lying with our heads together in the middle of a bed so vast it needed three sets of pillows to span its width. We were sharing the middle one, our bodies a small island in a sea of bed. I made a little *ha* sound. Cat raised her eyebrows.

'Say it,' she said. 'No one can hear you. We're in the guest wing.'

I pulled a face.

'*Say* it.' Cat took the covers and pulled them up over our heads. 'How about now?' Our eyes held in the dusky gloom of the sheets. 'Say it.'

'God, I don't know.'

'You don't *know* or you don't like to *say*?' Cat said. 'Don't tell me you can't see it, Robyn. Willa's family is seriously fucked up.'

In the morning Willa brought us tea and then sat on the bed with us, taking us through a box chock-full of the newspaper cuttings she'd collected about Laika, stories that ranged from serious pieces of journalism to tabloid reports of clairvoyants who'd wanted money in exchange for speculative titbits and implausible sightings. Later she showed me Laika's room, unlocking the door to let me into the sad untouched shrine of it, the belongings of a thirteen-year-old left exactly as they were the day she'd disappeared. After a bit I joined her at the window.

'Sorry about yesterday. You probably guessed this,' she said, her voice barely above a whisper, 'but things aren't that great between my parents.'

I took a moment to answer, trying to find something tactful to say. 'It must have put a huge strain on them when Laika disappeared.'

'In some ways that's the one thing that keeps them together.'

'You mean they support each other?'

'No.' She turned to face me, then added in a voice so low I could barely make out the words, 'I mean Mum won't leave the house.'

'D'you want to talk about it?'

She shook her head, and I pulled her into a hug.

We'd originally planned to stay the whole of Sunday, but instead we invented an excuse that meant we would need to leave after breakfast, and Bianka drove us back to the station, stopping off en route to collect the puppy from the vet. I'd already called my dad and he'd said there was always room for one more dog at theirs, and that if we could get the little floofball to London he'd happily drive up and collect him from ours. It made me grateful to think I had parents I could call in a crisis. I was even more glad to get away from the strange atmosphere of that cold, silent house. I realized I couldn't wait to get home to our tiny, noisy flat, where the beat of other people's music pulsed through the walls, and we had neighbours who laughed and shouted and argued and hugged.

We came to love that flat in the end. We lived there far beyond the time we could afford to move out. I asked Cat to marry me in its tiny galley kitchen, and it was the home we went back to after our civil partnership, and after our honeymoon in Greece. Our parents visited whenever they could, our brothers too. We held parties there that gradually became less wild over time, and eventually Cat got to indulge her love of the Scandi aesthetic, buying patterned rugs and vintage furniture with clean lines. It was a good place, a good home. But all the time we were saving like mad.

*

With no small sense of wonder we arrived at our thirties. Both of us registered some deep subliminal change, a growing-up. We were ready for the next stage of our lives, one that had been a long time in the planning. I met Willa at Postman's Park to tell her our news. I'd moved to Bart's by then and she had a job in a call centre that she had repeatedly assured me was the absolute worst. I told her first about the Victorian terrace we'd found to buy in Forest Hill, a proper house, with three bedrooms and a jungle out the back which the agent had said had the potential to be a 'perfect outdoor space' with a small amount of work. A doer-upper, I said. Cat would be in charge.

I smiled at her. I'd held on to the best news for last. 'I'm pregnant,' I said, 'twelve weeks.' Willa's mouth opened in surprise.

'Oh my God,' she said, each word falling over the next. She buried her head in my shoulder. 'I'm so, so happy for you.'

She held me so tight I thought she might not ever let me go. Gently, I pulled away. There were tears brimming over the lids of her eyes. She wiped a hand across her cheek. The tears fell.

'I'm so happy for you,' she said again. She laughed, then cried some more. 'Honestly, I don't know why I'm crying. I'm ridiculously happy for you, so, so happy.'

She cried again the day she first met Sophie at the hospital, holding our beautiful, precious daughter in her arms. For a long, secret time she gazed into our child's face, as silent tears worked tracks over the curve of her cheeks. She was so very far away that eventually Cat looked at me, her face etched with concern. Willa had gone somewhere that didn't include us. With a delicate finger she touched our daughter's cheek. Her tears continued to fall, but whether they were tears for a newborn, for Laika, for herself or for a child she didn't yet have, I didn't ever ask.

14.
Body parts

Willa

I first met Jamie at a bar in St Paul's. At that time I was working a three-month contract making props for a low-budget horror movie. My employer was a small, furious Scot in his fifties called Fen Roberts. He had a shock of sandy hair, strung-out eyes, and periodically panicked about our rate of production. After my first couple of weeks I came to suspect that Fen had undercut any other bidders for the job by some considerable margin. Most of the other temps were students from Eastern Europe who spent the day laughing, gesturing with their hands and talking at speed in a language I didn't understand. They also took regular breaks for coffee and cigarettes, which made Fen apoplectic with rage, something that amused the students no end. My job was to dob fake blood on various body parts. They needed a lot of dismembered limbs.

I'd arranged to meet Robyn for a rare, snatched drink after work. I saw so little of her in those days, less and less it seemed. Sophie was already a toddler by then and Cat was expecting the twins, so she was always keen to get home.

I arrived before her, of course. I found myself a tiny table tucked away in a corner and was half reading my book, half watching a group of three women, when I realized a man was smiling at me. A slow smile of approval, full of promise. He was standing at the bar on his own. I checked around to see if the smile was meant for someone else, then back at my book. The next time I looked up, he smiled at me again. He looked a bit older than me, with a large leonine head, a broad nose, tawny hair that curled over the back of his collar, a strong jaw and clear blue eyes. Handsome too, ridiculously so. A lock of hair fell across his face and he brushed it out of his eyes. I reckon he's an actor, I thought, an actor who specializes in period dramas, a natural at playing a crowd, he's got that confidence about him, and the smile of a man who knows he's the best-looking male in the room. Then Robyn arrived. Behind her back, as she bent over and kissed my cheek, he grinned at me and shrugged his shoulders apologetically, *Just missed my chance.*

The next night I went back. I told myself I didn't have any particular reason to hurry home, which was true enough. He was there again, standing at the bar, but if he clocked me coming in, he didn't let me know. I found my seat in the corner and took out my book, *Great Expectations.* I hooked a stray piece of hair over my ear and propped my chin on my hand. Then I read.

The next thing I knew he was standing in front of me.

'If this was a blind date,' he said, 'I'd be looking for the girl who said she'd be reading a trashy novel' – I held up the book to show him the cover – 'or, indeed, Dickens, one of the great classics. I'm impressed. Jamie Casteele,' he said. 'May I?' He didn't wait for a reply. 'Let me guess, you're a visiting professor of comparative literature swinging through London to give a TED talk at UCL.'

It was almost impossible not to warm to his wicked grin. 'Nothing like that,' I said. 'I just wanted to read English at university.'

'You *wanted* to. So you didn't.'

'No.'

'Why not?'

I took a breath. 'I wasn't in a good place.' I was going to leave it at that, but Jamie waited in silence, giving me a look of such patient concern that eventually I added, 'My little sister disappeared. Snatched, I mean. She's been gone twenty years.'

'Jesus. I'm sorry to hear that.'

I hadn't expected him to be so kind. A thing like a large, smooth stone appeared in my throat, painfully huge. I couldn't speak.

Jamie paused, then said, 'How do you move on from a thing like that? God, it must be hard.'

I couldn't answer that. The truth is, I'd never moved on. I'd never returned to finish my A Levels or gone on to uni, even though both my parents had told me I should. I hadn't had a career, just a series of jobs. I hadn't had a lasting relationship either. I'd dated over the years, of course I had, but things had never worked out. And it had always been me who'd ended things, me who'd made the decision that something intangible wasn't quite right. I was a master of self-sabotage. I longed for a family, but I'd never got to the point where that was even being discussed. And time was running out.

'Here,' Jamie said, 'give me your hand.' His was large, and warm. He held my fingers in his. He took a pen from his top pocket and wrote a number on the back of my hand. His head was bent close to mine, as if we were sharing a secret. He was so close that I could see the individual hairs bedded into his chin. His hair smelt clean. He wore a blue tie, and his pink shirt was crisp and expensive-looking, City clothes. Underneath the number he wrote JAMIE in capital letters that lifted and dipped across the bones of my hand.

'Ball's in your court,' he said. 'Call me.' His smile was open, sincere.

Two days later, we had our first date.

*

At forty-one he was five years older than me, with the easy confidence of a man who had his life pretty much set up the way he wanted: a nice car, a big group of friends, a career as an ambassador for Pearl River Wines that took him all over the world. He was easy-going and had a huge sense of the ridiculous. On dates I found him expansive, generous and irreverent, with a boyish charm he knew how to work. *Watch and learn*, he'd breathe, as he moved forward to beguile a waitress into giving us the best table in the house.

'I love an upgrade,' he told me in bed late one night. 'It's kind of like a secret challenge, working out what I can bag for free.' He laughed then, pulling me towards him and growling in my ear, 'You should see me when I don't get what I want.'

I'd never before met anyone who seemed so utterly at ease with life. I liked his jokes, his confidence, his spontaneity, even the artless way he swore. He didn't care one jot that I hadn't been to university. Neither had he; his own school career was far more chequered than mine.

'I accidentally got expelled,' he told me one morning over breakfast, 'twice, actually. Two different schools.' He grinned at me over his bowl of muesli.

'What did you do?' I asked him, a slow smile of amusement spreading over my face. It was still early days in our relationship, a time when all our conversations seemed to move fluidly between brilliantly funny and meaningfully intense.

'Racketeering, cheating, lying,' Jamie said cheerfully, 'you name it, I did it. I was forever in trouble. I had yet to learn the noble art of not getting caught. God, my poor parents.' He squeezed my hand. 'They'll like you, though.'

I was amazed anyone could be so blasé about their bad-boy past, so open and frank. Also, just a tiny bit concerned. *Oh, forget it*, I told myself, *people grow up*. And Jamie wasn't a clown; he had a serious side too, I knew that from the way he talked about conservation, his great love of the wild. He told me that one of the reasons he loved his job so much was that Pearl River Wines not only had vineyards but also owned a small private game reserve. It was mainly used to entertain their well-heeled guests, but Jamie got to stay there every couple of months, for free, whenever he went to Cape Town for work.

'How d'you even get a job like that?' I asked him. We were lying on his bed, flicking through an album of photographs he'd taken at the reserve. I stopped on an image of three lion cubs tumbling together in the long grass, the edges of their solid furry bodies glowing fire-red, backlit against a setting sun. 'Wonderful,' I said.

Jamie shrugged. 'Good luck, I suppose. Friend of a friend. I'd had loads of different jobs before that. I never really knew what I wanted to do with my life, to be honest.' He pulled a face and stuck his hands behind his head. 'So many options out there: that's the problem. And only one life to do all of it. God knows how you're ever meant to decide on anything.' For a long time he stared at the ceiling, as if lost in thought. Then he said, 'D'you like dogs?' I sat up, laughing, somewhat surprised by this abrupt shift in the conversation. 'Mum breeds spaniels. Someday I'd really love a dog. A little Staffy or something, you know, from Battersea Dogs Home. Get a rescue.'

I smiled. We didn't have dogs when I was growing up. My mother was always desperate for one – something small and cute, she'd said, a chihuahua perhaps, or a pug, but my father said he questioned why anyone in their right mind would invite a pissing, crapping, germ-laden, bollock-licking, arse-dragging, flea-ridden animal to live under their very own roof; and, while we were at it, he didn't much see the point of horses either, when cars were faster, less temperamental and didn't leave their passengers stinking of shit.

'Sure,' I said, 'I like dogs.'

I ran my hand through his hair. I loved that he loved animals. I loved too that he'd asked my opinion on that matter, and, even more, that his first choice would be a rescue. That was nice, I thought. It showed good character. That mix of sunshine and humanity reminded me something of Robyn.

I was drawn to him like honey.

Jamie was sharing a flat in North London when I first met him, renting a bedroom from Sam, an old school friend of his. It was an arrangement he'd made in haste, he said, not ideal, but a temporary measure until he got a place of his own. The year before he'd made something of an abrupt return from years of living in Cape Town. 'Beating a swift retreat from my disastrous marriage,' was how he actually put it. His ex-wife, Melissa, was still there. He showed me a couple of pictures of her once, a confident-looking blonde on a sun-drenched beach.

'Why didn't it work out?' I said. We were lying in his bed, late at night.

Jamie shrugged. 'I wanted kids. She didn't.'

Come on, I thought, there's got to be more to it than that.

'Isn't that the sort of thing you should discuss *before* you get married?'

'Yeah. No, we did. Melissa could be very' – Jamie paused, searching for the right word – '*contrary*. Don't get me wrong, I did love her. She was sharp, adventurous, spirited . . . but she could be a bit – hell, I don't know, *tricky*. Oppositional. The moment I said we should start trying for a family she said she'd changed her mind. Now she didn't want kids *at all*. And, no shit, I promise you she was *always* like that: didn't want the stuff she could have, irresistibly drawn to everything else.' He sighed, looking grim. 'Did the same thing with me, I suppose, got bored with me the moment we got married. We lasted only eighteen months. Yet another catastrophe as far as Mum and Dad were concerned: not just a divorce but no grandkids to dote over either. God.'

He sounded so dejected that I took his hand and squeezed it. We stayed like that for a while. Finally, he rolled his head towards mine. 'How about you?' he said. 'Do you want kids?'

His words moved through me like the first shoots of spring, all my secret desires pushing to the surface. I smiled. 'Yeah,' I said. 'I do.'

I would have let that special moment hang in the air, but he made a grab for me, laughing. 'Come here,' he said. 'We'd better get on with it, then.'

God, that was good. I almost enjoyed sex that night.

Cat had only just had the twins, so I said we should get ourselves over to visit. They would be my litmus test, and it was a good one, as it turned out: we arrived to what could justly be described as utter chaos. Sophie, wearing her favourite red dungarees and fairy wings, was marching up and down the length of the kitchen table performing magic tricks, most of which involved shouting *Ta-da* at the top of her voice while pulling random objects out of a hat. Meanwhile Cat, still in her pyjamas, was sheltering in the front room with the boys, both of whom were intermittently producing the sort of intense, keening noises only a new-born with colic can effect. Lunch was a selection of random stuff pulled out of the fridge.

'Is it like this all the time?' Jamie asked, looking bemused as he picked out bits of Lego from a salad made from carrots, lettuce leaves and a tin of chickpeas.

'God, no,' Cat said. 'It's not all sunbeams and roses. Sometimes parenting can be quite hard.'

I thought I saw a quick flash of horror sweep over Jamie's face, but later, as we sat together on their sofa, each of us holding a tiny sleeping child, he cast me a look so full of tenderness and wonder that I felt a soft wave of genuine love for him.

The universe had spoken: here was my match.

It was summer. We settled down easily, naturally, fluidly, almost without discussion. We visited galleries and went to the theatre. We ate in tiny bistros and talked endlessly. We walked through London's parks and lazed on the grass, sitting in puddles of golden evening sun, drinking glasses of Pearl River wine, Jamie's head bent towards mine. When I was on my own, I felt like singing the entire time. I smiled at strangers on the tube.

Even better, when my temporary contract came to an end and there were no more limbs to paint, Fen asked me to stay on. 'Not so much as a prop-maker,' he said. 'More as an assistant, a co-worker. I can't pay a huge salary, but it's a permanent job offer if you want it. I need somebody who can deal with people. I am aware,' he said with a grimace, 'that part of the job is not exactly my forte.'

Everything was falling into place. Within months we were talking about hunting for a place of our own, somewhere to buy rather than rent, a proper home with *two* bedrooms, maybe three if we could afford it. I told my parents the big news over Sunday lunch. My father placed his knife and fork on the side of his plate and fixed me with a flat stare.

'I need to meet this man. Get him down.'

I met my father's eyes. He smiled.

I'd already met his mum and dad. Now Jamie had to meet mine.

My father and Jamie got on. Over lunch they drank Pearl River wine while my father told Jamie all about the superlative auction prices achieved by Ming Dynasty porcelain. Later they stood outside, arms crossed across their chests, and discussed the comparative merits of their cars. Meanwhile my mother and I sat at the kitchen table trying to decipher a message somebody had posted a few days before on findlaika. I read it aloud for the thousandth time.

I see 1998 en picardie ilisabat et gentille Jabir.

'Clearly whoever sent it doesn't speak much English,' I said. 'The best I can make out is that somebody thinks they saw her in Ilisabat, in 1998. The problem is there's nowhere in Picardy called Ilisabat, in fact, nowhere in *France* called Ilisabat. I've tried Isles Abat and Isles à Bat, but they don't exist either. At a push, Gentille could be Gentilly, north of Paris. The police said they'd look into it but not to pin my hopes on anything. They said it could be anywhere French speaking: Monaco, Burundi, Haiti. Guadeloupe.'

'Not this again,' my father said as the two men came back in. 'It's a slow news day, is it? You know all about findlaika, do you, Jamie? Then you'll know just how much trouble it generates. The tabloids drag up some old story, then some jackass concocts a load of rubbish, and this one, without even telling us, jumps on a plane –'

'Once. I jumped on a plane without telling you *once*.'

'And buggers off on some wild goose chase halfway round the world.'

'This is the first sighting there's been for ages, Dad.'

'This isn't a *sighting*, Willa. It's complete gibberish, from which you have apparently extracted that someone claims to have seen her *twenty years* ago. It's clearly bollocks. This is just some donkey playing with you, Willa, a bored child. Leave it alone. I've told you before, that website of yours doesn't help with anything. Shut it down. It just upsets you.'

'You've got to admit,' Jamie said, 'it doesn't sound very likely.'

'Exactly,' my father said. He gave my boyfriend a slow nod. 'Good man, James.'

I shut the laptop.

At the end of the afternoon my father nodded his approval to me. To Jamie he said, 'She's a good girl, Willa, golden.'

'She is. And we certainly have a lot to look forward to,' Jamie said, beaming in my direction. 'I'm thinking maybe a little romantic getaway to Paris, then there's Christmas. And, fingers crossed, we should be in our own place by the spring.'

'Paris, eh?' My father reached out, shook Jamie's hand and then held it firmly in his grip. 'You and I should take some rounds of golf together. Ping me some dates. I'll introduce you at my club.'

'Fantastic,' Jamie said. 'I'll do that.' His face was a hearty mix of sincerity and appreciation. He gave the hallway a last look, taking in my father's collection of china and jade, the oriental rugs, the round mahogany table and silk flowers, the mounted stag's head on the wall. He shook my father's hand again, and then turned away, rolling his eyes at me behind his back. I had to stop myself from laughing.

I kissed them both goodbye. My mother said, 'He's lovely, darling,' loud enough for everyone to hear. Then she hugged me close, and, with her mouth right next to my ear said, 'Don't rush into anything.'

A couple of months later we had a long weekend in Paris, our first trip together overseas. We stayed in a hotel near the Musée d'Orsay and walked everywhere, stopping in tiny cafés for coffee and to pore over guidebooks. We visited the Louvre and Sainte-Chapelle, took a river cruise and had cartoons of our faces drawn by an artist at Montmartre – me all eyes, Jamie all teeth.

We were on the Pont des Arts when I saw my sister walking

in the distance, on the pavement below the bridge. I recognized her instantly – her dark hair, the shape of her back, the fast gait of her walk. One person, in a crowd of thousands, and it was *her*. She had an orange backpack flung over one shoulder, and she was moving at a good pace through the crowd. I watched her for a second, then dropped Jamie's hand and plummeted down the flight of stone steps to the bank below. I didn't have direct sight of her any more, but I knew the direction in which she was going. Above me, I could hear Jamie shouting my name from the bridge. There were people, so many people, too many. I shouted, '*Laika*.'

I hurtled along the bank, pushing through or darting around tourists grouped like slow moving ships. But she was gone. I couldn't spot the orange backpack anywhere. It was like she'd vanished into thin air.

I stopped and turned, spinning on the spot, looking in every direction, back into the mass of bodies I'd just passed, into the crowds up ahead, at the upper embankment, at the strangers sitting at the tables dotted along the pavement. My heart was thudding, my vision blurred with tears.

By the time Jamie caught up with me, he was panting heavily. He took my arm and turned me towards him. I could see myself reflected in his sunglasses, my eyes wild. He pulled me close and wrapped his arms around my shoulders.

'Hey,' he said. His voice was low and soft.

'It was Laika,' I said, breathless. 'I saw Laika. She was on the embankment. She –' I pointed in the direction in which I had seen her walking. 'She was going that way. We've got to find her.' I took a step down the pavement. Jamie pulled me back.

'Sweetheart,' he said, wrapping his arms around me again. 'It's not Laika.'

'It *was*,' I said into his chest. 'It was *Laika*. It was her.'

'How many years has it been? Twenty? More? Darling, think

about it, you wouldn't just spot her on the street. You wouldn't recognize her – you've told me that yourself. She'd be changed beyond all recognition. You're carrying around some vision of her as a young, healthy girl, a thirteen-year-old, but the truth is that, even if she's still alive, she's probably living rough or holed up in an institution. She wouldn't look the same. She could be missing teeth for all you know. It was somebody who looked a little like her, perhaps, somebody who reminded you of her, as she used to be.' He pulled me closer. I put my head against his chest and I knew in some clumsy way he was trying to be kind, so I closed my eyes and breathed until I no longer felt the urge to punch him on the jaw.

'Darling,' he said, his voice gentle but firm, 'your dad warned me this might happen. You're not going to see Laika on a street in Paris. You're not going to see her in London, or *anywhere*. Whatever awful thing happened to your sister, she's not coming home.'

Jamie asked me to marry him that night and I said yes. We hatched plans together and, as soon as we got back from Paris, I moved into the little flat he shared with Sam.

Three weeks later, Jamie went to South Africa for work. On the morning of his departure, he stood in Sam's hallway with his bags packed, cupping my face with his hands.

'I'll take you with me another time, promise.'

He gave me a flash of that wide smile, perfect white teeth in two perfect white rows, then, from the window, I watched him bound down the outside steps to the waiting taxi, the morning light catching his golden head as he folded himself in through its door. I watched the black cab disappear down the street until it turned the corner and was finally out of sight.

Then I ran to the bathroom and threw up.

*

I knew I was pregnant straight off, even before I could take an accurate test. My entire body felt fundamentally different: powerful, elemental, complete. With Jamie still away, I went about my days in a blur of happiness and exhaustion. In the bathroom I stood in front of the mirror, running my hands over the flat of my belly, dazzled by the magic going on inside. I was going to be a mother.

No, I already was.

15.
Satellite

Willa

Jamie's reaction to the news was a mixture of incredulity and pure joy. Given my age, I don't think either of us had really expected things to happen quite so fast. As soon as he returned from South Africa, and on weekends when he wasn't summoned by my dad to play golf, we started house-hunting in earnest. We began our search first in the nicer parts of Central London, a dream that was almost instantly moderated to the outskirts. I'd been putting money away since I left school, but I'd never earnt a lot. Even combined with Jamie's savings our little nest egg didn't stretch to much. We looked at grotty basement flats that stunk of damp or in which the windows rattled with each passing train. At one place the so-called second bedroom was a cupboard.

Three months into my pregnancy, I started to feel desperate. Sam's flat was nice enough, but obviously we couldn't stay there, not with a baby on the way, and, while Sam was lovely, he was Jamie's friend, not mine. Jamie himself was only living there as a favour, so I tried to make my own presence as unobtrusive as possible, arriving home after the others whenever possible. But I was tired, and still prone to bouts of sickness, and occasionally, very occasionally, I'd get home first.

Which is how I came to speak to Melissa.

The landline was ringing as I opened the front door. I dumped my bag and snatched it up, thinking it might be Jamie.

'Hello?'

'It's me,' a woman's voice said. 'Why aren't you picking up your cell?' A South African accent.

I paused. 'Are you calling for Jamie?'

'Who is this?'

'Willa.'

'What are you doing in Jamie's flat?'

Oh, no, you don't, I thought. 'He's my partner,' I said. I put a protective hand on the small swell of my belly. 'We're engaged.'

There was a moment of near silence, then a quick humourless laugh.

'Is that right?' the voice said slowly. '*Unbelievable.* Good luck with that.'

It was Melissa, of course it was, but Jamie arrived home at the same time as Sam, so I had to wait until we were in bed to tell him about the strange call.

'Ah,' he said. 'Okay. Sorry about that.'

'But why was she calling you? What did she want?'

'God knows,' he said. 'Perhaps she's heard you're on the scene.'

I let that sink in. 'What was she like?'

'Melissa? Messy.'

'That's it? She was *messy*?'

'I mean it. She was brought up by servants. It used to drive me mad. I'm a neat freak – like you.'

'Come on,' I said, half laughing. 'This is your *ex-wife.* You can come up with a bit more than that.'

Jamie glanced at me. 'Okay, then, feisty. How about that? A dynamo. Very single-minded about pursuing her goals. Not to mention combative: took no prisoners, shot from the hip. Melissa *loved* a good fight. She was forever arguing, running out of rooms, yelling at the staff.'

'The *who*?'

'The house staff. Christ, if you think that's bad, she'd even yell at *me*.'

I sat up. 'Hang on, why would yelling at *you* be *worse* than yelling at your staff?'

'*Of course* that's worse.'

'You can't yell at people you've employed.'

'Bloody hell,' he said. Now he sounded slightly irritated. 'I didn't begin this conversation expecting to have to defend myself. Or Melissa, come to that.'

'Wow. I'm just amazed you married her in the first place.'

'Come off it. Do you *really* want to hear good stuff about Melissa? She was a live wire, okay? She was good fun.'

'That's not what –'

'Look, we've been through this. I tried; it didn't work out. That's it. Now leave it, will you? Go to sleep.'

He pulled up the covers, turned off his beside light and rolled on his side, turning away from me in the dark. Minutes later, he was asleep.

I stared at the ceiling. The problem was we hadn't yet found a home. It was getting really urgent. The stress was getting to us both.

The next day we put in an offer on a basement flat. It was a bit dark and a bit dingy, and the tiny second bedroom faced a brick wall, but we could sort all that with mirrors and clever lighting. It would do.

'Ping me the details,' my father said on the phone. 'Let's have a look.'

A week later my parents invited us out for lunch, along with Jamie's mum and dad too.

'My treat,' my father said. 'Meet us at Hammersmith Station.'

It was a warm Saturday in early May. My father had booked a table at a ritzy little bistro and was playing the big-hearted host, putting Jamie's parents comfortably at ease as he led the little party on a winding route through the quiet residential squares of Brook Green. Eventually we stopped outside an elegant red-brick mansion block.

'What's this?' I said. It clearly wasn't a restaurant.

'A small diversion,' my father said. 'Indulge me, if you will.'

Jamie glanced at me, a fleeting question passing over his face. I replied with a look, *No idea*. Meanwhile Dad had produced a key. He let us all into the lobby, then up a couple of flights of stairs. On the third floor, he produced another key, unlocked a door, and the six of us stepped into the top-floor apartment.

'Have a look around,' my father said, 'and use your imagination. You'll see.'

We were standing in a spacious living room with two huge sash windows that looked out over the green, leafy square. Even with the dark-toned walls and patchy brown carpets, the room was full of light. Ahead of us was a good-sized kitchen with dated Formica units, and to our right a tiled bathroom. Further doors led to two large bedrooms, both with gently sloping ceilings under the eaves. The whole place was clearly in a terrible state of repair: strips of flocked wallpaper were peeling away from the walls and one entire window was veined by a thin tracery of dirt-lined cracks; but even in that state it was possible to see its true potential. It clearly had *good bones*, rooms that were light and beautifully proportioned. It was, in truth, everything I would ever want in a home. It was also completely unattainable. My father was nuts if he thought we could afford this place, or anything like it, and certainly not in Brook Green.

It was hard even to look around. I leant my backside against the sill of the cracked window, hit by a slow wave of exhaustion. All the stress of months of miserable house-hunting hit me in one go. My eyes filled with tears.

'Dad,' I said, 'we can't afford this.'

'It's on for a good price,' Dad said. 'Needs a complete renovation, not just updating. New electrics, plumbing, windows, everything. Flooring, plastering, the works. It's a lot of work. We're talking a good few months before it's liveable.'

'It's completely out of our budget,' Jamie said. He flashed me a tender look of apology.

'It's yours if you want it,' Dad said, 'fully paid for and in both your names. Think of it as an early wedding gift.'

Andrew, Jamie's father, said, 'You're not serious.'

'I am,' Dad said. He gave Jamie's parents an even look, his voice level and completely matter-of-fact. 'We can afford it.'

'*Bianka, Bryce* –' Jamie's mother said. 'I can hardly believe my ears. I mean, *look* at this place, the location alone –' She opened her hands and made a slow turn on the spot, taking in every inch of the flat. '*Jamie.* This place could be *gorgeous*.'

Jamie looked at me in stunned silence.

'It's too generous,' he said, turning to my father. 'We couldn't ever –'

'Look at this.' My father went towards the kitchen. Jamie's parents followed and, after a moment's hesitation, Jamie went too. 'Personally I'd take down that wall, open it up to the living room, put in a breakfast bar *there*, and make it one big space.'

'O-kay,' Jamie said, his voice drawing out the word. He glanced in my direction, then, after a moment, smiled. 'Yeah, that would work.'

'Leave it with me. I've got people who can sort that.'

'This is *wonderful*,' his mother said.

His father said, 'Incredible.'

Jamie nodded and crossed his arms across his chest, workmanlike. I could see he was starting to engage with the idea. He didn't understand. There was *no way* we could take the flat.

'Dad,' I said. My fingers gripped the sill. 'That's so generous and obviously we're both hugely grateful, but – look. We just can't. It won't work. The problem is' – I was thinking on my feet – 'it needs so much work and we need a place *now*.'

'Not a problem. The two of you can move in with us while the work's being done. Correction, the *three* of you.' He gave me an indulgent smile.

I placed a protective hand over the swell of my belly. Somewhere inside my daughter was orbiting my womb like some distant satellite, turning slow cartwheels, her tiny fingers and toes unfolding in the dark.

'You can have the guest suite. Willa, your old bedroom can be the baby's room. Laika's room can be the new guest room.'

'No.'

My mother hadn't said a word up to this point and her voice made everyone turn.

'We are not touching Laika's room,' she said. '*No one* is touching Laika's room.' There was a moment of silence.

'Of course,' my father said, giving her a slow smile. 'It's all just ideas at the moment, Bianka.' He smiled warmly at Jamie's parents, opening his hands. 'Propositions. The finer details can be drilled out later.'

'Jamie,' I said, 'we should really talk about this.'

My father placed a proprietorial hand on Jamie's shoulder. 'I'm sure we can all put up with a temporary bit of multigenerational living. Move in next week. I'd appreciate having my golf buddy a bit closer to hand, especially now the weather's good. What do you think, James?'

Jamie nodded. 'Great.'

His mother said, 'You *lucky, lucky* things.'

'Good decision,' my father said. 'Welcome to the family, son.'

There was a bright beat of surprise, then the sudden realization that a deal had been struck. My father beamed and held out his hand. After a moment Jamie beamed too. He shook my father's hand and then the four of them plunged into a small hubbub of congratulatory chat. I went over too, hugging each of them in turn and thanking both my parents, knowing that any tears I shed would be interpreted as joy. I knew that's what I should really be feeling, and not the bubbling disquiet that was gradually building in me. After a few minutes, using my pregnancy as a convenient excuse, I returned to my perch on the sill.

My father had a strange look on his face, a slight smile that almost wasn't there. I turned my face towards the window, looking not through it but at it, my eyes tracing the dark filigree of ragged cracks in the glass, a barely visible map of complicated fractures. It would take only one soft knock for the entire thing to go.

What just happened? My father's generosity wasn't in doubt, but there was something else too, something going on under the surface. There *had* to be. My father was a *brilliant* businessman. He didn't just give his money away, not to anyone, and that included me. *Everything* he did had a reason behind it, an end-goal, a transaction, an exchange. In fact, I now thought, most likely the mechanics of that entire discussion would have been pre-planned by him, including having Jamie's parents with us, encouraging and thankful, jollying everyone along. Behind the screen of their gratification my father had made a series of moves so subtle that they'd completely missed the cardinal point: a gold-plated bulldozer may be dazzling, sure, but it's still a sodding bulldozer. What did he want?

I gazed around at the flat that was suddenly, unexpectedly, effortlessly ours. A shaft of midday light fell across a living room that would, one day, be beautiful. Dust motes hung in the air. On the far side of the room, Jamie's parents were talking to my mother. Jamie and my father stood slightly apart from them, two big men, so similar in stature and height, deep in conversation. At one point, like perfectly timed synchronized swimmers, they both crossed their arms.

Oh, God, I thought. The answer was staring me in the face.

My father was buying two things that day. One was a flat. The other was Jamie.

16.
Shards

Willa

At twenty-three weeks the baby poured out of me in waves of blood and pain. We were living at Laburnum House by then, but only my mother was there at the time. Jamie was on a work trip to South Africa, and my father was away too, somewhere overseas.

At the hospital they gave her to me to hold, wrapped in a tiny white blanket that had the ward's name stitched along the edge in blue thread. I held my daughter in my arms and tried to burn her face into my soul. Everything about her looked perfect; her tiny hands, her tiny feet. Her tiny nails. She was utterly beautiful. She had a wisp of dark hair and everything about her was impossibly small. She was absolutely still.

I had listened to her heartbeat.

She had a name, Wren.

They let me hold her until my mother came, and then they took her away.

They discharged me with a plastic bag that contained a thick stack of pads and a thin leaflet on grief. My mother drove me back to their house and I lay in my old childhood bed while she stroked my hair, too hollowed out to cry. She never once said, *You can have another one*, and I loved her for that.

She alone could understand.

We had both lost daughters and they could never be replaced.

Autumn rolled in, spreading great blankets of felted mist across the Channel. I went for long walks along the coast path above the white cliffs. Fen had been generous, telling me to take as much time as I wanted, so I hadn't yet returned to work. I was back in a house that I had spent my entire adult life trying to leave, but still, I was glad to be near the cliffs. I needed the space, time by myself, the deep boom and hiss of a distant filmy sea, a retreat into the safety and formlessness of silence. There were times up there when I felt almost weightless. I needed Jamie with me, someone to keep me earthbound, but he never seemed to be around. His commute to London added hours to his day, and every few weeks he disappeared off for work overseas. At least we would have the weekends together, I remember thinking at first. I was wrong.

A Saturday breakfast in September. The week had been cool and bright, the first leaves yellowing on the old oaks, and Jamie and I had spoken about doing a long walk together, maybe taking a picnic or having a lazy lunch at some cosy pub.

'You'll need to get a crack on, James,' Dad said, spearing a round of black pudding into his mouth. 'I want to be on the road by nine.'

'What?' I said. 'Jamie and I have plans.'

My father furrowed his brow. 'Nothing I know about, James?'

'Well, Willa and I –'

'We need to check on the build.'

'Right. Yes.'

'Given the amount I'm paying out, I thought you'd be fairly keen.'

'No, absolutely. Of course.'

'Right. London, then. Lesson One, James: builders are lazy

sods. You've got to show them who they're dealing with. I've booked us a late lunch at my club.'

'Shouldn't I be there?' I glanced between Jamie and my dad. 'It's *our* flat.'

'Not possible, Willa. And so to Lesson Two.' My father gave Jamie a slow, droll smile. 'Pick an *all-male* club.'

Jamie laughed, not meeting my eye.

'And golf tomorrow, okay? I need you on top form. Bit of an early start.'

That turned out to be the pattern of every weekend. By November, things with Jamie felt strained, and a quiet distance hung between us like mist. Always so engaging and personable around my father, Jamie now seemed guarded around me, tight-lipped and reserved. Our sex life dried up. I forgave him. I forgave him *everything*. The cool way he spoke to me, his frequent trips away, the lack of physical touch. It was always going to be a little strange living with my parents, I told myself. We would just need to let things rumble along until we could move into the flat. Finally, December rolled in. We could be in by Christmas. Things would be different then, better, perhaps. In the meantime, we were very polite to each other: careful, solicitous, detached.

Mostly anyway. The night he broke my pitcher, the one that Chris had given me so long ago at his pottery, we openly fought. He didn't even *tell* me, didn't even say there'd been an accident. He just threw my beautiful sea-green jug away, leaving me to find it later, discarded in the bathroom bin.

It was late at night when I found it. I'd been reading, sitting up in bed, when Jamie, lying next to me, looked up from his phone. He gave me a quick glance, then scratched the back of his head.

'Okay, so my boss wants me in SA next week.'

'Why don't we both go?' I said. It would be good for us to be away. 'I've got the time.'

He looked back at his phone. 'It's just work. You'll be bored.'

'I won't be bored,' I said. 'How could I be bored? I'll just stay on the reserve all day, watching the animals.'

Jamie paused. He didn't look up. Then he said, 'Actually, you can't stay at the reserve.'

He wasn't meeting my eye. Suspicion leapt through my brain like a feral cat, wild-eyed and tight-limbed.

'Why not? What's going on?'

Jamie put down his phone. 'Can you just not?'

'Not *what*?'

'Ask all these questions. It's complicated, all right?'

'*How?*' I held his eyes. I crossed my arms and said nothing.

'Fine. If you really want to know, I'll tell you. But you won't like it.'

I waited.

Eventually Jamie said, 'Marc – the reserve's manager – is Melissa's brother. That's how Melissa and I first met.'

I let the implications sink in. 'So what?' I said. 'Does that mean, when you're in South Africa, you see Melissa?'

'It's not my fault if she shows up.'

'But you told me you didn't have *any* contact.'

'No. I didn't. I *never* said that. You just assumed that was the case.'

'Of course I bloody well assumed that. She's your sodding ex-wife.'

'I don't believe this. You don't actually trust me, do you?'

Astonished, I said, 'Are you making this about *me*?'

'It's pretty clear you don't like that I was married before.'

'It *is*?'

'Or we wouldn't even be having this conversation.'

I threw myself on my side, turning my back to him.

'Sweetheart,' he said, the tone of his voice now cajoling. He kissed the back of my neck, between the blades of my shoulders. 'Don't get paranoid on me, okay? Seriously, the last thing I need is a relationship with another uncontrollable child.' He paused, then added, 'Obviously I didn't mean *uncontrollable*. I meant out of control.'

I lay in silence, furious, wounded.

'Come here,' he said. He reached out a hand and jabbed it into the flesh just above my hip, his fingers tickling hard.

'No.' I turned round, snatched up his hand and held it by the wrist, looking him in the eyes. 'Do not tickle me. Just don't. Not ever.'

'Jesus,' he said. 'You can be so bloody uptight.'

Uptight?

'Screw you, Jamie,' I said. I leapt out of bed and stalked into the bathroom. That's when I found it, my pitcher, in the bin, in *pieces*. I picked out two large shards and charged back into the bedroom, feeling rage and fury move through me so fast I thought I might throttle him.

'Jamie,' I said, 'what happened to my jug?'

Jamie looked up from his phone. 'It just broke,' he said.

A jolt. Somewhere, deep in my memory, an echo of those words.

My father's voice: *It just broke.*

My mother's voice, harrowed and frantic: *Things don't just break.*

And, white-faced between them, my sister.

'*No*,' I said.

'It's just an old jug. I'll get you another jug. I'll get you ten jugs.'

'I don't want another jug, I want *that* jug. *What did you do?*'

Jamie looked amazed. 'Christ, Melissa,' he said, 'what is this, the Inquisition?'

'You just called me *Melissa*.'

There was a stunned moment of silence. I couldn't fight any more. I got into bed and turned off my light. *Everything* was broken.

17.
Harlequin

Robyn

It was a Friday morning in December and I had the entire day off, so I met Willa on the steps of the British Museum. We hugged as if we'd not seen each other for years, rather than the few months it had really been. She felt bony thin.

'Cat really doesn't mind?'

'God, no, she's delighted. Her mum's got the twins. She's completely thrilled to have a bit of time to herself. I promised I'd be back in time to collect Sophie from nursery.'

'How are the kids?' We were walking through the harlequin light of the glass atrium. Her voice was steady and I could only begin to imagine the effort it took to be that brave, asking after Sophie and our boys after her own awful miscarriage. *Precious, wild, wonderful, exhausting. And perfect*, I thought.

'Good,' I said. I squeezed her hand. 'This way.'

I pulled her towards the stairs to the upper galleries and we began working our way through rooms devoted to the sorrow and wonder of all things human: endless things made for the beloved, the dead, the ones left behind.

Finally, we arrived on the top floor and the galleries devoted to pottery and glass: cabinets full of ancient shards of early clay pots and countless finely crafted objects from every century since. It was quiet up there, with only a couple of other visitors, and the halls felt calm and peaceful. I let Willa go at her own pace, not wanting to hurry her, so it was only when we reached the very end of the main gallery that I turned to her and said, 'Surprise.'

We were at the entrance to a small temporary exhibition. Willa looked baffled for a moment, then her eyes moved to the overhead banner, and a look of wonder spread over her face.

'You are kidding me,' she said. I grinned.

'An exhibition of work by eminent contemporary studio potter Christopher Bee,' I read. '*Eminent*. Right here in the British Museum. *No shit*, Dad.'

'Why didn't you tell me? *Bloody hell*, Robyn, that's amazing.'

I followed her round as she peered into each of the cabinets. 'I don't believe it. This lot is basically just like the stuff we were using to *eat* from at your house. No, correction, it's *exactly* the same as the stuff we were eating from, and now it's here, *behind glass*, because it's so flipping good. I had no idea he was so celebrated.'

'*Eminent*,' I said, grinning. 'Check out this cabinet. Dad made this lot that summer you came to stay. These even have titles.'

I pointed at a tall, slender urn that Dad had named *Breathe*, crackle-glazed in bone ash and feldspar, the colour of sun-dried grass. Willa stood so quietly that I couldn't help wondering if she was experiencing the same summer storm of memories that I had when I'd first seen it. Lying in the meadow, looking at the sky. Stars and dogs and worked wood and talking. Swifts. The touch of her hand.

The final cabinet contained his *kintsugi* work. Willa read aloud the little nameplates for each pot: RESTORE, HEAL, MEND.

'Do you remember that day in the studio, and Dad telling us how mending a treasured thing makes it stronger?'

Willa nodded. Her eyes moved to a mounted screen next to the cabinet that showed a time-lapse video of a broken pot being repaired, all the separate pieces gradually growing into a complete vessel. The video had been made using stop motion, so it didn't show my father's hands, which gave the odd impression that the pot was making itself. As soon as it was made, the video went into reverse, and all the pieces came apart again one by one until they became a mass of disconnected shards on a plain white surface.

The pieces were broken. They came together. Then they separated.

They came together. And separated.

Together, apart.

For a long time Willa stood looking at the video. When eventually she turned to me, her face was full of reflection.

'I can't help thinking,' she said, 'that there's something here I should have understood years ago. I –' She stopped. 'Robyn, you are honestly the best person I've ever known. And I was so, so awful to you –'

I touched her arm. 'Let's get coffee,' I said.

'Jamie broke my jug' – Willa gave me a grim look – 'and, yes, before you say anything, I've got all the pieces.'

'So fix it,' I said, smiling. 'How is he?'

'I haven't seen him yet. He got back from SA a couple of days ago, but work's been busy so he's staying at the flat. I'm going there after this. It's *nearly* ready to move into. The bed arrived last week and now we're just waiting for the curtains and a few other things. But Jamie said he'd make do for a few days. I honestly can't wait. We really need that place.'

'God, poor Jamie. How has he found living with your parents? It must have been a bit odd, right?'

'*Really* odd. He seems to get on really well with Dad, though. They're always off somewhere together, drinking, playing golf. I swear he spends more time with Dad than he does with me.'

I went slowly. 'Perhaps he feels he can't say no. Your dad – look, stop me if I'm crossing a line – but the one time I met him, I got the impression that your dad can be a bit – I don't know, maybe quite a *strong* character.'

'You mean he's a bully.'

'I didn't say that.'

Willa chewed on her thumb, looking away. She took a while to answer. Eventually she said, 'He is.' A beat. 'He's less obvious about it these days. Less – physical.'

'*What?* I'd guessed he could be a bit domineering but – *God, Willa* – I never guessed *that*.'

'It stopped a long time ago. It wasn't me. He never touched me, Robyn. Not once. It was –'

'Your mum.'

'Yes. And Laika.'

'*Laika?* Oh, God.'

'Never me.' She blinked, eyes brimming. 'And I've always felt so *awful* about that. Guilty, I mean. Not somehow taking my turn, sharing the load.'

'Why didn't you tell anyone? Why didn't you tell *me*?'

She wiped away the tears, then looked me straight in the eye. 'I was ashamed.'

I held her hand, and for a while we listened to the sounds of the museum: mothers calling to children, the voices of baristas, china cups meeting china saucers, the metallic clatter of a spoon dropping to the floor.

Finally I said, 'Remember at school when I swore I could keep your secrets? That still applies, you know. You can talk to me. You can trust me with anything.'

She gave me a half-smile. 'Anything?'

It was the exact same question she'd asked when I was sixteen and I gave her the exact same reply, 'Anything. I swear.'

She squeezed my hand. 'That means a lot.'

I paused. 'How are you, Willa, really?'

'Okay. I've been grateful to have Mum around. At least I can talk to her about' – she took a deep breath – 'the baby. I never really discuss it with Jamie.'

'You don't?'

'Not really. It's not been particularly easy between us lately, to be honest. And obviously it's different for men.'

'Don't forget, he wanted her too.'

'Yeah, I know. We all did.'

For a long time she seemed somewhere far off, lost in her thoughts. 'It's made me think so much about Mum, what she's been through. At least I've had some sense of closure. That's been the hardest thing for Mum, you know, not knowing what happened to Laika. She lives with it every single day, that awful, *awful* not knowing. Not having a body, not knowing if her child is dead or alive, not having any resolution. Not having a funeral. Not ever being able to say goodbye. We're in a museum dedicated to the importance of all those milestones, loving other people properly, celebrating every point in their lives: birth, death, all of it. Mum can't. She can't heal. She's living her entire life in suspended time.'

I stood up, moved around the table and Willa stood, and I held her.

'You've got to go,' she said.

'I don't have to.'

'You do, I know. But I'll see you tonight, okay? Eight, right?'

I hugged her close. 'You okay?'

'I'm okay. Thank you. It's meant a lot, today. Seeing you, seeing your dad's work up there. It's been – healing. And important. I feel like I get it now, just how much that matters. To mend things. To mend yourself. To *allow* yourself to heal, to move on.' She gave me a small smile. For a long moment we looked at each other. I hugged her again and she turned to go, walking away through the clean light of the museum concourse. Then, as if spun by a thought, she turned back. 'You know, you've always been that for me: a sage or something. A catalyst. The person who changes everything.'

18.
Supper with friends

Willa

I see her. She is sitting at the very same table as me. My sister.

My eyes are fixed on Nate's girlfriend, Claudette. But she's not Claudette. That's *Laika*, my *sister.* But, of course, it can't be. It's impossible. I glance at Jamie, where he sits half-cut with one arm dangling over the back of Robyn's chair. *Lunatic*, he called me, a fucking lunatic for believing that Laika could somehow still be alive. That I would find her. That we would meet.

But he's right. It's not possible. Because Claudette is *French*. She's just someone who looks so much like my sister I want to cry. *It can't be. It can't be.* What would Laika even look like now, twenty-two years older than when I last saw her? Like Claudette, I think. She'd look exactly like Claudette.

It's Laika. It's her.

It can't be.

It's her.

Then she moves back in her seat and my view of her is obscured again by Liv, who is asking us to recall our early memories, and so we go around the table, each of us speaking in turn. My brain is short-circuiting. *It's her.* A story. I need a story. One about me. One Laika would know, so I say I remember being tickled. And that I wet myself. I don't tell them the details: my father's fingers jabbing hard into the flesh of my stomach, my mother's nervous high laugh, Laika's fearful face, my begging him *Stop* as the hot thin yellow stream leaked out of me, over him, soaking into his shirt, seeping into the white sofa. I don't tell them my age either, that I was far too old for something like that. My shame. No, none of that. I just tell them that I remember being tickled, and that I wet myself.

And then Claudette laughs.

Everyone looks at her.

'I'm sorry,' she says. 'I'm sorry, *Weela*, to interrupt your story. I have a little something in my throat.' She taps her chest, just below her clavicle. She makes a short coughing sound – not coughing, in fact, but an imitation of coughing – *hec hec* – to illustrate her point. She looks at me, straight in the eyes. *Is she smiling?* 'I apologize.'

'What about you, Claudette?' Liv says.

'Me?' she says. 'I remember breaking my arm. Oh, and also eating a cake.' She's still holding my gaze. *Cake?*

'Cake?' Jamie asks, smiling broadly. 'Was it a special cake?'

'Yes, very special, a beautiful big cake covered in tiny sugar flowers. It was on a marble shelf. And I was hiding under the shelf, eating the sugar flowers.' She raises her eyebrows at me, and something like little birds flitter around the inside of my chest.

My heart thuds. *It's her. It's Laika.* 'Was it your own birthday?'

'Non,' says Claudette, 'not mine. I was born in March.'

March? She can't mean *March*. It has to be *November*, November the third, Laika's birthday. Because Laika's earliest memory could very probably be about cake, and not any old cake either but rather the exquisite showpiece of my mother's thirtieth on a hot day in July. A cake she'd found in the pantry and smashed.

'And about how old would you say you were?' Liv asks.

'I was six.'

And I was nine. And I should *never*, ever have let that happen.

Liv tells Claudette that she is almost certainly remembering something almost exactly as it occurred. Then she tells Jamie that the memory he recalled is invented and, hammered as he now is, he scoffs, instantly arguing back.

'It's just a load of bollocks,' he says, swigging back the last of the red. To my surprise, Liv says the memory I recalled was fabricated too.

'No,' I say. I look around the table. 'That really happened.' There's *no way* I would have made up a memory of wetting myself. Why would I do that? Claudette holds my eyes for a moment and I think an understanding passes between us that is so unmistakable that I very nearly say *Laika* – but then, flat-eyed and without the smallest hint of recognition, she looks away again and starts talking to *Jamie*. It's not her. What was I thinking? Of course it's not. Sometimes it feels as if my whole adult life has been spent like this: lighting little fires of hope that are just as quickly put out.

'So, Jamie,' Claudette says, turning her gaze towards him and resting her chin on her hand, 'I'm trying, but I can't quite place your accent.'

I see Jamie attempt to sit up a little in his chair. He chuckles, apparently liking her attention, and the warmth returns to his voice. 'Well,' he says, his voice slightly slurred, 'I'm English through and through but I lived in South Africa for a while – ten years, actually, so you might be hearing a hint of that. Have you ever been?' He's in his element now, clearly enjoying himself. 'It's a truly magnificent country.'

'Non.'

'You should try Cape Town. Fantastic city. One of our favourite places.' I look at him sharply, but he doesn't seem to realize what he's just said. I've never even been to South Africa and I've certainly never been to Cape Town. Whoever 'our' refers to, it's definitely not him and me. Which leaves who? *Melissa*, I think. *Great*. The tricky ex-wife.

'But you and Weela live in London now?'

'We have a flat in Brook Green,' Jamie says. 'Very, very nice.'

Now everyone is listening to Jamie: to that slow, languid drawl of the pissed. I try to keep my face impassive, but it's an effort. The heat of shame starts rising up my neck.

'Yah, doer-upper. Total wreck when we got it, s'taken like, fucking, *months*. Cost an arm and a leg.'

I shoot Jamie a look, feeling myself colouring. I don't think I've ever seen him this drunk. Since our little squabble earlier, he's been *throwing* back the wine. Hacked off *and* bladdered: God, I think, that's a pretty toxic combination. Dangerous too. And he's still going strong. I can't keep still. My hands move to my lips, my throat, my chain, and my fingers find the little silver dolphin, tugging it out from underneath my dress, holding it like a talisman.

'Meantime we've had to bunk up with the paterfamilias: Lord and Lady Bryce.' His face makes an odd twitch. 'Yah. In their *massive* pile,' he says. He links his hands behind his head, tipping his chair so far back that it leans against the wall. 'Down on the coast. Fuck, what a place. You should see the security. S'like fucking Fort Knox.'

'Wow,' Liv says, 'what level are we talking, bodyguards and dogs?'

'Not quite' – Jamie makes a lop-sided attempt at a grin – 'but electric gates and a bloody great wall.'

'A wall,' Claudette says. Her voice is cool. 'Is it to stop Weela escaping?' Her eyes flash over to mine.

Jamie seems to find this immensely funny. 'Ha, ha,' he says, 'very good. But no. 'Cos of scumbag intruders.'

'You have a problem with invaders?'

'Yeah, all that lot you Frenchies should be keeping. Immigrant types.'

Dear God, I think, *no*. I can feel my cheeks glowing with embarrassment, no, not just embarrassment, more, a growing sense of horror. I don't think even *he* believes what he's saying. I notice Robyn steeple her fingers, tucking down her chin to form a barrier over her face. In fact, the entire gathering has fallen into an awkward silence, every last one of them. I can almost feel them squirming in their seats.

But Claudette leans in now, her expression bemused. 'You don't think refugees need our help?'

Jamie's eyes make a slow, uncoordinated blink. '*Look*,' he says, 'what you've got to do, *right*, is go to the *crux* of the problem. You've just got to tackle the problems back where they came from. I mean, it's bleeding obvious, right? Letting them all in here doesn't help a thing.'

'Don't you think, *Jamie*,' Claudette asks, her voice low, clear, and with a new level of intensity, 'that the reason refugees choose to undertake terrible, dangerous journeys, often alone, often at great expense, is because they don't have any other choice? You understand, yes, that they're leaving cities thick with poisonous dust, homes reduced to piles of rubble, places where there's no education, no sanitation, no fresh water, no medicine, *nothing at all*.' She leans across the table, holding Jamie's gaze. 'You've seen the news footage, right? All those kids riddled with diseases; babies so malnourished they can't even lift up their heads. We're talking about the completely dispossessed.'

'*Genuine* refugees need help, no one's denying that, and there are clear rules to be followed in those cases. But only a fraction of this lot fall into that category, insignificant numbers. You don't see women and children coming across the Channel, do you? No, they're all young men, the very ones who should be staying at home, building their countries back up, working. But instead they trek over here as economic migrants, looking for an easy life in a country with a generous benefits system.'

'*Yes*, there are women. *Yes*, there are children. And you,' she says, her voice rising now, 'you're going to sit here, or down there, in your tiny village, behind your big wall, and tell me you don't think these people are genuine refugees? That you don't think they have the right to try to make a better life? You should be *ashamed*.' Claudette's head snaps towards mine, her face a picture of disgust. 'And, *Willa*,' she says, 'this is what *you* think?'

No, I think, horrified. *Christ, no.* I open my mouth to tell her but she has already switched her attention back to Jamie, this drunk and belligerent man she knows is directly connected to me. I've got to apologize. I leap to my feet.

I watch a boozy smile spreading across Jamie's face. 'You're a funny girl, Claudette.' He waggles a finger at her, smiling. 'All poise and grace and whatnot, then *bam*. You're kinda like that thing in *Alien* when it rips through the chest of Officer Kane.' He laughs, then adds, 'Yeah, and has anyone ever told you just how English you sound when you get worked up? It's like your *entire* accent disappears. Brilliant. I honestly think you could pass for a Brit.'

Claudette instantly rises from the table, slamming her hands on its surface as her chiffon scarf fills with air, flying open like a frill of lizard skin. 'There is one, single reason why a person would leave their known life, one reason alone. And that one, single reason is that the unknown world is ultimately less terrifying than their actual homes, which are *hell on earth*.' For a second she glares hard at Jamie. Then she says, 'Sod this.'

She snatches a pack of cigarettes from her bag and marches towards the door. But, as she strides past, she slams straight into me, speaking so low and fast I almost miss the words.

'It wasn't *you* who pissed yourself,' she says. 'That was *me*.'

19.

Robber-child

Claudette

'You'll be okay?' Nate says. 'Sorry to abandon you.'

'Don't apologize. I was expecting to amuse myself.'

'I don't think you'll be bored. There's a lot to do in London.'

'I know. I'll be fine.'

'I should be back by five-ish. Six at the latest. I'll let you know if I'm delayed.'

'Nate, stop it.'

J'observe: my boyfriend, his dark eyes and closely cropped head, the taut ligaments at the back of his neck, the beautiful, rounded shape of his skull. We're talking in rapid French. There was a time, years ago, when I spent hours with a voice coach perfecting my accent. Nonetheless, I'd made it a rule to date non-native French speakers and I still stick to that. It would only take the smallest verbal mistake to be outed.

'We're in England now, Nate,' I say in slower, accented English. 'Your 'ome country. I should be talking English while we're 'ere.'

He smiles and switches to English. I like hearing him speak in his native tongue. His accent is an interesting mix of all the places where he'd spent his childhood – mainly a combination of London and New York, with drawn-out words and the odd glottal stop, but I can hear his mum's Irish influence in there too, something softer, a little more lyrical.

'Then tonight we've got supper with my sister and Robyn.'

'I remember.'

'They're good people, you'll like them.' He pulls me to him, tips my chin up and kisses me. 'Where will you start?'

'Right here' – I wave at the tangled sheets strewn across the bed – 'with a little meditation.'

'Okay,' he says, glancing at his watch. 'I'd better go.' He smiles, gives me a long look. 'I love you,' he says.

Nate is a wonderful man. He's easy-going and has an inner joy that bursts out of him at unexpected moments, an enthusiasm for life. He's smart, and talented in ways that he's worked hard to achieve. He has large, animated hands, and he's open and interested in pretty much everything. But, most of all, he's kind. He's a saint compared with me. He takes a genuine interest in other people's lives, and he's so passionate about his work teaching music that he gets tears in his eyes. In another life I'd have wanted to stay with him. By now we'd have started to explore ideas about the future, talked about living together, making a life. He is easy to love.

But that would be another life, not this one. We've been dating for over a year, longer than I've ever dated anyone, and it's already way too risky. I've seen it before. Gradually they start to question why there's a whole bunch of beads missing from the rosary. Then their questions become more angled, and, like sharp little stilettos slipped between the ribs, they find they've killed the thing.

And Nate will do that too in time, I know. I should have ended things ages ago, but somehow I've never quite managed to find the right moment. The truth is, I haven't wanted to. It's like he has a sacred heart, a love for me that shines so brightly it's practically visible, smack bang in the middle of his chest, blasting rays of light in every direction. And he's going to get hurt and there's absolutely nothing I can do about it.

'Okay,' he says, picking up his bag. 'And if you get tired of London and fancy a change of scene, you can always use the car, get out and explore the countryside a bit.'

I hadn't thought of that. Something inside me seems to contract.

'What?' he says. 'You're looking at me oddly.'

'Am I?' I remember myself. '*Oui, bonne idée.* So we keep London to explore together, yes?' He throws me the keys to the ancient 205 that we've borrowed from his aunt, and I catch them in mid-air.

'Don't forget to drive on the left.'

The Peugeot has a sat-nav, and the traffic moves slowly, so it's easy enough to find my way out of the city and on to the A22. In time, I'm driving on smaller roads and passing through pretty villages with greens and traditional pubs. It's a cold, sunless morning in early December. Skeletal winter branches stretch over the road, casting grainy silver light on the car's windscreen, flickering like an old home movie playing without sound.

Eventually, I pull up outside a barrier that bars the entrance to a private road. On a wide grassy verge a large sign reads PRIVATE, below that, RESIDENTS ONLY and below that 5 MPH. I draw in and stop. I think about parking up and walking, but I don't want to draw attention to myself. I'd be the only pedestrian. I'm still thinking through my options when a delivery van pulls up. He punches a code into a mounted keypad, and the barrier opens. And I just follow him in.

I drive slowly, keeping to the five-miles-per-hour limit, peering down each of the long driveways to large houses cushioned from the road by wide green lawns. A lot of them I don't recognize; old houses I once knew have been torn down and replaced by bigger, grander homes in a mishmash of horseshit architecture: I spot mock-Tudor, Edwardian, Regency, even Victorian Gothic. The whole thing reminds me of a job I once had at Disneyland Paris.

I pull up in front of a building site, earth churned up like the spilt guts of roadkill. A completely unnecessary sign announces the building of a new executive home. You couldn't miss the thing: it's only half built yet it already covers almost the entire plot. Behind it, a small tile-hung cottage is caged in by high metal fencing, like it might make a bid to escape. Everywhere signs read KEEP OUT, and sadness wells in my chest. I'd known this place when it was a secret garden, full of old roses and meandering pathways, fruit trees and vegetables. I put the car into gear and drive on.

Further along the road I park up at a pair of ornate gates topped by angled CCTVs with red lights that occasionally blink. On the top of a brick plinth is an engraved slate sign that reads LABURNUM HOUSE. I switch off the engine, step out into the chill day and look through the metal latticework of the gate. A long, gravelled drive loops around a central circle of grass, beyond which is a Georgian-style house with a white stucco façade and stone steps that lead up to a pair of solid oak doors. Off to one side of the house is a large conservatory, with three sets of double doors that lead on to a wide stone terrace; I've seen it before, once, a long time ago, but it's a part of the house I've never actually been inside. Craning my neck to look past towers of rhododendron bushes, I can just about make out the squat outline of a separate building that stands alone in the far left of the garden: the windowless bunker known as the pool house. Main uses: storage for chemicals and badly behaved children. I've been in there.

I find myself wondering if my mother is at home, and the thought makes something like a snake coil around the insides of my gut, a quiet and dangerous need to know if she's in. Or even if she still lives here. I push it away.

I wrap my fingers around one of the gate's fanciful scrolls, and the shock of cold iron whips needles through my palms. I shiver. They're new, as is the high brick wall. I wonder how they might open, say, if you needed to leave in a hurry. Would they just open automatically as you ran towards them? Or would you have to push a button?

So much easier not to have gates at all. Just to walk to the end of the drive, pause and, instead of turning right, as always, as expected, turn left.

And, just like that, as simple as that, it turns out you can leave.

I was wearing my school uniform that morning – a grey plaid kilt, white shirt, house tie and blue blazer. In my bag I had a plum, my grey school jumper, a pencil case, some pads and a book I'd nicked from my mother's bedside table. I was going to school, walking fast. When I got to the end of the drive, I stopped. It was still early and long shadows fell in a kaleidoscope of soft greens across the road. I ran a hand over my hair, and the short stubble bristled under my palm. My head felt strange and fascinating. And cold. I put my bag on the ground, took my jumper out and draped it over my head like a veil. Then I wound the sleeves round my head and tucked them in, making a sort of turban. I picked up my bag.

Further along the road sunlight glanced off the bonnet of a large silver car that was crawling along, edging its way over speed bumps. The road's residents always made a show of sticking to the speed limit, especially if they happened to find themselves in front of a delivery van. It was a point of honour never to hurry anywhere. I could hear wood pigeons.

Behind me came the sound of tyres scrunching on gravel. I

turned to see the builder's van bouncing down my parents' drive and stood to one side to let it pass. The van pulled up next to me, its rear end sitting on the driveway, front end on the road. The builder, Ian Cox, wound down a window.

'You're the Martenwood girl, right?'

'One of them.'

The silver car came to a slow stop on the road. Felicity Williams, a neighbour, sat in the driver's seat. A Shih Tzu sat next to her on the white leather of the passenger seat, its white hair tied in a little red ribbon above its head, revealing uncoordinated, bulbous eyes. From inside the car, they both turned to look at us and I noticed our neighbour's eyes had the same protuberant bulge as her dog's. After a long moment she indicated the partially blocked road with an exaggerated show of exasperation, raising her hands in a slow mime, indicating the van and widening her eyes in disbelief.

'Christ,' Cox muttered, 'you could get a fucking bus through there.' He stuck his van into reverse and a spray of gravel shot up from his tyres as he pulled back on to the drive. Felicity Williams plus dog returned their globular eyes to the empty road, as if the act of driving a car at five miles an hour took every fibre of their joint concentration. The car slowly rolled forward as Felicity Williams moved her head in a slow, deliberate shake, moving not a single hair from its assigned position on the blonde helmet of her head. She appeared to be speaking but it was impossible to hear her. She was hermetically sealed inside her car.

Ian Cox moved his van back alongside me.

'Waiting for your mum?' he asked. He glanced behind him, back up the drive, as if he half expected to see my mother appearing from the house.

I didn't say anything.

'Interesting headgear.'

I looked at the interior of the van, at the folded copy of the *Sun* on the dash, the old coffee cups, crumpled drinks cans and bits of greasy paper that littered the passenger seat.

'Don't say much, do you?' he said. He looked back up the drive. 'All right, then. Tell your mum I'll be at another job today, let the cement set. I've seen your dad.'

His eyes looked me up and down once more, from my grey turban to my black school shoes. I looked at his scruffy grey hair, his chequered red flannel shirt, the thrust of his belly against the steering wheel. He gave me something almost like a smile. I looked back up the drive.

'Sure,' I said.

'I'll be back tomorrow.'

'Sure.'

He gave me one last look. Then he revved up and took off fast down the road, the wheels of the van skidding over its speed bumps, black smoke billowing from the exhaust.

God, I thought, how incredible to have that freedom. To up sticks and go somewhere else for a day. To just drive away. I looked down the empty road. To the right was my known life, the walk that would lead me to a school full of girls who thought I was weird. Now they wouldn't even recognize me. When I'd last seen them, at the end of the summer term, I'd had long hair. And flesh on my bones. The beginning of breasts. Now my uniform hung off me. It didn't fit. Nothing fit. I didn't fit. My entire life didn't fit. I thought about the dull year ahead, the endless routine of classes and bells and homework and organized games. I thought about the half-curious questions my classmates would ask about the state of my hair, the sly, judgemental looks they'd exchange. They wouldn't be unkind, at least, not directly to my face. All of them were *nice* girls, already well versed in ways of dealing with undesirables, and, once they'd satisfied their curiosity, they would simply close the gates of their exclusive friendships, leaving me on the outside. None of them would ever risk talking to me again. Everyone knows weirdness is catching. That's just how it works.

I thought about Willa. She'd be nearly at school by now, walking fast, anxious about being late and seeing her shiny friends again after the long summer break.

I looked back at the house.

This was a life where I didn't belong.

So instead of turning right, I turned left.

I walked down the empty road, slowly. I would take a day out. Just a day. No one would notice. A sickie. I could fill it however I liked. I could lie in the sun and read that book. I started to walk more quickly. I could hear my feet on the tarmac, carrying me along, as if they'd already made the decision to go someplace else by themselves. It was the first day of September, and the day still smelt like summer. I walked through puddles of warm and cool air. Above me, I could hear a bird singing a triumphant rising song, a victory song, that of a blackbird, perhaps. I pulled the jumper-turban off my head. I put my face to the sun.

I kept walking.

I hadn't got a plan. I wondered vaguely if the school would contact my parents if I didn't arrive. Willa would be busy in the sixth form centre. It wouldn't matter to her, and anyway, she wouldn't have a clue if I skipped a day.

In the distance I saw another large car glide out of a driveway and that was the moment I knew, with a clear and absolute certainty, that I didn't want to be caught. Not today.

I nipped on to a pitted grey tarmacked drive and stood inside the deep shadows of an overgrown shrub. The car passed. Then I walked a little further up that drive. I'd always been slightly curious about that house anyway. It had a reputation, a mystery around it. First, it was the only house that couldn't actually be seen from the road, and, second, people said it was genuinely old, or, as my father put it, 'ripe for redevelopment'. Mostly people just called it the cat house.

I went slowly, picking my way along a drive that curved round beds of roses, until, at the last turn, I could see a tile-hung cottage with black metal window frames and thick ropes of ivy climbing up its walls.

I stopped. Standing on the edge of an oak-framed porch was a small elderly woman feeding a whole bunch of cats. There must have been eight or ten of them winding around her legs, their fat tails coiled into question marks, pink mouths open. The woman herself was wearing a tweed skirt, wellingtons and a thick brown jumper. I crept closer, keeping to a deep wall of shadow cast by overgrown plants, until I was near enough to see her fingers digging in a tin with a spoon. Her red knuckles were swollen, and her white hair was tied into a tiny scraggly bun at the back of her head. A black cat with yellow eyes looked me straight in the eyes and hissed. I froze. The old woman didn't look up. A pigeon rose unsteadily from the trees, its papery wings crackling in the morning air.

Once the tins had been emptied, the woman scraped the entire contents of a plate on to the ground too. Then she went inside and pushed shut the door. Keeping to the safety of the undergrowth, I edged my way down the side of her garden, ready to dive under the bushes if I heard a sound. I kept my eyes on the door. Around the back of the house the gardens were divided into a maze of thin grassy pathways. I sat in a patch of sunlight and pulled some dandelions out of a bed of overblown dahlias. For a while I watched a tiny spider sitting quietly in its web. I rolled my blazer into a pillow and lay down. Above me the shifting shapes of the clouds became one thing, then another. I pulled out the book I'd taken from my mother's bedside table. It had sat there for over a year, pristine and untouched since my mother had read the first few pages, declared herself more of a Jilly Cooper sort of girl and switched to *Riders*. I didn't think she'd miss it. It was the cover that had caught my eye: a painting of two women in red robes and white caps dwarfed by a high brick wall. I began the first page.

I didn't have a watch. When the light changed position, I did too. I read on; the book was really good. When I was hungry, I ate the plum. When I needed to pee, I squatted by a bush. I changed my pad and buried the old one in the earth. I slept too – I needed to. I hadn't slept one wink on the Saturday night, curled up on the gritty concrete floor of the pool house. And then, in the middle of the night on the Sunday, I'd woken up with cramps and a strange wetness between my legs. I'd put my hand down and when it came up bloody and I realized I'd finally started my periods, I'd had to creep along the landing and drag Willa out of bed so she could show me where she kept all her sanitary bits.

In the bathroom she washed out my pyjamas while I inspected my hair in the mirror. The cut my father had given me was an absolute shocker, a short, hard-edged, uneven bob with a fringe cut high above my eyes.

'It will grow,' Willa said.

'What, and let him cut it off again? Not a fucking chance. And I'm not having it like this either.' I grabbed the abandoned kitchen shears and held them towards her. 'Cut it off. All of it.'

Willa froze. 'Don't be stupid,' she said, 'you'll be in such shit.'

'If I can't have my hair the way I like it, I don't want any at all. Do it.'

'Dad will kill you.'

I pushed the scissors into her hand. '*Do it.*'

*

Eventually violet-tinted shadows spread cold fingers across the grass, and the pools of sunshine faded into dusk. I put my jumper on, then my blazer, then drew my legs up and tucked my hands under my armpits. I wondered if there might be an old summer house hidden somewhere, or an unlocked shed. I wondered what time it was. I thought about going home. I thought about being a fly, letting myself in through an open window and landing on a wall, seeing my mother ask my sister if she'd seen me, calling the school, listening to its out-of-hours message; perhaps she'd call her friends. She'd worry. She'd have to tell my father. I thought about the bruises on my arms, their shifting edges and deepening blooms of colour. Becoming one thing, then another.

I was cold, but it was thirst that got me in the end. Eventually I picked up my things and, keeping low, walked around the garden. I needed water – a hosepipe or an outside tap would do. But, as I neared the house, the front door opened and the old woman came out. I froze: she *had* to have seen me. Wearing slippers now, she made slow, unsteady steps towards a bird table with a tub of seeds and a handful of bread, and in the hazy light she walked straight past me. I'm already shapeshifting, I thought, into something else, a shadow, perhaps. A ghost. But the woman had her back to me now and the front door was open and, like some invisible robber-child, I slipped inside.

The dim, panelled hallway was hung with portraits, and ahead of me was a dark oak staircase. The first door on my right opened on to a small sitting room. Opposite an old TV was a deep green velvet sofa with a Chinese silk scarf thrown across its back and orange crocheted cushions; the entire room was stuffed full of books, some on shelves, others piled in great stacks on the floor. A tawny cat turned pale yellow eyes on me, and then opened its pink mouth into a yawn, showing small, white, pointed teeth. A carriage clock sat on a mantle above a tiled fireplace. It read 8.30, later than I'd thought. A small electric fire sat on a slate bed, two of its bars burning a soft red.

At the end of the hallway was a small kitchen with a black metal range and Formica units. A radio and pots of herbs sat on a window ledge, beneath which was a stained metal sink. *Water.* I had to be quick. I found a mug, turned on the tap and drank three lots in quick succession. There had to be a tea towel somewhere. I opened another door and found a pantry with shelves of cat food and several long wooden trays filled with onions, carrots, potatoes, apples, tomatoes and pears. There were jars of walnuts and a large metal sieve filled with fat green pods. I looked at the door. Only now I realized I wasn't just thirsty, I was hungry too. How bad was it to steal from an elderly lady? *Bad*. But still, I helped myself to a pear, and then, with another quick glance at the door, stuffed handfuls of the bright green pods into my blazer pocket.

'Elisabeth?'

I froze, my guilty thieving fingers still gripping the stolen peas, and moved behind the door, willing every molecule in my body to freeze, painfully aware of each too loud breath.

'Elisabeth?' A thin voice shaking with age, or hesitation. 'Are you here?'

Then the plaintive mewing of a cat.

'Well, girls,' she said, 'Elisabeth was here. There's her mug on the draining board, look. Elisabeth was here. And now she's gone. And she didn't even make me a cup of tea. She didn't even say hello.'

I should go, I thought. Right now, before she comes into the pantry, with its half-open door. I could hear the old lady moving around the kitchen, the chink of china, the opening and closing of the fridge door, her shuffling steps. Then, after a while, silence.

I looked through the crack of the door. There was no one in the kitchen. Slowly, I slipped my feet out of my shoes and held them in one hand. I moved silently into the kitchen. I crept back into the hallway where the portraits continued to frown at my shady behaviour. The door to the sitting room was open, and the TV cast an oblong of blue light across the hallway floor. The old woman would probably be sitting on the sofa in full view of the door. There was *no way* I could risk going past. I could scare her to death. She could just drop dead of a heart attack, right there. There was no way out. I looked up at the creaky-looking stairs. I crept back into the kitchen.

There was still one other door to try. I turned the handle and found myself in a cool tiled hallway where a back door led out to the garden and, as quietly as I could, I tried turning the handle. Locked. To my left was another, much narrower, set of stairs. Moving slowly and freezing each time they creaked, I made my way upstairs. At the top was a pink-carpeted landing with dark oak doors. I opened the first one and found myself in what had to be the old lady's bedroom, with a small double bed covered with a crocheted coverlet. An ornate free-standing wardrobe stood in one corner, and, in another, an armchair unholstered in pale pink linen. Under the window was a dressing table with a hairbrush and a few bits of jewellery: brooches, earrings, strings of cut-glass beads. I shut the door again and moved as quietly as I could down the landing.

Next was a small pink bathroom, then a small room with steeply angled eaves piled high with boxes, and finally a little room with a single bed with a padded silk quilt. The walls had paper speckled with tiny yellow flowers, and there was a small window that overlooked the curve of the drive. I sat on the bed. I was so hungry. I picked a bright green pod out of my pocket, ran a nail along its pale seam and watched it spring open, revealing a line of perfect peas. I picked one out with my fingers and put it on my tongue, rolling it around my mouth before biting down. It was, I thought, perhaps the loveliest thing I'd eaten in my entire life. It was dark outside now. I lay down, tucking myself under the quilt, cocooned in a mattress that was deep and old and soft. Outside I could hear the wavering call of an owl.

Just one night, I thought. Then I'll go home.

I closed my eyes.

I thought, I am going to be in such deep shit.

It was thirteen hours since I'd left home.

Five hours since I should have arrived back.

Nineteen hours since I got my first period.

And fourteen hours since my father had come into my bedroom on the Monday morning. Everyone else was up. From the garden I could hear banging, hollering, the noise of a truck pumping out concrete. Willa had already left for school, and I'd spotted my mother through my bedroom window, walking rapidly down the drive with a large bunch of flowers. She'd be going to the neighbours' house, I imagined, the bouquet intended as some sort of compensation for their smashed-in windows. I wasn't late. I still had plenty of time to get to school. I just wasn't in a hurry. I stood in front of my mirror and inspected my head. I was pleased with the result. Willa had done a great job. The ragged bob my father had given me had gone. *All* of it had gone. A couple of dark tufts stood upright in small clumps. In other parts the pale skin of my skull showed through. I looked like a baby chimp.

I didn't hear my father coming until he stopped short in my doorway, 'What in the hell?' He came closer. 'Jesus Christ, you stupid bloody little cunt. How are you going to explain that to your school?'

'You gave me a haircut, remember?'

'Not *that* one. You lying little bitch.'

He made a swipe for me. I ducked, feeling a small triumphant bolt of joy whip through my heart: *No hair to grab now.* He came at me again. This time his fingers found my silver necklace and he yanked it hard. I felt the chain snap and the whole thing came away in his hand. He dropped it on the floor.

'That's mine,' I said, bending towards where my little silver dolphin lay glinting on the rug. But before I could pick it up my father gripped my wrist and jerked me upright. I looked him straight in the eyes. 'Careful you don't break it,' I said, 'again.'

That's all it took. With both hands he slammed me against the wall. My head whacked the plaster and he put his face so close to mine I could feel the heat of his breath. 'This family is sick of your wacko behaviour, Laika,' he said. 'Me, your mother, Willa, all of us. You think you've got all the answers, don't you? Making out you're better than the rest of us, prancing around like some little tart, spouting off.'

'*What?*'

He let go of my arm and jabbed me hard on my breastbone.

'Wait till you get out into the real world, find out then what happens to smartass little sluts.'

I righted myself, took a moment, then shoved him back as hard as I could and, before he could come at me again, I grabbed my bag and ran.

'How did you get in?'

I opened my eyes. The old woman was standing over me, holding something, a folded towel. *Shit.*

I looked towards the window. Through a small crack between the curtains I could see the sky was already a pale grey. I looked back at the woman. My brain was playing catch-up. I swallowed. I opened my mouth.

I said, 'Sorry.'

I sat up a little, propping myself on one elbow.

'When did you get here?' the woman said.

'Um,' I said, 'last night. Just last night. I mean, only last night. What I mean is, I've only been here one night.'

I sat up a bit more. Tiny deltas of lines ran from the corners of the old woman's eyes, skirted the beak of her nose and dipped into the hollows of her cheeks. Her hair was white and as light and fine as spider's silk. She looked worried.

I said, 'I'm so sorry. I didn't mean to –' I pulled myself fully upright. I said, 'I can go.'

She smiled and the rivers of lines lifted. 'But, darling,' she said, 'you've only just arrived, and I've been waiting so long.'

She sat on the edge of the bed and picked up my hand. Hers was as small and light as a child's and clouded with blooms of pink and brown skin, under which the blue lines of her veins draped in knotty threads over bird-like bones. I sat very still.

'They hurt you,' she said, examining my wrist. Her hands worked their way up my arm, turning it gently to examine its deep purple bruises. She looked up and met my eyes. With her other hand she leant forward and touched my cheek, then ran a finger along the edge of my shorn head. 'They hurt you.'

Her eyes, red-rimmed and wet, moved between the two of mine.

She said, 'But you're here now. And you'd better get up because they bring the lunch so early.'

She patted my hand. Then she left.

I edged my legs out of the quilt and sat on the side of the bed. I was still fully dressed. The old lady had left the towel on the bottom of my bed. On top of it was a toothbrush, still in its plastic wrapper. I got to my feet and remade the bed, trying to make it look the same as when I'd arrived. Then I stuck my head round the door. The landing was empty. I walked on tiptoes to the bathroom. I sat on the loo and looked at my pad. Now there was only a small amount of blood on it. I wrapped the thing in wads of paper and stuffed it deep into the bin. Now I had to flush the toilet, a sound that was going to be too loud, too real. I stopped, my hand hovering above the handle. I looked in the mirror and my dumb face looked back. I brushed my teeth. Then I took some more paper and dried the sink. I would need to leave everything exactly as it was. That was important.

Okay, I thought. And now I'm leaving. I flushed the loo, grimacing at the sound. I went back to the little room and picked up my school bag. I walked slowly down the main staircase, running my hand along the smooth wood of the dark banister. I could see the front door ahead of me. I thought, *I'll just go*. Then I thought, okay, no, first of all I'll say goodbye. And thank you. And then I'll go.

I stood, listening. Other than a slow-ticking clock, the house was quiet. I took the last few steps down the stairs and stopped. I turned towards the kitchen.

The old lady was standing by the table and didn't seem to notice me at all. She was fumbling with a metal tin opener, attempting to get it to grip on to a tin of cat food, the thickened knuckles of her fingers trembling with the effort. On the kitchen table were three more tins. I watched her for a moment.

'Here,' I said, 'let me.'

She let me take the tin from her hands and I opened the lid. Then I did the other ones and helped her to carry all of them out to the porch, where the cats were waiting. I helped her to feed them. It was still early, after all. I wasn't in a particular hurry.

I thought, I'll go, just now.

I said, 'Is there anything that I can do for you? I mean, anything you need doing?'

'Well,' she said, 'I could really do with a cup of tea.'

I boiled the kettle and then we sat across the kitchen table from each other, our hands wrapped around matching brown mugs patterned with orange flowers.

'I can't begin to tell you, dear,' she said, 'how nice this is.'

I smiled. 'Have you lived here for a long time?'

'Yes,' she said, 'I think so.'

Her eyes moved into the distance, and for a long time she didn't say a thing. Eventually she said, 'Well, this is nice.'

We were still sitting there, both of us, at the table, when I heard a car pull up. *Shit*, I thought. My ears felt hot with listening. Then I thought, perhaps it's just the postman, but, before I knew it, the front door was being pushed open.

'Hello,' a woman's voice called. 'Mrs Laschamp.'

There were heavy footsteps in the hallway. I looked at the old lady, then at the kitchen door. Then I jumped out of my seat and dashed into the pantry. I held my breath.

'All right? Here's your lunch, then. I'll put it on the side.' The voice was very loud. 'It's Tuesday today, innit, Mrs Laschamp? So it's pork. You've got a mushroom sauce and that there looks like mushy peas.'

I put an eye to the crack of the pantry door. I could see the old lady still sitting at the kitchen table, while a large woman in a plastic apron unloaded a plastic bag of groceries. I could see the two mugs on the kitchen table, and, tucked just under one chair, my school bag.

'Then there's a nice pink blancmange for your pudding, and some cheese and biscuits to save for your tea. Do you want to eat this now, or save it for a bit?'

'I think I'll have it later.'

'D'you want me to make you a cup of tea before I go?'

'I've just had one, thank you, dear.'

'I've got it down you're not meant to use the kettle, Mrs Laschamp,' the woman said. 'We don't want you getting a nasty burn.'

'Somebody made it for me.'

'That's nice.'

'I have a visitor.'

'Did you?'

'My sister.'

'That's nice. Where's she based, then?'

'I haven't asked her yet.'

'That's nice. I'll just take yesterday's plate, shall I?' Through the crack in the door I could see the woman checking her watch.

'Thank you, dear.'

'Right. That's me done. That your list? I'll be off.'

I heard the woman's heavy footsteps retreating down the hallway, the door closing, then the sound of a car turning in the drive. Then silence.

I came out of the pantry. On the draining board sat a plate on which a few gristly-looking lumps floated in an oily puddle of grey sauce, alongside a thick scoop of pond-green mush. There was also a flaccid pink dessert in a miniature plastic bowl, a single slither of yellow cheese and two plastic-wrapped crackers. I looked at the clock on the wall. It wasn't even nine o'clock.

'Is this okay?' I said. 'I mean, does it actually taste all right?'

Mrs Laschamp smiled. 'No, dear,' she said. 'It's completely inedible. I give it to the cats.'

'So what do you eat?' I said.

She gave me a resigned look.

I said, 'You've got vegetables in the pantry.'

'I grow those.'

'You could make a vegetable soup.'

The old woman raised her small red hands and held them aloft in the air. They fluttered like prayer flags.

'Jazz hands,' she said. A smile rolled over her face like a wave through quiet water, lifting the corners of her mouth.

I said, 'I can probably make soup.'

'Well, then,' she said, 'if you did that, we could both have soup.'

All right, then, I thought, first I'll make some soup. Then I'll go.

I made a sort of minestrone, adding dried pasta for bulk. It took a while to clean and chop the vegetables, to sauté them in oil, then to heat the whole thing through. Mrs Laschamp sat at the table and talked to me. She told me her husband, Ted, had died five years before. She told me she'd been born in Germany, then she'd moved to France when she was a small girl, then she'd returned to Germany, which, she said, had not been a good time to go back. She'd come to England after the war.

Later we sat in the garden together. I told her about the book I was reading. She said it sounded very good, and perhaps I would be so kind as to read it for her? She loved a good story, but her eyes weren't so good any more.

I said, 'I can if you want, but there's a bit in the bedroom you might not like, and sometimes she uses the *f* word.'

'Darling girl,' Mrs Laschamp said, 'I wasn't born yesterday.'

So then I started *The Handmaid's Tale* again, from the beginning.

We ate the soup in the late afternoon, and she told me it was the best one she'd ever had.

I thought I'd better do the washing-up and clean the kitchen before I went. After that we sat in the sitting room and watched a little TV. She gave me a toffee from a box she kept under the sofa.

'I'm not really meant to have them,' she said. 'I have to hide them from Ted's niece.'

Maybe, I thought, I'll just stay one more night, then I'll go. I didn't want to appear rude. I hadn't finished reading her the book.

*

I was better prepared for visitors after that. The next day, and in the following days, as soon as I heard a car in the drive, I disappeared up the back stairs and lay flat on the carpet of the landing until the woman in the plastic apron had finished and gone again. I never had to wait very long. Five minutes, max.

And we got into a bit of a routine, Mrs Laschamp and me. I cooked. I read her the book. Then I read her other books. I cleared the veg patch and pulled up hundreds of potatoes. She taught me how to prep things for freezing and bottling. We talked. Her mind worked in interesting ways, and I liked that. It was a bit like a radio being tuned, moving between the stations. One moment she'd be talking about one thing, then she'd stop, and when she began again she might be on a completely different wavelength. Sometimes she spoke to me in other languages. I'd studied French at school, so I was okay with that, but when she spoke in German I'd just nod and smile until she switched back into English.

In the evenings we watched TV. Mrs Laschamp especially liked nature programmes and *World in Action*, but, on my fifth evening there, we watched the news. I was the second item. I felt the insides of my ears prickling. I kept very still on the sofa, looking straight ahead, not looking at Mrs Laschamp at all. Mrs Laschamp kept her eyes on the TV too.

Busted, I thought.

A photo of me filled the screen while the newsreader introduced the piece. It had been taken at the start of the summer, when I'd had long hair and a fringe that covered my eyes. The blood was rushing in my ears so loudly it was almost impossible to hear. The theory was that I'd been abducted. They named my town, my school, my road. They showed a photo of a white van. They said a 46-year-old man was helping them with their enquiries.

A 46-year-old man? Who was that, then? My father was in his fifties.

They'd find me soon enough, just as soon as they worked out I'd run away. Or perhaps the woman in the plastic apron might spot something was out of place first, realize there was an impostor in the house, perhaps someone holding the old lady hostage. I imagined helicopters overhead, searchlights trained on the house, armed police bursting in through the door shouting *Clear* and then shooting me in the head before they bundled the old lady off to safety.

At the end of the news, Mrs Laschamp switched off the TV. I waited for her to say something. She opened her mouth and sighed. She shook her head. She gave me a long searching look.

'Would you care for a toffee?' she said.

It took another three days for the police to visit the house. They arrived when the Apron was delivering the lunch, so I was already upstairs.

There were two voices, a man's and a woman's. I strained my ears to hear.

The policewoman spoke first. 'It's just routine. We're speaking to all the neighbours. People are often convinced they haven't seen anything and then we show them a photo and – hey, presto – it all comes flooding back.'

'This one?' Mrs Laschamp said.

There was a long silence.

'Laika Martenwood. Laburnum House.'

'I see.'

The Apron joined them at the door. 'Dreadful business that,' she said. 'I thought you had someone in custody.'

'And you are –'

'Carol Atkinson. A-T-K-I-N-S-O-N. Mrs. That's it. This here is Mrs Laschamp. Elfrieda.'

'And you live here, Mrs Atkinson?'

'Me? Lord, no,' she laughed. 'I'm from an agency. I do mornings. I do her personal care, her cleaning, washing, help her with her bath, anything she needs doing, really. Bring her meals and that. Get her basics in, sort her meds. Bit of cooking. Keep her company mostly. Read to her. Anything what needs doing. All of it. You know.'

'And you're here every day?'

'That's right, every day, like clockwork.'

'And you drive here?'

'Yes, yes, I've got a little car. That one. The yellow one. The Fiat.'

'And your hours?'

'That depends on what needs doing. I get here, well, eight, maybe, nine, and then I'm off later, you know, two o'clock, one-ish sometimes, perhaps.'

'No,' Mrs Laschamp said, 'I don't think so.'

'Yes, that's right, isn't it, Mrs Laschamp? I do your mornings.' She lowered her voice to a stage whisper. 'She gets a bit confused, you know.'

'So you were perhaps driving along this road at approximately seven forty-five on Monday, the first of September?'

'Well, yes,' the Apron said. 'I suppose I would have been.'

'It's possible, then, that you saw a young female walking along the road, heading west, towards town?'

'Laika Martenwood. Lord, no. I'd definitely remember. No, there weren't nobody when I came along. I'd have noticed. It would stand out, you see. You never see anyone walking round here.'

'Or any vehicles, a white van perhaps?'

'No, nothing.'

'Mrs Laschamp,' the man's voice, 'is it possible you've seen this girl?'

'Don't ask her. She don't go out much, do you, Mrs Laschamp? She don't see nobody 'cept me.'

'And Elisabeth.'

'What's that, Mrs Laschamp?'

'Elisabeth. My sister.'

'Your sister, Mrs Laschamp?'

'My sister came. In the morning.'

'In the morning?' The man's voice.

A brief hesitation, then the Apron's voice again. 'In the *morning*. Yes, that's right. I remember now. She had a brief catch-up with her sister a few days ago *in the morning*, when I was here, doing my hours. I'd forgotten. *Elisabeth*. Frieda's *sister.* That's right. Lovely lady.'

'Is this Elisabeth?' Mrs Laschamp said. I angled my head slightly to look through a gap in the banisters. I could see Mrs Laschamp tapping a finger on a photograph. Time's up, I thought. I'll get my bag.

'See what I mean?' the Apron said. 'She gets awful confused.' She raised her voice as she spoke to Mrs Laschamp. 'Your sister's, what, about your age, I'd say, give or take, yes? And that there's the missing girl, the one what's been on the news. The one what's been kidnapped by that Cox bloke, whatsisname, Ian Cox. The builder.'

'Mr Cox has been released, Mrs Atkinson.'

'Has he now?'

'Without charge.'

'That can't be right. You sure?'

There was a moment of silence.

'Well,' the policeman said, 'thank you both for your time. Do please let us know if you see anything.'

'We certainly will,' the Apron said, 'don't you worry about that.'

*

About a month later, a new person turned up. It was the middle of the afternoon. The bell went, then the knocker. Then I heard the letter-box opening. I lay flat on the carpet at the top of the stairs.

'You in there, Frieda?' a voice said. 'It's me, Linda.'

Frieda opened the door.

'How've you been? It's me, *Linda*, Ted's *niece*.' Just like the Apron, this visitor pronounced each word clearly, as if she were talking to an imbecile. I felt a bit cross. I thought, she's not deaf, you know. Or stupid.

'Hello,' Frieda said.

'You going to let me in?'

Footsteps. I angled my head so I could see this Linda through a gap in the banisters. She was short, with a small turned-up nose and thin blonde hair in a bob.

'This is a nice surprise. You look well,' Frieda said. 'Would you like tea, perhaps? Or a coffee? Some nice biscuits, all homemade?'

'Yeah, you're all right. I'm not staying. Just thought I'd better check up on you, what with all that trouble that's gone on round here.'

'I'm fine, dear.'

'Amazing, the stuff that can happen on your doorstep.'

'Is it?'

'Yeah. Unbelievable. Anyway. They didn't take *you*, then.' I saw the woman looking around, her hands on her hips. 'God,' she said, almost to herself, 'so much junk.'

'How are you keeping, dear?' Frieda said. 'Now remind me, are you still at the shop?'

'I'll get Steve round sometime, give you a hand clearing up.'

'I'm perfectly fine, thank you, Linda.'

'You can't live like this, Frieda. How d'you know where all the important stuff is?'

'Important stuff?'

'Your papers and stuff. Where d'you keep everything? Your will, for instance? Where d'you keep that?'

'It's all tucked away, dear. And you needn't worry about that. I've always said, when my time comes, I'll always look after my family. Would you like a biscuit?'

'No, thanks. How d'you cope?'

'I have help.'

'That exorbitant home help.'

'And Elisabeth.'

'Elisabeth?'

'My Elisabeth. Elisabeth Oppenheimer.'

'Who's that, then?'

'My sister.'

'I don't think so, Frieda.'

'What was that?'

'I said, I don't think it could have been your sister, Frieda.' She raised her voice. 'It can't have been Elisabeth.' Then, practically shouting, *'You haven't got a sister, Frieda.* You're *confused.'*

'I do. I was talking to her just this morning.'

'Bloody Nora, really?' Linda said. *'You're mixed up.'*

'I don't think I am.'

'Okay, Frieda. I've got to go.'

'Always in such a hurry. Next time you visit, could you perhaps bring me a new toothbrush? I like to keep a spare. Actually, now I think of it, could you please bring two?'

'Two? What d'you need two for? God, never mind. Give us a tenner, then.'

'Goodness, do they really cost that much?'

'There's petrol too, though, isn't there? To get to the shops.'

She waited in silence while Frieda located and rummaged around in her bag.

'All right, dear. Well, thank you for visiting. It's always nice to have company.'

I knew it was wicked, living with Frieda. I tried telling myself that I was helping her, that what we had was a mutual arrangement, which somehow made it okay. But, of course, it wasn't. I was bad. I was as bad as Linda. Probably worse. Where did moving in uninvited and unannounced with a little old lady fit on a rising scale of criminal activity? Was it somewhere between trespassing and fare dodging, or shoplifting and petty theft? Or was it even worse? What would they do me for? Fraud, I thought. Deception, impersonation, theft.

The news reports about me appeared less often. After about two months, they stopped altogether. I thought, I can't be that hard to find, can I? Have they just given up? I missed my mother. I missed Willa too, painfully. I missed lying together in the garden plotting out our futures, swimming, playing tennis, even all that nutty advice she'd try to ram down my throat. And I worried about them. How they'd be doing, how they were coping. If they were worried or scared. I imagined walking back along the road and going home, sitting at the kitchen table as if nothing had happened. What if they blamed Frieda? I could fake amnesia perhaps. Say I'd been taken by aliens or just point-blank refuse to answer any questions. Say I didn't know.

I wasn't going to stay away forever. Just a little bit longer, to make my point. Meanwhile, I was happier than I'd been in a long time. I felt safe. And I genuinely liked Frieda. She was good company, I liked the ever changing cloud of her mind, the fluid way it moved and shifted between ideas. Sometimes she'd want to discuss something she'd seen on the news, ask questions and debate my answers; then at other times she'd tell me the same thing three times in a row. Sometimes she talked about her life, her childhood in Munich, her parents, her school, her first ever cat, Petit Chou. She could be outrageously funny one minute and lose track of what she was saying the next. And that was okay too: it was just a different way of thinking. It was like her brain was a spiderweb with a whole bunch of broken threads: if she walked down one and found nothing there, she just reversed and trotted off down a different strand. A conversation with her wasn't always linear, but it all made sense; you just had to stay with her, walk with her, follow wherever she wanted to go. She only ever seemed *genuinely* confused when there were other people about. Sometimes I even wondered if she were putting it on.

She did sometimes call me Elisabeth, but when she did that I pretended I hadn't noticed. But still, sometimes I slipped on Elisabeth for size. I ran the name around my mouth. She felt older than me, wiser, neater, less of a mess. A better person than me. I looked in the mirror and mouthed *Elisabeth* at my reflection. It was such an elegant name, all those syllables. And I didn't want to embarrass Frieda by correcting her. So I never said *Laika, my name's Laika*. And that wasn't even a lie. I'd seen the news. Everyone knew it: Laika had gone.

20.
Memory box

Claudette

Then it was November the third. My birthday. I didn't tell Frieda that, of course. The day was thick with gunmetal clouds and far too cold to walk around the garden, so in the afternoon she and I went upstairs and sat together in the room full of boxes, Frieda on a chair and me cross-legged on the floor. She wanted help finding something, she said. She directed from the chair as I sorted through boxes of clothing, holding up shirts, jumpers, dresses, old ski trousers, shoes, things she'd once loved, she said, things that at one time she'd never wanted to let go. Things she said would fit me.

It was photographs she was after. First, she showed me the photos of her wedding to Ted in Aldershot, holding hands, both of them dark-eyed and smiling.

Her eyes grew soft. 'He was a lovely man,' she said, 'a violinist. He helped me, you know. He got me out. Then we came here and got married and I became Elfrieda Laschamp. Before that, I was Elfrieda Oppenheimer.'

'Did you have children?' I said.

The moment it was out of my mouth, I knew I'd asked the wrong thing. She went still for a bit, her eyes moving somewhere distant.

'No,' she said. 'We wanted them, both of us. But my body

wouldn't cooperate. It had some healing to do. I had some healing to do. And by then it was too late.'

She examined each photograph, holding them up close to her nose. There was Ted playing a violin, Frieda in a polka-dot bikini, Frieda and Ted in a boat on a lake.

Eventually she found the one she was looking for.

'That's her,' she said at last.

She passed me a photograph of a young girl on a beach, a girl my age, perhaps, with dark eyes and long hair, blowing bubbles through a metal ring on a stick.

'That's Elisabeth.'

'She's beautiful,' I said.

'Yes.'

She passed me the photograph, and I could instantly see the likeness to Frieda in the shape of her cheekbones, her lips, her brow. It must have been a warm day. The light touched her shoulders. The stream of watery bubbles hung glistening in the air.

'I took that photo,' Frieda said. 'It was one of those perfect days, the ones you hang on to for the rest of your life.'

'It shouldn't be here, stuck away in a box.'

'I think you're right. I'll keep it with me from now on.'

She went quiet for a few moments, lost in her own thoughts.

'Now, then,' she said, 'd'you think you can move that thing?' She pointed at a heavy wooden chest next to the wall. 'You'll have to move those boxes first. Can you lift them? No? Well, just shove them, then. That's it. Clear that space by the wall.'

I followed her instructions, even though I couldn't see the point. There was nothing there but a wide section of skirting board.

'That's it. Now put your fingers under there, yes, that big bit of wood, and pull.'

'Pull? It's solid.'

'You'll have to work your fingers under. There. That's right, try again.'

The next time the board came away in my hand, revealing a small crawl space hidden in the eaves. It looked like a triangular-shaped coffin, with hard boards below and a steeply sloping ceiling. It was probably just about large enough to contain a small adult, lying flat.

'I had Ted make it for me,' Frieda said. 'Turn that panel over. See on the back? Once you're inside, you use those handles to pull the board back into place. There's two little wooden swivels too, so it can lock from the inside. There should be a light switch somewhere, so you can read – well, there was a light once, I don't know if it still works. I used to keep a pillow in there, and a blanket. It was all perfectly comfortable.'

I peered into the claustrophobic hole.

'Did you ever – *use* it?'

'I never needed to, not properly. But Ted made it for me, and it was just nice to know it was there. We all need a safe space. Well, that was mine. Put your hand to the right now, will you? Have a feel around – can you find anything?'

I lay flat on my stomach and poked around until my fingers touched something angular and hard.

'A box, I think, yep, a box. There's a box.'

'Good. Bring it out.'

I pulled out a box the size of a thick hardback book and passed it up to Frieda. She drew a wavering line through the grey dust on its surface, revealing a glossy stream of chestnut-coloured leather. Then she opened the lid and pulled out a creased black-and-white photograph of two serious-looking girls with deep, pool-like gazes.

'This was us,' she said. 'It's the only one I've got of us together.' For a long time she sat in silence. Then she ran a finger over the faces and put it to one side. She turned again to the box in her lap, picking out things and holding them out for me to see: a fabulous necklace with diamond clusters, a bracelet strung with sapphires, a gold watch.

'Wow,' I said, 'that's one serious box of treasure.'

'It is,' she said. In a quiet voice she added, 'And I'd have given the entire lot of it in exchange for a ticket for Elisabeth.'

For a while she stared open-eyed at the wall. Then she seemed to gather herself. She held up a pair of pear-shaped emerald earrings, each one topped by a huge diamond stud.

'These were my favourites,' she said. 'Ted gave them to me for our wedding.'

'They're beautiful,' I said. 'Put them on.'

'No,' she said, 'I can't wear these now. Look at my earlobes. They'd look ridiculous on an old lady. You put them on. Go on.'

I held one up to my ear.

'There's a little mirror in that box,' she said. 'Can you see it?'

'Yup.'

'Now, then, what do you think?'

'They're beautiful.'

'You have them.'

'Me? No.'

'Go on. I'd like you to have them.'

'No,' I said, 'really, Frieda. I can't do that. They're yours.'

'There's no one else I want to give them to.'

'No,' I said. 'Thank you. Really, I couldn't.' I placed them in the box, pushing them back into their bed of old red velvet.

'In which case,' she said, 'perhaps you'd be so kind as to put that box back where you found it. Put this photo on top too, please, I can't lose that.' I placed the photo of the two girls on top and closed the lid before I pushed the box back inside the hole, under the eaves. She watched me put the panel back in place and it disappeared seamlessly into the wall. 'One day I fully intend to shut myself in there and that will be it.'

'Don't say that.'

'I didn't say *today*.'

'You shouldn't –'

'What? Acknowledge I'm going to die? Sweet girl, we all have to do that.' She fixed her gaze on me and I noticed the way her irises changed from brown to grey where they met the whites of her eyes, like quiet water lapping on a beach. Then she turned back to the pile of photographs in her lap, lifting each one with trembling fingers, to examine close up.

'Did Elisabeth get out?' I said.

The atlas of lines on her face folded and dipped.

'No,' she said, 'she didn't.'

'I'm sorry,' I said, 'I'm so, so sorry.'

After a while she looked up. She said, 'You're that girl, aren't you?' I didn't reply. I felt as if a glistening bubble was about to burst inside my chest. 'The one from the news. The one that disappeared.'

Shame warmed my cheeks. I felt the blood in my ears. She bent down and touched the edge of my hair, still short but no longer patchy. I looked up at her.

'Do you want me to go?'

She looked at the window, where rain had started to lash against the pane. For the longest time she looked into the dark.

'I didn't have a plan. I didn't know what I was doing,' I said.

'People *always* know what they're doing,' she said, her voice firm. 'Don't let anyone ever tell you any different.' I held her eyes. 'There's been an almighty manhunt for you, you know.'

I felt my cheeks reddening.

'And, in the meantime, I've been busy wondering whether I'll be going to jail for harbouring an escaped fugitive, or kidnap.'

'I never thought about it like that,' I said. 'I don't know how to explain.'

'You must have had your reasons. But' – she tipped her head sideways like a bird – 'there'll be people missing you. People worried sick.'

I knew that. I thought about them all the time. I thought about Willa, my mother, her gentle grey eyes. But each time I thought about them, I saw my father too, looming up behind, his iron breath on my face; I saw myself being smacked, slapped, manhandled, my head cracking against the wall.

'Don't think you can stay here indefinitely, hiding away. No – stop – I managed perfectly well until you came along, thank you. Believe me, I can look after myself. And I won't be around forever.' She tapped her chest. 'Dodgy ticker. Or is it a dicky todger?' Her lips lifted and her eyebrows rose into thin half-moons. 'Now which one is it? I always get those two mixed up.'

Her eyes were bright and full of amusement. She waited. I said, 'I think you mean the first.'

Her face opened into a smile, then grew serious again. 'The truth is, I've had enough. I know that's hard for a young thing like you to hear. People your age don't like to think about the end. But life hasn't been the same for me, since I lost Ted.' She lapsed into silence. After a while, she said, 'You'll meet people you'll always wish you could have walked with a little longer. You'll know when you meet them. You hold on to them fast. They're the important ones.' She went very quiet, and I sat watching her, her eyes fixed somewhere in the past. 'This was always going to be fleeting, wasn't it? Of course it was, Laika. Breathing space, I suppose you could say. Don't think I say this lightly; I've rather enjoyed these past two months. But you'll need to go your own way soon enough, and I will go mine.'

That was the first, and, as it turned out, the only time she ever called me Laika, and my face must have registered the shock because she reached for my hand. 'You've already made hard choices, getting yourself this far, and, when you're ready, you're going to have to make some more. You have a life to live.' I wanted to say something, but I thought I might cry. She took my hand and squeezed it tight. 'Some of life's most important journeys you have to take on your own. Certainly the hardest ones. You just have to be brave.'

Ted's niece, Linda, came back. She brought with her a sour-faced man in a T-shirt that had FUZZY BASTARDS written across the front. Silent and hidden at the top of the stairs, I watched them talking to Frieda.

'Remember Steve?'

'Is he your husband, dear?'

'Something like that.'

'I don't think we've ever properly met.'

'He's gonna take a load of stuff to the dump for you, stop you getting vermin.'

'I don't need that. I've got my cats.'

'You should get shot of them too.'

'I should not. And I like my things.'

'All right, Frieda, calm down. Course we won't take any stuff you *use*. We'll just clear out the rubbish, yeah?'

'I don't have any rubbish.'

'Why don't you take Frieda into the kitchen, Steve, yeah? Make us all a nice cup of tea, and I'll just have a quick look around. Check the window locks and stuff.'

Movement, then fast footsteps coming up the stairs. With a pinch of panic I leapt up, dived into the box room and stood behind the door. I could hear Linda moving about in Frieda's bedroom. She'd be in the box room next, I knew it. I had moments to act. I put my fingers under the wide bit of board and pulled, then I backed into the space and used the handles to pull the board to. I turned the two small wooden swivels.

Then I lay quietly in the dark, letting my eyes adjust to the gloom.

Moments later I could hear someone outside, the sound of boxes being moved. Behind the false panel, I stilled my breathing.

'You up there, Linda?'

'Yeah. Hang on.'

More footsteps, heavier.

The man's voice, 'What you up to? I'm stuck downstairs with the old bird.'

Linda's voice, 'I'm looking for something.'

'What you doing?'

'Checking stuff. Anyone could break in. She hasn't got any security to speak of.'

'So get her into a home.'

'D'you have any idea how much those places cost?'

'It's not our money, though, is it?'

'It bloody well is. Think about it. I'm Ted's niece, so *technically* that makes me her only living relative, right? By marriage, anyhow, and that's gotta count. No kids, and she definitely hasn't got anyone else, meaning it's all coming my way sooner or later. Stick her in a home and she could go on for years. We'd have to sell this place to fund it. There won't be a penny left. At least here she might do us all a favour and fall down the stairs. Help me shift this box.'

'Linda, *wake up*: this stuff is trash. Did you not see that TV downstairs? It's got to be at least twenty years old. Older, probably. You'd have to *pay* someone to take it away.'

'She's got a load of decent jewellery somewhere, I know she has. Ted spoilt her rotten. And I do mean seriously expensive stuff. The real McCoy.'

'It won't be in here, then, will it? It'll be in her bedroom.'

'I've already checked. Nothing but junk.'

Then Frieda's voice, close by: 'Have you finished checking the windows, dear? There's tea downstairs. And biscuits, special ones, homemade.'

'Yeah, everything's fine up here. I was just wondering, d'you want me to look after anything for you, Frieda?'

'Not that I can think of.'

'What about your jewellery?'

'My jewellery?'

'Yeah. You've got a few little bits tucked away somewhere, haven't you? D'you want to dig them out? I can take them to my place for you if you like, keep them safe.'

'Why should I want that? Silly, I know, an old lady like me, but I am very fond of my beads. I like to wear them, look.'

'Not them glass ones, Frieda, other stuff. Emerald earrings, diamond rings, stuff like that.'

'There's nothing I can think of. I'm sure I'd remember if I had anything nice like that.'

'Have a think, then.'

'I *am* thinking, dear. I think you must be getting confused.'

The Apron took the week off between Christmas and New Year, so I turned the radio up loud and sang along while I decorated the entire house with bits of holly. Or at least I did until they played Wham!'s 'Last Christmas'. Then I froze, gripped by a sudden vision of our Christmas Day the year before. My father, stuffed with pudding and port, had fallen asleep in the drawing room, so the three of us had retreated into the kitchen, where Willa and I had spent the next hour alternatively laughing and then shushing each other as Mum, using a giant turkey drumstick as a microphone, had mimed along to her beloved George Michael. *Oh, God, I missed them so much.* A hard pressure started building behind my eyes, and I ran to the radio and turned it off.

On Christmas Day itself Frieda and I had a lunch of rice and roasted vegetables and played gin rummy until the Queen's Speech came on. Later we watched a Bond movie together, both of us curled up on the sofa. I gave Frieda a cake I'd decorated with miniature marzipan cats, and Frieda gave me an old, embroidered silk purse in which she'd placed two twenty-pound notes. The purse also contained a large wad of French francs.

'Well, they were in there already,' she said. 'So I didn't bother taking them out. I've no idea what they're worth, probably pennies. Useless, I suspect, but I suppose you could always try exchanging them at the bank.'

Four days later, Frieda got sick. She didn't want the TV on. Rather she wanted to listen to some of her vinyl records – a Debussy sonata, Ysaÿe's *Poème élégiaque*, Messiaen's *Quartet for the End of Time*. She was very quiet; I couldn't tell if she was listening or sleeping.

She said she was too tired to face the stairs; rather, she would sleep on the old velvet sofa. I kept the curtains half closed and draped the embroidered orange throw over a lamp, bathing the sitting room in a soft amber glow. It was like being suspended in a tank, both of us floating, weightless. Waiting.

She stopped eating, then talking. She lay with her eyes shut, breathing slowly, barely awake. 'Let me call someone,' I said. 'A doctor. An ambulance.'

Her eyes fluttered open. She said, 'Non.'

I felt a growing pressure in my chest, a rising sob that wanted to erupt from my core, a howl. Her lips moved. I bent closer to hear, her voice was barely there. *So brave*, I thought she said. It was only years later that I realized she'd been talking in French. *Soit brave*, she'd said. Not *so brave*. *Soit* brave. *Be* brave.

She had one hand resting on the tawny fur of a cat. I took

the other, all tiny bones and thin transparent skin, and held it in mine. She took a slow, rattling breath. The pale half-moons of her eyelids stayed shut. The cats stretched and yawned. Fauré's *Élégie* for piano and cello came to an end. I didn't want to let go of her hand to lift the needle from the vinyl, so I just let it turn. Anyway, I liked the steady repeat of the hiss and the skip: soothing, constant, certain. I stroked Frieda's white hair.

Two hours later, she died.

It was New Year's Eve.

I held her hand and cried. I'd known Frieda for such a short time but I loved her, I really did. I didn't know what to do. The Apron would be back in the morning. Then there would be ambulances, the police, Linda and Steve tearing the place apart. And what would happen when they found me there? It wasn't my home. I didn't belong. There would be questions and they wouldn't understand. I wouldn't be able to explain.

I had to go home.

I closed my eyes and imagined walking into my house, finding my mother in the kitchen or the den, waiting for me. Her tears, then the rolling surf of her love and anger and bliss. Willa running down from her room, holding me like she'd never let me go. Every time I'd had these thoughts before I'd pushed them away, but this time I let them flood my mind. I felt a painful blooming inside my chest, an urgent desire to run to the house and bang on the door and shout *I'm home*.

And I *wanted* to go home. I'd always wanted to go home, the whole time I'd been there. I just never had. Somehow a single night away had turned into four whole months.

I pulled on the old black ski trousers and a thick black jumper, socks, a pair of old black boots. I took everything else that belonged to me: my school uniform, the toothbrush I'd used, the embroidered purse, my mother's book. I kissed

Frieda's pale cheek and tucked the blanket around her body. I opened a bunch of tins and fed the cats.

Outside, the freezing air cut right through the jumper, so I grabbed a coat off the peg, an old donkey jacket that must have once belonged to Ted. I shrugged it on. It was several sizes too big: a giant heavy hug of a coat. There was a woolly hat in one of the pockets so I put that on too. At the last minute, I went back and took the photograph of Elisabeth blowing bubbles and another of Ted and Frieda in a boat and tucked them between the pages of the book. I put the purse in the deep inside pocket of the jacket. Then I closed the door behind me, hearing the click of the latch, and finally I hid the key high up in a crevice in the old oak porch. Then I started to walk down the drive, the clear night sky above me speckled with stars. When I arrived on the empty road, I stood for a moment, looking at the outside world: everything was just as it had been. It was about ten minutes to midnight. I started walking.

At the end of the drive I stopped by the dark wall of rhododendrons, honestly stunned by the sight of my own home, at once both familiar and strange. The house was in darkness, its huge white façade inked lavender by the night. In fact, only one bedroom light was on, and not any bedroom light either: *my* bedroom light, shining like a beacon. Like a *vigil*, I thought, warmth filling my chest; maybe they keep it on all night, a sign for me to come home. Then a figure stepped up to the window and a head pressed against the glass. *Willa.* Willa was in my room, and for some reason up in the dead of the night, *awake.* Every atom of my body felt pulled across the void between us. I started to run towards the house, ready to bang on the door and shout her name, yell over and over *It's me.*

Two steps, in an almighty bang made me jump out of my skin. *A gunshot*, I thought, *an explosion.* I threw myself to the ground, then rolled into the deep cover of the glossy rhododendrons, at hidden layer of brambles tearing at my face, jabbing barbs into my skin. From there I looked up, feeling like an idiot as fireworks flared across the sky, spraying vast arcs of brilliant sparks through the night, lighting my sister's pale face at the window. I'd forgotten it was New Year's Eve. *Shit*, I told myself, *stupid girl*. The sky boomed and crackled and hissed. Willa wouldn't even hear me knocking over all that, so for a while I just lay there on the freezing grass, watching my sister as she stood at the window, hands pressed against the pane. Like a spaceman, I thought: Major Tom, remote, distant and somehow adrift.

Eventually the fireworks faded into nothing and I stood up, brushing myself down. Okay, I told myself, now. Take a moment. *Just one moment*. I'd learnt so much that Willa needed to know. Things about myself. Things about her. Things about all of us. I *had* to compose myself, find the right words. I watched her as she walked away from the window. Then the light in my bedroom snapped off.

Not a vigil, then. I stood for a moment, thinking about that.

I was about to move again when a car turned into the drive, gravel crunching under its tyres as it passed within a few metres of where I stood unseen, just one more shadow in the night. *My parents*, I thought, spotting the two dark figures inside the car's interior. *They'd been out*. My heart drummed in my chest, too loudly. They parked beside the house and the front doors flew open, throwing a long trapezium of golden light over the winter lawn. Willa ran down the stone steps and all three of them hugged. I saw my mother laughing. I could hear voices, *Happy New Year*.

My father took my mother and sister by their hands and slowly, graciously, assuredly led them into the house. I could hear my mother's heels clicking up the steps. Then the front doors shut behind the three of them, leaving the garden in darkness. Okay, I thought, well, they're all in there now, okay: good. I was everything at that moment: excited, pensive, scared. I took a breath, a step towards the house. But then something truly extraordinary happened: a colossal structure at the far end of the house burst into light and the sight was so startling, so completely, utterly unexpected, that I stopped in my tracks.

I thought, *What the hell?*

I knew what it was. It could *only* be one thing: the brand-spanking-new conservatory.

Staying outside its long rectangles of cast light, I edged towards the extension until the whole thing came into view. It had just been foundations when I'd last seen it. And now it was finished. And it was vast. *Wow*, I thought.

Then I thought, *Fuck*. They built the conservatory.

Through its huge glass windows, I had a good view of my father. He was sitting in a stuffed white armchair, a bow tie loose around his neck. Then my mother walked towards him, crossing that vast golden room with a cut-glass tumbler in her hand. She'd taken off her outdoor coat and now I could see the outfit she was wearing: a cocktail dress, a shimmering midnight blue. My father took the glass from my mother's hand. I saw him pull her towards him, draw a hand slowly across her backside and say something. A slow smile moved over his face.

I looked away. At the far end of the space there was a huge Christmas tree, brightly lit and festooned with gold ornaments. They'd had Christmas, I thought. A normal Christmas. A normal Christmas with presents and a tree. They'd celebrated. They'd gone to parties. They'd got on with *everything*. No wonder they never found me, I thought. They weren't even looking. I was *missing* and they built a *fucking extension*. That's what they did.

I turned around. Outside, everything was still. The wide, dark lawn; winter trees like blackened sticks. The lights from that immense glass building gleamed on the black surface of the swimming pool, casting a strange bronze glow on the cement bunker wall.

Nothing has changed, I thought. Everything is exactly the same as it was.

What did I know about anything? I was fourteen and blind-sided and angry as hell.

That's when I decided. I had forty pounds in my purse and a wad of French francs.

I wasn't going back.

21.
Cleave

Claudette

It was morning, sunless and cold. My mind felt fuzzy from lack of sleep, my limbs leaden and heavy. I'd arrived in Dover. I left the train and was funnelled down a maze of grubby corridors towards the ferry at the Eastern Docks, eventually finding myself in a large hall lined with banks of grey plastic chairs. The ticket booths were to one side. I rehearsed my lines in my head, *Single foot passenger to Calais*, and, if asked, *I'm visiting my aunt.*

'Passport.'

I blanked. *Passport.* I couldn't believe I'd been so stupid. The woman looked at me, her unsmiling mouth set in a thin pink line. I made a show of looking in my bag, stalling for time, digging through the pockets of my old school jacket, leafing through the pages of *The Handmaid's Tale*.

I looked up. I said, 'I think I must have left it somewhere.' I heard my voice wobble slightly. 'Is there any way –'

'Next.'

I caught sight of someone reflected in the booth's glass window and it took a moment to realize it was me. I looked ashen and small, my eyes too big in my face. The oversized donkey jacket and woolly hat made me look exactly like what I was: a child. I turned away, hollow and dumb. It was hopeless; the whole thing was impossible. I didn't know what to do. And I was hungry. *So* hungry. At Frieda's house I'd grown used to eating good food and lots of it too. From somewhere across the concourse the smell of fried food and coffee filled the air and made my stomach rumble. I needed to eat.

Five minutes later I was sitting at a plastic table with a mug of pale tea and a slice of plain buttered toast, the cheapest things I could find on the menu. I wrapped my fingers around the mug, trying to warm my hands, to shake my slow brain into gear. Consider my options, or at least try to work out if I had any.

'This space free?'

The man didn't wait for my answer but settled himself into the seat opposite mine with a loaded plate: bacon, black pudding, eggs, sausage, fried bread, beans. Despite my own hunger, my stomach turned.

'Looks like you could do with a bite. Want some?'

I glanced up. The man smiled at me, revealing a bank of nicotine-yellow teeth. 'No, thanks.'

'Suit yourself.' He shovelled food into his mouth, yolk catching on the scrub of grey bristle that jutted from his chin. I could feel his eyes taking me in.

'Going to France?'

I looked up. He smiled again, waiting for my reply.

'Maybe.'

'Still thinking about it, are you? Funny place to make up your mind.' He grinned broadly.

'I've got family there.' I held his eyes, daring him to call me out. 'Grandparents.'

'Good on ya. They'll be glad to see you.'

'Yep. Okay, well, I guess I'd better go.' I stood up.

'Found your passport, have ya?' His face was open, still smiling. 'That was me behind ya in the queue. Shit, innit. Can't tell you the number of times I've left somethin' or other at home.

Now the wife makes a list, sticks it on the fridge and makes me check it off before I go. She's an honest-to-God lifesaver, that woman. Don't know what I'd do without her.'

I looked towards the ticket booths, then the exit back towards the trains.

'No rush. It's ages till the next crossing. Perhaps between the two of us we can sort out a way to help you out. Two heads better than one, right?' He smiled again, his mouth full of food. 'I've got kids myself, as it happens, boy an' a girl. Hang fast, I'll bag us a couple of hot drinks and we'll figure somit out.'

He walked over to the counter and hovered there, ordering, his eyes flicking back every now and again to where I stood, unsure of myself. Waiting. Then he was back with two steaming Styrofoam cups and a bag of croissants.

'Here,' he said, his voice lowered, 'take this – hot chocolate – an' listen – I've had an idea.' He gave me a conspiratorial wink and leant towards me. 'As luck would have it, I've got my daughter's passport in the van – you can use that. She looks like you an' all. Just let me have it back when you get through customs on the other side. Then, when you get to your nan's, you just get your folks to mail your own one over for the return. See – sorted – told you I'd think of something, right?'

'They'd see it wasn't me.'

'Border control? They barely look at the things. Been over three times this week and they didn't ask for it once, the lazy bums. You've just gotta have one in your hand, that's all. Come on – we'll grab it, then you can sort out your ticket. I can even give you a lift in the van if you like, save you wandering 'bout on ya own.' I stood, hesitating, torn. 'Up to you,' he said. 'I'd just like to think if my kid was in a bind, some nice bloke would do the same for them.'

He turned away, leaving.

I hesitated for a long moment, watching him walk away through the doors. My one and only option. Then I followed.

Outside the terminal doors was a space like a vast amphitheatre, ringed by concrete barricades, a circling flyover, and behind that the curved wall of the scrubby white cliffs and the heavy dome of a granite-lidded sky. We were walking diagonally across a car park at a good pace, past rows of cars and lines of massive haulage trucks, heading towards a livestock lorry that smelt of pure terror, where the wet eyes of calves peered out darkly between the gaps in its side. I felt a sudden reluctance to go any further. I thought, *This place is hell.* Rain started to fall.

'That's me,' he said, indicating a blue Bedford van half hidden behind the truck, rust mottling its flank.

'Jump in. Keep yourself dry.'

He opened the passenger door with a key. I glanced at him, then back at the squat terminal building, now just a grey block in the distance.

'Get a move on,' he said. 'I'm getting wet here.' I hauled myself up on to the seat and he slammed the door behind me. He got in on the driver's side.

'S'better. Just realized I haven't even properly said hello. Jerry, Jez.' He held out his hand. I took it. He waited.

I stayed silent.

'Never mind,' he said. 'You don't hafta say. Right, don't let your chocolate get cold. Here – have a croissant.'

I was so hungry. I took a bite of the stale pastry and chewed. Rain drummed on the windscreen.

'Just in time.' Jez shoved a load of old food wrappers off the seat between us. 'Sorry 'bout the mess. I practically live in this van. Sleep in it too sometimes – see that?' He nodded towards the dark back of the van, which, as my eyes adjusted, I could see was almost entirely taken up by a stained mattress and filthy-looking duvet. 'Here, give me that.' He took my bag and threw it in the back.

'I even got curtains, see?'

He reached across the windscreen and tugged together a pair of green curtains attached top and bottom by lengths of elastic cord; then he did the same with the side windows, and the cab filled with a strange greenish light, like I was under water, looking up from the bottom of a pond. I felt the hairs on the back of my neck prickle and rise. My eyes flicked towards the handle of the door.

'Right, then. Let's get you sorted, shall we? Find that passport.'

He leant across me and tugged open the glove compartment. His body suddenly felt very large and very close to mine. I could smell his head, the dirty smell of unwashed hair. I pushed back in the seat.

Shit, I thought, what was I thinking? *Stupid girl.* Stupidstupidstupid. *Do something.*

The moment he sat back up, I yanked open the door-handle and, terrified he might somehow pull me back in, dived out, falling hard on the wet tarmac, hitting it with my hands and knees. I scrabbled to my feet and ran, rounding the truck of calves and out into the open space, my heart jabbering in my chest. I'd almost reached the other side of the car park before I understood he wasn't following. My breath came in ragged gasps. I put my hands on my knees and retched. Slowly, I took account. I was okay; I was in one piece. It was fine. I was fine. But also I was a complete *idiot.* I needed to wise up, and fast. I turned towards the terminal, feeling strange and weightless, and only then did it hit me: I didn't have my bag. In it was my old school uniform, the book and, inside that, my photographs of Frieda and Elisabeth and Ted. The woolly hat had gone too. But there was no way I was going back, no way I was going to risk being hauled back into that foul-smelling van. Freezing rain soaked my head and trickled down the back of my neck. My hands hurt, and when I held them up I saw they were badly grazed from my fall on to the tarmac. My shoulder throbbed under my coat. In panic, I patted the inside pocket. Thank God, the purse was still there. But that was it. I had the clothes I was wearing, a few pounds plus some old French francs. And nowhere to go.

I looked up. Ahead of me were three massive container trucks, each one dressed in a familiar gold-and-purple livery, and, in giant letters that filled the entire side of each, a single repeated word: MARTENWOOD.

That was my choice: go on or go home. On was the entire world, unknown and utterly terrifying; home was heaven and hell.

I thought about my father. The bolt of fear that shot through me as a child whenever I heard his car pulling up on the gravel drive. Hiding in my room, flattening myself into a thin blade, pressed between my chest of drawers and the wall, or under the bed, making myself as small and silent as I could. The slap of his hand, the crack of his belt. Being made to touch my toes for an hour as a punishment for rudeness, watching the minutes of the clock tick past, every muscle in my body screaming with pain.

I thought about my mother and my sister, how much I longed for them. My squeaky-clean, dependable, wonderful big sister lecturing me on how to be good. My beloved, funny mother singing us George Michael songs in the bath. For a long time I stood there, thinking about the two of them, letting blooms of love open soft velvet petals inside my chest.

I knew exactly what the cost of going back would be, what punishments I'd face. But I had to anyway; I didn't have a choice. I found a telephone box and dialled the number of my parents' house, a clutch of ten-pence pieces ready in my bloodied palm. It rang. I heard the sound filling the spaces of my home; tears filled my eyes as I imagined my mother dashing towards the phone in the kitchen or their bedroom, snatching it up – *Lai?* My eyes drifted over the cards stuck to the board behind the phone – ads for women with oily-looking breasts and bums: busty and fun, strict discipline, mature, hot schoolgirls, sexy massage; a blonde with her eyes blacked out and the words REAL PHOTO scrawled across it in pen.

Please pick up, I thought, and then *Let it be Mum.*

Pips. I shoved my money in the slot.

'Martenwood.'

I took a breath. 'Dad?' My voice caught in my throat.

Silence rang in my ears.

'Where are you?'

I took a breath. 'Dover.' Then 'I'm at the ferry port.'

'What are you doing there?'

I knew only a straight answer would do. 'I was going to France.'

'And then?'

My voice was small. 'I didn't have my passport.'

Pips. I shoved another coin into the slot and waited.

'Stay where you are. I'm on my way.'

It had a good view of the entrance, so I did stay exactly where I was, hidden inside that old phone box, but even then I almost missed him because he was driving a Martenwood works van and not his own car. I stepped out of the box and held up my hand. He stopped next to me. I got in. We circled the car park once, then he parked up. He turned off the engine.

'Wait here.'

My father got out of the van and slammed the door behind

him. I twisted in my seat, watching him walk into the terminal building. I sat, waiting. Five minutes later he was back. He sat back behind the driver's seat but didn't start the engine. Instead he stared straight ahead. I could see his tongue moving about under his cheek.

I said, 'I'm sorry.'

His jaw moved forward and he turned to look at me.

'Is that right. So the girl who's done *everything possible* to *ruin* me, is sorry.' Silence fell between us. I sat very still, my heart beating fast. 'Let me tell you something about me, Laika. I was thirteen when I started working for my old dad. Up at the arse crack of dawn, cracked round the head when I fucked up. Full time at fifteen. Age of twenty, I said to him, you're not going to make proper money messing about with a piddling fleet of Lutons – put me in charge – I'll show you how it's done. And he did, didn't he? Old bastard wanted to see me fall flat on my arse. Didn't, though, did I. Martenwood Removals became Martenwood Haulage and, as they say, the rest is history. *I* did that, Laika. *I* took that business from a couple of old removal vans to five hundred trucks. *Me*. Five hundred trucks and hundreds of staff, everyone doing exactly what I say, when I say it, not one of them putting a foot out of place, every one of them just that little bit scared. That business, *Laika*, earned me my right to live on the best road in the county, earned me my place on the golf course, my right to hobnob with judges, lawyers, CEOs, anyone I want, people *born* with money. I *earned* my place at that table, and don't they know it. Earned myself the cars, the watches, the beautiful wife. Earned my right to have *everyone* jumping up and down. And you know who's brought that business to its knees? *You*.' A small tremor moved through his cheek. 'You take off and next thing I know I've got the pigs on my tail. The police took away *every single fucking truck*, interviewed *every single fucking driver*. Went through every lock-up.

Went through all the books. Went through the entire lot *again*. I lost *hundreds* of contracts. The moment you took off, Martenwood Haulage started haemorrhaging money out of its arse. You turned something of a spotlight on me there, Laika. And I'll bet you think you were being that little bit clever, *right*, shining the light straight back at Daddy's eyes?' He paused, his face hardening. 'Yet here she is, here's Laika, tried living in the real world and found it a little bit tough. Thinks she'd like to come home for a bit. See what other havoc she can wreak. Show me your hands.'

I turned my palms over, showed him the cuts, the lines of drying blood.

'Want to go to France, do you? Want to make it on your own? Never did me any harm.'

He took something out of his top pocket and handed it to me. My passport and, tucked inside its pages, a ticket. I said, 'But, Mum –'

His voice dropped dangerously low. 'Your mother, Laika, knows *exactly* which side her bread is buttered on. She has a very nice life, your mother. See her anywhere, do you? See her rushing down here to bring you home? No? Why not? Need it spelling out? *Your mother* picked a side, my girl. She always has and she always will. Mine.'

22.
Paris

Claudette

I never meant to run away from home. I hadn't planned or prepared for it. And I didn't want to go to France either. That flash of resolution I'd felt standing in the bronzed shadows of my parents' house at midnight had quickly faded away in the cold murk of the day. But, sitting by myself in that grey terminal, I didn't know what else to do.

What I wanted was to get caught. I'd seen the photo of me they'd used on *Crimewatch*, taken when I'd still had long hair and a fringe. Okay, so I didn't look exactly like that any more: my hair was short now, and I'd filled out a bit. But surely I was still recognizable: only four months had passed. And I still had to be on a list somewhere, I thought. All I needed was for someone to notice my name. For someone to *do* something. Someone to stop me. To call the police.

At the border the guard was shouting something to another official a little way off. I walked straight up and stood there in front of him, holding out my passport and waiting for a pause in their conversation while all the other foot passengers just waved their documents and walked straight past. When he didn't take it, I almost *thrust* it at him. I wanted to say *Please*. Perhaps that was my mistake. Perhaps I was *too* eager, *too* keen. He glanced at me once and just waved me straight through.

*

From the back of the ferry I watched gulls wheeling and diving in the hazy air: drawing a double helix, a heart, a Möbius strip. Everything was white: my pale clouds of breath, the screaming birds, the filmy sea. The cliffs grew fainter, then disappeared into nothing, like sleep.

I knew I was going to die.

I wondered how long I'd survive before something did me in, weeks maybe, a few months. Then I wondered what would kill me: hunger, sickness, something worse. I imagined my body in a ditch, or else propped upright and bloody somewhere remote. I wondered whether I would fight, or whether I would simply give up. If I would be scared. If it would hurt. If I would ever be found.

Then I thought, *Fuck that.*

In France I learnt fast. I got good at not being noticed. Not meeting people's eyes. Standing in the shadows. Never asking for directions. Memorizing maps. Clocking people before they even became aware of me. And, even though it was out of season, I found work, on a farm in Picardy where the owners kept a skeleton staff on through the winter. There were six of us: four men, one woman and me. We worked fifteen-hour days, slept in bunks in a barn and, after vast chunks had been deducted for accommodation, bed linen, food, heating, electricity, water, taxes, insurance and something called retainer fees, received a pittance in wages. None of us would complain. None of us *could* complain. We were all illegal there, somehow or other, that was clear enough. None of us ever asked direct questions or even looked one another straight in the eye. I guessed every last one of us had a story we didn't want telling. You gave a name and got paid in cash. I was Elisabeth.

At first I was so miserable that I didn't really look outside of myself, so it took a few weeks before it dawned on me that I probably wasn't even the youngest one there. That place was almost certainly taken by a tall, thin, silent boy who would throw himself to the ground whenever a tractor backfired. He had beautiful green eyes and blooms of ringworm on his arms, and he slept in the bunk next to mine. We all went to bed fully dressed, but one night in February, when a biting cold pulled me out of sleep, I saw he was staring through the skylight at the moon, his eyes spilling over with terror and tears. I reached over for his hand and he took it silently, curling his fingers around mine as a single silver line worked its way down his cheek, like a riverbed filling after a drought. That was about the extent of our friendship. In the daytime we mostly ignored each other just like everyone else. But I was fairly certain French wasn't his first language, because he pronounced my name the Arabic way, Ilisabat. Of course, we didn't stay in touch. All of us were on the move and none of us had phones back then, access to the internet or even a forwarding address. Jabir, he said he was called, and I've thought about him a lot over the years, worried about him, in truth. So many times I've found myself wishing that I knew where he was, or just that he was doing okay. Because this is what I've learnt: the shy ones, the gentle ones, the sensitive ones, the good ones, they're the ones that don't survive out there.

And I am none of those things.

As soon as the weather began to improve, I moved south and started harvesting work. And I was lucky. I found work on a farm with some good people, Basile and Agathe Abadie. Not just good people but rather truly beautiful people, whose kindness and generosity I repaid with betrayal and theft. They had a child, a daughter about my age who'd been born with severe learning difficulties and needed constant care: she had to be turned and changed, to keep her clean and safe. Despite the fact she couldn't walk, or talk, or see, Basile and Agathe were always talking to her, singing to her, touching her, always comforting her, wheeling her into the orchard so she could feel the breeze on her face. They always let her know they were close. In all my life, I don't think I've ever seen such love given to another human being. Sometimes something like a smile would pass over her face, and those were the moments her parents would live for and celebrate. In fact, they seemed to celebrate everything about her, each and every day she was alive. I think they knew they could lose her at any moment. And they were kind to me too, so kind. Too kind. Looking back, I realize it can't have been easy, having someone like me around, so similar in age to their daughter but living an active life, walking and talking, doing normal, everyday things. But if they felt that, they never showed it, not once, and at the end of the picking season they invited me to stay on with them, to help in the house, and I did. I actually stayed with them for more than two years in the end, cooking, cleaning, working in the fields; later even helping with the admin and books. They trusted me, Basile and Agathe, they let me into the absolute heart of their family. I lived in their home. And, gradually, I got to know that house inside out, where everything was kept. The daughter's name was Claudette. And during the time that I was living there, I borrowed, no, not borrowed, I *stole* her birth certificate and applied for a passport. With my photograph. I *stole* from the very people who had been so good to me. I *stole* from a disabled child. And I became Claudette.

That meant when I turned seventeen and moved to Paris to start waitressing, I could work legally. I've always stayed in touch with Basile and Agathe. Whenever I go back to visit, I call myself Elisabeth. Whenever they come to Paris, I'm always too busy to meet. Both these things fill me with shame.

I can never tell them what I did. I can never tell anyone.

I have lived in Paris for twenty years now, renting a flat in the 20th arrondissement, an area populated by students, immigrants, musicians, painters, beatniks, free spirits and dropouts. It's a tiny one-bedroom place, on the seventh floor of an old apartment building that does not have a lift. I suppose I could move now, if I wanted to. I could probably afford to. But I like it. It's *me*.

For my first few years in France I thought about home all the time. I had vivid dreams about my mother and sister. I'd wake up with tears running down my face. I was desperate to see them, desperate to go home. For a long time I told myself I would return to England when I was eighteen. Then I told myself, to be absolutely assured of my adulthood and independence, better make that twenty-one. Then I pushed it back again. Twenty-five, I thought. But, at some point, I just *became* Claudette. I *wanted* to be Claudette: this girl who'd lived her entire life being loved for exactly who she was. A different me. How I saw it, Ilisabat was loneliness and terror; Elisabeth calculation and survival; Laika, impulse and rage. As Claudette I could be something else. As Claudette I could be composed, self-possessed. Balanced. I felt steady, and stable. I took up yoga, and eventually gave up waitressing to teach it full time. I liked the way it made me hold myself, the way it taught me to breathe, the way it made me think. Yoga gave me strength and I changed, all of me. I had dates. I had friends. It may not have been my own life, but it was one I enjoyed.

And I didn't look back. I *chose* not to look back. When thoughts of my mother and sister crept in at the edges of my consciousness, I pushed them straight back out of my head. When eventually I got the internet, I never even Googled them. If ever I felt the urge, my fingers pausing on the keys of my computer, I made myself think about that gargantuan glass house. I would close my eyes and force myself to look inside it, to see them there: my father, smiling; my mother walking through that golden space in a midnight-blue dress. They could have found me if they'd wanted to, I told myself. But they didn't. They were too busy going to parties and building that bloody thing. And if they weren't going to look for me, why the hell should I look for them? I wasn't even Laika any more. I was Claudette.

And then I met Nate.

He signed up for my evening class, arriving loose-limbed and smiling. He worked hard, laughed a lot, had all the kit. Sure, I liked him. He was confident, talkative, lean. I had his picture: he was someone, I thought, who would give yoga a few tries, find it all a bit quiet and at some point just stop showing up.

But he didn't. He kept coming back.

After a few months he asked me for a date and, when I turned him down, he was good-natured about it. After a few weeks he asked again. Then again. Eventually I thought, okay, we'll have one date, maybe two. He seemed pretty easy to be around – it could be nice. Maybe we'd end up in bed, enjoy ourselves for a few weeks and then just agree we'd be better off suited as friends. So finally I told him okay, yes, one date.

I arranged to meet him on the Left Bank, well away from my flat. He'd told me he wanted to take me to a concert, but the moment I saw him standing there, grinning with his hands in his pockets, on the corner of Rue Saint-Jacques, I knew I should have asked for more details.

'Where are we going?'

'It's a surprise.'

'I don't like surprises.'

Nate beamed, and I could see he assumed I was joking. I wasn't. My entire life was built on knowing exactly what, and who, was around the next corner. I felt my heart dropping. I should have known better. This wasn't going to work.

'I'm serious,' I said, but he was already talking about his sister, filling me in about her life and kids in London, while, only half listening, I pulled up my mental map of Paris, checking each passing small side street for a quick way out, a fast escape into the dark.

My sense of dread built. We were somewhere in the Latin Quarter. I was just about to pull a fast migraine and excuse myself when he stopped outside the entrance to a dreary community hall.

'Nate –' I said.

'We're here.'

I could hear shouts and hollers coming from the inside, and I threw him a questioning look as he held open the door. He stood back and, because I had to, after a moment I stepped inside a room full of young men tearing about, shoving each other and laughing. This couldn't be it. We had to have come to the wrong place. It was a joke. As the group massed around Nate, I edged back, towards the door. It would be easy to leave. Nate had his back to me. I could be halfway up the street before he noticed I was gone.

'Eh, vous là!' he shouted. 'Bougez-vous les fesses, on n'a pas toute la journée.' Instantly there was silence, and, in the sudden quiet, I froze, my hand already on the door, waiting for the racket to start up again so I could just slip out.

'Okay,' he said, 'guys, true to my promise, tonight I have something truly special for you: your first ever audience.' Nate turned towards me and held out his hand. The group of young men turned too and I was met by a sea of wary faces. That's when I realized they were really just kids. Nate grinned and after a moment I stepped forward a little, pretending I hadn't been about to disappear. Nate pulled me to his side.

'Eh, les gars,' he said, turning his attention back to the group, 'I'll tell you now: not everything tonight is going to go right. There's going to be mis-notes and duff chords and cock-ups and bits where we stop and start from the top. It doesn't matter. Just support each other, go with it, it's okay. Fall in love with the music, give yourselves over completely, plunge in. But, most of all, this is your moment. Show us what you can do and be proud of yourselves. Allons-y!'

Two plastic chairs appeared in front of the assortment of scrappy-looking instruments, and Nate and I took our seats.

He put his head close to mine. 'To say they're a little rough around the edges would be an understatement. But they're truly great kids, seriously, every last one of them. They all want to learn.'

We were the only members of the audience. As they began to play, I saw the boys' guarded caution start to slip away, and in its place came first the buzz of excitement, then true and absolute euphoria, their faces breaking into grins. They were changing before my eyes, and I was so – *moved*. Sitting, listening to them play, I felt something swimming up from deep inside me, something like hope. These were street boys with scabs and scars and knocked-off clothing and broken noses and shorn heads. Boys who'd never got a chance in life. These were boys like Jabir.

At the end of the last number, Nate and I leapt to our feet, clapping, our hands held high over our heads, shouting bravo. The concert had been rough and chaotic and full of mistakes and also utterly transformative, a wonder, a delight. It was honestly the best music I'd ever heard in my life.

I didn't want to fall in love with Nate, but I did. It was an adventure, utterly magical, like learning to swim in a tropical sea, our sex like starlight and storm. And, yes, I would want to walk with him a little longer. Of course I would. I would hold on to Nate forever if I could. But I always knew I couldn't stay with him always. I'm not who he thinks I am, and I carry that fear of discovery like a drowning man carries stones. The truth is, I could *never* bear to tell Nate that I'm not the person he believes he knows, the person he loves, that deep down I'm really just a thief, a fake, a runaway fraud. He is so honest, so straight, so decent, so *good*. His disappointment in me would be too much. I couldn't bear seeing it, the truth of myself reflected in his eyes and, worse, the kindness he would show me then, the pity. I always knew that I would need to end things sometime, before he started to discover the gaps in my narrative, the tiny bits that didn't quite add up. So when he asked me to go with him to London for six months, to set up his street-music project there, I knew the time had come. I couldn't, I told him. I had commitments, arrangements, work. Anyway, it was England, I told myself, the last place I wanted to go. Not that I needed to be afraid of anyone recognizing me, not after more than twenty years. No, it was just an ideal time to end things. And, I told myself, I would do it in such a way as to mean there was no turning back. I would wait until he was already over there, totally involved in his project, and then I'd do it snappily, by email or text, so he wouldn't hear the heartbreak in my voice, nor I any in his. And I would have to be absolute the moment it was done, not waver. Change my number. Not answer his calls. Let him find happiness with somebody else, someone better than me. Hard as it would be, I knew that *Claudette* could do that. She was strong enough. Wise.

But still, the pull of him was like a moon over a mountain.

I said I would come for a week.

23.
Supper with friends

Claudette

A woman opens the door in a rush, her cheeks flushed.

'Thank God you're here,' she says to Nate. 'I can't begin to tell you.' She throws her arms around his neck and hugs him, hard. Nate laughs.

'Good grief,' he says, as she releases her grip. 'How late are we? The traffic –'

'Hell, don't worry about that. Just get in there and lighten the mood. Claudette,' she says to me, 'sorry, I'm being rude. It's brilliant to meet you at last. I'm Cat. Nate never stops talking about you.'

She kisses me on both cheeks, then follows it up with a hug. She's a beautiful woman and feels instantly familiar: my boyfriend transformed into womanhood. She's slender, with high angular cheekbones, the same cropped hair as Nate and clever, quick-moving eyes. We're still standing on the doorstep.

'Come in,' she says as she takes our coats and the bag of goodies I've brought them from Paris, 'you're letting the cold air in. Shut the door. And don't even think about going up to see the kids tonight, just wait till tomorrow, okay? If you woke the boys up, I'd literally have to kill you.'

'What's going on, then?' Nate says, grinning, and with a quick upward nod indicates the kitchen door, behind which we can hear the voices of their other guests.

'Nothing, really. Willa was having a moment.'

Willa. There must be more than one Willa in the world. Nonetheless, the name feels like a sly pinch in a playground. I reach into my bag and pull out a pair of glasses with heavy tortoiseshell frames. The lenses aren't prescription. I used to wear them a lot, hardly ever now. These days they're more like a comfort blanket than anything else. We move towards the door.

'Hey,' Cat says, stopping in her tracks with a hand on Nate's chest. She looks at me and says, lowering her voice, 'Don't forget I told Robyn you don't speak English.' A wide and wicked grin spreads over her face. 'Do me a favour and play along for a bit, will you? Just enough to see her squirm. Believe me, languages are not her forte.'

Cat goes first into the warm glow of the kitchen, and I follow behind Nate. My boyfriend is instantly at ease, hugging Cat's wife, Robyn, and greeting Michael and Liv, all of whom rise from the table to greet us. There are two other guests too. At the back of the kitchen, standing behind the table, is a large, heavy-set man holding a slim woman in a close embrace. The woman has almost-red hair and she's the only other woman in the room, so this must be my sister's namesake, Willa. I do a double-take. *Jesus*. Despite the fact her face is turned away from the rest of us, pressed into the chest of the large man, this woman *is* my sister, Willa. I feel it with every atom of my body. Instantly my nerve endings are snapping and fizzing. I freeze. I think, *No fucking way*. I take a sharp intake of breath. I look again. It's her. I can feel my heart spinning like a freshly trapped wildcat. I need to leave. Right now. Before she sees me. Before she turns round and says *Laika*. I step towards the door.

'Et voilà,' Nate says, sweeping an arm around me, 'je vous présente ma magnifique Claudette, ma petite amie.'

'Please tell Claudette, Nate, that we're all thrilled to meet her at last and are looking forward to getting to know her better.' Standing beside Robyn, Cat nods at me, holding my eyes and smiling, her lips puckering with the effort not to laugh. I glance at Willa, but she's still completely preoccupied. In fact, she hasn't even noticed there's a newcomer in the room. She's far too busy canoodling with the big bloke. I stand frozen beside Nate.

'And, Robyn,' Nate says, 'I'm right in thinking you speak some French, right?'

His sister's wife nods, a look of barely contained panic in her eyes.

'I can certainly give it a go.'

Concentrate. Her French is hesitant, but the basics are all there. In truth I'm barely listening anyway. Nonetheless I join in, and blather something in return, talking as fast as I can, gesturing with my hands for the full effect and to keep her eyes on me and off Cat and Nate, both of whom are in fits.

'Claudette speaks fluent English, Robs,' Nate says, laughing. He grins at me, a wild and happy look in his eyes, his arm slung around his sister's shoulders, and another part of the picture of him falls silently into place. Robyn takes it gracefully enough. If it were me, I would have thumped him. In fact, right now I'd thump anyone. But, worse, I've missed my one chance; there's no way I can leave now. In which case, I need to get in control. *Breathe*, I think, *get a grip.*

I switch to English and smile at Robyn, who already seems far too nice to be the butt of such a joke. 'Thanks for having us and I'm really sorry we're late. That honestly wasn't my idea.' I automatically use just the right amount of accent to indicate that English is not my first language. Plus, it's grounding for me, Claudette. I'm Claudette. And, evidently, I'm French. I feel calmer. Perhaps it's not my sister. It can't be. I've been thrown into panic over nothing. I haven't even had a good look at her face. It can't be my sister. She's not my sister. She's not.

We've kept everyone waiting, so the food is already being placed on the table, and in the hubbub of all that action the other woman and I are not introduced, which does somehow feel like a happy accident. I need time. Right now I feel as if I have a whole bunch of ants marching through my veins and some of them aren't even going the right way. That's not good. I take a few silent minutes to still my breathing first and then my mind, shutting myself off and drawing myself quietly back into a place of certainty and peace, using every technique I've learnt over the years. The voices around me recede. I shut my eyes for a moment. I'm okay.

As I bring myself back, I become aware of some good scents: ginger, lime leaf, basil. Plus music: Nina Simone, 'I Loves You, Porgy'. The comfort of candlelight. Nate's voice, wonderful food and, clearly, good people, people I'd genuinely like to know better. Robyn's eyes meet mine, and she beams at me. I smile back.

But it's Willa I really want to see. Or even hear. I keep glancing towards her, but we're both sitting on the same side of the table, so it's hard to get a good look without making it obvious. I strain my ears to try to catch the sound of her voice, but she's barely said a thing so far. That's odd. In fact, thinking about it, that wouldn't fit with my sister at all, trained as she was by our mother to be the most socially appropriate person in the room. If that was my sister, right now she'd undoubtedly be leaning across the table, nodding, smiling, politely joining in. So it can't be her, then, just someone who looks like her. And for further proof: there's no way my sister would have somehow ended up with this leering goon of a man opposite me, Jamie, a man who hasn't taken his eyes off Liv's cleavage the entire night. So that woman can't be my sister. She's just someone who looks so much like her I want to cry.

'What's your thesis about, Liv?' Cat asks, as she and Robyn

clear the main course and bring out a long wooden platter filled with fruit.

'I've been looking at the corruption of memory,' Liv says, 'by which I mean how memory can be changed, altered with time. I'm a psychologist.'

'Interesting stuff,' I say, and I mean it.

'It is,' Liv says, meeting my eyes. Hers have a new brightness in them, that sort of inner light that switches on when somebody touches on a subject that truly fascinates them. 'It really is. I've been looking into false memories. It's truly extraordinary how easily the human brain can be tricked into believing it remembers something that didn't happen. You'd be amazed.'

I look around the table. Everyone's listening, and within minutes everyone is joining in, asking questions, bashing ideas around and wanting to know more.

Then a voice from the other end of the table speaks up, shaky but clear. 'But how are we ever meant to know?'

My thoughts rise like startled birds. It's my sister's voice, I'm absolutely sure. It's changed certainly, matured by over twenty years, but still hers. It's her voice. That's my sister. I look down the table again, a quick glance. Love and terror flood through me. I want to meet her eyes and at the same time I feel an urgent need to avoid them. What if she sees me, stands up and says *Laika*? Then what? Deny it? Fess up, right here? Opposite her, and in my direct line of sight, is Nate, my honest, straightforward boyfriend, a man who trusts me. Nate, who knows me as I am now, the me I've worked so hard to become. Nate, who thinks I'm *French*, for fuck's sake. No, I sloughed off Laika a long time ago. This is my life now. A life I've *made*. *Mine*. And it's definitely not a life I'm about to throw away at a moment's notice.

I see Willa glance down the table. *Shit*, I think, she's clocked me. Heart jumping, I shift back in my seat a little, using the other guests to block her line of sight. Thankfully no one else seems to notice my little dance; they're all preoccupied by Liv, who is now talking about how people can sometimes actually absorb other people's memories, how it's not always easy to know if our memories are even credible in the first place.

'Here's a simple example,' Liv says. 'Think about your earliest memory. Okay, done that?' She looks around the table. 'What is it?'

Must we? I think. Believe me, only someone with a happy childhood would come up with that game. My earliest memory is my father jabbing me so hard in the ribs in the name of 'tickling' that I actually wet my pants. Fuck this, I think, I'm not playing. But instantly I'm powerless to stop another memory that comes barrelling out of the dark. A different one. The worst.

I'm a child again.

Deedee plucks a baby bird from my hands and feeds it to her dogs.

I howl. I'm sent inside and I am hiding under a shelf in the pantry when two adults almost fall inside, slamming the door behind them.

A cake tumbles, smashes on the floor. Thousands of sugar flowers orbit and fall.

I am smeared with sticky white cream.

My father and I stumble out into the kitchen. Also, the woman in the red dress. My mother is there, and Willa too, wide-eyed and twisting her hands.

I look at the woman and say *sexetary*.

My father pushes me forward. He says, *It just broke.*

My mother says, *Things don't just break.*

Take her to the hospital, my father says, *tell them she fell off her pony.*

And my mother, eyes pink-rimmed and brimming, says, *She doesn't have a fucking pony.*

'Willa?' Liv says, and I snap out of it, opening my eyes.

'I remember being tickled,' she says, 'by my dad. Bit embarrassing, really, I wet myself.'

My mouth drops open. Are you *shitting* me? She's going to claim *that* as her earliest memory, even after Liv has gone to such lengths to explain that *stealing* other people's memories is her exact area of research? *That was me. Me* who got tickled, *me* who pissed myself, *me* who got hit. *Not* Willa. *Willa was watching.* It's so outrageous that a hoot of astonished laughter flies out my mouth. Everyone turns to look at me, so I have to quickly cover it up with a fit of pretend coughing.

Liv says, 'What about you, Claudette?'

'I remember breaking my arm. And also eating cake,' I say. I keep my eyes on Willa. *Remember?*

'Cake?' Jamie asks. 'Was it a special cake?'

I speak slowly, holding Willa's eyes. 'Yes, a birthday cake. On a marble shelf. Inside a pantry.'

'Was it your own birthday cake?' Willa asks, and I know *exactly* what she's doing. She wants me to say, *No, no, my birthday is November the third.*

I glance at Nate. 'Non,' I tell her, 'mine is in March.' This is true. Claudette's birthday, the one on my passport and, more importantly, the one my boyfriend knows, is in March.

'And about how old were you?' Liv asks.

'I was six.'

Then Liv tells Willa her memory is just a generalized impression, and a happy one at that.

Willa blinks rapidly. 'I never said it was *happy*,' she says, and, to my amazement, glances over at me, like she's asking for back-up. Fucking cheek.

'Yeah, well, that's what she said to me too,' Jamie says. 'Anyway, forget it. The whole thing is hogwash.'

'Coffee anyone?' Cat says, and as she moves away from the

table, I catch a look of pure irritation on her face. Interesting, I think. It's not just me who doesn't like Jamie. And Liv too, she's definitely not a fan. What the hell is Willa doing with him? I've got to work this one out. And I suspect with Jamie there's an easy way to do it. Time to turn on the charm.

I smooth my expression into a decent impression of female interest.

'So, Jamie,' I say, propping my chin on my hand. 'I'm trying, but I can't quite place your accent.' I give him a playful smile.

Too easy. He laughs, instantly basking in the spotlight of a woman's attention, a slight swagger in the movement of his head. 'Well,' he says, 'I'm English born and bred, but I lived in South Africa for a while, so you might be hearing a hint of that.'

I make my voice as rich as double cream. 'Of course it's easy to pick up an accent if you are hearing it all the time.' Dead easy, actually. I glance at Willa, then quickly back. I need to keep Jamie's focus on me and I suspect I'm on limited time: his face already has the fuzzy look of a man who has drunk way too much – slow, uncoordinated blinks and the sort of speech that suggests his tongue is taking up way too much room in his mouth.

'You should try Cape Town,' he drawls. 'Fantastic city. One of our favourite places.'

From the corner of my eye I see Willa's head snap up. *What?* I think. What happened then? I desperately want to read her expression, but I can't afford to take my eyes off Jamie. I need to keep him with me for as long as this takes. But there was definitely something not right about that; I just can't quite place my finger on what it could be. Okay, move on. I still haven't found out where they live.

'But you and Weela live in London now?'

'Yah, Brook Green,' Jamie says. 'Utter shit hole when we got it. Total wreck. Forced to hole up at the family citadel, Martenwood Towers.'

They're living at *Laburnum House*? You've got to be shitting me.

'Fucking great wall, drawbridge, hot oil –'

Jesus. What is she doing with him?

'What do you need a wall for?' I say, feeling my voice harden. 'Is it to stop Willa from escaping?'

I'm looking at Jamie, but I can feel the intense focus of my sister's eyes on me, listening to every word. The others too. 'Nah,' he says, 'keeping out the garbage. Vagrants, scumbags. Immigrant types.'

'I'm sorry, *what*?'

'Yah. We've got a serious problem with immigrants in this country. A load of spongers, if you ask me.'

Christ, I can't believe what I'm hearing. My heart is scudding in my chest and it's all I can do to keep my face expressionless. I try to keep my voice from shaking.

'You don't think refugees need our help?' I realize I'm gritting my teeth. He's *got* to get this. I try again. 'You understand, yes, that these are people coming from places where simply to cross the street is to take your life in your hands? Where every day babies die silently in the arms of their mothers, because they don't even have the strength to cry? We're talking about people in *dire need*. People with *nothing*. People living in *terror*.'

I flick my eyes towards Willa. What the fuck is she doing with this prick? Unless – *fuck* – does she believe this shit too? Who is she anyway? It's twenty-two years since I last saw her – is this what she's become? How could she even *be* with someone like that, unless – the breath catches in my throat. I look at her again, at that expensive green dress, the enormous diamonds stuck through her lobes. What kind of woman is she? Someone so wrapped up in her own comfortable life that she's no longer capable of looking beyond the end of her own nose? I look down the table, feeling an unstoppable fury rising inside me, *Laika* working her way up through my flesh like a chip of old bone. 'And, *Willa*, this is what *you* think?' She jumps to her feet, looking for all the world as if I've just put a knife to her throat, and that's when I notice it – the tiny silver dolphin on a thin silver chain around her throat, glinting like a torch in a wood. Shock charges through my body. *What is she doing with that?*

I whip back to Jamie. 'You should be *ashamed*.'

Jamie pushes his jaw towards me. Keeping his eyes on mine, he leans back in his chair with a sneer on his face. 'What in God's name happened to your accent? You sound *exactly* like a Brit.'

And there it is. *You arsehole*. Of all the possible buttons he could have pushed at that moment, he somehow picked *exactly* the right one. I feel revealed, viciously exposed. I stand up and slam my hands on the tabletop. 'Leaving home is *terrifying*. There's only one reason why anyone would do it and one reason alone. And that *one, single reason* is that place is *hell on earth*.'

Nate gives me a look that says *You okay?* No. I'm not. I can't be around this pig. I'm leaving. Right now. I snatch up my bag and storm towards the door but, without warning, Willa steps into my path, a movement so fast and so unexpected that I end up banging into her. She staggers. I grab her, feeling a flash of pure rage. She got *everything*. *Mum*, her *own real life*, *my* necklace – hell, she's even laid claim to my fucking *memories*.

I pull her upright. My mouth by her ear.

A heartbeat to decide.

Say nothing – or break this whole thing apart.

'It wasn't *you* who pissed yourself. *That was me*.'

24.

Paper chains

Robyn

It's the morning after our supper party, a night that came to a particularly abrupt end: Nate following Claudette out of the door and Michael calling for taxis for the others, while Willa stood encased in the fortress of Jamie's arms, silent and unreachable, as bright tears coursed down her pale face.

I'm still trying to process the whole thing when, shortly after ten, I hear Cat answering the front door.

'*Claudette*,' she says, 'it's just us today. Come and meet the kids.'

I stick my head out of the kitchen, my hands covered in flour, to the hall, where our children are already tackling Nate like the Eiger.

'You've got to check out our mad tree before we head out,' Cat says, hauling Nate plus entourage towards the lounge. 'The kids decorated it. Sophie's making a paper chain long enough to go round the entire house.'

'It's a lot quieter in the kitchen,' I tell Claudette, and she follows me in, dumping an orange backpack on a chair while I turn down the radio a notch.

No mention is made of the spat with Jamie. By all accounts she is back to the zen-like woman we met at the beginning of last night, a picture of serenity and calm. I tell her about the plans for the rest of the day: how she, Cat and Nate will take the kids to see the Christmas lights while I prep the food for tonight.

'I can stay and help if you like,' she says. 'I like to cook.'

'Are you sure? Wouldn't you prefer to see a bit of London?'

'Non. I can stay. We can talk.'

Perhaps she's tired, I think, after the madness of last night. Anyway, she seems pretty sure about it, so I put her to work with a chopping board and a big pile of veg.

'So how did you break your arm?' I ask, after Cat and Nate and the kids have found all their kit and eventually headed out. 'I did mine falling off a ladder in my parents' kitchen. I was seventeen.'

'I was six. Actually, it happened the exact same day as my story about the cake. The exact same minute. Those things happened together.'

'Ouch, how did that happen?'

She glances towards the door, almost as if she's checking that we're definitely alone, then gives me a long look, like she's deciding whether to say something or not. Finally, she gives a little Gallic shrug, an almost *what-the-hell*, and, with her face completely composed, says, 'My father was fucking his secretary in the pantry.'

I stop kneading the dough. '*Wow.*'

'I was already in there, hiding under a shelf. And because of the noise they were making and because I was little and didn't understand anything, I thought he was hurting her. So I crawled out from my hiding place and said, *I'm telling Maman.*' She pauses, no doubt taking in the horror on my face, then continues, 'And I tried to run out of the pantry, but my father grabbed hold of my wrist and yanked me back so hard my arm snapped. We *literally* heard it break, me, my father, his secretary, all three of us. Then we all just stood there for a moment, I remember that very well, because I was exactly head height to his dick and his trousers were still around his ankles. So I screamed and then the secretary screamed and ran out of the pantry. And my father let go of my arm and I crashed backwards, straight into my mother's birthday cake and the whole thing smashed.'

'Shit.'

'Yes, well. My father was a brute. He filled our home with fear. My mother was afraid. My sister was afraid.'

'Wow.'

'Me, I was not afraid,' she says, each of her words shimmering with an intense energy. 'I was angry.' She holds my eyes, then shrugs, and the heat that surrounds her seems to ebb away. 'I don't see them any more.'

'I'm not surprised.' Thoughts orbit my mind like the hazy photographs of some distant galaxy, shadowy and unfocused.

'By the way, I want to say I'm sorry about last night. About the argument. I should have done better than that. I'm usually better at dealing with dickheads.'

'Forget it. That was quite a performance from Jamie. We should probably be apologizing to you.'

She shakes her head. 'Some people are very ignorant.' She pauses, then says, 'And his girlfriend, Weela, does she think like that?'

'God, no, Willa's lovely. She can be a bit fragile at times.' I put down my rolling pin and face her. 'Something truly awful happened to her, years ago. Her sister disappeared. I mean she vanished, into thin air, without a trace. She never got over it. Well, you wouldn't, would you?'

She doesn't respond the way most people do when they hear that story. Most people express sympathy or concern. I've seen it a hundred times. They're curious too, keen to hear more: details about the case, exactly what happened and when. Specifically they want to know about the missing girl. But

Claudette just looks at me blankly and her next question feels like an odd one, because it's not about Laika at all.

'And you met Willa when, just after that? How was she then? What was she like?'

I pause, playing for time as I try to bring a thought into focus. 'Why?'

She holds my eyes, and for a moment it feels like I'm looking at somebody very familiar, rather than somebody I've only just met. It's the oddest sensation. I feel like I've known her for years. 'She wasn't in a great place. Not then, and not now.'

That's all I'm prepared to say, so I look down and start rolling out the pastry to bring the conversation to an end. For a few minutes we work in silence, listening to the Christmas songs on the radio: 'Fairy Tale of New York', 'All I Want for Christmas', 'Jingle Bell Rock'.

When Wham!'s 'Last Christmas' comes on, Claudette says, 'God, I haven't heard this song for *years.* My mum was a *huge* George Michael fan.' I stop rolling and look up. Claudette is looking down, placing the knife thoughtfully along the line of a carrot. But, for me, the spinning earth stops turning. Because in that single, shining moment, I know *exactly* what she's going to say even before she's opened her mouth. 'She used to sing us Wham! songs in the bath.'

The previous night's events rip through my mind, and I see Claudette standing over Jamie, the absolute force of the words she'd hurled at him: *Leaving home is terrifying.* I feel as if my heart has actually physically stopped. I am looking at *Laika.* Without any shred of doubt, I know it. *Laika* is alive, and *Laika* is standing next to me, here, in my kitchen. And Laika is . . . French?

How is that possible? My eyes whip over her, this dark-haired woman, this mix of serenity and fire. Again, I hear her shouting, *Leaving home is terrifying.* And now too I hear Jamie's voice, his casual, flippant reply, *You sound exactly like a Brit.*

I look at her again. It *is* Laika. I am absolutely certain of it.

But, if it is, why didn't she and Willa run straight at each other and not let go? Did she know? Was she pretending she didn't? God, no wonder Willa was beside herself. What the hell was going on? And, if it is Laika, how could she not have let Willa know where she was years ago, that all this time she was okay? How could she have seen all the posts on Willa's website, all the endless poems and letters and photographs and all the *love* and not have *instantly* got in touch?

Is it possible she hasn't actually seen it?

'Come here a moment,' I say, wiping my hands on my apron. 'I want to show you something.' I'm trying to sound composed, but my heart is yammering in my chest.

Claudette puts down her knife and comes to join me at the kitchen table. I push aside a bunch of papers, photographs, packets of basil seeds, letters, bank statements and picture books. I open up my laptop and navigate to findlaika.

I angle the screen towards her and then I watch her face as she scrolls through the hundreds of posts. Her breath quickens.

'I'm an admin,' I tell her, 'so you can see all the direct messages too if you want.'

I tap on the mailbox, and she reads through all the contact we've had over the years and our notes about our attempts to follow them up. She stops on one, reading it first in French and then translating the words into English: *Picardy. She was Ilisabat, and kind.*

'When was this written?'

'About a year ago.'

'Jabir,' she breathes, 'oh my God.'

Watching her scroll through the posts, one hand moving to her mouth, eyes filling with tears, I know then that this is the first time she's ever seen the site. She didn't know any of it, and

I am filled with tenderness for this woman, and sorrow, this woman who, I'm now sure, is Laika.

I have one chance to get this right. Time it badly or use the wrong tone of voice and she'll almost certainly deny everything. I put my hand on her arm. I leave it there. When she looks at me, I speak.

'Laika.'

She folds her lips over her teeth and I see she is biting down, physically sealing her lips as her eyes move to the ceiling, filled now with strange light. I give her all the time she needs. Eventually, she turns to look at me directly and, in unaccented English, says in a voice that is quiet and clear and completely direct, 'Yes.'

We stay in the kitchen, talking for a long time. I tell her everything I know: the number of times we went to investigate a sighting. The places we went to, the people we met. She tells me about their childhood, things I didn't know, things Willa has never been able to say. She tells me she's not Laika any more, that Laika is gone, that she is now one hundred per cent Claudette. I tell her about the love that I know Willa and Bianka have carried for her over the years, the weight of their loss, their endless cycles of hope and grief.

'And rage?' she asks.

'Rage?' I'm not sure I've heard her correctly.

'Have you ever felt true rage? No, or you'd understand my question straight off. It's volcanic, uncontrollable. If you've felt it even just once, then you spend the rest of your life trying to stay in control of it. You have to know your triggers. Do you understand what I'm saying? When you're filled with napalm, you'd better make damned sure you know where the matches are kept. Rage is *terrifying*. We all had it. All three of us: me, Mum, Willa.'

'*Willa?*' I say. 'I've never seen Willa get angry in her entire life.'

She looks at me like I've totally missed the point, 'No,' she says, 'neither have I. But, believe me, she's got it. I know it's there and, more importantly, so does she.' She shrugs. 'Trust me. It's in our DNA.'

There is so much more to say. But, first, I need to ask her about the thing that has sounded in my mind like a small alarm since we first started to talk.

'How did you get to France?'

For a long time she holds my eyes. Then she says, 'I had my passport. My father met me at Dover. He gave me my passport,' and her voice is so steady, and her eyes so direct, that I know without a shred of doubt that she is telling me the truth, and that I am hearing a truth that is so terrible, so *stunning*, that I am almost knocked off my feet. All this time, through all these years of watching Willa and Bianka go through endless cycles of hope and disappointment and heartbreak and loss, Bryce knew *exactly* where Laika was. The whole bloody mess of it flies through my brain. The absolute *betrayal*.

'You've *got* to tell Willa,' I tell her. 'They stayed at the flat last night. Let's go.'

'Well, they're in,' I say, as we draw up outside the block in Brook Green. 'The lights are on,' and we run up the stone steps as a woman on her way out holds open the door.

'Thanks,' I say. We're in.

The two of us climb the wide stairs to the top floor. I knock and a voice shouts, 'Hang on. That was quick.'

Wearing only boxer shorts and a crumpled shirt, Jamie opens the door. 'Oh,' he says. He glances between the two of us, looking somewhat rattled. Embarrassed, I suspect.

'Surprise,' I say. 'Expecting someone else?'

A beat. 'Delivery,' he mutters. We are not invited in.

'Any chance of a quick word with Willa?'

Jamie glances down the stairs, then clears his throat. 'Willa's not here, actually. She went home this morning. To her parents', I mean. The coast.'

'Shit,' I say, 'we really need to talk to her.'

For a moment we all just stand there, Jamie blocking the flat's entrance with his bulk. 'Is this about last night?' he says.

'No,' Claudette says, her voice flat. She adds, 'It's about Laika.'

'Jesus, Robyn,' Jamie says, 'don't get Willa all fired up about her sister again, okay? Bryce really doesn't want that. According to him, she was trouble.'

'And you *believed* that?'

My voice is needled through with such bright threads of anger that for an instant Jamie looks like he's been slapped. 'Hey,' he says, holding up both hands, 'don't shoot the messenger.'

'Any chance I could use your loo?' I say, and, when he doesn't move, I add, 'Jamie? Then we'll be off.'

'I'm just a bit –' He stops, glances behind us, then runs a hand through dishevelled hair. 'Yeah, I mean. Of course.'

Still he stands there. We wait, and after another long moment he shuffles aside. The three of us go in and, as he closes the door, Jamie says to Claudette, 'So, uh – I should probably apologize for last night. Obviously we didn't get off to the best start.' I hear her say, 'You think.'

For such a newly decorated apartment, the bathroom is a mess. The basin needs cleaning, a tap is dripping and there are damp towels discarded on the floor. *God*, I think. I had no idea Jamie was so slovenly. That must drive Willa mad – she and I shared a bedroom for almost two years and she's just about the tidiest person I've ever met. It's all I can do to stop myself from cleaning up.

'Thanks,' I say as I step back into the living room. 'Jamie, I hate to say it, but you look terrible. Maybe drink some water. Get some rest.'

He really does look ill. I give him a grim look. Jamie returns a wooden smile and in that moment of silence I hear a quiet scrape, followed by a rattle. Now all three of us turn our heads towards the source of the noise, listening. It is the unmistakable sound of a key in the door.

Moments later a woman steps over the threshold. I recognize her instantly. She's the woman we passed on her way out, the one who held open the downstairs door. She's carrying the keys and a bottle of champagne in one hand, and a couple of plastic flutes in the other. She stops.

'I see we have company,' she says to Jamie, a distinct snip in her voice. With some emphasis she adds, '*You should have let me know.*'

Little switches flick on and off in my brain. 'Who are *you*?'

She turns her head to look at me, a quick up-and-down. 'Melissa. I'm Jamie's wife.'

'Err, *ex*-wife,' Jamie says, looking uncomfortable.

'What are you doing in Willa's flat? Does *Willa* know you're here?'

She examines me coolly with flat brown eyes. 'What's it to you?'

'I'm her best friend.'

She raises her eyebrows. 'Well, then,' she says icily, 'I think we can be fairly certain she will now.' She purses pink lips, a long-suffering look on her face. Then, as if deciding to share a confidence, she takes a step towards me and says in a slightly lower voice, 'Obviously she had to know sometime. To be absolutely honest I'd told Jamie that if he didn't get on with it, I'd tell her myself, woman to woman, you know.'

'Stop right there,' I say, holding up both my palms. 'Don't you *dare* invoke the sisterhood.'

Claudette says, '*You conniving bitch.*'

Melissa turns her head, slow-blinking. 'I'm *sorry*,' she says in a slow voice riddled with condescension, 'and you are –'

'*Laika.*'

I throw the car into reverse. 'I'm taking you to Laburnum House, but do me a favour, will you?' I toss her my mobile. 'Can you call ahead and let them know we're on our way? Leave a message if you have to.'

'Sure,' Laika says. 'I'll stick it on speaker so you can hear what she says.'

The phone connects, then rings.

'Robyn.'

'No, it's me' – a beat – 'Robyn's driving.'

I hear a soft breathy sound, a taking-in of air, then the sound of Willa's voice fills the car. 'Oh my God,' she says, a sob in her voice, '*Laika*.'

'We're coming down to see you. Right now.'

'I don't believe this is actually happening. I thought I'd lost you all over again.'

'We're on our way. But, listen, Willa, there's something you need to know, now, before I get there.' I meet Laika's eyes and in that instant I catch a flash of something cross her face, a look of bright, savage illumination. 'Dad knew I was in France. He's always known. He met me at the ferry terminal at Dover. He gave me my passport.'

There is a moment of silence. Then the howl that rises from the telephone is so animal, and of such extraordinary pain and fury, that, even reduced to the scale of a handset, the noise flies through me like electric-hot wires.

The line goes dead.

25.
Fragments

Robyn

By the time we reach the South Downs the winter sun is already sinking fast.

The metal gates to the house jolt open and we head up the drive. Across the other side of the lawn a labourer slams a lump hammer into the walls of an old bunker-like building, but stops work at the sound of crunching gravel, stands upright and, with a halo of silver hair backlit by the low December sun, transforms into Bianka.

'*Mum*,' Laika says, her voice ripped by emotion. I slam on the brakes.

Laika throws open the car door, jumps out and starts sprinting just as Bianka starts hurtling towards the car. Willa steps from the house to the terrace, sees the car and starts running too.

I climb out of the driver's side and, from a distance, I see them collide on the lawn, the three of them coming together as one, finding each other, arms, hands, heads, three bodies connecting perfectly, the silver light of winter between them closing, and then disappearing altogether.

I turn away, pull out my mobile and call Cat.

'Where in God's name are you,' she says, 'and where's Claudette? We've been out of our minds.'

It's not like Cat to worry. I can hear the strain in her voice, fear thinly disguised by irritation, and I'm instantly filled with remorse for not having let her know we were safe. I turn away from the others and walk slowly down the garden so I can fill her in, giving her the astonishing story of the day piece by piece and she listens, occasionally interjecting into my account the words *Holy fuck*.

Finally I say, 'Look, if it's okay with you and Nate, I think we'd all better stay here tonight. I can't rip Laika away so soon, and, also, I need to find a way to talk to Willa about Jamie. I'll bring Laika back tomorrow. She said she'll call Nate later tonight. She's going to tell him everything and then we can let them talk more in the morning.'

'Okay,' she says, 'fucking hell,' then, after a moment, 'I love you, you know.'

And I do, I absolutely know.

The day is plummeting into night, a pearl moon rising out of a flood of brilliant air. I stick my phone in my pocket and hug my coat tightly around me, tucking my chin deep into my chest. On the ground by my boot, something glints in the fading light. I bend down, pick it up and discover that it is a small shard of pottery covered in black-and-gold scales. A little further away, I spot a second piece in the grass. I pick that one up too, and place the two together to see if they might fit. I'm about to turn back towards the house when I see another bit, then another. I stop picking up the pieces and start to simply follow the trail, and they lead me across the lawn until finally I am standing by the side of a deep pit, which after a moment I realize must be the old swimming pool. In the deep gloom of the falling night, it looks uncannily like an open mouth, ringed with ancient, tiled teeth. In the deep end a syrupy violet puddle surrounds a vast ragged island. The gathering dark makes it hard to see, but, as my eyes adjust, I see it is, in fact, a heap of old clothing: suits, jumpers, jackets, jeans, shirts, socks. Shoes. Also framed photographs, papers. Box files, golf clubs, a suitcase, leather bags. Broken gin bottles with heavy glass bases. And, scattered over the entire pile, are hundreds and hundreds of shards of broken pottery, and all of them, every last piece, glimmering with the lustre of tiny golden scales.

'There you are.'

I jump. 'Willa. I didn't hear you.'

I turn towards her. In her arms she carries a pile of heavy winter coats, beautiful, desirable things made of cashmere and thick wool. In a small, mechanical action, she opens her arms and lets the entire lot drop into the deep end of the empty pool.

'Mum's getting it filled in tomorrow,' she says. 'She's decided she'd rather have a rose bed there instead.'

I turn towards her slowly. My breath forms soft, empty speech bubbles in the chill winter air.

'Where's your dad?'

'Gosh,' she says mildly, 'overseas, I suppose. We never really know what he's up to these days.' Her eyes gleam in the iridescent night.

I pause, and for a beat we just stare at each other.

I say, 'How d'you get that scratch on your face?'

Her hand moves to her cheek, and her fingertip delicately traces a thin red line. Then, in a voice as soft as the silken night she says, 'Mum and I were doing some gardening earlier. We had a to-do with some brambles.'

They talk into the night, the three of them starting a journey of healing and understanding that I imagine will take them years. At some point I tell her about our visit to the flat and she listens in silence, then tells me she's okay. 'It's over,' she says, 'and I'm okay.' Eventually I leave them at the kitchen table and make my way to bed.

But I don't sleep. I can't. I stay awake all night, staring into the gloom with open eyes. Above me, the nebula of my thoughts blooms and unfolds. I think about all the small things that build and destroy us, all those little things we choose to hide and reveal, forget and forgive. How we all carry hidden histories that we continually circle back to, the things that make us soar, or slowly unwind. I think about the life I have lived and all the things I know. The vows and promises I have made to others and those they have made to me. I think about my duties and obligations as a mother, daughter, sister, wife, friend. As a decent human being. The things that I have always known and understood, the things I'm prepared to stand up for, put my name to, hold myself accountable for. I think about my beautiful parents, how their love has allowed me to grow into the person I am. What it means to love at all. I think about Willa.

And what I've got to do.

Willa, Laika and I leave the next morning after breakfast, the sisters promising to return later that day. I am moon-eyed from lack of sleep.

'Jamie sent me a text this morning,' Willa says, as I pull out of the drive and turn on to the road. 'He said he's very sorry and that he hadn't meant for things to turn out like that or for me to find out the way I did, and, also, that he hadn't known how to tell me.'

'*All* the excuses.'

'Personally I think you had a close escape,' Laika says. 'From what I saw, you were engaged to our dad.'

'Jamie's not a monster,' Willa says, 'and it's not entirely his fault. He didn't start out like that. He changed. Dad got to him, I think.' She pauses, then adds, 'Anyway, I'm not even sure if I like men.'

'Good grief, Willa,' I say, '*that* I could have told you years ago.'

She turns to me, laughing, and for a moment I see her as she once was, back in our shared bedroom at school, finding out who she really was, so far away from her father's control. And finally, *finally*, something slips into place. Bryce would *never* have accepted us as a couple. If she'd stayed with me, her mother would have lost both her daughters. She didn't choose me because she *couldn't* choose me. She wasn't ever free.

'What a mess,' Willa says. 'There's so much to sort out. Selling the flat for a start.'

'So keep it. Buy Jamie out.'

'Not possible,' she says, 'not on my pay.'

'*Stop.*' Laika slams her hand on the dash. I slam my foot on the brake and we come to a sudden stop in front of a large, churned-up plot. Beyond the mountains of frozen mud is a small tile-hung cottage caged behind a wire fence strung with multiple signs reading KEEP OUT and DEMOLITION SITE.

'I still can't believe you were here,' Willa said. 'It's been empty for years. Your friend Frieda left it to her cats – did you know that? It was all over the news – and, trust me, there's nothing the press love more than a story about a batty old lady. There was a massive legal battle over the will – it must have practically bankrupted the claimants. Anyway. Nothing could be done: it was completely fixed in stone. She'd stipulated that the house had to be kept warm and all of the kitties had to be fed and watered and cared for until the end of their natural lives. It took almost a year for the courts to agree they could even be neutered. The last one died only a couple of years ago. It must have been bloody ancient.'

Laika grinned. 'I told you she was wonderful. Come on, let's take a look.'

She jumps out of the car, and a moment later we follow, stumbling our way over the clefts of frozen mud towards the old house. Then Laika feels around the inside of the roof of the porch and to our utter amazement produces an old key hidden inside a deep crevice. We let ourselves in.

Inside is a real mess. It looks as if the place has been done over, drawers and cupboards left flung open, oak panelling ripped away and left in heaps, revealing a carcass of bare plaster and struts. In the kitchen Laika wraps two old brown mugs patterned with orange flowers in a tea towel and places them carefully inside her backpack. Then we head upstairs, looking first at Frieda's bedroom and then at the little room at the end where Laika slept, still with its wallpaper of yellow flowers.

Finally we visit a tiny box room. It's clearly empty, but Laika drops to her knees and starts tugging at a wide section of skirting board. Nothing happens.

'What're you doing?' Willa says.

She pulls again, and Willa gives me a look of surprise as this time the board comes away in Laika's hand, revealing a small crawl space under the eaves. Laika sticks her arm inside and feels around, then pulls out a little dusty leather box. She flips open the lid and lifts out a photograph of two serious little girls seated side by side.

'That's Elfrieda,' she says, tapping on one of the girls, 'and that's her sister, Elisabeth.'

She looks at the image for a long time, then passes the rest of the box to Willa.

'Look after this for me, will you?' she says. 'I've got what I wanted.' Willa looks inside the box, her face baffled for a moment, then utterly amazed. She holds up a necklace clustered with diamonds, her mouth opening in surprise.

'Take that one. Use it to help buy out Jamie. Think of it as a ticket from Frieda, sister to sister. Nate's group could do with a few new instruments too. As for the rest' – she turns to me, searching my eyes – 'Robyn, d'you reckon you could help me track down Jabir?'

'He's clearly checking the site.'

'I think so. Yeah, he must be. So maybe we could put a cryptic announcement on it. Something he'd understand, a message he'd know could *only* be for him, to let him know to get in touch. I'll think of something. He's the one who needs that lot the most. The rest of that box is for him.'

26.
Family album

Robyn

My father is dying. He has cancer of the pancreas and there's not a thing we can do. In London, Cat has put her arms around me and let my stunned soul empty out. Through all my years of training and experience, an entire career spent working with cancer patients, I have not prepared for this. My beloved father, a man who can fix anything, cannot be fixed. How did I miss it? How did any of us?

We don't know how long he has; he's still pretending it's forever. It's high summer and we are gathered at my parents' house on the hill. After weeks of rain, the skies have cleared to a blue so cloudless and deep it looks like a summer sea. On the small patch of lawn in front of the house, picnic blankets, deckchairs and tents are scattered on daisy-speckled grass, and beyond the low stone wall is the wild and healing moor. The swallows are back, dipping and diving above bone-coloured grasses, also house martins, and skylarks too, heard but not seen. My father sits in a deckchair watching it all, a look of peace on his face. By his side is Scrap, his beloved ancient lurcher, long ago rescued by Bianka from the top of the white cliffs, and my father's constant shadow and companion throughout the years since.

My mother touches my father a lot these days, placing a hand on his thinning face, the back of his hand, on his tanned and sinewy arms. Before we drove down, she phoned us in London to put new house rules in place. Cry if you must, she said, but only if you have to and definitely not in front of Dad, no big speeches. He's still here, she said, so just enjoy the now. And she's led by example since we all arrived. You'd think, watching her pottering around the kitchen, that there's nothing wrong. The atmosphere in the house is joyful and relaxed; there's music, terracotta pots spilling over with flowers, mountains of homemade food. And my mother hasn't stopped talking since we arrived, throwing her arms around all three of her grandchildren, pulling them to her, wanting to know every last detail of their little young lives.

'I'm fine,' she tells everyone. 'Don't you worry about me,' but on our second night there I find her alone at midnight in the kitchen garden, pulling out weeds with an unremitting fury, her eyes brimming with tears.

We've hauled out boxes of old photographs from the attic and taken many more, recordings, videos too. So many of our conversations seem to begin with the words *Do you remember* – and then the retelling of some old story that all of us know, sometimes embellished, other times not. We all have our personal favourites. I listen to my father. What I want, I realize, is to remember his voice, the slow cadence of his speech; the way he listens, smiling, his head resting in the crook of his hand; the way he flares his nostrils when he's amused. At our request, my mother has dug out her tatty old exercise book, the visitors' book she used to give her accidental guests, and all of us have written in it. My father's entry reads, 'Good days and long views up on Tea Mountain.'

In the past couple of days he's found moments of quiet time to spend with Sophie away from us all. She knows what's going on. Cat and I have decided that she's old enough and we want her to knowingly lay down her memories of him, to have the chance to say goodbye. We haven't told the boys. Right now they are racing around the garden with a football and their uncles Michael and Nate, stopping every five minutes to beg us to take them to swim.

Liv, who now wears a gold band set with a delicate opal on her ring finger, sits with Laika and Cat. Laika shifts on the picnic blanket, trying to get comfortable. It is over two years since she blazed into our lives, and now she's almost seven months pregnant. Cat and I never wanted to find out what we were expecting, but she and Nate know they are having a girl. She even has a name, Elisabeth Elfrieda, or Elfie, as Nate has already started calling her, which is just too cute.

'She's here,' Ned, our youngest by five minutes, shouts, '*at last.* I am *starving to death.*' To make his point he drops to his knees and keels over on the grass, spreadeagled, tongue out, eyes rolled back. I shade my eyes and look down the track to where a blue estate car is bumping its way unsteadily up the hill.

For someone so far along in her pregnancy, Laika is surprisingly light on her feet. She's the first to the car and, as the passenger door swings open and Willa jumps out, she presses her sister to her in the longest hug, swaying with her from side to side, both of them laughing and crying tears of real joy. Willa looks wonderful, happier and more relaxed than I've seen her in years. Her hair is pulled up into a chaotic bun from which a few loose strands have escaped. She's wearing sandals, a faded blue A-line skirt and a white embroidered blouse.

'Finally,' Cat says. 'Right, let's get some food into these boys.'

Like most of our meals, lunch is a picnic of savoury tarts, bread, cheese and salads: good food sourced straight out of the kitchen garden, and laid out in a vast, chaotic spread on a long line of faded tablecloths arranged across the grass. The group of us gather, sitting cross-legged on cushions, or otherwise perched on low wooden stools and canvas chairs, passing around beautiful stoneware bowls thrown by my dad. We are all talking at once.

I watch Nate smiling, talking, as ever relaxed. He calls his girlfriend Laika now, having made the switch the moment he found out the truth. Cat used to check in with him a lot in those first early days, keen to make sure her little brother was doing okay. I know the whole situation worried her. After all, she said to me late one night in bed, it takes a certain kind of person to fake an accent, to fabricate an entire life. 'She had me,' she said. Hugely protective and typically direct, finally she asked Nate straight up whether Laika could ever be totally trusted.

Nate had shrugged it off. 'You're overthinking it,' he said. 'Everyone reinvents themselves to a greater or lesser extent. Anyway, she was never trying to *actively* deceive *anyone*. She was just doing whatever it took to survive.' I'm pretty sure Cat must have accepted his reasoning because she never mentioned it again after that.

Willa's face breaks into a wide and wicked grin. 'You'll never guess who turned up at the flat the other day. *Jamie*.'

'You're kidding.'

'For some reason he wanted to let me know that he and Melissa had split up again. I think he was after a bit of sympathy.'

Laika rolls her eyes. 'What a knob. I hope you told him where to go.'

'I felt a bit sorry for him, really.'

'Now tell me, how is your mother?' Mum asks Willa in a quick change of subject.

'She's doing okay,' Willa says softly.

'I do so feel for her,' my mother says, 'abandoned like that. Do you *ever* hear from your father?'

Willa replies without hesitation. 'We think he must still be somewhere abroad. Going for a completely fresh start, I imagine. Unfortunately, we have absolutely no way to contact him – he must have changed both his mobile number *and* his email. He always was famously bad at keeping in touch.'

'You wouldn't want to report him as a missing person?'

'Gosh, no,' Willa says mildly, 'we wouldn't do that. I mean,' she adds, 'we're not *really* worried. I'd say we've *some* idea where he is.' Momentarily her eyes flick over to Laika's, then mine.

'That poor man,' my mother says, her voice full of compassion, 'imagine having no idea his precious daughter came home.'

'Yes,' Laika says, speaking in the same even tone as her sister, 'but there's all sorts of reasons why someone might just disappear. Perhaps it's in our DNA.'

'And your mother – she's all right, is she, living all alone in that big house?'

'I don't think she'd want to move now,' Laika says. 'She *really* loves that garden. You should see it. She's made this gorgeous rose garden where the old pool used to be. It's full of lovely blooms with wonderful names like *Sweet Child of Mine* and *Champagne Moment* and *Brilliant Result*. Every time Willa and I visit she makes us sit on the terrace and admire it.'

Willa turns her head towards mine. She gives me a quiet smile, and, after a moment, I smile back. It is, after all, an innocent conversation, unweighted by anything other than the gamut of human concern. Bryce is away, and no one has a clue where he is or when he'll be back. That's all anyone knows.

It is all I know, really.

After lunch Cat says, 'Are you lot up for a swim? Only I promised the boys we'd go when Willa got here and they're driving me mad.'

'*Love* to,' Laika says, 'just wait till you see my *enormous* swimmers.'

'Don't get too excited,' I tell her, 'you can't do lengths. It's about the size of a plunge pool, at the top of a waterfall. It's kind of like a big natural jacuzzi. But it fills up only in years when there's been a lot of rain, so it does feel a bit special. The boys love it.'

We go, all of us, the entire family, walking along the top edge of a steep combe where the bright temples of beech trees plunge steeply downhill to a distant river below. Edged by glossy rocks and surrounded by ferns, the small pool is crystal clear and, deep in the middle, its whorl of ever moving water a glistening celadon green. It's fed by a hidden stream which appears like magic out of the ground at head height, its entrance hung by strands of tiny green leaves. Cat and I sit on one side of it with Sophie, next to my mum and dad.

'Don't get too near the edge,' my mother says. 'Boys – I'm talking to you.' The twins are lying flat on their stomachs where the pool plunges over the top of the combe, racing sticks over the edge. They have Nate on one side of them and Liv and Michael on the other. They'll be okay.

Willa and Laika are the last to get in. Standing by the water's edge, Willa turns to say something to Laika, her words lost to the rest of us by the sound of conversation and birdsong and the fast-running stream. Laika laughs, then Willa smiles and places her hands gently on the round of her sister's growing child. Submerged up to her shoulders, I see my mother's pale hand reaching for my father's beneath the bright water. With a voice gravelled by tenderness, he says, 'That child will be loved.'

It is a blessing.

I can feel the faint warmth of Cat's body through the water. I don't need to look to know that she's there. Rather, I'm looking at Willa, this beautiful woman whom I have known and loved for more than half my life, with whom I have travelled to unknown places, and to whom I have made, and kept, unbreakable promises. A woman about whom I know everything and nothing.

For a moment she and Laika stand in their bathers by the edge of the pool, holding hands for balance, then together they dip under the silver lines of its bright surface, gasping with the shock of the cold. And now the tiny pool is packed with bodies, so the sisters end up perching together under the actual stream that feeds it, letting the water pound over their shoulders and backs. Willa pulls her hair from its band and the almost-red of her hair catches the light and flashes like strands of pure gold. Then she and Laika tip their heads back and laugh like children as they let the water flood over their heads. The water is ice cold and as clear and bright as a new day. And it strikes me now as a strange sort of magic, how fresh water can appear from an underground stream, how it just keeps coming, how all of it is just endlessly replaced. And the water plunges into the pool and rushes past all of us and plummets over the edge and just disappears.

Acknowledgements

First, I would like to thank my brilliant, amazing agent Felicity Blunt. Thank you, Felicity, for your guidance and keen insights, for your good humour and huge support, and for always pushing me in the right direction. You've made this whole thing a joy.

I count myself unbelievably lucky to have had the chance to work with two exceptionally wise and generous editors: Harriet Bourton at Viking in the UK and Amy Einhorn at Crown in the US. Thank you both for everything. My deep and heartfelt thanks also go to Ella Harold at Penguin and Lori Kusatzky at Crown. I'd also like to thank Donna Poppy for her eagle-eyed copy-editing. I'm incredibly grateful to all those people who have worked tirelessly to design, produce, and bring this novel to market, and my especial thanks go to Emma Pidsley for producing such a stunning cover design. At Penguin, I would also very much like to thank Kayla Fuller, Chloe Davies, Laura Dermody, Emma Brown, Sam Fanaken, Autumn Evans, Kyla Dean, Eleanor Rhodes-Davies and Annie Underwood; and at Crown, I am deeply grateful to Mary Moates, Heather Williamson, Dyana Messina, Julie Cepler, Chris Tanigawa, Liza Stepanovich, Natalie Blachere, Michele Giuseffi, Karen Ninnis and Chris Brand.

I would like to thank the entire team at Curtis Brown but especially Rosie Pierce, Florence Sandelson, Sophie Baker, Katie Harrison, Camilla Young, Katie Battcock, Jennifer Kerslake and Alice Lutyens. My grateful thanks go to CBC Creative and especially to Charlotte Mendelson for being such an inspirational tutor. Not only was the three-month novel-writing course challenging, uplifting and great fun, but it also introduced me to the most perceptive, talented, spirited and supportive group of fellow writers that I could ever hope to meet. Thank you Tessa Sheridan, Kas Twose, Jo Agrell, Paul Baird, Brooke Maddison, Jen Faulkner, Lucy Evans, Ange Drinnan, Kate Finnigan, Sam Olsen, Marise Gaughan, Roberta Francis, Sarah Gardner Borden and Anni Walsh. You are all absolutely the best.

Thank you Tony Cabon and Hélène Heurtevent for sorting out my French!

I would also like to thank Olubunmi Adesanya at Oxford University together with Dr John Ballam and my fabulous Creative Writing classmates. For their outstanding teaching, incisive feedback and unfailing encouragement, I am deeply grateful to Lucy Ayrton, Claire Crowther, Elisabeth McKetta Sharp, Jeremy Hughes, Daisy McNally, Aleksandra Andrejevic, Michael Johnstone, Shaun McCarthy, Nicholas McInerny, Helen Jukes, Amal Chatterjee and Elizabeth Garner.

Thank you Paul Doctors, Giles Easter, Caroline Easter, Ali Flind and Jan Rayner for helping me out with all those things that are so absolutely beyond me. Caroline and Giles, thank you for everything, I don't know what I would do without you. Gi, relax. See? You're really not in it.

Thank you Camilla Luard and Katherine Luxford for reading my first draft and, together with Annabel Turner, Andrea Dingley, Carolyn Heath, Christina McGregor, Emma Johnson, Natalie Lockhart, Kirstie Horgan, Fiona Gosden, Naomi Cudmore, Jill Davies and Rachel More, thank you for being there along the way, and, as always and ever, for your steadfast friendship and support.

Families are at the heart of this novel and I would like to acknowledge mine, and most especially my own Mum and Dad, who were both wonderful. Thank you to my wonderful son Luke Easter, for being there at the start and for cheering me on. Thank you for believing in me, Peter Collins: without you this story would never have been written. Finally, thank you to my beloved Siddley, my beautiful, loyal and gentle friend, who was by my side from the very first word right the way through to the last. Gone now but absolutely not forgotten.